ANNE ZOELLE

CROWN of STARLIGHT

EXCELSINE PRESS

Other Books by Anne Zoelle:

The Awakening of Ren Crown

The Protection of Ren Crown

The Rise of Ren Crown

The Unleashing of Ren Crown

The Destiny of Ren Crown

House of Scepters

Cage of Shadows

Crown of Starlight

Tender of the Garden

Contents

SCAND
DENMA
Helsgir
MORU
Lisso
SHOUNE
RABA
ZAGA
CARTHA
MEDIT SEA
LIBU
ERSINE
TYRAS
ORSO
OLBIA
YALE
AXSAINA
ANCY
MEMFI
KEMET
KUSH

THE FEHL EMPIRE
SCYTHIA
HELIP
TOMYR
CASP SEA
ZENURIT
ZENUSET
ZENUT
ZENUN
ZENURE
HEIT TERRITORIES
LYNDEL
RA
TEHRAS
AHRA
LORAN
HERAT
TEHRASI
PARSA
HLAKA
CUIPSIN
HOSFURI
KROKOLA
A
NURFINE
FEHLA-DA
FEHL SEA
INDI

CHAPTER ONE
ENDS AND BEGINNINGS

RONE

(Cuipsin)

With Taline's arm looped around his neck, Rone stumbled to an outcropping near a small seaside village in Cuipsin. The slivered moon had set, leaving only the starlit sky. Moonrise at dawn would herald the approach of the dark moon that they had labored toward since Ninli had made her oath with the Shadow Prince.

The new moon would rise upon their failed states.

Taline was nearly unconscious—and Rone's heart clenched as she vacillated between laughing and sobbing. He had never been equipped to deal with emotion and regard.

But now, he wanted to—and this want was its own double-edged sword. He wanted to be the person who she could turn to, yet seeing the emperor—and seeing the man's awareness as he had looked at Rone's powered hands—was a reminder that Rone had been born wrong.

Rone closed his eyes. He felt scraped raw—like exposed skin flayed in a sandstorm. Ninli had healed the burns and broken bones he had received from the emperor, but it felt like nothing could fix Rone's twisting emotions.

Ninli and the Shadow Prince stumbled next to them in a similarly twined position—though who was clutching and who was holding up the other was indeterminate.

Hate curled in Rone's chest.

Ninli's fingers moved over the Shadow Prince's neck—light tingling from her fingers as she tried in vain to connect to the magic that no longer flowed around him. The prince's fingers curled around hers finally—to stop her from trying.

Grief and grim despair slivered through the air, hovering like one of the shadows that Kaveh ul Fehl could no longer cast. Satisfaction joined

Rone's hate. Fehl looked drained of all that he was—his eyes unfocused, his posture stooped. He was a mere shadow of the man who had commanded armies and destroyed kingdoms.

The Shadow Prince had been broken. He had no more magic, no more father, and no more empire to believe in. Rone's gaze slipped down the unprotected back of his half-brother, and he felt the press of cold steel in his sleeve. He thought of the easily pierced human skin beneath Kaveh ul Fehl's heavy cloak. Ninli's gaze was connected to the Shadow Prince's. In her present state, she would be unable to stop a blade from reaching its target.

"There is still hope," Ninli said to Fehl. "There are still avenues available, but we cannot linger long." Her gaze shifted to the interior landscape with deep sorrow in her uncovered crimson eyes.

Rone's gaze followed hers. In the distance, banners, tents, and torches spread across a vast expanse of land under the starlight. A great military encampment stood outside the walls of Krokola, Cuipsin's capital city and busiest port.

Rone had no idea what was happening in this layer, their home layer, other than the drivel the pentalayerists had taunted them with. But from Ninli's expression and the presence of the man she was holding, sorting truth from lie did not seem as though it would take long to parse.

His lip curled derisively as Ninli pressed a hand to Fehl's nape. She had found a wounded bird in the godforsaken Shadow Prince. Damn Summoras.

"Why are we here?" Rone asked grimly. Ninli had deposited them in this location for a reason.

"The Ninth Scepter is in that camp." Her tone was both wistful and sad.

Ice and rage filled him. "Taline suffered every time a scepter was used here."

Ninli jerked. "I—"

"Aros was using the scepters," Fehl interrupted, voice grim and deep. "Whatever happened, it was not from Nin. Aros is to blame. For everything."

"So you say." Rone knew Ninli would have done everything in her power to limit any damage to

Taline, but he was angry. After trekking through an unforgiving, hostile terrain and keeping Taline barely alive for the last five days, Rone felt as if he hadn't slept in years. "Aros has the other scepters. He will track this one."

"We aren't going to take it," Ninli said. "But its presence will help overshadow us until he claims it. It will give us time here beneath its shade."

"You mean to stay here?"

"No, but—" She looked at the Shadow Prince with an expression that made Rone uneasy. "Kaveh, your camp and followers, your forces—"

"Won't follow a magi without power."

She firmed her lips and her gaze slid to the camp and its unholy light. "You don't know that."

"I know." The Shadow Prince's voice was implacable.

"In Raba or Scythia, we could—"

"I killed a quarter of the military forces in Raba a week past." Kaveh ul Fehl, once the monster to slay all others, looked west to the Fehl Sea. "And Aros was likely behind whatever happened in Shoune, stirring the forces against us there. Scythia hates the empire. They would see us dead."

"But Raba, Zaga, and Scythia are not part of the empire yet. Not without you at the front. Aros can't—"

Rone cut a hand through the air. "Why are we here, Ninli? Why is he here with us?"

Ninli looked calmly at him, though he knew all her tells—the pulse that was beating too fast at her throat, the shaking fingers that were quick to clutch her cloak, the lift of a royal chin that would accept no defeat. "The empire hovers on a precipice. On a dagger's point. We need to set it to rights before it is lost."

A sound of disbelief escaped him. "The empire is already lost. And it can burn. I look forward to its destruction."

Her royal chin lifted higher, her red eyes as calm as they ever were when she was holding her mind together by a thread. "We can save it."

"I don't want to save it."

Ninli said nothing for a moment, then nodded in understanding. "You do not have to. But I will do what I must."

Never asking, always accepting the choices of others. Damn her, damn her, damn her.

"Aros has the Scepter of Darkness, Ninli. Aros has all the scepters but one if what you are saying is true. And if he doesn't have them all, he will soon."

The Scepter of Darkness would find all the others. It would also gift the wielder with the powers of all the others.

Sehk-Ra, they were all dead—living on borrowed sand.

Ninli tilted her head, listening to something on the wind. "The ninth is here. Aros is not. That he's not here means—"

"He's securing the throne." Fehl's voice sounded like heavy stone dragged across gravel. "He needs to do it while he can control the narrative of what happened to the emperor. He'll have plenty of time to finish us off."

Taline shifted against Rone and the heat of her forehead brushed his throat. He cursed and set her carefully down. Ninli detached herself from Fehl and rushed to her side.

Rone looked at the Shadow Prince—the former Shadow Prince—easily taken down without Ninli providing cover and protection. Rone fingered the knives in his sleeves.

"How long until Aros finds us?" Taline asked tiredly, pulling Rone's attention back to what was most important—her safety. He could mete out Fehl's fate later.

Ninli touched Taline's skin, checking her temperature, then her burned palm, unable to keep her hands still upon her sister's flesh. "Long enough."

It was a lie.

"No." Kaveh ul Fehl watched the three of them with eyes cut from stone—stark and hard—then focused so completely on Ninli that it was as if Rone and Taline didn't exist. "You need to hide."

"Not yet. We aren't completely without plots of our own."

The Shadow Prince's eyes narrowed.

Rone could only unwillingly agree. Rone, Taline, and Ninli were in both better and worse positions than before. Kaveh ul Fehl had no leash upon them anymore. He was powerless. The only tether that remained was the one he had leashed to Ninli's emotions—a tie Rone would sever. But the empire possessed the Scepter of Darkness now.

And although Etelian ul Fehl had never learned what the Second Scepter of Tehras was capable of, the same had not been true for Aros. Rone allowed his eyes to slip close for a moment at the assassin's fate. Aros had killed his own son in order to release Irsula of Denz. With Sher Fehl dead and Kaveh ul Fehl incapacitated, there was no more dangerous man who could sit upon the throne.

Aros ul Fehl held the Scepter of Darkness. His power would soon know no bounds. He would place a permanent leash upon them—for a monster could only become more monstrous upon a throne.

"We are with you," Taline said.

"We are not," Rone hissed. "Not with him."

Ninli looked at Rone. "You don't have to be. But I could use your assistance. Just for one task. Will you accompany me? The two of us, to complete one task and save a family? They have little time."

"The two of us?" He motioned harshly and incredulously. "And leave your sister with him?"

"Kaveh won't hurt her."

She had gone mad. Rone couldn't look away from her, disbelief making his stomach jump. "You've gone mad."

"Rone," Taline said.

"She's gone mad."

"He won't hurt her," Ninli said, fingers light on her sister's cheek. Her fingers were not shaking; her chin was normally set.

That meant she believed it. Unease swirled. "Why only the two of us?"

Ninli touched Taline's pulse. "I can't take Tali in her current condition—the gambit will not work." She grimaced. "And as for Kaveh...when the Scythians see he is without magic, they are apt to kill him as soon as listen."

Rone was in agreement with that.

Ninli ran a finger down Taline's cheek, then looked at the Shadow Prince. "You will guard her?"

It was barely a question. For all its absurdity as an inquiry, she was not asking him if he would guard Taline—the expectation was foregone. She trusted him. She trusted the monster.

The Shadow Prince stared back at Ninli. In a less tense moment, Fehl's gaze might have made Rone avert his eyes as he watched the starkness give way to despair—and devotion, for the briefest of moments.

What the ever loving Sehk had happened here?

"Yes," Fehl answered.

Ninli rose. Taline said nothing—her trusting gaze on Ninli.

"No," Rone said. He trusted none of this. Monsters and devotion? It was simply a gambit before the strike.

"Go." Taline looked at him with hazy, beautiful brown eyes.

Unfairness curled, and weakness. But he had been too long as caretaker to shed such commitment now. "No." Rone was implacable.

"He won't hurt—"

"Because he doesn't have magic? He doesn't need magic to hurt her, Ninli." Rone knew that better than most. And everything in him said not to leave Taline. The traumatic circumstances of the past weeks couldn't be brushed off like water from skin.

"He won't hurt her," Ninli said, voice solemn. "He wouldn't hurt her even if he still had his powers."

"Am I the only one lacking madness? Is there an infecting strain I have yet to catch? I will not leave her with him."

Ninli said nothing for a moment, as if considering whether Rone really meant it, then turned and opened three gates. Two gates revealed war-torn landscapes. The third displayed a well-appointed tent.

Ninli looked at Fehl. "Collect our things and anything you need. And…speak to your generals before Aros does."

"No."

"Kav—"

"They will only follow someone with power—one who can instill fear."

She sighed, then nodded in the calm acceptance that was so aggravating. "I will reopen the gate in ten minutes' time."

Fehl touched her cheek. "Do not reopen it if Aros comes."

Rone narrowed his eyes.

"All will be well," she said. And Rone could see that the prince did not believe Ninli's soft words, but that he believed in Ninli. Pretended to believe. Anger unfurled larger wings in Rone's gut. He would believe nothing when it came to the Shadow Prince. The prince was not going to be part of their plans.

The prince stepped through the gate containing the tent. "Close it," he said, without looking back.

"Take care," Ninli whispered, then closed the three gates. Opening three gates was an obfuscation tactic to hide the true exit destination, but Rone didn't think it would buy much time.

Ninli stared at the dissipating motes of magic, and Rone did not like the expression on her face. She turned to him, expression wiped free, but an anxiety that had not previously been there vibrated her frame. "We need make haste, for we will get no further opportunity to save the Scythians, and if we dally, Aros will discover Kaveh in the camp."

Rone didn't like the plan. He didn't like any of this. But at least the Shadow Prince was gone. "The three of us will go to the non-magic layer after we save whoever has targeted your heart."

"No."

"Ninli—"

"We aren't leaving him."

"We aren't keeping him."

"Running only means a few days longer to live before we do so in constant fear. We have this one chance, to get ahead of Aros, if only by a bit."

"Running? As opposed to what? Fighting?"

"Yes."

"Fighting—fighting the Scepter of Darkness?"

"Yes."

"You are mad."

"I've always been," she said, gaze direct. "But we will prevail. We will prevail with the four of us aligned and fighting together."

He curled his fingers into his palms to stop himself from reaching out and shaking sense into her. "We aren't warriors, Ninli. There is only one warrior, and he is currently without power."

"A warrior but needs a reason to fight," she said softly, and she looked at him as if looking into his soul. "We are all warriors."

He hated that look. He hated how it made him feel—as if all his secrets were laid bare. "You will send your sister to war?"

"A war will come for all of us. It is our decision whether to prepare or run. If we stand together, we will have a chance."

"The Shadow Prince has no shadows. And if he did, I'd want him dead even faster." The warning in his words carried a maliciousness she could not misinterpret.

"I know."

He hated her. He hated Fehl. He hated himself. "So long as you do."

"I have a plan."

"You always do," he said grimly.

"As do you." She tilted her head. "Will you accompany me now?" Relentless. Implacable. Soft. Calm. The vise of a silk grip.

Mirthless laughter spilled from him. "You know I will." But his gaze shifted east. The Shadow Prince knew where Taline was—just beyond view of the camp. He could call upon anyone to grab her.

"But we take Taline with us," he said.

"We can't."

"We aren't leaving her here alone."

"Taline can defend herself."

He knew she could, but he bristled, even so. He motioned even more harshly to her fevered state. "In her condition? Like that?"

"I'm right here," Taline responded, eyes shut. "And my ears are the one thing working just fine."

"See? The only—"

"I don't prefer to leave her either, Rone, but Kaveh won't hurt or hunt her, and she will be in greater danger if she's with us—and we will be in greater danger if she comes. People will die if we don't do this now." She tucked herself back against Taline's side and touched her sister's undamaged hand, wrapping a bottle into her palm. "Do you have enough energy to change Rone's clothes? Courtly dress?"

Rone looked at Ninli, and fully took in her garb. Her skirts and wrappings were dirty and torn from being thrown around, but they were of the finest materials and cut in the latest fashion. Ninli had been at court. Of course she had. They had just come from the Imperial Palace.

Taline dragged a shaking, battered hand through the air and Rone's clothes freshened and brightened, and silken cords drew small details over his chest into the designs of the empire. He could feel magic smoothing along his cheeks, ferrying away dirt and grime. He could feel the soft, soothing charms making all imperfections melt away.

Taline gripped Ninli next, and Ninli's clothes repaired themselves in a moment of time—like the blooming of a flower from husk to full beauty.

Rone looked at the bottle Taline was holding. He had seen the two girls work together many times. Ninli had always offered herself to Taline as a fresh, unending energy source.

It said something that Ninli had asked Taline to do the spells—and that she had given Taline a bottle of stored magic to do the spell instead of giving directly from herself. Rone wasn't sure he had ever observed it before.

Taline hissed; her fisted hand curled inward and dropped the bottle in the aftermath of her usage. Ninli clasped her fingers around Taline's, magic sluggishly opening between them, and Taline's muscles relaxed.

"You can still do magic." There was relief in Ninli's voice.

Had it been a test then? No, something was still off.

"Hide, if someone comes," Ninli murmured, rooting through the travel bag they had carried in the non-magic layer. She tucked something in the crook of Taline's arm. "Or use this. We will be back soon," she whispered.

"I know."

Rone grit his teeth.

Ninli rose and touched each of her own eyes. They bled from crimson to the muddled brown color of dried blood. From past to present. Transformation complete, she held out her hand. "Rone?"

Rone growled. That hand had been thrust before him at his lowest points. Trust me. What did he trust? Who did he trust? He had already been through this revelation about the girls.

It was the Shadow Prince's presence that he questioned and didn't trust.

"Fine." He grabbed her outstretched hand with his. Ninli would never harm Taline. He trusted in that.

Ninli opened four ripgates—one each to what looked like Memfi, Ancyra, Tyras, and an antechamber in Tomyr's royal palace in Scythia. The latter he knew intimately from having spent an illustrious weekend in the palace a few years ago with a cousin of the queen, a lady of insatiable tastes and risky desires.

Rone expected Ninli to open more ripgates to Scythia, but Ninli breathed heavily, then motioned to the antechamber. "Quickly."

Apprehension shot through him—what family were they saving?—but he stepped through the ripgate. She closed the ripgates quickly, leaned heavily against the wall as if to catch her breath, then straightened abruptly and opened the door to the throne room.

Servants jumped and spells shot forth, but before they hit, three guards had absorbed the spells.

"Mistress." They bowed.

Apprehension became dread. Scythia had not been part of the empire when Rone had left, and the respectful address to Ninli was not a good sign. Rone was starting to see why dragging Taline's half-dead body through the halls would not have lent itself to a "state" visit, or whatever this was.

The imperial guards at the archways leading to the hall snapped into even more rigid positions and saluted Ninli as they would a commander. Rone felt himself descend into the surreal as she gracefully stepped toward them and inclined her head. The pentalayerists' comments about Ninli becoming the right hand of the Shadow Prince were starting to feel real.

"I am here under the command of the Imperator General to question the prisoners," she said. "Do not disturb us."

"Yes, mistress." The man halted for a moment, indecisive. "The imperial oaths have—"

"Yes." She nodded. "Something went askew with the magic a half tick of the dial past. The emperor is dealing with it."

The guard looked relieved. He snapped another salute and stood tall in his position at the right side of the dungeon door.

That meant Aros was already shifting imperial oaths to flow to him. Sehk. Ninli had not been wrong in her assessment. They had little time to change anything in this newly paved hell. He picked up speed.

Ninli strode through the door and Rone followed, shooting a too-bright grin at the men who looked at him askance as he passed. But he wasn't questioned—and they weren't stopped.

"Ninli, what exactly happened while we were gone?" he asked as the door closed behind them.

"Later, I promise." She hurried down the stairs, fingers weaving in the way that she did when she was crafting intricate spells.

When they rounded the dungeon stairs, it was still unreal to see the Scythian royal family and chamber servants behind bars. The royal servants immediately formed a barricade in front of their charges. Ninli's gaze went to the smallest princess and the servant clutching her and he started to realize exactly why they were here.

"Come to finish us off?" one of the elder princesses sneered.

"Valeran!" another voice exclaimed.

Rone blinked and located the girl he had spent the lovely weekend with, but he couldn't be bothered to bring forth any amount of charm. He had put his trust in Ninli, but his gut screamed at him to hurry. And he could see Ninli felt the same.

"I know him! Rone ul Valeran is—"

"He's an imperial child," another hissed back.

"Why are you here, Mistress of Death?" The king stood tall behind his servants.

All gazes turned to Ninli, who stared directly at the king. "The emperor is dead. Aros ul Fehl has taken the throne. I offer you a choice."

The silence of the dungeon fell to shouts.

"Aros!"

"The emperor is dead!"

"We can't trust her," someone said.

"She stopped Nera," someone else hissed.

"The Shadow Prince—"

"What is this choice?" The king held up his hand for silence and moved in front of his servants. "And the price?"

"Your freedom for the chance to fight another day. All we ask in return is for a simple alliance."

"With the Shadow Prince? How is he not the one on the throne?"

"He will be," Ninli said, voice simple and direct.

Rone cringed automatically. Every decision that had gotten him to this point with the girls had been preceded by that voice. If whatever she said in that voice wasn't already true, Ninli would make it so.

The king's eyes narrowed on Ninli. The moment hung.

"Yes," the king said. "We will accept your offer."

"Father!"

"Sire!"

But Ninli was already unlocking the door, and even the vocal opponents were eyeing the spelled bars with gazes hungry to be free.

They filed out of the magicless space and Rone tensed as the antechamber became a room crowded with opponents—some quite powerful. He was exhausted, as was Ninli—it was obvious in her strained expression and posture and the spells that were barely holding around her—she was only just holding herself upright. There had been more than one reason Taline had cast those spells for her. They would be hard-pressed if the Scythians decided to attack.

"Give three destinations," Ninli said to the king. "From those, I will choose the one best suited."

Voices clamored. "Destinations where? How?"

The king held up a hand, silencing the room again. His eyes narrowed on Ninli. "Your eyes bleed, Dark Mistress, Mistress of Death, Wraith of Shadows."

"As do all broken secrets," Ninli acknowledged, eyes tinging red as the strength of her spells dissolved. "Time dwindles, Your Majesty."

"We can take back the castle!" someone shouted. "We can oust the intruders!"

"Aros ul Fehl holds the Scepter of Darkness, as well as all the others of Tehrasi," Ninli said, never disconnecting her gaze from the king's. "Do you wish to remain, fight, and await his arrival? Or do you wish to continue the plans you've already discussed—your armies already seeking to gather in the north?"

"How—?"

"We have a traitor!"

"The shadows!"

The king held up his hand again. "Cius, Sagada, Axion," he said, listing three destinations.

"Father!"

Ninli opened ripgates to all of them instantly.

Gasps rang out and surrounded them. Rone, preparing himself for an assault, let a little more magic drip into his palms.

"Gatemaker!"

"A Barrini?"

"She's a Carre!"

"They are all dead!"

The king and Ninli paid no attention to the chaos that reigned around them, as if they existed in their own space. Ninli knew Rone would protect her back. He felt only resignation at the knowledge. It had always been a myth to believe that he would be free of her web.

Ninli pointed to the gate that led to Sagada. "You will go there. Do not tarry."

The king surveyed her for a long moment. "And so it will be done."

Ninli stepped to the side. "Farewell, Your Majesty. May your rebellion be smooth and unbroken."

"We will never be part of the empire after this," the king warned, not yet taking a forward step.

"No," she said, her voice again simple and direct. "But maybe someday, we will all be part of something more."

The king narrowed his eyes, then nodded sharply and strode through the ripgate. The others were quick to follow.

When the last person was through, Ninli closed all three ripgates. She stumbled and Rone reached out to catch her.

"Got yourself in quite the pickle, little beetle," he murmured, his mind churning on the move that had just been made. Allies—strong ones from outside the empire—who now owed Ninli their lives.

"Yes." She dragged a shaking hand through her hair. "Six more stops. Quick ones, but none so perilous as this."

"Are you sure?" he asked quietly.

She looked at him. "Time dwindles. Nothing matters right now but time. I will be on a leash forevermore after this hour until we fix this mess."

"The Shadow Prince—"

"Trust me."

"You will explain."

"Yes."

He held out his hand.

They made six more jumps, three of them inside Tehras to spots that held enchanted boxes that Ninli quickly filled with spelled messages, and three more to other provinces that held similar communication drop boxes, before finally, finally, returning to where they had left Taline. No more than fifteen minutes had actually passed, but it felt like an eternity. Taline clutched a knife in her hand, which went limp with relief as they appeared.

Rone found his feet moving toward her without his say-so. Before he reached her side, an explosion rocked him from his feet. In the distance, he could see spell lights flaring and soldiers darting to safety.

"That is the fourth explosion," Taline said tightly.

"They've found him." Rone felt an odd sort of numbness that echoed strangely in his voice. He had never...experienced it with the Summoras. They had always been trustworthy—irritatingly so. But Ninli had sent Kaveh ul Fehl to his death. "You sent the broken prince into an arena without power or weapon, and they found him."

Rone didn't care that Kaveh ul Fehl would die. He welcomed it. But that Ninli—

"No," she said calmly. "He is not without weapon. Nor without power."

Ninli was already kneeling to open another ripgate—her hands shaking, her expression tight, her magic stripped and raw—unable to open it without using the earth as a base.

She was going to save the Shadow Prince, no matter the cost to herself. Of course she was.

The strange numbness fled, and easily gathered ancient anger resolved once more. "Leave him to justice, Ninli. He's a monster. He's not worth pity or distress."

No monster was. Rone felt his own magic stir. He felt the monster that slept deep in his chest. He felt it wake and reach from its cold, chain-filled pit. He could stop her. He could stop this. With a flick of his magic, he could stop hers. It would only cost him everything.

Rone touched Taline's arm. Sleep. Her eyes fell shut.

Just this once he would use his power. No one would know but Ninli—and he could save her from herself.

He reached forward and let his power curl.

CHAPTER TWO

OF DARKNESS AND LIGHT

KAVEH

(Cuipsin Military Camp)

Ten minutes prior…

"Take care," Nin whispered. Her ripgate dissolved, taking the image of her with it. With a heart that bled for others, her mission was easy to deduce. Kaveh would make the Scythians pay if they harmed her.

The darkness of the tent descended without starlight to aid, and he automatically reached out with invisible fingers to the power that always answered his call.

Nothing whispered, nothing was revealed, no shadows answered the call.

His flesh fingers curled into fists. Like a thought that resulted in no action, there was no pain, no backlash to the reflexive, shadowed demand. Instead, there was a simple absence of result to a mastered command—like a limb that no longer worked, but that continued sending phantom sensations of availability.

Powerless. He closed his eyes and clenched his fists. He was an animal ripe for slaughter.

He had seen the look in the traitor prince's icy eyes. He knew the man meant to end him. Kaveh looked at his shadowless hands and the dormant air hanging limply around his ankles. He was the predator who had become prey.

Kaveh stood in silence and darkness for long minutes, wrestling with and absorbing this new reality he desperately abhorred. He wondered at Sehk-Ra's plan, at the cursed life he now found himself within.

Kaveh's fists clenched harder. Perhaps he would allow the bastard prince his wish, but it would be after Kaveh watched Aros fall. He focused on the objective and stepped forward.

Even without the enhancement of shadowed sight, he had no need of torch or light. But where his eyes were accustomed to the dark, his senses screamed at the loss of everything he had been. Shadows no longer curved around space to tell him of all the secrets that they found. Unheard were the tales from all the nooks and crannies and the shifts of life and death. Lost, were the secret ways that edges and curves could become allies and hide subterfuge.

The tent flap lay at rest—the only thing separating Kaveh from being seen by the rest of the camp. If someone entered the tent, Kaveh would be a pathetic target in full view. The lack of separation between areas inside the tent was an obstacle he had never needed to consider before. He had never needed physical barriers of privacy—not when shadows could grow into impenetrable obstacles at a thought from his mind. Not when a mere desire could rend the flesh and blood from whoever crossed his path.

No shadow would answer his thoughts or calls now. His fingernails bit into his palms.

Without the lens of magic that had always permeated his vision, without shadows to focus his sight, the tent—the world—felt...less. It was the loss of a sense—like touch or smell or taste—that the body could continue without, but that made the world feel incomplete.

He stepped across the space, eyeing the flap and hating every guarded step. Who was he now, that he had to step softly like a commoner crossing the capital promenade?

He had seen the victims of his father's power—ones who had been stripped of power and the ability to do magic. Some survived. Most did not. He wondered how long it would take his mind to compensate for his loss. He wondered whether it ever would.

His fingers grazed the delicate, bejeweled headdress Nin had taken from her living quarters in Tehras. He had no idea of its origin, but she had looked upon it with fierce longing and sadness. He could no longer feel anything but the faintest mental whisper of her, and it was more likely a desperate delusion of his mind, that whisper.

His fingers slipped over the blue silk veil. He wondered who had gifted it to her—or whether it had been a gift at all. His fingers automatically lifted it and tucked it inside his cloak.

His gaze went from one bright comfort to another, looking at the tent through naked eyes. Nin had permeated his ascetic space with color and texture. Like the increasingly rich food that had appeared each night, her advent into his life had meant an increasingly vibrant world surrounding him instead of the stark one he had maintained before.

It had been exhilarating. The world felt stark once more, though, and the contrast was debilitating.

He lifted her bag and belt and slung them around his neck and across his chest—securing Nin's things before approaching any of his own. What was there to take that was his, anyway? He had always traveled with his own powers wrapped around him. They had been all he had ever needed.

He touched Nin's belt where it touched his heart.

He lifted a knife from the table and slid it into his belt, then lifted an extra cloak from the stand. The darkness inside of it writhed and the shadows bit along the inside of his skin before retreating. Unrecognized, recognized, then uncertain—some fled, bursting into the darkness; others remained, cautious. But he sensed they, too, would eventually flee.

He considered leaving the cloak, but the ache beneath Nin's belt caused him to tuck the cloak into her bag.

Without a way to hold the shadows to him, everything would flee.

He lifted a heavy bag of gold—a "gift" from one of the countries he had recently conquered. Sensation skittered across his skin and Kaveh waved an absent hand to crush the foolish magi on the other end of the eavesdropping spell. The drumbeats of feet and the blaring of the camp alarm were the only things that answered.

"Sehk." Kaveh dove.

No one had dared set an eavesdropping spell in his tent in years. That meant Aros had already made a move. Barely an eighth turn of the night sky and he had moved against Kaveh on his own field.

Without a connection to the shadows to warn him of its existence, the security spell had done its required job—the job it did on all humans it touched. And without his magic, there was nothing he could do after he tripped it.

With little furniture and no barriers, there were few places to hide as his own soldiers tore open the flap to capture or kill him.

"The Imperator Gen—the Emperor Killer is here!"

Kaveh automatically swiped both hands to crush the figures hurrying through, then swore as the giant gaping maw of nothing rose from his palms. Sehk, he had no patience for failure.

He flung the cloak stand at the tent flap as the first soldier's palm formed heart-rending fire. The man jolted in pure terror—as if the stand were made of Kaveh's shadows—and lit himself aflame with the fire in his hand.

Kaveh dodged the blast sent by the second soldier. Had it not been for the man's shaking fear, Kaveh would have been felled. As a consequence, the blast ignited half the tent, lighting the sides and exploding the sleeping linens. Singed erialdown feathers engulfed the tent. It had been a big enough blast to take out a single man—if aimed correctly without shaking hands.

The soldier on fire screamed in agony and stumbled blindly into the men attempting to gain access from outside, creating chaos.

"Move away! Grab that soldier! Flee! The shadows live!" A young voice, vaguely familiar, screamed outside. "The news ball lied! The shadows live! Flee!"

Another explosion rocked the camp, quaking the ground.

Chaos would give Kaveh precious moments before they tried again—and try they would, if Aros had already gotten word out. That still left the one soldier inside.

The soldier looked like a man who had decided to fight Sehk-Ra himself and was regretting everything that had led him to that decision. But, to his credit, he relit his trembling palm. "They say you lost your powers when you ki-killed the emperor. You ki-killed the emperor. I will ki-kill you."

Another explosion rocked the ground. The man drew his quivering palm back.

Kaveh thought distantly of the world-breaking spells that people had tried to kill him with since his birth—spells that had leveled cities, that had destroyed kings and kingmakers. He thought of the god-level spells he had faced, and here, he was going to die at the hands of a simple military fire enchantment wielded by a man he would never have noticed on a battlefield.

An unknown feeling coiled in his gut. Like too-rich or badly spoiled food hitting his stomach. No. It was...worse. A strange, detached feeling of knowing there was no remedy. An emotion so totally foreign to anything he had ever experienced.

Was this fear? This certainty of failure? This vulnerability in the absence of any power or might?

He snarled. Magic or not, he refused to be prey.

He threw the knife from his belt and dove toward one of Nin's scalpels.

The fireball left the figure's hand. The soldier let out a cry as Kaveh's knife drove through his palm and into the wooden pole of the tent. But he was a soldier in Kaveh's forces, and other than his fear of facing the former monster in charge, he was a battle-hardened fighter. He pulled the knife from his hand.

Kaveh grabbed the scalpel between his fingers and whipped his hand forward to throw the blade. A figure flew into the tent. In the middle of the motion, Kaveh had left himself open for a clear kill shot by the second figure—a shot that couldn't miss at this range, even if the second figure also possessed shaking hands.

Death at the shaking hands of a simple soldier. The irony. He, who had held off entire armies single-handedly, today would be beaten by two men—the second the size of a stripling lad.

The second figure deflected Kaveh's thrown blade and wrapped a hand around the back of the neck of the fire thrower just as the fireball left the first's hand. A box was tossed at the soaring fireball, consuming it in midair and sucking up its tail in a giant, greedy grasp, before pulling the rest in like a crocodile wrested upon the riverbanks. The box dropped ignominiously to the floor, along with Kaveh's thrown blade.

The first soldier followed—dropping like a stone. Unconscious, but not dead, he joined his captured flame on the carpets.

The second figure unhooked a bag thrown around his shoulder and chest and checked the downed man.

Kaveh felt a sigh build deep in his chest—he knew those stupidly heroic movements designed to incapacitate and shield, not torture or kill. The face of the boy resolved into one Kaveh knew all too well from the past few weeks.

Kaveh retrieved another scalpel but forced his hand not to release it. Another explosion went off outside. Kaveh distantly realized the voice yelling earlier and the subsequent explosions could probably be directly attributed to the boy before him.

Nin's lead duckling, Akel, threw his bag to Kaveh. "Hurry, Imperator General. You must leave. Aros ul Fehl's edicts are moving on swift wings across the empire's communications."

Akel moved the guard into a position away from the growing fire and turned to put himself in the path of the flap, back stiff. Kaveh recognized this guarding position as well—they were always practicing new combinations of shields and disabling spells whenever Nin passed by in camp.

Kaveh looked at the boy's stiff, thin back and the fire consuming the tent around them. Kaveh understood devotion. Kaveh had been devoted to the emperor and empire. However, this effortless gathering of devotees that Nin collected without force or a show of might was still out of reach of his mind.

"Why?"

"You are tied to her, are you not?" Akel asked tightly, not turning.

"Not anymore." He touched his wrist. He didn't like feeling the bare skin there.

"But you still travel together. She supports you. I can feel her magic lingering here. She opened a ripgate here not thirteen minutes past and is opening another one now just outside the camp's boundaries."

Kaveh narrowed his eyes. He felt a pressing urge to kill Akel, and anyone else who knew about Nin's powers. All the ducklings...if this one knew, they all had to know. The more a specific magic was used around a competent magic user, the easier it was to feel. They had to have known for a long time and been keeping it secret.

"I have no power," Kaveh said.

Akel looked over his shoulder at him as though he were crazy. "You have the support of a goddess."

The tent was on fire, Kaveh's powers were gone, and the entirety of his earthly belongings were going up in flame, and the slip of a boy was telling him he had everything.

He looked at the burning tent. He thought of fate. "I am of no use."

"Use is in the eye of the wielder. And she never abandons those she considers hers." Akel tilted his head. "She will save you. She comes now. I feel the ripple."

"She has physically suffered more than anyone today. She may not be able."

Akel looked solemnly at Kaveh. "Then you will save her."

Kaveh stared at him as the tent burned around them. He could hear people yelling and feel the onrush of water spells falling. Steam rose in great waves.

How had Nin engendered this feeling of loyalty that was so strong a boy was literally bathing in flames for her? Kaveh looked at his powerless hands, as well, to ask it of himself—for he was obviously willing to forsake all for her.

He looked back at Akel as a fourth percussion rocked the ground outside. "Go," he said to the boy.

"She comes," Akel said. "Save the goddess and your empire."

A ripgate tore into view. Akel's eyes went wide and he yanked a glass vial from his belt and threw it through the ripgate, like a target knife toward a competitive stand. Kaveh's gaze and body shot toward Nin, but he was too late. He could only watch as the vial sailed past her and hit Valeran's hand. Valeran cursed and fell. Nin remained unharmed. Kaveh stuttered to a stop.

"Akel?" Nin said. The cacophony and alarms echoed strangely through the ripgate, from the hill within sight of camp. Nin looked between the boy and Valeran, then to Taline sleeping behind. Something in Nin's eyes shifted, but she turned back to Akel with a calm and quiet expression. "All will be well."

Akel smiled—a smile far too bright. The flames had grown in size and volume within the tent. "Mistress Ferra! Of course it will! Now that your blessings are upon us."

The ripgate flickered and Nin motioned with a hand. "Come. Come with us."

Akel looked at the flickering ripgate and resolve descended upon his face. "You have your work, mistress, and we have ours," he said gently, raising on the balls of his feet, ear cocked to the yelling growing closer outside, leaning away from the flames licking toward his clothes.

"Akel." Her voice turned urgent. "They will punish you! You have—"

"Blessings upon you."

Kaveh felt the shove before he realized the boy was moving. Kaveh twisted his body as he fell through the ripgate, just long enough to see

Akel swipe the cloak stand through Nin's magic, slicing the stand where it touched.

"Akel!"

He could feel Nin reach out—could see the magic that shot from her through the closing space to the boy inside.

Kaveh landed on the ground.

Rone ul Valeran was cursing, clutching his hand. Taline ul Summora was unconscious next to him. Nin was frantically pressing her hands to the dirt.

Kaveh knew when relief washed over her face that Akel was alive. From the pulse of magic and from knowing Nin, Kaveh could guess that a ripgate had opened beneath Akel and dropped him in his own tent.

The feel of Nin's magic changed, and the distant camp lit up in a fiery wave of shadow wings. A great beast of darkness lit by flame rose into the air, then dissipated. Screams and flashes of magic lit the camp—some flinging magic to fight the beast, some to defend against it.

Nin took a shaking breath and pitched forward.

Kaveh caught her against his chest and checked her pulse. Beating too fast, but beating, nonetheless. He looked at her face and cataloged the bruised lines and the sickly paste of her skin. Exhaustion. Hopefully, nothing more.

He pulled his cloak from the bag he somehow still clutched and wrapped Nin carefully within it. Larger explosions from camp rent the air. "We have to go," he said.

Valeran grimly positioned himself in front of Taline ul Summora and glared at Kaveh. Hatred and death stared between them. "We aren't going anywhere with you. And our best method of travel just used her last bit of magic to save you."

"If you hadn't had your fit over me staying in this spot, things would be different."

A chill air swirled around Valeran. Taline shifted and murmured in distress. The air abruptly swirled clear.

Kaveh wondered what Valeran had been doing when Nin had opened the ripgate. He wondered what had caused Akel to attack. Nin had not immediately put Valeran down, but Nin trusted too much. Kaveh lifted her, slung the loose bags around his right shoulder and headed toward the coast.

"Where do you think you are going?" Valeran asked bitingly.

"North."

"Not with us, you aren't."

Kaveh shrugged. It would be easier without them. He could even honestly tell Nin that it had been Valeran's choice.

"Not with her," Valeran stressed.

"She can decide for herself when she wakes."

"That's rich. As if she's been making her own decisions these past weeks?"

"Yes." Kaveh's gaze shifted to Taline. She had been conscious last he had seen, and although in pain and exhaustion, she had not looked on the verge of passing out. "Are you certain it is I who should be questioned thus and not you?"

Valeran gave an ugly laugh. There was something inwardly focused about it. "You won't survive the new moon." It was a promise.

Kaveh unleashed the full force of…nothing. Not a single shadow answered his will at the threat. No magic connected to his command. He closed his eyes, then took a step forward. "Neither will they, if you have to carry them both."

He didn't wait for Valeran to respond. Either the man would kill him and try to carry both women, or he would follow and bide his time.

Kaveh had studied all the intelligence gathered about Rone ul Valeran when deciding how to handle his half-brother should he return with the scepter. Valeran was rarely hasty. He held grudges that could not be reasoned with or removed. He was one to plan and plot and slice through with an assassin's blade in the night.

Biding his time was Valeran's forte.

So Kaveh kept his back to the man and continued forward. His fingers wrapped protectively around Nin's unconscious form, and the bag from Akel wrapped around his flesh.

Akel had helped him secure the parts he had needed to make the shadowglass for Nin, but Kaveh had been nothing other than a terror in the night to those beneath him. He might not have terrorized Akel directly, but he had not cared for the riffraff of the army at his fingertips.

Kaveh had kept countries in line by exerting power and creating fear—all things which had made the emperor appear even stronger as the holder of his leash.

Now it was Nin who made Kaveh stronger. Made Kaveh appear worthy of saving.

He was shadowless, powerless, and easy prey—but Akel had protected him. Akel had helped a man who had stepped over his carcass weeks ago and left him to die. And tonight, in the greater camp chaos, Akel's plan had probably been supported by all the other ducklings Kaveh had brushed aside. They had helped because someone had helped them, because someone had believed in them and cared. Because Nin had cared.

What was power then?

Kaveh curled his fingers around her form and looked at the night sky with eyes that held no answers and no shadows.

CHAPTER THREE

ALLIES AND ENEMIES

TALINE

(The Kiffian Desert)

Taline dreamed of darkness. She dreamed of anger and despair and the wrenching away of all that she was.

She opened her eyes at the first rays of dawn to see Nin waking as well. Her sister was wrapped within the Shadow Prince's cloak, and the Shadow Prince was watching Nin with the intensity that he did everything. Nin stretched carefully in the way cautious soldiers did after great muscle fatigue and weariness.

"I'm awake," Nin murmured, running a hand along the shoulder of the Shadow Prince. A diagnostic spell slipped across his skin. "Sleep."

"I can't."

Nin was watching the prince with sad eyes. "Just for a bit. I'll keep watch." He didn't answer for a long moment, then gave a short nod. Nin squeezed his shoulder softly, threading a sleeping spell over him.

Taline frowned. She cataloged her own internal exhaustion and wakefulness. Had someone slipped a sleeping spell over her? But Nin would have asked first. Nin always asked first, even if in gesture—the Shadow Prince obviously knew well enough what was being asked when he had nodded.

Silence descended until the Shadow Prince's breath evened out. Nin kept running diagnostic spells across his frame.

"You should sleep, too." Nin's chin turned in Rone's direction, but her gaze never left the Shadow Prince.

"The sleep of death," Rone said. His gaze met Taline's, then skittered away, something tired and grieving in them. His eyes closed, though Taline wasn't deluded into thinking he was sleeping.

Taline wanted to demand to know what was wrong, but what wasn't wrong?

She looked over at the Shadow Prince, discomfort and fear mixing with a strange kind of sympathy. It was...beyond odd to see him asleep, exposed to the world, no magic, no shadows swirling in vicious readiness around him. Taline could slip a knife between his ribs.

She knew Rone had likely already sharpened his with intent.

Taline let Nin sort herself out for a few moments, fingers moving over her patient.

"I'm angry with you," Taline said.

Nin paused her ministrations. "I know."

"You left me." That hadn't been what Taline wanted to say. But once it was out, she understood its truth. "You wanted me to leave you."

"Yes," Nin whispered.

Taline sat up—the blanket sliding to pool in her lap—and addressed the emotion that had been simmering for weeks. "You don't get to make that choice for me."

Nin closed her red eyes. "I didn't want you to be hurt. I never want you hurt."

"I know." Taline gripped the blanket tight. "Which is why, though I'm angry with you, we will get through it. But not by me leaving you."

Nin let out a choked little sound. Taline pulled her against her chest, disregarding the abominable cloak draping Nin with its wisps of clinging shadows and the previous owner who was far too physically close.

"It's all a mess," Nin murmured into Taline's neck. As if the fire and control had drained from her completely, Nin seemed so much younger in this moment. "Kaveh, Tehrasi, the scepter, Aros, the empire."

As far as Taline was concerned, the Shadow Prince could expire quietly in the forest or loudly on the tip of an imperial spear, but she valiantly kept silent and continued to hold her sister.

"But you're here," Nin said against her skin. "And you're alive."

Taline clutched her close. In the end, it was that simple. Forgiveness was simple. They were together again, and anything could be forgiven for making that happen.

"What happened?" She pulled back to see Nin's face. "And why are you keeping him safe?"

Nin's gaze flitted downward and her fingers ran up and down the cloak's patterned edge. "I found a reason to fight."

"For the empire?"

"Yes."

"But the emperor was going to…" Taline pressed her lips together. "The scepter showed me what was happening. I followed its hook."

"Yes."

"And you wanted to fight for an emperor who would enslave you as well as cause you harm?"

"The empire is not the emperor. It was created and imbued by him, but it can be other. More."

"You see kings in villains," Taline said tiredly, "when most people see villains in kings." Nin had always seen the good in people—even people who deserved no consideration. Either due to trauma from her past, or perhaps a way to justify her own existence—an existence born from cruelty.

"It is a question that all those born without true light seek—can a monster become a hero?" Nin's fingers moved aimlessly, and her voice took on a distant tone.

"You aren't a monster," Taline said sharply. "Nor born without light."

Nin's lips pulled into a smile—sad and fond. "Not enough of a monster in a family of fiends—that was its own curse. But also not born to the path of sunlight. We must choose and walk our path. Do you believe those born without light can rise when given it?"

Caution stayed Taline's primary response. Nin's family had always been her greatest anchor. She chose her words carefully.

"A villain cannot become a great king, no." She thought of Etelian and his selfish and cruel pleasures. "But then, a villain is a villain by his choices, not by birth's light."

Nin reached up and curled a hand around the back of Taline's neck. "Yes."

Taline licked her lips, uncertain what she had just agreed to—knowing that she had doomed herself to it even as she felt the warmth of Nin's regard in her chest. There was an expectation of maturity now that Taline wasn't sure she could meet. It was the curse of loving Nin—that her expectations of greatness forced one to want to rise to them.

"If a person wants something—powerfully wants something that requires change..." Nin removed a strange looking glass from her pocket and held it between her fingers. A small shadow moved inside the glass. A trick of the light, Taline told herself. "Change on the inside is a most powerful choice."

"Sher Fehl—"

"Was a villain in many contexts, but before he became emperor? He was trying for his people. He succeeded in giving them opportunity by combining lawless groups under one firm and progressive rule. He wasn't the monster whispered about in the night. Not at first. Not even at the end."

Taline's eyes skittered to the Shadow Prince. To the monster who was at the center of the empire's iron hold and expansion. "And him?"

"He is still making his choices. People follow him naturally from strength and fear. It will be up to him if he wishes to seek other paths."

But Taline could sense doom in the way that Nin stared at the Shadow Prince, as if she already knew he was going to choose correctly and was simply waiting for everyone else to see it. "Nin, you can't fix him."

Taline had seen her work on his locked magic from the moment she and the prince had stumbled from the palace ripgate.

"No." Nin gazed at the dormant air around the man, where once there had been writhing, shuddering activity. "In the end, it will be fixed from within the Fehls or not at all."

Taline frowned. "The emperor's magic is permanent. No other Fehl wields that power. There's nothing anyone can do."

Nin stared at the looking glass in her hand, tipping it to the left and right. "Yet here it is, still trapped within."

Taline moved sharply, throwing the blanket from her lap over the glass. "That is his magic?"

Nin sighed and softly pushed the blanket away. "A remnant. A memory. But where there is life, there is hope."

Taline fought the powerful urge to bat it from her sister's fingers. "A memory of what?"

"A gift," she said softly. "One that required his abilities to give, and yet..." She twisted the glass. "His shadows and powers, like all magic, live for a brief time without renewal or aid." Nin touched her cloak and the thinning shadows inside.

"You think the prince's magic can be restored within a time frame." A shiver went through her. Taline didn't want that. She could see her sister did, but the image of Kaveh ul Fehl returning to his former self...

A strange expression passed across Nin's face. "I know it can. But time...yes, time will tell. And a price paid."

"What kind of price?"

Nin shook her head. She tucked the glass back inside the cloak. Taline wanted to rip both of them away to burn in the fire. But she had seen this look on her sister's face before. She had seen her tend and restore one wounded lamb after another.

Taline had not succeeded in ridding Nin of Rone, and she would not easily rid her of this prince either.

"I know you have questions, Tali. And I have some answers, though not all."

"Tell me." Make me understand.

Nin began her tale. Of how she had been threatened by the emperor, beaten mentally by the battlefield, bound more tightly to Kaveh ul Fehl—but this time by her own overpowering will to make it so—and finally how she had been unmasked to the empire.

"Aros knows the name to which I was born."

"He isn't the only one." Rone spoke up for the first time in the hours it had taken for Nin to recite the tale, confirming the notion that he had never planned to sleep and had only pretended to in order to give them a mask of privacy.

He and the Shadow Prince had both obviously stayed awake while Taline and Nin had slept. Rone really should have taken the chance to rest. She wondered if he couldn't allow himself to yet.

It was reminiscent of the night they had spent before entering the Scepter Temple—neither man trusting the other. Only this time, the power did not rest with the Shadow Prince, and the Shadow Prince had put himself in Nin's hands.

"The Scythians saw her eyes," Rone said.

The tale of the Scythians had come at the end of Nin's story. And though they seemed tentative allies, the Scythians would not be able to stand against the Scepter of Darkness in the hand of a man who already controlled their capital.

"The Scythians may be long in showing their hand, but Aros will spread her heritage." Taline frowned. "He'll use the Carre legacy against Nin. It will benefit him."

"Which is why we should go to another layer." Rone rose and looked at Nin pointedly, no longer bothering to feign sleep.

"There is nowhere we can hide."

"Not with Kaveh ul Fehl, no. Ninli, he is the reason you are in this mess in the first place."

Nin's gaze went remote. "And yet he is also the reason I am here. He saved me."

"You saved him, too. Debt paid. You are even."

Nin looked as uncomprehending at being "even" as ever. "I will save him again and again, if that is what it takes. He is mine now."

"Sehk," Taline swore.

"Ninli," Rone growled.

"I will understand if you seek other fields." She looked at Rone and there was something old in her eyes—ancient and accepting. "You know I will not hold you here or make you do that which you do not choose."

Taline carefully lifted her blanket back onto her lap, examining its rough edges. She did not want to see the agreement on Rone's face or the moment when he said he was leaving. She did not want to see the moment his body turned. She did not want to see the charming grin as he walked away.

She would never forget his help. But he had
done his part. He had no reason to stay. Not with
the stakes so high.

It would be better for everyone if he left.
Really, it would. Taline could already feel herself
separating from him—a self-preservation tactic
she had too often needed and used. People
didn't stay with her. Only Nin had held her close,
and even Nin had tried to leave.

No, she thought. Nin had not left, but she had
encouraged and accepted Taline's leaving, and
that had hurt all the same. But then, Nin was a
little broken—they all were. And without Taline,
Nin's broken edges made it harder to make
smooth choices.

And maybe that was what made Taline push
against the separation straining to overtake her,
and to tell Rone what she desired instead.

"I wish you to stay." Taline's fingers shook a
little on the thin blanket, worn and torn from
traveling for weeks without mending aid.

She struggled to lift her gaze, giving in to a
last bit of vulnerability before she had to be
strong again. She finally looked up, expecting

a witty, deflecting comeback, but his lips were parted and his eyes wide. Her gaze skittered away, confusion and something that felt like hope pushing against each other. "If you wish to stay," she added.

"Aros will hunt us," Rone said flatly.

But in the grim resignation of his tone, she felt only relief. He would stay. At least for a bit, he would stay.

"Aros is clever and smart." Nin shook her head. "And a step ahead in this. He knew the only one with the ability and standing to cage Kaveh was the emperor, and the only ones who could stand against the emperor were Irsula and the emperor's favorite son. But since Kaveh would stand between his parents, the emperor would likely prevail in such a scenario."

Nin looked to the distance. "A singular dilemma, then—how to get the emperor to take Kaveh's magic? For the emperor loved his son. And Kaveh was a dutiful one—he was the crown of the Fehl Empire, the Sunlight Empire, the envy of all the others of imperial birth. How to remove him from the field of play? For when had the emperor ever punished him? Kaveh succeeded at all he attempted before the scepter came into play. And the emperor was the only one who could punish him. Without the scepter, even the emperor couldn't have stopped Kaveh had Kaveh chosen to fight back when the emperor took his magic."

Taline had heard the recitation of events during Nin's summary, but thinking of the planning behind them churned her gut. But then, Aros had always been a threat to Nin. Nin had never trusted her own bloodline.

"Aros waited. He schemed. And when he saw opportunity, he put events into play." Nin swallowed and Taline saw her agony—for Nin had been part of that opportunity. Kaveh ul Fehl had made a choice for Nin.

Taline looked at Rone, who shook his head slowly, gaze fierce. Don't feel for the prince. Don't feel for the monster. Don't feel for Kaveh ul Fehl.

"Kaveh sacrificed himself to his father," Nin said. "And that sacrifice cost the emperor his life—for Kaveh was the only one who could have stood against Irsula. Aros knew—he knew if he could take Kaveh out of the play and release Irsula, the emperor would not survive. It was his only play, really. The emperor was too powerful—and his hubris, not his power, was his downfall. Aros couldn't take out the emperor on his own. He had to plan around him. He had to put his play on Irsula and Kaveh." She moved her fingers along the edges of her shadow-damned cloak. "He had to pit Kaveh against the emperor. But how? Kaveh loved the emperor. And the emperor was Kaveh's only weak point. Kaveh could destroy Aros easily. Aros could not stand against him. Aros has always known this. Kaveh with his powers could possibly destroy Aros even with the scepter in Aros's hand. Possibly."

Rone's gaze turned stormy as he looked at Nin, who was carefully looking away from him. "And then he will pick the scepter up, and what then, Ninli?"

"He will destroy it. We will destroy it."

Rone barked an ugly laugh. "Ninli, you will never convince me of that."

Ninli said nothing for a long moment, then nodded. "You think he will become worse than all the wielders before."

"I know he will. Did you see Irsula of Denz, Ninli?"

"He is not his mother."

"He is a monster."

Nin looked at Rone, and instead of anger, there was only compassion. "No."

"Ninli—"

Taline frowned at them. "It matters not. The emperor's powers are absolute. We need to discuss Aros." When neither of them responded, her frown grew. "Aros will grow stronger with the scepter, but the scepter will lead him to madness. Can we not...wait?" Wait for madness to descend and consume? Wait for the scepter to drop and search for a new body to control?

"In his madness, he will destroy." Nin's fingers ran along the cloak. "He will become a true Carre."

"He will become what he desires," Taline said pointedly. "Blood is only what you make of it."

A small smile bloomed across Nin's lips, warming Taline where the fire had failed. Nin tipped her head. "Our best play—Tehrasi's best play and the empire at large—is to restore Kaveh's powers."

"No," Rone said, voice implacable.

Taline blinked slowly at Nin. "You think the emperor's powers will undo with his death?"

"Perhaps." Nin looked down and away."

Taline's eyes narrowed. "How do we heal him? You said you could not." And though Taline felt the press of Nin's stories and the irrefutable proof of the magicless Shadow Prince laying a pace away, she was reluctant to trust in the notion that this direction was right.

Nin said nothing for long moments. "There are options. Rites, waters, rituals. One of them might work."

"People have searched for ways to heal themselves after the emperor has taken their powers. None have succeeded." Taline frowned and turned to Rone. "That relic you—"

"I destroyed it." Rone's voice was implacable.

"But, there might be anoth—"

"There is not."

She narrowed her eyes and wondered. Had he not destroyed it? There was a secret there—a truth he was unwilling to disclose. "I don't deny reservations on curing the Shadow Prince. But Nin trusts him."

"Ninli trusts everyone. I could create odes to her stupidity. She trusts in the worst people."

"She trusts me."

Rone nodded. "Exactly."

But where it would have been harsh and cruelly said before, she felt her shoulders relax a measure at the almost playfulness of the word. He was too angry and distressed to be truly playful, but she understood that it was as near to levity as he could come at the moment.

"It is hard to trust people who are capable of making hard decisions. Because sometimes the hard decisions are ones that are not for the trustee. Sometimes decisions are made that benefit more or other than the one who trusted," Nin said softly. "If the decisions are fair or right, then I go to my death in peace. I can ask for no more than doing my part for humanity."

Taline frowned. "You are still trying to make up for a past you had no part in."

"We all have a part. And the realization of suffering—even if you aren't who caused it, is it not within you to try and ease it?"

"You trust too much in the good of people, Ninli," Rone said coldly.

In me, went unsaid clearly.

"Just the right amount, I think." She looked at him.

Rone gritted his teeth. "I won't."

"I know." She said it in that simple way she had. A statement of fact that asked nothing in return—that made the other person feel the personal responsibility of their own actions curl irrefutably. The choice was always theirs. Taline always felt comfort in that choice. Rone clearly did not. She could hear his teeth grind harder together.

What wouldn't Rone do?

"She doesn't trust Etelian," Taline pointed out. "And we haven't been stabbed yet."

"I'm going to stab you."

"No you aren't."

"I put a sleeping spell on you outside the camp," he said harshly, avoiding her gaze as he said it. "That's why you slept."

A tension she didn't realize she had been carrying released. Part of her had recognized and gripped the abnormality and uncertainty was sometimes worse than knowledge. "Why?"

"I was going to get rid of the Shadow Prince." He looked pointedly at Nin. "I still plan to."

But Taline wasn't going to let them have their own conversation again. "Why did you put a sleeping spell on me in order to do it?"

His palms curled. A trick of the light almost made it look like a faint sheen of blue surrounded them. "Because I'm a monster."

She touched his arm. "You were trying to keep me from seeing."

There was pain in his eyes, and a strange desire that he shoved down too quickly for her to inspect. "You trust too easily."

"I don't. You know I don't. Just don't do it again."

"I won't." There was something ugly in his tone, inwardly focused.

"I know," she said simply. It was an easy enough deduction. He wouldn't look so upset about it otherwise.

He growled and turned in his blanket, putting his back to them as if he was going back to sleep.

Taline frowned. "Good. You need to sleep."

Nin pulled the bags to her lap and started going through the contents—sorting and cataloging. She frowned at a glass ball, setting it carefully to the side, before tucking through her belt and spreading herbs upon the blanket in count. "How are you feeling?"

"Empty." The expanse of hunger stretched.

"Scepter sickness." Nin ran her fingers across her cheeks and checked her eyes. "I can make a cordial to help."

"Inebriated sounds nice."

Nin shook her head, smiling. "Let's go for a gentle soothing."

"But it will go away? This...this feeling of loss?"

Nin's fingers tapped and her eyes tightened. "Eventually."

"Eventually?"

"You are tied to the scepter's magic. Addictions don't just cease, even when the user takes a first massive step away." She looked at Taline. "You let the scepter go, though. The strength that requires..."

It was reflected in Nin's eyes again—an awe and expectation that Taline wasn't sure she could match.

"The scepter made promises—about who I could be." Taline looked at Nin. "I decided to be Taline ul Summora—and she was already who I was."

Nin squeezed Taline's hand gently, and her smile—shaky, but bright—grew to solar proportion.

Overwhelmed, Taline looked down and searched for another subject. Her gaze caught on the orb that Nin had removed. "A communications orb? From where?"

"From Akel." Nin lifted and turned it in her fingers, sorrow threading through her words. "It's what the camps use."

Akel had featured highly in Nin's recitation. Taline looked forward to meeting him. "I'm sure he is fine." Nin had used the last of her magic to make it so.

Nin stared at the orb. "The commanders know who he served. Who all the youngest served. They will have to either disappear into the ranks or run. And I fear disappearing won't be possible under Aros."

"What do you think he will—"

Taline felt a pull in her gut and Nin's head jerked west. Magic from the three of them spread immediately over the camp, dousing the flames and pushing their residual magic field down. Rone flung aside his blanket and crouched with them, a faint blue light in his palms.

But she had no time to wonder, as their attention focused west, toward the oasis they had originally landed in and walked from. Brilliant lights lit in the oasis. As if speaking of him had spurred him to action, Aros was looking through Nin's ripgates.

The Scepter of Darkness could feel the ripgates Nin had created. Time hadn't improved their chances, only distance.

Their eyes met. Nin wouldn't be able to open a ripgate without Aros following.

Nin gently touched the Shadow Prince, removing the sleeping spell. He opened his eyes, at once. Taline shivered at his sudden alertness. Were they really going to try to rearm this man?

"Aros is at the oasis," she murmured.

Long, tense minutes passed as they waited for the light show to end. When it finally did—when Taline felt the pull leave her gut—Nin rose.

"He is gone, but he will send scouts when he has reached the end of the gates I made. We must be ready."

She lifted the orb, and the shadow cloak slithered from her shoulders and pooled on the ground.

She stepped forward, toward the oasis, eyes scanning the distance.

"The dark moon rises in six minutes. We—"

The pull yanked at Taline again, more intensely. Taline stumbled, Nin stumbled, and a beam of circular light ripped through their campsite.

"Hello, cousin."

CHAPTER FOUR

THE NEW EMPEROR

NINLI

(The Kiffian Desert)

Nin didn't pause to watch Aros step through the rift. She pulled the world out from underneath him.

Stillness became frenzied movement as the silence of the camp was ripped by activity.

Golden light streamed overhead and Aros dropped from the sky in a fall of gilded robes. "A lovely little trick that I finally get to utilize." Aros rose and smiled at her in the midst of their mad scramble to break camp. His smile had a maddened edge. "Hello again, cousin."

Taline was lunging for their belongings, Rone was throwing daggers, Kaveh had his hands extended, and Nin was trying—and failing—to pull the world out from under Aros again.

"That was your one chance, cousin." His hand rose menacingly. "The scepter shows everything."

In a hurried arc, Nin erected a three-pace dome, the automatic defense to any scepter that could slice.

A blast scorched the campsite and Nin darted left, opening a ripgate a hairsbreadth outside the dome and in front of the blast. No ripgate could form inside the erected dome for the period of the spell and she didn't want to test the dome against any scepter blast that wasn't a direct aim to slice in half. Ripgates had been used offensively and extensively to execute people in the palace by removing body parts. She knew exactly how to do it, but she could not slice Aros's hand off while he was holding the scepter. The Scepter of Darkness automatically protected its wielder against ripgates. She had to be creative.

Aros smiled. "How long can you keep it up, I wonder?"

Nin pulled a massive ripgate over him, but he swept the scepter through it, shattering it into motes. His eyes glowed with power, even above the sunken, tormented circles beneath. Only one night with the scepter, and Aros's eyes already showed the changes. Whatever blood enchantments Nera had placed on her eldest at birth to make him look exactly like her were sliding away like paint in a thunderstorm. Once-brown irises were now streaked with red—blood spilling over encasing amber.

Nin swung right, opening two ripgates three paces to each side of Aros, allowing Rone to throw a knife through one and have it spew out from another at Aros's back. Taline pulled out a clutch of papyrus and swirled it into the air.

Everyone was in motion, except Kaveh. Kaveh's hands were extended. His body was frozen in disbelief and torment.

Aros's pleased gaze focused on him as the scepter automatically erected a shield that devoured Rone's daggers and obliterated Nin's ripgates. "Oh, Kaveh," he said as he turned the scepter. "Look at you. I can't imagine your agony. Let me take it from you."

The scepter glowed brightly, and Nin gave up on trying to throw Aros somewhere else. Seeing his deadly intent, Nin pulled the world around her, forcing it to slingshot her out. She threw herself over Kaveh. The force of the scepter burst around them, and she used her momentum to spin them into the ground.

They spun up again behind Aros. Dirt exploded in a shower where they had been standing seconds before.

She hastily erected a second ripgate-resistant dome, but feeling the energy drain immediately, she prepared her next move carefully. She kept Kaveh behind her and clasped his hand to her waist to secure his position.

Aros turned. Hunger and anticipation suffused his expression as he batted away Taline and Rone's efforts from beneath the first dome. "Join me, cousin. Think of the things we could do. We can carve a new way forward for the empire. For people like us."

Ignoring his overture, she felt out along the paths that joined together in her mind as her magic splayed outward like a living enchantment, showing her all the ways that she could manipulate space. She had been practicing her craft these last few weeks. Practicing in a way that she had never been able to before.

Like Aros, she had been constricted by the curse of her birth in an empire that would not allow the free use of a gatemaker's power. But during her time with Kaveh, his protective shadows had freed her to use her powers and practice new moves and skills. And in that time, she had learned a few tricks.

She dropped a tree through a rip in the sky above Aros's head. "We had our day."

His eyes widened and he threw a cutting enchantment upward with his hand, forgetting about the scepter's abilities for the moment. Large chunks of the trunk crashed toward him. The scepter pulsed at the danger to its wielder and the tree exploded.

Aros stared at the scepter and a slow smile pulled his lips outward. "How delightful. The scepter seeks to protect its wielder. Irsula really is a marvel—that she was able to overcome such inherent defenses."

"It will drive you mad!" Nin shouted while she rifled through landscape points until she found oppressive heat.

Aros reached out with his free hand. "The scepter cannot return that which is lost. What use have I for sanity? It is in our blood—madness. Along with the power to wield it."

She yanked at the layer. "It is in our blood to be consumed by it," she said as lava poured from the sky. "Who was the boy you sacrificed?"

Aros thrust both his free hand and scepter into the air, and the lava poured around him in a canopy of sizzling red. The streams of red darkened to black as they fell.

Aros displayed a natural predilection for wielding a scepter, and there was no doubt in Nin's mind that he had studied everything he could find about them. In secret. In readiness. Until the day he could claim his birthright. Until the day he could be what he was born to.

She pulled at a landscape point she had actively avoided and buzzing soon overwhelmed the space as a swarm of confused locusts poured through.

The scepter swiped through large swaths of insects, and the irritation caused Aros to split his concentration.

While Aros's attention was temporarily overwhelmed by the mass of insects, Taline had been pressing pieces of papyrus into Rone's hands. Rone required another ten seconds to complete his task.

"But never chained." Aros snarled, while swiping at the locust. "Cousin, think. The pentalayerists, the scared, those who wish to see us not reach our full potential." Another swipe, this one larger and more irritated. "Scared of an ability instead of the person wielding it."

"I think they were quite scared of the people wielding it," she said gravely, moving to the right with Kaveh behind her—putting Rone and Taline behind Aros, as Aros chose to mirror her movements while still speaking. "Who was the boy?"

Aros's expression turned frenzied.

"He was your son, wasn't he? Blood matters to deals with demons." Nin had long speculated that only Lorsali's fear of their parents had held her back from sacrificing Nin for something both grand and petty.

Aros narrowed his eyes strangely. "You will tell me how to return him."

It was obvious that the sacrifice had devastated him on a level he had not been willing to accept previously. A man who had been without tight tie had found a measure of connection with another—and he had sacrificed that person in order to achieve his goals. That he felt remorse meant he was human. But it didn't mean she had to feel pity for his actions. He had made the choice.

"There is no return," she said softly.

"You lie. I remember each of you. I memorized every interaction we had with the Carres with avaricious eyes, especially during the ceremonies for the Festival of Blood. I remember Lorsali. And I remember the tiny wraith of a girl who stood no higher than her waist—who everyone marveled would be as strong as Savvan. I remember Lorsali's jealousy and petulance."

Nin stuttered to a stop, swallowing. Her countdown became lost in the scramble of memory. "You know nothing of Lorsali's petulance."

"No?" He laughed, while rotating and thrusting the scepter toward Rone and Taline.

Nin pulled them safely to her as Aros threw a hail of ice shards. Frost decorated the ends of Taline's hair.

"I think you'll find that I'm quite knowledgeable. And I can hurt you irreparably."

Fire burst through the air in ripgates that were so close that she could feel the blast of heat as they opened. Only by being in motion and gathering all four of them in a double ripgate with one exit, was she able to flip them out of the way of certain death and deposit them in the catacombs of Rasse in a tangle of bodies.

Lorsali had always targeted those around Nin first. She had known exactly where to hurt. The reminder of her only focused Nin more.

"Ninli, did you intend to trap us?" Rone's voice was tight as they all scrambled upright.

Nin pushed back the memories and readied herself for the next assault, pushing them behind her into a corner of stone several bodies thick. "He will annihilate us in the open. I can't hold fully functional domes and fight. And I can't save all of us from full assault attacks from multiple ripgates."

It was like encountering Kaveh that first time. There were only so many times a surprise maneuver worked. It was the downside of showing one's spells to a powerful wielder—they learned your techniques and used them against you the next time.

It was the justification that had held up the progression of Tehrasi and other civilizations throughout history—the rich and powerful not wanting the weaker or cruelly born to rise or become equal. For that meant there was nothing special about the elite, an ignominious death.

During a fight to the death, Nin had a little more empathy for those not wanting to share their best maneuvers and stratagems. But knowledge was inevitable. The only thing to do was learn new techniques.

She would catalog every move Aros made.

"The domes... When he realizes he can simply slice us all in twain if he gets the opening right, we are done." Taline's voice was grim.

Aros appeared in a blinding collection of sunlight in the thin hall—stone crumbling around him. His eyes were frenzied and oddly lit. "Trapped, cousin. You are trapped in your feelings for your sister. I can see it, and I know this pain. We will free ourselves. Build a new, better civilization, ruled by those who know power and pain."

And it was all she had ever wanted—to build a better world for her people—to be a good force in the layers.

"Fight with me." Aros thrust out his free hand. "And I will spare those at your back."

"No," said a voice behind her.

Aros looked over her shoulder and bared his teeth. "Kaveh, dear brother of my heart, but not my flesh, your time is at an end in this. Be silent."

"You will die for killing the emperor."

"Will I? With what? Your shadows? I feel nothing from you." Aros tilted his head, his voice dripping with disdain. "Not a sliver of energy. You always had so much capacity—flexing your powers constantly, calling forth darkness with every breath. And now, nothing. You don't even rate as the least of those with the faintest power. A pity."

Kaveh stiffened against Nin's back, then she felt him wrench his arms downward, felt him clutch at something.

"Shadow Prince," Rone murmured with warning.

Aros's brows rose as he watched. "Disrobing for your death? I approve. Perhaps I need not worry about you after all. The Valeran bastard will take care of sweeping up for me before I sweep him to dust."

Nin desperately wanted to look behind her, but she couldn't afford to look away from Aros.

Aros smiled. "There is only one way to save them." He reached out.

She stepped back, pressing the others into the thick wall behind.

Then suddenly heavy cloth was wrapped around her, and Kaveh was gripping the cloth at the front of her throat in the vise of his fingers. "Take us back!" he hissed in her ear.

Aros's brows shot into his hairline. "Killing her will not save you. I'll simply resurrect her."

Nin could feel Taline and Rone grabbing Kaveh's hands. "Take—"

But Aros's eyes pinched tight suddenly and he raised his hand. "What is this? What have you done? I can feel your sickened, frozen strings of black and silver again but not her—?"

"Back to our things!" Kaveh said harshly in her ear, fingers stabbing his gryphon cloak pin into place at her throat. "Now!"

She automatically heeded the command in his voice and dropped them through a ripgate in the floor and straight into the desert campsite.

Rone and Taline stumbled in confusion and panic, but Kaveh landed in a crouch and sprinted for where they had slept. He scooped up the cloak she had slept in and threw it around his shoulders—replacing the one newly wrapped around her body.

"What—?"

"Grab everything!"

"Aros will follow!" Taline spit, but she was already pulling things to her in the moment they had before Aros tracked them.

"Grab everything!" Kaveh roared.

Rone looked as though he were contemplating fratricide. But his hand swooped out and their last things rolled into a pack just as golden light split the clearing.

Nin heaved in a breath as Aros's gate took shape, and focused.

"Take us to a city," Kaveh ordered. "One meant for you—with gates."

Taline grabbed Nin's arm, comprehension dawning. "To a dark moon temple! It is almost upon us."

Nin didn't let herself think. As unnatural golden light overtook the rising dawn, Nin opened a flowing ripgate that scooped up all of them, depositing them in southern Skudra. The magnificent city of Bekli stretched its massive arms between the curling northern cradle of the Purattu and Idiqlat Rivers. Nin dropped them right in the city center—ripgate edge cutting through a vendor's stand.

People shouted and jolted away. Nin swore and yelled out an apology to the stand's owner, who stood frozen in shock. She never used her abilities in areas where people were present for two reasons—not wanting her actions to be observed and not wanting to kill people accidentally.

Rone shoved her forward. "No time." No time for niceties when death stalked your steps.

Turning a corner, they skidded to a stop, as they reached the town center and an impasse of bodies.

Thousands of people bent forward in the dawn's light, crowns bowed toward the sky where the dark moon would rise and command a new moon cycle. Starting fresh—a celebration of the dark moon. There would be a festival tonight to celebrate the new cycle, and people would travel through the moon gates to visit other cities.

Once something became tradition, it was accepted and desired. Praying to the moons, honoring their rise, worshiping at gates, and paying homage at a moon or sun temple powered to transport people to other temples was welcomed. But accepting and honoring a magi who could open gates without going through the land's authority? That did not sit well with people who imagined all the ways that power could be used against them. No one wanted a magi they didn't agree with to have power over them.

She wasn't unsympathetic to Aros's anger, but she also wasn't unsympathetic to those who didn't trust people like the Carres.

Golden light spilled behind them and familiar hands prodded her forward through the crowd, toward the grand round temple rising into the sky. She called out apologies as they tripped over worshipers.

Streets filled with humanity stretched before them. There were no khursifas or mechanical magics moving during the silent dawn celebration. The city winds were shut down to travel—most of Bekli's regular citizenry were bowed in the square or crammed into the side streets, while all Bekli's elite were in the distant temple facing east-northeast, bowing to the moonrise.

In Nin's eyes, Tehras would always be most magnificent, but Bekli—like Ur, Babil, Memfi, and countless other cities of significance—was its own wonder to behold.

The temple at Ur celebrated all things moon related and it would have been a good choice for their needs, but at the center of Bekli was the great temple honoring a specific aspect of the moon—the dark moon—and the magic there was undeniable.

"You couldn't have dropped us within the temple itself?" Rone huffed, hands flinging a shield into existence behind them. "We'll never get through the crowd."

She cringed. "There will be hundreds of people worshiping in there. I'd have killed at least a dozen in a ripgate opening."

"Aros is going to kill all those in the crowd around us."

Despair wound around her throat in a choking grip. She pulled up another ripgate, but was pushed by the crowd, losing the motes of magic.

"How did you hide your string, cousin?" Aros demanded, suddenly appearing in a flash of gold light that split two worshipers in twain.

Nin's fingers spread out automatically to stitch their bodies back together.

Unexpectedly, Kaveh pulled a staff from someone in the shifting tide of bodies and jabbed it into Aros's throat. It struck true.

Aros choked, curling forward.

Taline grabbed Nin and shoved her sideways. Rone threw a spell skyward.

She saw Kaveh raise his hands again, then curse. His fury grew stronger with each unsuccessful but automatic cast of magic he tried, and failed, to make.

A screeching voice echoed through the square at the bloom of Rone's enchantment. "Aros ul Fehl is trying to kill everyone in the empire on the dark moon with the Scepter of Darkness! Run!"

Bowed heads turned and the people who were not already screaming started to do so as Aros lifted the scepter.

"There!"

The crowd reacted. They rose and pushed together in pockets of panic.

Nin used the opportunity to scoop the four of them into a flipping ripgate between one pocket of citizens and another just as Aros's beam hit the spot where they had been.

Wails of pain and terror echoed behind.

People yelled and screamed as the mass of humanity shifted wildly in the overflowing square. The crowd began stampeding—fleeing from Nin as quickly as from the man who held a scepter and whose eyes bled red.

The skies, previously cleared of travel, filled as the investigorii of the city—the Ravens of Bekli—descended in screeching waves from their perches.

"Halt!" The Ravens screeched to a stop above the crowd at their commander's voice. The Investigore of Bekli looked between Aros and Kaveh; his hand hovered in the air, hesitating, gaze intense.

Tyre ul Fehl, Padifehl of Skudra, would have been notified immediately as to what was happening in one of his principal cities—what he would order his investigorii to do was the question, and the hesitance of the Ravens highlighted that indecision.

Then the investigore's hand moved—straight at the four of them. Against them.

Nin felt the pulse from the scepter vibrate up her spine as the Ravens dove. Despair rocked through her. She stared at an alley to the right of the temple—and focused on the only empty balcony one up from street level. She kept her gaze fixed as she whirled and grabbed the three in her arms, neck straining against the balletic movement, and she pushed them through a surgically precise ripgate.

The scepter blast ripped through the street, scorching her heels as she closed the ripgate with moments to spare.

Voices clamored and yelled from inside the living quarters where they had landed. But before anyone could react, Rone leapt off the balcony into the alley crowd below, with Kaveh, Taline, and Nin following right behind.

They raced around partly bowed bodies, some of which wore looks of confusion, too far from the mass panic in the square to understand what was happening but knowing that something momentous was occurring. They were mere paces from the temple.

As the dark moon rose, so too did the chanting of the citizens.

Nin scrambled into the temple and pushed through the circular foyer as people shouted and magic flew.

"Where are you going?" Rone demanded.

"To the travel room!"

"We are trapping ourselves," Rone yelled, but kept pushing through. "Aros doesn't even need to track you, Ninli. Our destination is obvious. And yet, here we are again, in a temple of the moon, running." They pushed inside the main chamber.

"Clear the room," Kaveh said grimly to Rone. "Or Nin will worry about the innocent."

Rone cursed profusely—at Kaveh and Nin—but a wave of magic pulsed from him, blasting inside the temple's coffered rotunda, blowing most of the people inside off their feet.

"Do not think to command me again, Fehl."

The blast of wind sent the thousands of enchanted prisms that hung from the ceiling into motion, clinking against one another as they swung from their long pendulums. Light glittered and flew wherever torchlight, sunlight, or magelight hit the enchanted glass. Reflected light spun madly around the rotunda, briefly lighting the circular arrays carved into the floor and creating a chaotic feeling of endless movement.

Each array represented a gate accessible by the dark moon's energy hitting the appropriate prism with light.

"Keep destroying then, Valeran, and see what happens."

The people waiting to enter an array were scrambling to their feet from where they'd been blown down by Rone's spell.

One man dressed in fine silks and linens surged upward. "Investigorii! Someone! Grab their oaths!"

Kaveh grimly punched the man. The glittering from the swinging glass flitted over Kaveh's stark features like far-flung starlight.

Aros suddenly appeared in the center of the dome in a swirling gust of wind, setting the prisms in motion once more, and making the spot he was in completely imperceptible for the barest moment due to the refracted light,

"Brother. Cousin." He smiled between the pulsing lights as he descended. "You'll have to do better than that."

He walked forward and people scrambled—trading their places in the long lines for safety as the rotunda emptied with a panicked press of bodies.

"I can follow your ripgates, cousin, despite whatever trickery you used to hide your string.

Such bold red and silver hidden from my gaze. How did you do it?" Aros tilted his head.

Nin saw the fierce elation rise in Kaveh's gaze. She didn't understand it, and wished she could enjoy it, but the scepter was rising.

"No answer? It's no matter."

Aros pointed the scepter at Taline and touched his forehead with his left palm. "The feeling of another wielder is embedded within your sister's skin." Golden light rippled over Aros's face. "Lilac and gold—what a lovely string she has—and the scepter has it now, no matter where she goes."

Nin tensed. So did Kaveh.

"Will you run through another crowd to shake my perception temporarily? I will have to level the next crowd then. Will you leave her behind, instead? Etelian dearly wants to see her." He cocked his head, smiling. "Giving him a tracker to her location may even be enough to soothe the burn of me taking Tehrasi from him."

"Never." Rone tensed so fiercely that Nin could feel it.

"You will not have her," she said softly.

"Poor, Zehra. I can find you whenever you use your magic and I can find her no matter where she is." He touched his forehead again, light rippling. "Come now, cousin. I'll leave your little band of friends alone for the moment if you come willingly. You can't save her any other way."

She felt the pull of the statement—the exchange required—her, for them.

"No," Kaveh said.

Aros swatted the scepter at Kaveh, and only Nin's use of a ripgate stopped Kaveh from becoming a new pattern etched in the floor.

The prisms tinkled above them in the unnatural wind created by the ripgates. Lights flashed as they swung and clanked against one another.

"I think I will get used to this lordsmanship over you, Kaveh. It feels...right." Aros smiled. "Now, cousin, come along. We are the last of our line." His smile remained static, but the edges of his eyes pinched.

"You can't control it." She knew what he wanted from her. Nin inched left, assessing all the angles in the room and places where she could throw the others. Luckily, Taline, Rone, and Kaveh had bunched together, understanding that it was easier for her to move them as a whole.

"Control? I've been in control all my life, Zehra—"

"My name is Nin."

"I have waited and plotted and been a dutiful son. I am unhindered now. Don't you want to let your powers free?"

Aros looked more hindered than she had ever seen him. Active madness lurked behind bleeding amber eyes. "I understand your desire."

"Our desire. I have been constrained by the emperor, by my very birth. Since the moment I screamed into life, I've been silenced. I know you understand."

Nin wouldn't deny it, but with understanding came vicious certainty. "The scepter will tempt me—in the same breath it tempts you. It will use us against each other. There will be no respite, now that it is in your hand."

"But you have resisted that temptation. You let the scepters lie within Tehras for ten years. And you knew where the Scepter of Darkness was all that time."

"Resisting temptation requires sacrifice," she said. Just like this conversation did, allowing Taline, Rone, and Kaveh to ready themselves beyond Aros's immediate view.

"I know the sacrifices required."

"Your son?" Nin didn't wait for him to answer. "Nera? Each sibling you share true blood with? You will run out of things—or people—to sacrifice eventually," Nin said. Control was only the first thing to slip. True madness lay in the slips beyond.

"You underestimate my desire and fortitude. Don't make me overestimate yours. Embrace your true past and destiny." The Fourth Scepter appeared in his hand. "Wield the scepter you were born to wield."

She stared at the Fourth Scepter with mixed feelings of pain and anxiety.

"It was this one, was it not, that Lorsali the Lovely held?" He rotated it in his palm before deep red-brown eyes pinned her. "But it was meant for your hand."

She felt the pull, like she did every time she was in the presence of her family's scepters. The Fourth had always been exceptionally potent, and everything about it—sight, smell, feel—screamed with memories of Lorsali.

The scepter disappeared, taking some of her anxiety with it, and the Ninth appeared in his left hand instead. "And this one, you wielded it just two days past. I can still feel your magic clinging to it. I can feel you reach for it now, even blocked as you are. Ah!" Understanding bloomed in his expression, vicious and precise. "The cloaks. Kaveh's missing magic still resides within. Shadowed shields that hide all, even from such relics of power. But not for long."

Nin opened a ripgate just as Aros ripped through the space himself. She deposited the three of them as Aros countered. Kaveh, Rone, and Taline appeared stagnant in the shifting, while Nin moved the air around them.

She saw Rone freeze at Aros's words as the three of their positions changed without physically moving their bodies. Rone ripped open the bag wound across his chest and stared inside. She saw his fingers hesitate. She saw Kaveh's eyes widen and his own hand dive for what was inside.

Rone's fingers wrapped around Kaveh's wrist, and Nin could see painful lightning run through their limbs as she scooped them into three more spots in the chamber as Aros appeared in five places of his own.

She could do this dance endlessly in a chamber this size, but Aros could target her at any moment. Kill her, take her body, resurrect her elsewhere. That he wanted her to join him of her own volition was an imperfection in his otherwise solid plan.

Kaveh grit his teeth and the wrist held by Rone spasmed, but he didn't let go of whatever he was trying to grab. "That's why I put the cloak on Nin. The shadows still live, even if the power no longer resides within me. Taline, put it on."

And Rone must have hesitated, because Kaveh ripped an old cloak free—a cloak with fading shadows, but ones that still existed.

Taline's sharpened gaze flew to the cloak with a mixture of hope and dismay.

Aros reappeared, just as Taline fumbled with the clasp.

"Come, Zehra, come join me. Join your family."

With the cloak...she could send them away to safety. Taline could hide. Kaveh could hide. Rone could hide.

Sacrifice. She had always understood it.

She stepped forward.

CHAPTER FIVE

OLD PLANS AND NEW

RONE

(Bekli, Skudra, Temple of the Dark Moon)

Rone silently cursed. He understood the fundamentals of Ninli's plan only because he knew the stupid shape of her mind. He understood Fehl's plan only because it relied on the powers that the other man held sacred. He understood Aros's plan because he was a bastard.

Aros held the scepter. And Rone had put two thin strings of blood magic ties into its shaft—Fehl and Carre. He had not known who would hold it after Taline—the emperor, Kaveh, Aros, Aros's son, or Ninli—so he had used that which he had of Ninli and himself and hedged his bets.

Rone started to weave the threads of the activation spell in the hand angled behind his back, while moving three paces from the other two.

Aros pointed the scepter at them, but before he could cast a spell, there was a jet of light, a ripgate of gold, and Rone felt the unpleasant tug in his midsection that always accompanied one of Ninli's gates when she wasn't in full control. By moving, Rone had forced her to use two ripgates instead of one.

He whirled through the other side of his ripgate to see Taline and the useless Shadow Prince exiting theirs. Taline blast a spell at Aros that was easily deflected but required his action. Rone curled a finger into an interior pocket in his cloak and dug out the small paper buried within, slipping it between the palmed slit of two fingers, as he would a cheat card.

"You are hidden in shadows now, too," Aros said to Taline, though he, too, was physically positioning himself to account for the new battlefield positions—uncertain why they would separate. "But it won't last long. The shadows upon you are weak. I can almost suss you through them. You won't last long. And this one..." He pointed the scepter toward Rone—who stood alone—and beckoned with his other hand to Ninli. "The scepter already wants his death. I do not know why the emperor wanted him alive, but that is all the more reason for him to die. I will give the scepter what it wants in this, unless you come Zehra. You have some care for the useless ones."

Rone knew what Ninli would do, and also what she would choose at the end of this fight should it not be in their favor.

"Don't let the sister of your heart suffer," Aros crooned. "Don't let them suffer from a choice made of love. I will kill the one she strains toward, then turn her over to Etelian."

Rone pushed his rage down—he couldn't afford it—and breathed deeply as he placed the hidden paper inside the spell he had woven in his left palm behind his back.

He concentrated on the head of the scepter, waiting for the life-ending spell to emerge. Wrapped into the grains of the staff pointed at him, his spell waited.

He had put the spell in place to give a split moment to either save or run. One shot. A split moment of time. One-time use and no more. He had readied it to use against Aros when he had postured with the scepter upon lifting it in the palace, but Ninli had reacted first and used her own powers to rip them free.

Neither Ninli nor Rone's powers would work against the scepter directly. And though Kaveh ul Fehl wasn't his mother, who was spawned of Darkness, he had practiced with his powers since birth, unrestrained, unlike either Ninli or Rone. He might be able to sever the scepter from Aros's hand.

But then he would lift it, and that end was too terrible to contemplate after seeing Irsula unrestrained. What could the Shadow Prince become with the scepter in his hand? No. Never.

Unlike the Shadow Prince, Rone had let his own monstrous power wither, only using it sparingly. He couldn't risk the failure if desperation and might didn't succeed.

The scepter knew when it was being targeted. Rone had figured that out quickly when Taline first held it in her hand. Taline, who had so little magic compared to Aros, had been immediately protected from harm. Rone hadn't required further testing to know that the scepter would protect itself from direct assault—that even Rone's monstrous powers wouldn't work against it.

An indirect assault was the only answer.

Rone understood why the emperor had needed to have the scepter—why he believed no other should wield it. The emperor would have had an extremely difficult time trying to overcome another magi with the scepter in their hand. Eventually, he might have succeeded. Even the Carres who commanded their scepters had fallen to greater might and trickery.

And the latter was where Rone consistently placed his bets. Trickery beat might when one had patience and time. He had lulled the scepter into a false sense of security, laid an easily unnoticed and dormant seal upon it, and waited for his moment to strike.

The dark moon rose and the lights shifted along the prisms hanging from the ceiling.

Any spell used directly against the scepter would be deflected. A spell inside the scepter would be easily burned, but it would give them a moment.

One moment.

"Come, Zehra."

Ninli stepped forward and Rone tapped his chest with a single finger of his right hand. She would choose to go with Aros, when faced with no other option to save them. But if Rone gave her one...well, he could complain about her stupidity in trusting others until his voice no longer worked, but she would take his hand.

It was his hand that would fail. For after this, the scepter would know. It would know exactly who had placed the spell and how it had been achieved. After he activated this measure, the scepter and Aros would know what form of magic Rone possessed, and although the scepter might seek him to add his power to its own, Aros would make certain he died.

One chance.

"My name...is Nin." Ninli swung a hand through the air and Aros stumbled back. She whirled and blew a spell that twisted Aros to profile, holding him fast, giving Rone his moment as the full length of the scepter stretched in front of him.

Aros was already powering a retaliatory blast that would likely rip limbs from Ninli's shaking body as she tried to freeze in place a power far greater than her own.

The prism light shifted and glowed through the chamber. The scepter pulsed. Rone crushed the spell in his palm. "Begone," he whispered.

The power around the scepter froze and Aros roared. Ninli fell to her hands and knees. Aros's hand shook around the staff, making the scepter—deadened and unlit—wobble wildly in the air like a long balancing rod wielded poorly by a new hand. Aros swung toward Rone with surprise and the beginnings of terror crossed his face along with a hastily erected shield made by his own hand, not the scepter's power. "You, you—?"

Rone held out blue fingers toward Aros and began to curl them inward.

Taline whipped toward him, mouth dropped in confusion and astonishment. "How—?"

Rone hesitated. Monster. He knew her expression would turn from confusion to horror as blue turned to black. She would know.

Aros's enraged gaze swung furiously between Rone and Kaveh. "You—?"

Power started to sear around Aros again in Rone's peripheral vision, but he couldn't look away from Taline. His hand extended toward Aros, his fingers starting to curl...no, yes, no, yes, he had to—

Scepter light outlined Aros, pulling the magic back. Ninli pulled herself upright and blasted Aros through a ripgate as the dark moon crested past dawn.

Lights sparkled in endless waves around the Temple of the Dark Moon and all the arrays lit in golden light. Rone dropped to his knees. The moment he had set in place was...gone. He hadn't been able to let Taline see. Monster. Useless. A useless monster. But a monster she had not seen.

"How long will it last?" Ninli asked, breathless, stumbling forward. Fehl barely caught her before she fell again.

"A few moments, no more," Rone said, breathing hard. Useless. "Choose wisely."

Choose better than Rone could. He looked at Taline and the soft way she was looking at him in concern. No—there had been no choice for him.

"Aros won't know which we choose," Taline said urgently, understanding without explanation. "He won't know which array we choose."

Each array was a gate activated by the dark moon that would take them to the place specified within. The arrays were already lighting. People would start stepping through at any moment.

Unlike the critical nature of seconds in the non-magic layer, here, the temples were all designed to hold and spread the magic of the moons. They could travel from one temple to another in a span five times as long as what was available in the first.

Ninli nodded, eyes old. "This one." She pointed.

As they emerged from the Bekli array into Atale's, Rone felt the cool, but jagged edge of Taline's magic as she wove enchantments around them, setting upon them new faces hastily created. Helpful, kind magic, not like his own destructive powers that took and took and drove him to destroy.

He curled his fingers into his palm, feeling the end traces of the magic he had wielded in the dark of night while Taline had thrashed.

Useless.

But a tiny bit of unspent power remained, hovering, and he grabbed it and forced himself to form a shield—layering the thin layer of nothing around the edges of his body and mind. He would not be the reason they were caught. He would not be the reason Taline was found by Etelian.

They ducked around the temple chamber crowd as they exited. Lines of people stepped into and out of arrays, and few looked at the four people with morphing features stepping out of Bekli's.

Most people were eagerly waiting their turn to step through an array, unaware of anything wrong in the empire. But more than one pair of eyes in the Atale to Bekli line narrowed and followed them. If one was paying close attention, Bekli's otherwise empty array would be noteworthy. Dozens should be streaming through around them.

They couldn't afford to linger.

Rone ducked his head and followed Ninli, Taline, and Fehl as they hurriedly strode through the temple corridors of Atale, Scythia with its curving moon temple halls.

What Rone wouldn't give to cast Fehl through one of the wide stone windows and be rid of him for good. Taline wouldn't object. Neither of them wanted to be dragging along the prince who had wanted to kill them. The prince who now stood as if he would protect Ninli with his body, should it come to that.

Rone grit his teeth. Taline might object at this point, because she, too, knew exactly why they were still dragging him along.

"Valeran has no shadow cloak," Fehl said, as they gained some distance from the temple and entered Atale's bustling center. Dark moon ceremonies were wrapping up—people collecting their relics and mats.

"I don't need a shadow cloak." Rone did not trust the Shadow Prince. He would never let his shadows touch him. He would never help him. He would never let him be at his back. Rone just needed the right moment to get rid of him.

Exactly like you just got rid of Aros?

Ninli's eyes were serious as she focused them on Rone. "Aros will figure out how to trace your magic, too. The scepters—"

"I'm fine," Rone said grimly. The body shield he had pressed against his skin felt empty and wrong. "I need nothing for five days."

It was the longest he could go without true sleep. And if he could figure out how to keep this accursed power activated at this level, even in sleep, he could extend those days.

It was a new day and a new moon. A new, cursed life.

"You feel muted now." Taline looked at him as they hurried through the moon crowd that was breaking up in the aftermath of the dark moon's rise. "What did you do?"

"I have a small relic," he said dismissively. "Single use and active, so I can't transfer it."

Ninli's gaze slid sideways. Thankfully, Taline and Fehl weren't looking at her and her nonexistent game face.

"What did you do to Aros?" Taline pressed. "You did something."

Rone didn't bother to dissemble or mislead. "I activated a seal I put on the scepter."

"What seal? When?"

He could see her mind working uneasily. Everything in her posture and voice underlined her disquiet. She didn't understand yet that her unease was the edged, instinctive fear of knowing a monster was in one's midst—the natural unease of knowing one was close.

"While you were asleep," he answered. "The last night. I placed it under the scepter's notice, dormant."

"Like one of the seals we'd been using?"

His eyes slid away. "Like that, but lighter—only useful for giving a single moment in time, in case we could take advantage of a pause."

A measure put in place to drag the scepter from her or to save her from the next wielder. He let his eyes rest on the Shadow Prince. The worst scenario had always been the emperor, the most likely of wielders, but the Shadow Prince had been a close second.

"Thank you." Taline touched his hand.

Rone barely stopped himself from jerking away as his latent power jumped to consume hers. Once provoked, power wanted to be used and it was one of the reasons he never used it. He covered his flinch with an overaggressive bowing motion and grin as he stepped back. "Of course, narsumina."

Taline's eyes narrowed. She frowned and looked down at her hand. He begged that she didn't use her cleverness to see what he didn't want her to see.

"You thought about going with him, Nin." Fehl's deep voice was grim. "You thought about going with Aros."

Rone hated Fehl, but he could only be desperately thankful for the diversion as Taline's gaze narrowed in on Ninli. The relief—temporary, blissful relief—almost made him release his shield. He grabbed it, scrambling.

"Yes," Ninli answered.

Fehl stared at Ninli with lips gone pale with pressure.

"Just like she went with you, Shadow Prince," Rone said, relief and tension curling easily into contempt for their fourth member, and continued irritation for the one who bound them all. "To save us. A curious and irritating self-sacrificial trait. Do not be surprised when she truly leaves with him, in the end."

For she would. Rone counted on it already. And it was obvious that the new emperor knew it, too, from the way he had addressed her. Rone would have to interrogate her further about their interactions to determine what else Aros knew.

They were back to their beginning gambit again, but instead of Kaveh ul Fehl chasing them with all the might of his power and empire behind him, now they had Aros ul Fehl doing the chasing with the might of the scepters.

The Summora girls really were a curse.

Rone pushed a branch out of the way, so it didn't hit Taline as they walked through the small grove patches that stood to the sides of the city gates. Outside the city walls, fields and groves stretched in all directions.

Taline pulled the shadow cloak she was wearing out of the way of the snagging branches near the hem. She looked at the cloth with a curled lip. Rone approved. "How long will the shadows last?"

The only reason Rone hadn't demanded the cloak's removal was because it was obviously working. Aros would have appeared before them by now, otherwise.

They had carried that damned cloak through the non-magic world. He supposed he had to be grateful he hadn't dumped it. He wondered whether it would have made a difference to put it on Taline in the non-magic world. Could it have kept the pentalayerists and Aros's son from following them?

Rone felt a moment of pity for the boy. Rone had tried to keep him out of it, and he had tried to resurrect the boy on the throne room's floor. But Aros had followed Osni's footpath in destiny.

"I don't know." Fehl shrugged in answer. "I've never needed to renew shadows. They did my bidding automatically. They just...were."

Powerful, monstrous Kaveh ul Fehl, who had never been without his monstrous power, stared at his own cloak, and Rone felt vindictive glee. The blessed of the blessed, the one who had held power and future from birth, and here he was without a shred. Rone was unforgiving in his satisfaction.

"Shadows obscure sight," Fehl said. "They hide everything within their obscurity."

"That's why you were always so hard to see coming in those days before the oath," Rone said laconically, thinking of the hundred ways the Shadow Prince had shown his might while chasing them. "We could have almost missed you."

Fehl looked coldly at him. "No one saw me when I didn't want them to."

"Right, because announcing your presence like the fiend of the deep is just so useful."

"It is extremely useful for those who wish to live."

"Wished. Wished to live, isn't that right, Your Imperial Highness? Because"—Rone swept a hand at the Shadow Prince's body—"you can do magic no more."

Taline looked uneasily between them, still not internalizing that the Shadow Prince was no longer prince of the shadows.

Ninli stared at Rone, but Rone held to his spite.

No, Ninli, Rone thought viciously; you don't get to be disappointed in this.

Fehl's gaze was cold. "Better to have lived fully for twenty-two years than to have lived a half-life for twenty-one. You were abandoned by your mother, were you not?"

"I seem to recall seeing your mother abandon you just yesterday, Your Empty Highness."

KAVEH

Kaveh stared at the Valeran bastard and felt his fingers curl and extend into the sign of certain death—sending shadows that would split the man in two.

Valeran smirked, gaze drifting to Kaveh's extended fingertips and the nothing that was coming from them. Valeran opened his mouth and Kaveh grabbed the scalpel at his belt.

"Enough," Nin said quietly.

Kaveh let the scalpel fall back into its too-big sheath and curled his fingers inward, digging crescents into his palms. He wanted to slice Valeran's tongue from his mouth with cutting darkness. He wanted to flay the flesh from his frame. He wanted to send a shadow diving down his throat, then rupture it and rip the organs from his body.

Nothing happened. As in everything that came with the new state of things—nothing happened when Kaveh wanted it to.

Nin's warm fingers curled around his wrist and her fingers moved to his bag, where light pulsed inside. She lifted the sand ball that Akel had given him. A small lightning bolt shot wildly around the glass. "A message is being passed through the camps." Her gaze swept the grove for stragglers, but most people were within the city walls, and those outside were not lingering. She let an imperceptible bit of magic seep inside.

The multicolored sand and crushed gemstones swirled inside the glass orb, then resolved into a panoramic view of the golden throne room in Fehlaka, complete with marble pillars, opulent ornamentation, and lavishly dressed people.

There was no sign of decimation—no fallen marble pillars or strewn slabs or crushed statuary. The orb bloomed with false recreation to hide the actual evidence and chaos.

Ninli pushed more magic and the enchanted sand recreated the memory of the room in finely, detailed mosaics of color, life, and definition, pulling the eye within and expanding the interior in a living image. This was his father's room, built by stone, sand, and magic.

It was not the new reality, stained with his life's blood. It was the last setting Kaveh would ever be able to picture his father standing alive.

The sand and crushed gemstones swirled into the figure of Aros with glittering browns and golds, casting his robes into the gold and greens of the Farin Sea's sandy shores. The sand could only capture so much detail in their intricately shifting and forming mosaics of a thousand dots, but the finally tuned enchantments on the orbs ensured that the vision was close.

Aros's glittering, defined sand mouth turned downward as his gold-tinted features took on a doleful expression that made Kaveh curl the shadows around him into sickled blades, ready for his to throw.

But nothing wrapped his fingers. Kaveh shut his eyes. No blades, no shadows—only his nails digging into already moon-pocked flesh.

Soothing magic filtered into his hand from Nin's small one. "After he left us, he went immediately to the palace to make this announcement," she murmured. "He is shaken."

Aros's hands lifted in supplication and the sand swirled strangely around his right hand where the scepter was—hidden in the enchantment, but hinted at in the confused recreation. He stood on the dais, speaking directly to his royal siblings, but documented for all to hear. "Good citizens of the empire, I bring you sad tidings on the birth of the dark moon. The emperor, Sher Fehl, is dead."

He let the statement hang for a charged moment, along with his hands in the air. The sand in the ball vibrated in tense reflection as he slowly lowered his arms.

"Our emperor, my father, was assassinated in a surprise attack last eve by Kaveh ul Fehl, who sought the Crown of Sunlight for himself. A vicious monster, Kaveh ul Fehl murdered the emperor and released his mother, Irsula of Denz, Night Terror of the Land of Darkness and Mistress of Shadows."

Siblings stepped forward.

"Kaveh ul Fehl killed the emperor." Darona.

"Kaveh ul Fehl killed the emperor." Tyre.

"Kaveh ul Fehl killed the emperor." Omari.

Kaveh did not realize that the pit of emptiness in his gut could open further.

The ball whirled and more imperial faces appeared—Baksis, Simin, and Sarvar among them—reciting the same sentence. Some siblings were more rote in their recitations than others, but the unification of the message across so many blessed imperial children solidified rumor into fact.

He—Kaveh ul Fehl—had murdered the emperor.

Fierce impotency overtook his fury, because he could do nothing.

Voiya, Padifehl of Fehla-da and Nera's fourth child, was last to appear. "Along with the assassination of our beloved father and emperor, we have also uncovered ties to indicate that Kaveh ul Fehl was behind all of the recent royal assassinations. Beloved Shiera, Carsue, and Urful—they all fell to the monster Father lost control of. It was only due to the brave actions of our brother and eldest among us, Aros ul Fehl, that Kaveh's treachery was revealed and we survive. He, who drew upon the myths of our people and was gifted with a scepter of great power to aid his just cause, ensured that the Shadow Monster did not slay the rest of us."

Kaveh would kill them all.

"Three padifehl deaths?" Valeran asked Nin grimly.

Kaveh stared at the line of blessed children with cold hatred. He would kill all of them and raze the palace to the ground. He would conquer their lands and lay waste to their loved ones. He would find a way to regain his powers, then he would destroy all of them.

"Look at him, Ninli." Valeran's grim voice seemed very far away. "Look at your precious new dove and the look upon his face and tell me he is not the monster."

Kaveh would be the monster. Oh, yes.

"Rone..."

Voiya clasped a hand to her well-decorated chest in the orb. "By the grace of Sehk-Ra, we found the beloved Padifehl of Bahra, Rayd ul Fehl, alive. He was beaten and starved by the royal family of Scythia—who are in league with Kaveh ul Fehl—but he is alive. Rayd would have suffered the same fate as Urful, Carsue, and Shiera—may they rest in the glorious arms of Sehk-Ra forevermore."

"Beloved ruler?" Taline asked skeptically. Ever since they had stopped to watch the orb, she had been doing something with an intricately designed silver box. "Rayd was only slightly better than Etelian."

"Complications. A larger plan," Nin murmured as Voiya made a gesture in the sand ball.

"The Imperator General held a strong military presence these long years," Voiya said in a voice so like her mother's, "and he could have continued to make our empire strong under the sure hand of our father—as our brother, our general. Alas, he was driven to madness by his tainted blood."

They were dead, all of them. Dead magi pretending at life until he executed them.

Sarvar stepped forward. "As Padifehl of Syra, I extend my deepest blessings to all who are saddened by this news. However, in an uplifting turn of events, prior to his death, the emperor stripped Kaveh's powers as his final act—the emperor guaranteed that the Shadow Prince is no longer. He can harm no others. Since no other has the ability of our father, we submit this to you, the citizens, as a permanent piece of evidence against the thirteenth blessed child of the emperor, who shall forevermore be stricken from the annals."

The sand slid into Aros again, but Kaveh had stopped feeling emotion.

"Aiding him are conspirators against the empire," Aros said. "Chief among them is Rone ul Valeran, who is considered a mortal enemy of the crown. He is to be killed on sight." There was something strangely fevered in the statement. "Ninli and Taline ul Summora are victims of the men's machinations and should be subdued and delivered to the investigorii unharmed, as soon as possible. Here are all the facial aliases that they have assumed."

Kaveh cared nothing for Valeran's fate. But Nin's...

Her fingers clenched to white around the orb as visions of her different guises appeared along with her sister's. Included were the guises they were in right this moment.

Taline ul Summora dropped the silver box in her hands to the dirt and scrambled for another she had been fiddling with—pressing glyphs on the side as soon as it was in her palms. Magic slid over each of them immediately, changing their features once more.

Those new unused features appeared in the orb next. Taline made a strangled sound and started grabbing small boxes, vials, and containers from her satchel. Nin and Valeran hunched in instinctively to form an inward circle—attempting to conceal their features from outside view.

Kaveh's emotions were dead, but his mind still processed. Aros must have started collecting information from the moment Nin had disappeared from the Palace of Tehras. Kaveh had witnessed his hungry expression but had been too content in his own arrogance and abilities to care. Aros could never touch him as they had been. Kaveh had only cared that the emperor not find out. He had not given Aros's hunger further thought until he had realized the depth of his plans. Aros had made no secret of the fact that he had guessed Nin's heritage and that he planned to use that knowledge in the future.

But to take it to this depth of research... Obsession.

He looked into Nin's eyes, once more an unexceptional shade of brown as her sister flipped new features onto her. His gaze drifted over her throat to where his imperial cloak pin was fastened.

He wondered at how Aros must have rejoiced upon finding a Carre alive—upon finding a Carre alive right under the very nose of Etelian, sitting upon the throne Aros had always viewed as his. The irony of it.

"Kaveh must not be allowed his freedom," Aros continued, directing his comments to the citizenry. "As he has no magic, I urge all to go forth in earning a monumental bounty. You owe it to your late emperor, and to your new emperor—whoever he may be—to avenge Sher Fehl's death."

"Our new emperor must be you, Aros!"

Kaveh felt cold, killing rage at Voiya's obsequious words. Aros would die first. She would die second.

"First born!" another shouted. "Save our empire!"

That speaker would be third.

Aros sighed and knelt, then reached for the Crown of Sunlight. "It is with a heavy heart that I place this crown upon my head."

When the emperor had not awarded Tehrasi to Aros, he had decided to take everything. It would have been an unimaginable thought, days ago. The healthy, powerful emperor had always been the impediment that made such desires unimportant. Succession would have become important to Kaveh only when the emperor neared death in forty years or more.

No one could have slayed the emperor, especially not with Kaveh near. It was a fact he had built his life around.

Kaveh's stomach gave a strange heave when Aros rose with the Crown of Sunlight glittering upon his head. It felt as if his stomach were traveling up his throat. Kaveh touched his midsection against the weird feeling. Perhaps it was a consequence of Taline's spellwork as she hastily crafted new disguises on each of them.

"What about the council members?" someone in the orb inquired. The council had always been against Aros. They had been the ones who had stood between Aros and Tehrasi.

Aros tilted his glittering head. "In additional grievous news—"

The feeling of unease bubbled further. Was his stomach fighting to be free? A small hand shoved his head sideways and he watched in fascination as the contents of his last meal splattered upon the ground.

Nin's hand rubbed his head while the other held out the shaking orb.

Kaveh blankly looked from the ground to the orb. His stomach lurched again. He didn't understand what was happening to him. What was this malady? He felt his stomach give another unacceptable twist. What was this?

Aros shook his head sadly in the shaking, reforming sand. "Half of the council was obliterated in the same attack by Kaveh ul Fehl. Irreplaceable. My father relied upon their wisdom and counsel. I have every faith that new council members will step up during this time of great change and be the force of will and visionaries that the empire needs to progress."

"What about protecting the front and extending the borders? Without the Imperator General—"

"Our father was aggressive in extending the empire. And we will continue to bring our vision of the future to other countries and territories. For now, though, I believe we should look internally—to the empire we have now. Let us aid our own countrymen first. Then, when we are ready to expand once again, I will appoint a new Imperator General—a strong one who will be revered, not feared."

Rage gone cold, stomach now empty of protest, Kaveh remotely examined Aros's expression in the sand. It was the weakest point in Aros's argument, and he seemed to know it, if his tightened lips were anything to go by. Kaveh had been soundly feared, but there was no denying that he had been revered by those who fought with him and who served the empire. He had been the empire's monster—and no one could hurt you when you had a monster on your side.

"Now it is time to grieve and move on," Aros said. "Kaveh ul Fehl was stripped of his magic in the battle with my father. He will be easily subdued and killed. The sooner you deliver his head to me, along with the head of Rone ul Valeran, the greater reward you will receive. Here are the faces and identities of possible conspirators. Onward with the empire!"

Faces were displayed again—names, activities, places conspirators were known to frequent.

Nin's fingers clenched around the globe.

Enemies of the empire. It was not unexpected, but it was unwelcome, all the same. This would be a different flight and fight from when the three had run from Kaveh weeks ago—a single agent who had held all the power in his hands. They would be running from a hundred thousand smaller, zealous eyes, plotting and following, hands slicing and mouths spitting.

"Well, that was a lovely little recitation," Valeran said coldly.

Taline's brows furrowed and she whipped through the last spell boxes, enchanting facial hair and altering features on Valeran. "He is targeting you specifically, Rone. Why?"

Kaveh's eyes narrowed on them. It was true. Aros had put entirely too much significance upon Valeran. Why? What had Valeran done? What had Aros been trying to say before Nin had cast him through her ripgate? What had been in Valeran's magic?

Kaveh no longer had the ability to see.

Valeran's mouth firmed and he looked away. His hair remained garishly bright with its red and gold streaks under his hood. "He wants both of you returned to him, for different reasons, and I stand in the way."

Taline's full-body shudder made her miss the way that Valeran's gaze slid unerringly back to her with deep resignation. Truth inside a lie. Aros had not targeted Valeran for that reason, at all.

Kaveh looked sharply at Nin and tensed at the clenched expression on her face as she looked between Valeran and Taline. She knew whatever his secret was. She knew what Valeran was hiding. Taline might not have enough power to know what lay beneath Valeran's magical strings, but Aros did, and so did Nin.

Nin had taken Aros out of play, not faltering for an instant, when Valeran had hesitated to do...whatever it was that he had been trying to do. It had looked like he meant to crush Aros with magic. Why had he hesitated?

Nin took a deep breath, filling her small rib cage. "Aros knows that the more time that passes, the more likely it will be that Kaveh figures out how to return his magic, or that he convinces the other Fehls to move against Aros. Aros can't risk either of those outcomes."

Valeran's gaze jerked to her. "Did we watch the same orb, Ninli? The rest of the imperials are aligned behind Aros."

"They have to be." Nin tilted her lovely head. "The council members who objected or who despised Aros are dead. Aros wields the scepter. The blessed children know disagreeing with him means death. But that doesn't mean they won't be amenable if the situation changes."

"You seek allies in shifting sands," Valeran said harshly.

"Those who stay in power frequently shift upon the sands in order to do so," she said.

Kaveh's eyes narrowed. Baksis and Simin would seek to retain their power. Namir and Omari would guard Kush with all their might. If that meant bowing to Aros temporarily while they plotted, they would definitely do so. Indefinitely, even.

He looked at Nin as her quick mind worked. Her quick mind was the equal to her overwhelming empathy for everyone who crossed her path.

"Your ducklings..."

Brown eyes that were familiar, yet unfinished—like an artistic render without the right shades and tones—fastened their gaze on him. "They will be watched." She swallowed, delicate throat moving above the pin that was his.

Like she was his. His to protect.

He had to regain his shadows. He needed to get his powers back.

"I slipped Akel back into his tent," she said, "but I don't...I don't know if he's... I don't know what might have happened afterward. And any contact with him is a risk of his life that I cannot take. Not yet. Not before we have a plan.

Not before we are ready to march against the throne."

And they would—they would march against the throne. He would, with this woman at his side.

He touched her cheek. "I will kill Aros with the scepter in his hand."

Nin looked at him with eyes filled with emotion. Emotion for him. Her gaze traveled to the others, strangely. There was resignation and acceptance in equal measure. "I will find a way to make it happen," she murmured, gaze returning to him.

"We will. We will find a way," he said intently. For he would not leave her or have her undertake a mission apart from him.

She smiled at him, a small, burgeoning thing, and he clasped it and let it soothe the acidic feel in his stomach—let it fill all of the empty spaces opened by Aros's words. He would protect this. He had to.

"We can kill Aros without your powers," Valeran said, shrugging—like speaking of killing a scepter wielder was nothing of note. "Without you."

"You did little against him today," Kaveh said harshly.

"With planning, anything is possible." Valeran made a motion with his hand. "Aros might even do it to himself. The scepter drives all who wield it mad. We simply need time."

Taline looked down at her cloak and the wispy shadows curling along the edges. "How much time have we?"

Valeran's expression went bleak before smoothing out. "We'll figure out how to hide you and Ninli." Valeran's lips were firm. Resolved.

The only thing Kaveh agreed with him on was protecting Nin. And in that, and only that, he was thankful that if something happened to him in his useless state, there would be someone to watch over her. He didn't like feeling any particularly good thoughts for Valeran, though.

Nin's fingers curled around his. "We will fix this," she murmured. "We just need..." She turned her gaze downward. Strangely. As if avoiding looking at something in particular. "We just need to find a cure."

He felt the words in the hollow of his stomach. The empire had never found a cure, and there were many who had sought just such a thing in order to put a check into place against the emperor. For if his powers could be undone, the power of his ability was lessened.

"You said Omari ul Fehl helped you," Taline said quietly. Her gaze unwillingly shifted between Kaveh and Nin. She hated him for good reason, but she wanted to help her sister. It was an interesting dilemma, and one that he could only recently understand.

"Omari cleansed the last of the cuff's magic from me," Nin said. "But the emperor's cuffs didn't take magic; they just suppressed it. Cleansing the remnants allowed me to use my powers immediately."

Omari had the gifts of her mother in her vines and connection to the earth, but she, too, had the slightest breath of the emperor running through her magic—though in opposition.

"She can purify—she can't return," Kaveh stated, in case the others didn't understand.

Nin nodded. "The emperor's cuffs were destroyed, and the binding was within them—not elsewhere. He didn't take my magic with the cuffs—the cuffs were to be used to control me. Omari purified the remnants of the binding."

Kaveh felt his stomach do that strange turning again. Was this ailment a result of losing his magic?

"So she's not your solution," Taline said.

"She's not."

"Is Etelian?" Taline asked, voice tense. "Can we force Etelian to unlock the emperor's power?"

Valeran stiffened oddly. But then, he seemed strangely protective of Nin's sister. And Etelian's interest and past with Taline was easily deduced from his words in the throne room.

"Etelian has not the skill," Kaveh said. "A disappointment in every way. My condition is permanent until another is born to the power."

Taline looked blankly at her hands. "Perhaps Etelian hasn't been pushed hard enough yet. Maybe if we—"

Valeran's hand chopped through the air. "We aren't going to Etelian for anything."

"But if Nin—"

"No."

Rone ul Valeran loved Taline ul Summora.

The realization rang clearly in Kaveh's mind. Kaveh watched them argue, his mind distantly and automatically seeking how to use the realization against the other man.

"I don't seek to put myself near his powers, Rone," Taline said quietly. "If I never feel power that can take away another's, it will be too soon, but Nin trusts the Shadow Prince and we are in danger until—"

"We will find another way to unseat Aros." Valeran's voice was implacable, and a strange hatred hardened his features. "One that does not involve the emperor's or Etelian's powers."

Taline nodded slowly. Her distaste for such power seemed only to be matched by her relief. That she had no desire to see Etelian ul Fehl ever again was obvious. That his powers terrified her was also apparent. But then, Kaveh had seen few who truly understood the emperor's powers who weren't terrified of Sher Fehl. It had been one of his key strengths.

Valeran's expression went bleak for a moment, then smoothed into pleasant lines.

Kaveh's eyes narrowed. Valeran had a secret. Valeran was...afraid. Valeran loved Taline, but he was also terrified of her fear. What secret did Valeran hold?

TALINE

Taline didn't want to think of Etelian ul Fehl. Ever, if she could help it.

But he was out there, hunting her. She had seen it in the sand ball. She had seen his face as the guises were shown. He would hunt her until she was caught.

She shuddered.

Invisible fingers of memory made her feel the remnants of his magic stripping away hers.

The broken pieces from the scepter moved in jagged, echoing edges under her skin.

She lifted the box she had dropped and busied herself with her concealment containers and enchantments. All the guises she had preset had been in Aros's orb. Sehk.

Her hands shook. What did that mean? She stole a glance at Nin. It meant Aros knew her sister well. Worse and worse, matters grew.

As they started moving again, Taline crafted new disguises in her main box that was attuned directly to Nin and her, tweaking new features. Uneasy, she tried to mix her recollections, but forced herself to stop. Everyone had a style—and a clever person, when looking at Taline's previous guises, would likely be able to pick out new ones.

No, no memories could she use. She would use the features of the next people they met as the base. As long as those people weren't Fehls or assassins trying to kill them, it should work. Start new. Start again. Be flexible. Be creative. Be vigilant. It was an old refrain, and one that had saved her many times before.

She stole a glance at Kaveh ul Fehl.

Such a refrain used on a man like this...one who had been all-powerful and was now completely without...could he rise from his ashes? Taline had been stripped of her abilities—some of them permanently, due to the repeated damage that had occurred. She knew what it was like to start again, weakened. But this man...could he rise again without?

She did not particularly want to return the Shadow Prince to his former glory, but she could see it was important to Nin. That somehow, in the moon cycle when they had been separated, Nin had taken this man into her heart.

And even if Fehl wasn't special to Nin in some unique way, Taline knew from countless circumstances—from countless people they had saved—what it looked like when Nin refused to be dissuaded. And that dogged look currently graced her sister's face.

In Taline's experience, only ill could come from a Fehl.

Taline looked at Rone and her expression eased. Perhaps the ill came from those who retained the name and ties. Rone ul Valeran was powerful—far more powerful than she—but his power was varied and mercurial. It wasn't harsh or unforgiving.

Though...it felt strange, at present. She wasn't sure what it was about the relic he was using that made her feel unease.

"If you seek to unseat Aros as you are," Kaveh ul Fehl said, continuing their argument on the road, "you will be destroyed."

"Then perhaps we won't unseat him at all," Rone said idly. "Perhaps Aros will lead your empire to greater heights. Perhaps he will be a far better leader than your father was."

The Shadow Prince's fists curled. "He was your father too, Valeran. His blood runs through your veins the same as mine."

"Then perhaps a Carre should be the one on the throne."

"No," Nin said softly. "No Carre should be on the throne."

"You could rule," Fehl said harshly, whipping toward Nin. "All would bow before you in surrender." Muscles taut and expression fierce, the former Shadow Prince's body was angled in a way that said he would kill all who dared to say otherwise.

By the grace of Sehk-Ra...

Taline closed her eyes. Fehl believed in Nin. Taline's desire to see Kaveh ul Fehl's powers returned was only slightly above her desire to see Etelian again, but this man would see cities burn for Nin.

And Nin would need that. Taline had seen Aros look at her sister and hunger for her knowledge. Nothing good would come of Aros's desire to secure scepters, lineage, and throne with Nin as the jewel in his collection. Not when Aros was ruled by the Scepter of Darkness.

Taline felt the shifting emptiness inside her—the ache and desire—the emptiness of not holding the scepter in hand and the gnawing need to have it back. She had released the scepter, and still it had a hold on her. Aros would be consumed.

Taline needed Nin to have every ally she could possibly find. "We will get the Shadow Prince's powers back."

Rone jerked. "What?"

"We will get—"

"No."

Her stomach clenched hard and she stumbled.

Rone caught her. "Taline, Taline, what—"

"I am well." But she was not. She could feel the gnawing, choking feel of the emptiness. A half-moon more. Maybe a whole moon cycle if she stretched.

She needed Nin to have a chance. Should Taline throw off the shadow cloak and call the scepter's magic to her location in a fit of craving—the promise to have her feel it again whispering in suddenly disjointed thoughts—she would plan ahead for her own doom.

Rone steadied her. His eyes narrowed. "What is this?"

She lowered her eyes, unwilling to let him see the hunger that couldn't be satisfied.

"Scepter sickness." Nin put her hands upon Taline's forehead and then her brow against Taline's own. "It calls to her, like a dependence that can't be salved."

"She got rid of it," Rone said vehemently. "She let it go of her own will."

Taline felt humiliation curl. She was supposed to be strong.

"Yes, and she will get through this, too." Nin's cool fingers brushed across her skin, pulling the sweat and fatigue from her flesh. The headache that had been building, receded. "There are a few things we can do to quicken the cleanse."

Rone let Nin remove her from his arms and looked tightly into the distance. "If we cleanse the scepter from her mind and skin, will she return to normal?"

"I'm fine."

Rone turned and stared at her, eyes intense. "You are more than fine. You dropped the scepter of your own accord. You will make it through this, too. Ninli's correct."

The humiliation receded. She felt tears well and spill.

Rone knelt and touched her cheek, pulling the wetness away. She could see pain and anger in his eyes. "But you will suffer until the pull ends." He closed his eyes. "Aros—and Etelian with him—will be able to track you as long as the scepter is embedded in your skin. We will rid you of that cloak. We will free you from the empire, Etelian, and...all those who can control you."

"We don't have time to cleanse her," Fehl said.

"We don't have time to return your powers," Rone said, far too pleasantly, not looking away from Taline.

"We have time for both." Nin sounded tired. "Until the world closes upon us. We don't have power or plan, but time is the one thing we have right now."

"In finite supply. Extremely finite supply," Rone said.

"Yes," she agreed. "But we can seek answers and solutions."

"Until the cloaks run out."

Nin looked at Taline's cloak with its wisping, fine shadows. "Until the cloaks run out."

Nin's eyes strayed to Fehl. "We need to remain invisible. The enchantments will wear off in another week, two at most. But the base enchantment..." Everything the Shadow Prince had put into place was unraveling like a tapestry pulled of its threads. "Such an enchantment is alive in the Land of Darkness."

Silence met her pronouncement.

"That's why you chose Atale." Rone didn't sound surprised. He sounded resigned.

"Yes," Nin said quietly.

"Too many people saw us in the temple, Ninli. Aros will know. He will know where we head."

"Aros will not venture inside the Land of Darkness. Not until he has gathered his power more. Did you see him look upon her?"

"I saw his face when he looked upon Irsula of Denz." Rone grimaced. "She is as god to him."

"And that is why he won't go," Nin said firmly. "He reveres her. He fears her. She killed the emperor while the emperor was holding the scepter. Aros won't take that chance. Irsula is a threat to him, especially while he is learning to control the scepter."

Nin leaned forward. "And he'll think we are trying to hide behind Irsula. When Kaveh does not come after him fully powered tomorrow or a quarter moon from now, Aros will think his success is assured. He will think the options he fears might exist to bring Kaveh's powers back didn't work. He won't think we are seeking another solution."

Rone tensed.

Taline looked between them. "What other—"

"There are other cleansing items," Nin said. "Items of myth—"

Taline's shoulders tightened—for she knew Rone ul Valeran's reputation for missing relics perhaps better than anyone, and she knew Nin better than all. "No."

"The Eternal Spring is said to be accessed only through the Land of Darkness." Nin spread her fingers.

Rone swore.

"Absolutely not," Taline said.

Nin waited them both out.

Taline got tired of waiting. "The Eternal Spring is a myth of everlasting youth."

Nin nodded. "The waters unwind time in the body."

"You think it can reverse the prince's state before the absence of his magic?"

Nin looked at her. "I think it might rid you of the scepter addiction—the sickness. And that, in turn, will make it harder for Aros to find you."

For without the scepter, Taline was...nothing. The wiggling worm of addiction ran through her mind and she pinned it. No, not nothing. But without the tie, she would be unnoteworthy to the scepter.

Nin looked at Rone. Her gaze was crafty. "And we might discover other things."

Rone's shoulders stiffened.

"Dip me in a pool of magic," Taline said tiredly. "By the heel. So that only that is traceable. Then cut off my foot."

"It shouldn't come to that."

Taline winced and bowed forward. Sweat poured down her face, matting her hair.

Nin's fingers were smoothing it back and she didn't have to look up to feel Rone and Nin exchange looks.

"I'm fine."

"Is she?" Fehl asked coldly.

"She will be," Nin murmured. "We will travel through northern Scythia and beyond. Through the Land of Darkness. Beyond, to the churning spring in the shape of a serpent, to the pitcher made of jade, cinnabar, hematite, and gold and fashioned with a snake around the lip."

The weight of the words sunk upon the hollow—the myth wrapping like the serpent of its tale.

Rone sighed. "You want to cross Irsula of Denz's lands and see if she'll behead all of us as well?"

Nin cast a glance at her former oath mate, who was staring at the ground. It was surreal to see the Shadow Prince conflicted—to see any emotion that didn't include intense disregard or death dealing. "Kaveh?"

"Yes?" He looked up at her.

Taline shifted uncomfortably at that look. It was the type of trusting expression you would find on a human.

"The spring might be able to restore your power. Maybe the Eternal Spring can restore us all."

"The Eternal Spring is a myth."

"It is. Just like the Scepter of Darkness is a myth."

Taline's lips pressed together and she wiped a hand along her damp and clammy brow.

Kaveh ul Fehl nodded. "I will go."

Nin's expression, still gentle, edged with exasperation. "We will all go."

"I'm not going with him," Rone said.

"Rone—"

"I don't give a Sehk's damn about returning the Shadow Prince's powers. I'm happy they are gone."

"I know. You've said it enough times," Nin said tightly. And there was something charged in the look between them that Taline didn't understand. "But the Land of Darkness serves other functions, like hiding and recovering."

The Shadow Prince—or former Shadow Prince, she supposed—wasn't paying attention. But then, he must be used to people hating him.

"Aros—"

"Will grow more unstable. He will be overly paranoid, but unable to track everything at once. He will become hyper focused. That gives us an advantage, for he can't focus on hunting us down if he has to secure the empire—no small task. We are a threat, but the empire will fall beneath his feet, if he focuses on us alone."

Rone looked at Nin with a narrowed gaze.

"He has studied you. He thinks he knows you." Rone nodded at something in his head, his gaze remote. "He will focus elsewhere because he thinks you will capitulate eventually. He thinks you will go with him."

Taline went cold.

"You've already said that, Valeran," Kaveh ul Fehl said warningly.

"Well, princeling, don't be surprised. Don't say you didn't know she would leave you to save you."

"She won't."

Rone's eyes narrowed. "You don't know her then."

"I know her better than you do."

"You know nothing of sacrifice, Kaveh ul Fehl—sitting in your shadows, killing all that which was in your way. Rolling over all that didn't fit with your plans, doing what your father bid. You know nothing of those who sacrifice."

"Again, our father, was he not?"

"Your father. A monster just like you."

Fehl's eyes narrowed. "What are you scared of, Rone ul Valeran?"

"I won't help you get your powers back, Fehl. Nothing can make me do it."

There was a strange vowed quality to the words, as if Rone could help him, but would choose not to.

"Rone, if you want to go a separate way, you still can," Nin said softly, calmly—in the way that she always gave people a choice. A true choice—for she would still help them later, if called. She was honest in her expectations of nothing past whatever someone wanted to give. A leftover trauma from a childhood full of people taking anything and everything they wanted without consent.

Taline looked down. Rone's words to Fehl and his past choices matched in this. He had chosen to stay the first night. That did not mean he needed to continue to do so.

When she finally looked up, Rone was looking back at her, his eyes unreadable.

He turned away. "We are all hunted. Again, better for us to be hunted together."

Relief made her stagger in place and she put her hand out to stabilize herself against a tree trunk.

Kaveh ul Fehl's eyes narrowed on her, uncovering the weakness she couldn't hide, but she didn't care. Not right now when her relief was too fierce.

The irony didn't escape her.

There would be no relief in the Land of Darkness. No Kaveh ul Fehl to keep the monsters away from sheer fear. Instead of taking the biggest monster with them, they would be heading toward the biggest one themselves.

CHAPTER SIX

HEADING TOWARD DARKNESS

NINLI

(On the Scythian Way)

Getting to the Land of Darkness was no easy feat. Traveling was a balancing act between taking off road trails for stealth and on road paths for speed. A ripgate would have saved them three days—Nin had the perfect coordinates for half a day's walk from the forest's southern border. But while Aros was not in Scythia searching for them himself, if he felt Nin creating a ripgate, he would appear.

Still, Nin would have liked to spare Taline those three days to rest while she cycled in and out of wellness and sickness—a terrible curse she had never asked for.

In northern Scythia, on roads and ways made for travel, the largest pitfall was passing imperial agents and setting off ear-shrieking alarms.

The imperial agents struck.

Iron struck iron, the metals singing as blades met. Spells struck shields in sparks of white.

The imperial agent in front of her lunged and Nin slid left, leaving Rone to guard her flank as she struck a second man in the nose. Rone took out the one at her side as Taline dispatched the third of a five-man unit. They converged on the last two, who were inching around Kaveh, and took them down.

The illusion box of simulated shadows Kaveh held in his hand had done its job—the agents had been too nervous to attack Kaveh directly. If Aros thought Kaveh had his powers back, it would give them some protection, too.

Nin and Taline had worked hard on it, and the illusion box had earned its reward when the first set of agents had been briefly stunned into inaction. Even Kaveh and Rone had looked unwillingly entertained at the agents' reactions to the box. Having Aros believe in the possibility would be the greater coup.

Kaveh and Rone's shared reaction didn't mean they were getting along or had become one mind about their goals, though. It was just a moment's reprieve from bickering and baiting one another.

"Just let me turn Fehl into a donkey," Rone said as Nin put sleep-healing charms on all the agents.

"Valeran, I will slit your throat if you suggest something similar one more time."

"You can't even slit your own linens. We'd get better use of you as a mule. You'd finally carry your own weight and we'd become a group of three."

They had been carefully dodging hunters and agents since leaving Atale, but the imperial agents were beginning to stop all groups of four now. Although they had avoided notice in numerous circumstances, the cloaks were wearing thin and they hadn't been able to avoid complete notice.

"A group of three won't matter as soon as they pass you," Kaveh said grimly, as they dragged and hid the bodies behind a small hill. They had been leaving the agents to wake without memory of the past three days, but with the box in place that morning, she had started leaving them with some memories. They would only see shadows. Neither Rone nor Kaveh had been a proponent of leaving any agents alive from the start, but Nin had argued hard against it.

These were imperial agents who bled for the empire—and the dead emperor they sought justice for. They would side with Kaveh, when truth was revealed and justice prevailed. Until then...

"You mean as soon as they pass Ninli and me. You simply swan off ahead. Perhaps feeding them information?"

...until then, they would all make do with trying to only maim each other with words. Kaveh and Rone had been bickering back and forth in the way that two men of unequal temperament, but equal stubbornness, did. Where Kaveh was cold and serious, Rone was glib and careless. But underneath they had the same intensity—as if it were within their natures to feel the same.

Nin hoped that as they traveled, the two men might come to an accord—that Rone might examine and reconsider choices that he had always spurned. The looks between Rone and Taline had grown fiercer. There had always been tension there, but now it was of a different sort—broken of the acrimony and animosity, there was heat of another kind. A different form of unrealized tension—one with far more consequences.

As they inched closer to the Land of Darkness, agents appeared more frequently. Aros obviously knew their destination, even if he did not know how they were getting there or what they looked like. He wanted to stop them before they reached their goal.

So far, the agents had been quickly dispatched. Either the lesser foes were faster to stumble upon them, or the greater foes were still to come.

The lesser foes were welcome, frankly. A few days of careful travel without overwhelming incident had allowed them to recover physically and to allow Kaveh to exhaustively investigate every holy spot and temple in northeastern Scythia, as they wound a fast, serpentine route to keep trackers off-balance.

"Yes, Valeran, that is exactly what I've been doing, feeding information instead of allowing you to avoid attacks five times over by me scouting ahead."

Kaveh had been especially good at reconnaissance and rumor gathering. With only one of Taline's physical enchantment boxes in his pocket to maintain a different face, Kaveh had no other magic—and no imperial oaths—to set off any alarms, making him nearly invisible to those tracking them. He exhaustively searched for any mention of ritual or rite amid the gossip of the empire.

They had clocked hunters and assassins at each site of note. Only their extensively enchanted features and long-range scouting—and the dwindling enchantments on their cloaks—had kept them from triple their engagement so far.

They couldn't entirely avoid the empire in Scythia. But they had advanced warning of attacks, which made dispatch far easier. As long as Nin didn't use a ripgate and the cloaks held up, they would deal with whatever agents appeared.

"Someone is going to put the pieces together soon, and they will enter the Land of Darkness ahead of us—a place you can't scout," Rone said viciously.

"Irsula will treat any who enter her domain as a threat."

"Your cursed mother will treat us as a threat."

"We are, all of us, a threat." Kaveh frowned at the box he held in his hands.

"A threat? You are now a simple bloodstain waiting to happen."

Nin's gaze met Taline's, and her sister rolled her eyes and carefully re-disguised them as four older Scythian men traveling together on horseback.

"You rely on such things often, do you not?" Kaveh rotated the box of simulated shadow between his fingers with a frown, then turned to Taline. "A way to deal with the paltry magic at your command?"

Nin cringed, but Rone slid in front of her sister—standing between Taline and Kaveh as if Kaveh were a direct threat. "You will take care with your tone. You are using that paltry magic right now."

Kaveh's gaze was even. "You do not like acknowledging the truth, do you, Valeran?"

"Her containers are the reason you haven't been destroyed yet. Taline is incredible," Rone said coldly. Another change—Rone calling Taline by her first name. "As are her paltry magics. Those magics made that device you hold in your hand. How does it feel, former prince? Relying on the magic of others to get you by?"

"How does it feel, Valeran, to know you will never be able to shed that hood?"

No matter what Taline did, Rone's hair held enchantment in its very roots. His hair needed to be hidden at all times—it was a dead giveaway to his identity—but it was easier to hide in a group of working men with dull and uninteresting sun coverings. People looking for disguises were a lot less likely to look at a group of day laborers traveling from town to town.

"You know, Fehl—"

Taline nudged Nin to her horse and the two mounted and took off, leaving the men to catch up.

Nin had attempted to mitigate arguments at first, but it had only served to make things worse when arguments blew past their seals. Both men seemed to crave fighting with each other to relieve steam. The last three days had been a long expanse of travel broken only by Kaveh's cold jabs and Rone's heated mocking.

"Thank you," Nin said to Taline. She took careful stock of her sister. Sweating a bit at the hairline, she otherwise looked fit, indicating the scepter sickness was in a lull period for a few hours—a boon.

Taline just shook her head as they navigated the brush and rounded back onto the way. No matter sickness or health, Taline always made things work.

Nin examined her sunworn male hands in the light as they maneuvered back onto the golden path. "Incredible disguise, as always. You are incredible."

Taline went pink at the restatement of Rone's words. Nin smiled.

The way ahead was clear for now, but they would have to navigate knots of travelers again soon.

Most hunters and agents were still mistakenly looking for two men and two women in a group of four, and they only ever realized their mistake after they grew close enough for identification spells to delve beneath the fading cloaks and sturdy guises.

Fleeing only made them chase harder, so there was little to do to avoid imperial notice when agents grew too close—but Taline had outdone herself on their disguises, putting a lot of effort and imagination into making each of them look similar enough to each other to pass as a group, but different enough not to attract attention that way either.

Because their old faces and disguises were useless, Taline had taken the guises of the first two older men she had seen who raised no conspicuous glance, then tailored the other two disguises to match. The intense efforts they had made in their previous role as the Hand had made it so Taline knew the spells to temporarily transform across gender. It gave them the edge.

As the two men caught up but continued to snipe, Taline rode closer to Nin—her new, aggressively masculine features unable to properly sustain the feminine tilt of her head. Nin withheld a smile. Taline would get into full disguise as soon as they passed a city threshold, but out here, with only the four of them currently on the Scythian Way road, she wasn't bothering to hide her own mannerisms.

Taline stared at the bag strapped around Nin's waist in contemplation.

Nin tilted her head in question.

"The glyph papers," Taline murmured, looking at the bag strangely. "Rone used the last one on me during the scepter fight. I had thought them finished."

A drop of gathered sweat slid down Taline's face. Nin let some of her magic slide over to try to alleviate the first touches of a new bout of sickness.

"Glyph papers?"

"The seals to hold...well, you...after you would have claimed the scepter."

Nin maintained her expression with difficulty, focusing her gaze on the road ahead. She didn't say anything for a long moment, trying to figure out what to say. "Rone used the seals on you."

"I had...trouble with the scepter. With not using it."

Nin reached out to grab Taline's left hand. "Everyone has trouble with the scepter. That you chose to continue fighting is the most important factor." She squeezed her fingers.

Taline squeezed back and they let go. "I don't know that I would have been able to fight it without Rone."

Taline looked over her shoulder, and Nin's gaze followed to the two men behind whose hands were both inching toward knives. Nin cast a quick shield enchantment between them.

"How did...?" Nin cleared her throat, turning back around. "How did it feel? The seals? To have the seals placed upon you?"

Taline cocked her head in a way that looked rather funny in her heavily masculine disguise, but Nin could concentrate on little but her answer. "The scepter worked against the magic, so it was unpleasant, but the seals contained your magic—and Rone's. And even though Valeran and I were not partners in the beginning, I trusted his magic."

Relief and hope poured through Nin, and she smiled tightly. "Remember that."

Taline's expression went funny. "Remember what?"

"Remember that so we can make more seals to fight Aros." Nin focused on the road ahead. "Look up ahead—frogdeer."

"That's not what...you are dissembling."

Nin could feel Taline's eyes narrow.

"What are you hiding?"

Nin considered how to answer, watching the frogdeer jump across the path. "Remember that trust. Rone has always had a soft spot for you. I knew it when I made him promise to look after you. That soft spot has only grown. I know his exterior is sometimes abrasive, purposefully so, but—"

"Nin." Taline's hand was pressing against her stomach and Nin wondered whether she was stopping butterflies there. She hoped so. She hoped it wasn't sickness rising up. Taline and Rone could help each other. "What exactly is his pow—"

"What are you two discussing?" Kaveh asked as he rode up.

Nin turned to Kaveh with a bright smile. "That we should stop in Galit."

"There is a holy site there. But we could push through."

"Push you through a wall," Taline muttered, hand dropping from her stomach.

That response brought Nin only relief. Lightly cantankerous Taline was a Taline who might be able to stifle a wave of sickness—and it came in waves. Taline was doing well, considering, but she needed rest. Good rest.

"We can push through," Nin said, "but the holy site there is worth inspection, and this is a good opportunity to hear what new rumors have spread." And to let Taline rest at an inn.

Kaveh nodded and Rone joined them. That meant Taline couldn't ask her question. Nin would never give up Rone's secret, but it was a tight line they walked now, and it would do their party no good for it to be revealed in anger. Rone was too terrified and volatile. He would leave. He would take all hope with him.

Whispers and rumors greeted them in each new city and town—a new emperor, the assassination of Sher Fehl, the assassination of the council members, the bounties on the Shadow Prince, the equally large bounty on a lesser known imperial child with strange hair. Then there were the tales of two girls—did anyone know of the Summoras? Why was that name familiar? Wasn't there a Summora somewhere out east?

Kaveh's mounted grip tightened. Each new whisper seemed to infuriate him more—to set within him some destiny of revenge. Each failed try at obtaining information or tonic to alleviate his condition made him more grim.

And something that they had been forced to acknowledge with the increasing attacks: they had traveled long enough that the cloaks' spells had started to thin, leaving peeping traces of Taline in different spots regardless of their care in modifying memories. The idea that there might be four men—or four women, or any combination thereof—traveling together would soon take hold in the rumor chain.

Then Rone really would be pushing to turn Kaveh into a donkey.

But regardless of whether he could, it wouldn't save them. And they needed to guard their reserves and save their tricks for use in the Land of Darkness, which came with much bigger threats.

In the uplands and steppe of the Plateau of a Thousand Rocks and the Lake of Despair, the next attack upon them was both expected and a surprise.

The three assassins were expected and quickly dealt with. The cadre of pentalayerists making a move on the final note of the first attack was not.

The pentalayerists rolled out from behind the boulders at the edge of the plateau—eight strong. Garbed head-to-toe in light brown and green wrappings to blend into the landscape, only their eyes and mouths showed.

That there were more magi shielded behind rock was in no doubt.

Taline, Rone, and Kaveh stepped back from where the unconscious bodies of the assassins lay.

The pentalayerists grabbed their four horses, as if they suspected the four of them might flee. They should have let them flee. They would have made far easier targets.

A man stepped forward, studying Kaveh with a piercing gaze. "It is true, then, what the lying Carre bastard says—the Shadow Prince is no more." The fabric wrapped around the man's face could not hide burns that had not yet healed.

Rone hissed next to her. This then was the man who had chased them. Nin looked at the pentalayerist's leader.

"He stands before you," Nin said softly, though she let her voice carry on the breeze.

"He stands as a man, not a force." The leader's eyes shifted away from Kaveh. "He is no longer a concern of ours."

"A mistake." Kaveh bared his teeth.

"Perhaps." The leader's gaze shifted between the four of them. "Three others to sort. One of mystery and possible threat, the woman tainted by the scepter who no longer holds it in her hand, and the man who defended the wielder. Why does the Carre bane who claims himself the new emperor want you dead, defender?"

Rone smiled sharply. "I suppose I'm simply too good-looking to live."

"We will help you to your end, then," the leader said brusquely, but his gaze focused back on Taline. There was a strange, feverish hunger in his brown eyes. "I can feel the scepter's taint on you from here, but yet it is not still in your hand. How are you still alive?"

And although Aros was without a doubt their main concern, this shared obsession was why the pentalayerists were more concerning than agents of the empire. The pentalayerists had specific tools and skills to locate scepter wielders and gatemakers. Nin had only kept herself hidden so well because of the powers in Tehrasi's blooded lands. She had used them extensively, and until Aros showed his hand, exclusively.

"I released the scepter," Taline said.

The pentalayerist's eyes narrowed. Old eyes in a young face. "Impossible."

"And yet, here I am," she bit out. "Defying your claim that I would not be."

Nin sharpened her gaze on the leader and his feverish hunger held back by disbelief. He had a strange stake in this. She realigned what she had been told about their encounters in the non-magic layer. Those burn marks had been acquired in their chase. He was a high-level pentalayerist who traveled between layers. He was a magi who had tracked them well. And there was something...

The pentalayerist leader tapped his fingers against his staff. "We shall see, wielder."

Nin let out a touch of power to prod at his. There was something...

He turned piercing brown eyes—filled with bitterness and hate—on Nin. "But first there are other tales I need to confirm. Tales within our halls that the one who lit the Ninth Scepter at the side of the Shadow Prince is of the Carre bloodline. A bastard child gifted with the power of the gates."

She said nothing as other pentalayerists crept into position at his tapped command.

"No answer? Whether you are a bastard child, or someone from a completely new line, matters only esoterically. You are clearly of powers that do not belong in a free world."

The bitterness and hatred in his voice turned into something fiercer—deeper and more turbulent.

She pulled her magic back, finding the answer to her question. To find yet another after so many years thinking there were two, when there had been four.

"A free world denotes that all are free," she said, shifting. She understood this fight. This man would see her permanently severed from the earth. And nothing would dissuade him. He hated himself as much as he hated her.

"A world free of magi who could use their powers to change that freedom."

Using a ripgate would bring Aros to them. Aros, who would wipe the pentalayerists from the earth in the way that they wanted to wipe Aros and Nin, born of the Carres.

But in bringing Aros, he would extinguish more than the pentalayerists.

She took another careful step. "All who hold power can change a given state of freedom. Any person can use their power for ill."

Rone, Taline, and Kaveh all shifted minutely as well, as did the pentalayerists—positions being sought and secured across the steppe.

"You speak glibly of freedom and power, gatemaker, but not all have the power to threaten the layers themselves—the landscapes and lifeblood that make up our very world." There was something old and dead in the leader's young eyes. A hatred that ran too deeply to reach.

The Carres had been hated for many, many reasons.

"No, some of them could just threaten the people who live within," she said softly, for she understood. She understood the hatred.

The leader paused, eyes narrowing further, looking her over. "Not a Carre then. A mistake perhaps. One who is trying to rectify the error and repugnance of her birth to powers that should not exist?"

The leader's gaze slid to Rone, and there was a question there, unanswered—or perhaps, an answer sought, but not expected to be found. She stepped deliberately, drawing the leader's eyes back away from Rone.

There was a trap here. A large one. In her answer and in the way things might turn. "Mistakes are to be rectified, are they not? But some mistakes serve a greater purpose."

Hatred and resolve still burned, but consideration joined them. "Our spies in Tehras say your goal is to help the people. To advance the good."

Another trap.

"Not everyone who advances is good."

The leader smiled. "No, they are not. Interesting." His head tilted. "No Carre would have thought that."

"No," she said quietly. Not even Memni or Allit, scholars both, had doubted the true dominance of their family.

And neither had Nin. Nin hadn't doubted it at nine when firmly within her family's grasp. She had doubted her own family's practices within the palace, but all that happened outside its walls had been far removed from her view or a contrasting understanding. Not until she had been on the streets had she seen the impact and understood.

She had been raised in an environment and she had accepted that environment as truth. Only being forced from it had made her question that truth.

Wanting to save her handmaidens from her sister had been an entirely separate notion from wanting to save the populace from her family. And yet, the emotion was the same. It had only been the scale and understanding—the connection of thought—that had been different.

Not until she had been able to connect the greater world outside to her own views inside the palace had she truly understood. When she had seen the faces of her handmaidens reflected across the greater populace. When she had looked back in memory on the faces and expressions of terror, resignation, or fervor that she had seen while she stood above the sacrificial platform at the Festival of Blood or any of the other ritualistic ceremonies she had been expected to attend.

Only through a different, newer lens had she understood what her family's desires, aims, and traditions had done to those they ruled.

That the population had allowed it, that a portion had even embraced it, hadn't made it less wrong.

The Carres had held the scepters, the power—they had held absolute dominance. And they had made the streets run red with it.

Only when she had stopped being a Carre could she see outside the notions given to her from birth.

"Not everyone who advances is good, but not everyone who stops such advancement is either," she said carefully. "I see hatred in you, raging and deep. What notion do you carry from the ghosts of your past?"

He smiled unpleasantly—a stab of lips between layers of cloth hiding his features from grasp. "What notion do I carry? Only those notions of justice and peace. The ending of all that threatens and all that has been done. A cleansing of our world. A cleansing of the Carres."

She took in his features and the skin that was unblemished by burn. Late twenties, perhaps. Younger than Aros, but older than Kaveh. That would put him in his late teens when the Carres had been extinguished. A number of possibilities that would stew vengeance were available. The Feast of Sustenance and Renewal—colloquially called the Festival of Blood for the amount that flowed down the steps of the palace—had run the streets increasingly red as the empire grew stronger and the Carres grew progressively more uneasy. They had sacrificed civilian after civilian in order to increase their magic stores.

Personal.

"How do you plan to deal with Aros and the Scepter of Darkness?" she asked, just as carefully as she had the other questions.

"Are you offering a deal, gatemaker? To save yourself by killing him?"

"Do you deal with the demons of the deep?"

"A stay of execution, perhaps, until the greater problem is brought low?" He smiled grimly and drew his sword. "No, I will not even grant you that. I want nothing of such powers as yours to remain. We will deal with you, then we will deal with him. Both in unmarked tombs."

"You speak so glibly of mistakes." Rone twirled a knife in his fingers. "But it seems as if you learned little from yours in the non-magic layer."

"I learned that the Scepter of Darkness is not one to underestimate. And do not worry, Rone ul Valeran. I learned that neither are the two of you." He withdrew a box.

"Rone?" Nin looked at the box with caution. Her caution only grew as Rone stiffened.

"Did you collect all that we left behind?" Rone asked lightly—too lightly. "How obsessive of you."

"Which one?" Nin asked, not taking her eyes away from the box. She ran through the list of the boxes Taline would have had on her when they disappeared. There had been a number of detonation boxes.

"The most devastating."

No. She was already diving, dragging Kaveh with her as Rone dove alongside her with Taline when the explosion went off.

CHAPTER SEVEN

DARKNESS FALLS

NINLI

(Plateau of a Thousand Rocks and the Lake of Despair)

The explosion gobbled air and earth as it charged toward them. They wouldn't make it. But they were together. A ripgate formed in Nin's mind—

A tsunamic wave of water rushed overhead and hit the explosion with a great crash. The wave reformed, reversed, and swept toward the pentalayerists. Nin pulled her forming ripgate back and hugged the ground with the others. Three of the pentalayerists—chiefly, the leader—dodged in time, but the other five exploded backward into the boulders they had first hidden behind. Water crashed, sending waves of liquid and power in all directions.

The ten additional pentalayerists who had been concealed behind the boulders scuttled out and sent their own spells at two other emerging figures—opponents hiding among them.

The assassins—then the pentalayerists—had been expected, but the two men completely clothed in brown and green like the pentalayerists were on an entirely different level. It was in the way they moved together and apart. One stood waiting, two swords drawn, features obscured by wraps and spell. But the one who wielded the sea moved forward.

She knew it was this figure who had cast the spell, for the strings of his magic were the same as from their strained trip across the Casp Sea and back.

Kaveh was stiff beneath her hands, giving further evidence to the recognition.

Simin ul Fehl examined the pentalayerists from behind his face-shielding coverings. "How lovely, that you decided to make your move so close to a lake."

"Another assassin?" Rone murmured. He would have had as little reason—lesser reason—to be near the watercaster as she had before being bound to Kaveh.

"No," Kaveh said, tone curt.

Simin's head tilted to them, focusing intently on Kaveh's position for a charged moment, then back to the pentalayerists, who were cautiously shifting. "We could, of course, let you kill them and clean up afterward, but we have explicit instructions on how these four are to be dealt with."

As if by signal, the two figures and the pentalayerists engaged. Everyone around her did as well. Taline pulled Kaveh behind the short boulder they had tumbled toward and Rone and Nin moved to flank them, putting their bodies, but not their heads, behind the easily compromised rock. They could easily see the fight.

Simin and the other man were downing the thirteen remaining pentalayerists with ease.

"We could kill all of them," Rone said, voice low. His fingers moved over a box that he pulled from his pack. "We have a force stunner. Useless against the scepter, but against magi fighting in close quarters? We could deal individually with each as they lay stunned."

Coldly execute each person as they lay upon the ground?

"Rone—"

"They will continue to hunt us, Ninli. Both the pentalayerists and the empire. The latter will just kill the prince and me. But the pentalayerists will kill you. And they won't let Taline survive."

Kill Simin and the pentalayerists? She had never had much in common with the pentalayerists' means, but their aim was to protect, or to destroy, for the good of the people. Did she have a right to decide their deaths?

And Simin...despite his words...

Nin looked at Kaveh, but there was no acknowledgment in his expression. He was watching the second figure with the swords as he fought with ruthless efficiency—intelligently identifying each opponent and their moves, then using the momentum of each to easily and efficiently move his body around them and his weapons through them.

She knew who the second figure was as soon as she gave it thought, though she had never seen him fight. He was with Simin, fighting like they were born of the same mind separated into two bodies. Second or third best at everything—here was the evidence that the combination of that skillset was devastating.

"It's Baksis," she murmured. "And Simin."

Taline jolted, eyes sharpening on the fighting figures. For she had likely not identified either of them. Rone looked sharply at Nin, then back at the men, cold consideration and caution in his gaze.

"So which type is he?" Taline murmured, harkening back to their conversation so long ago now about what type of man Baksis was and what type of leader he might be—moderate or vengeful?

She had less experience with Baksis—the night of palace revelry contained her greatest amount of data. She had watched him vocally spar with Namir—and she had been reminded of

Taline and Rone. That corollary had made her predisposed to like him.

But Omari and Baksis, along with the others, had publicly proclaimed Kaveh responsible for the emperor's death. They were all playing deep games. And the game of who to believe was a madness all its own in uncertain times.

"Should we not kill them then?" Rone asked idly, though his gaze was narrowed and cold.

"No," Kaveh said.

"Let us see," Nin said, hurriedly. For Rone would not acquiesce to a command coming from Kaveh. "Let us see what they have to say when they are done."

Taline looked her way but said nothing.

"He already said they had instructions to deal with us, Ninli." Rone's fingers curled around the box. "Surprise is a commodity that requires precision."

Baksis was dealing with the pentalayerists one after another while Simin supported his efforts by sweeping water and wave in cascading arcs to finish opponents off. They were playing with their prey. Nin wondered whether there was some message to Kaveh in it.

"Better to fight two instead of twelve," she said. "Baksis and Simin will turn against us immediately if we attack. We will deal with them if they choose to follow Aros's instructions."

Rone didn't look pleased, but he understood waiting and striking against fewer enemies as well as anyone. Nin looked at Kaveh. All they could do was see if they had placed their faith correctly.

The pentalayerist leader lunged toward Simin. "You are just as bad as Aros, if you allow such magi to live, Simin ul Fehl."

Simin gave a little bow as he sidestepped the blow. "Ah, but I promised my brother's head would be taken by one of our hands, so I can't let you have it by yours."

"Take your brothers. We don't care about the former Shadow Prince. He's a dead man walking. The world is better for it." The leader's eyes flashed. "The last good thing the emperor did was to take his powers. But there are others who need to be dealt with. Leave the two women to us."

"Ah, but the new emperor wants them most of all." Baksis pulled the pentalayerist leader against his chest and twisted the blade he had inserted. He had slipped behind the man sometime during the argument, all the remaining pentalayerists on the ground.

Blood gurgled from the pentalayerist leader's lips. "We will hunt you, too." His fingers curled into his cloak.

"No, you won't." Baksis plunged the blade further inside—a killing strike, if not dealt with immediately.

Nin stepped out from behind the boulder, hands palm down and out to the sides in surrender. "Let me heal him." Harsh voices behind her demanded she return.

None of Baksis's features showed behind his assassin's coverings and spells, but his posture tightened.

"Sweep them away," she said, "but—"

The pentalayerist leader's expression twisted and the coin beneath his fingers glinted.

"Release him!" Simin yelled.

Baksis did before the man could take him along with a twist of the travel coin in his hand.

Nin's path forward halted as the man disappeared.

Simin didn't wait for further gambits. A great wave of water swept through, lifting the remaining pentalayerists and sweeping them to the other side of the lake in a great rush of water. They continued past the tributary and out through the slim river—tumbling and slamming the ground with great force, end over end.

They might not all be dead wherever they ended up, but they would be worse for the wear. The four horses, though treated to a ride upon the waves instead of within, were unfortunately swept away with them. A concern for later.

More pressing was the leader's disappearance. He, who had viewed ripgates and those who could make them with hatred had just proved his own lineage.

There were many reasons people hated the Carres…

Kaveh moved in front of her, physically blocking her back. "Baksis. Simin."

Baksis touched his head wrap and it unwound with the spells keeping his features from notice. Simin followed. Nin moved to the side, elbowing Kaveh when he again tried to block her.

Nin could see the shift in Rone and Taline's forms at the confirmation of their new foes.

The pentalayerists were one thing. Even with their numbers, without the box they had stolen, Nin and Rone could have contained them. Baksis and Simin were in a completely different category—their category—both Level Nines. And Baksis and Simin knew how to work as a combat team—easily seen in their fight against the pentalayerists.

Nin, Taline, and Rone could fight together, but they were a stealth and evasion team—not a team trained for combat.

And Kaveh…

Headwrap thickly falling along one shoulder, Baksis was eyeing Kaveh, slowly examining him from head to toe. "It is strange to see you so diminished."

Kaveh firmed his lips.

Baksis tilted his head. "All the darkness—everything that makes starlight interesting—gone, to leave simple emptiness behind."

Kaveh's eyes were cool, gaze remote. "And yet emptiness still stands. What is your goal?"

"Well, that depends." Baksis's eyes went to Nin and stayed there. "The Lost Princess." His head tilted toward Kaveh, but his eyes didn't leave Nin. "You knew."

"Yes."

Baksis nodded and focused on him. "Aros wants her."

"I know."

"He will do whatever he needs to get her. He seeks Carre knowledge like a cawserpent's mating quest."

"He won't have her."

"You cannot defend her."

"As I am now, no. As I will be again...defense and more."

Baksis and Simin didn't look away from Kaveh—but there was a nonverbal exchange between them nonetheless. "You think you will gain back your powers?"

"I will."

Baksis's gaze moved in the direction they were traveling. "By whose hand? Irsula? The Osirin temple? The Eternal Spring?"

"By Sehk's will, if I have to gain it."

Baksis examined him, but it was Simin who answered. "We shall see then."

Kaveh minutely relaxed. Nin allowed herself to do the same, for Kaveh knew Simin and Baksis far better than she did.

Baksis shrugged negligently. "Namir would have my legs if I delivered the healer to Aros without other options being probed. Omari favors her. Two to release, then." His gaze went to Valeran.

"But that one... Aros wants that one dead. It would do us well to deliver his head to Aros at the expense of saving yours."

Rone's eyes slit with his curving smile. "Do try."

Nin wet her lips, shifting at what that smile meant.

Baksis's gaze went to Taline. "And for that one... Etelian grows more dangerous as he loses control. And for her, he might give me his throne—not that it is worth anything with Aros already sitting upon it."

Rone's cold smile curved more wildly. "Do try."

Nin slid another step closer to Rone and Taline.

Simin watched silently from his side. Gathering intelligence, like he always did.

"I don't much need to try, Rone ul Valeran," Baksis said cuttingly. "She is the way we found you. That, and you, in particular, are easily seen once proximity is gained—through the spells that tie you to our house."

Nin's lips firmed. That was how Kaveh had been able to tell who Rone was in Urshna. Once he had gotten close enough, no disguise had kept Rone from Kaveh's view.

Baksis and Simin would hold similar imperial vow threads that identified imperial children specifically. Of course they would. Aros and Etelian would have them too. As well as Nera and Voiya and all the others of Nera's line.

Sehk.

"The Lost Princess has the freshest protection and the most reward—she will outlive the rest of you by many moons. Your time alive dwindles, Rone ul Valeran. Aros wants you dead. Why, I do not know." Baksis's eyes sharpened with interest. "But it is enough that he does wish you dead that I am tempted to let you live."

Relief nearly made Nin stagger.

"I will not aid the empire," Rone said, lips curling unpleasantly. "Any of you."

Baksis's eyes slid across the group, landing on Taline. "We'll see. We'll see what aid you do or do not offer."

"You rise against Aros then?" Nin asked.

"Rise against Aros? No." Baksis raised a brow. "I play at servitude and do what he asks while I await, like the others."

"Await what?" Nin said, hope blooming.

"The others?" Kaveh asked.

Baksis's gaze moved between them hypnotically. "The factions and splits that have always been present. Many wait. They are holding off on casting their stones. They await a strong leader. The generals still have their hopes, despite the story Aros is trying to sell. They follow him because he has the scepter and the current throne, but they will waver, if other choices are presented."

Nin felt the solidification deep within her—the solidification of what she had hoped. If Kaveh was presented with his powers restored, they would follow the one the emperor had chosen to inherit. Only Kaveh had seen a throne that he thought would always hold his father.

"They will depose Aros?" Taline asked.

Baksis looked at her askance. "No one will depose Aros while he wields the Scepter of Darkness. He is only getting stronger and growing madder. He pores over the scriptures in the library of the palace in Tehras, he tortures and questions Osni ul Crelu, and he grows more powerful with each breath."

Simin shifted, and Baksis looked at him and nodded. "Aros has taken over the Palace of Tehras and throne as well," Baksis added. "Aros reassures Etelian that as soon as the imperial palace in Fehlaka is rebuilt, Etelian will be reinstated."

Nin could read between the statements without adding the curve of Baksis's lips.

The imperial palace in Fehlaka would never be rebuilt. Tehras would be the new seat of the empire. And Tehrasi had no need for a padifehl if the emperor sat the province's throne.

"But Aros and Etelian aren't the only ones working shadows that have no more ruler," Simin said.

"Nera," Kaveh said grimly.

"Nera waits, like all, in the imperial bower. And without the emperor, without you and Irsula, she is free to rule. She has tried to get Etelian into another province, but he has become more than obsessed with you." He looked at Taline. "And you will rue that obsession."

"I already have," Taline said, clipped.

"Nera will make you rue it. Don't underestimate the pain you have introduced to her plans for her most spoiled child."

"The other blessed?" Kaveh asked.

"Some have cast their lots. Others wait. They wait like Nera, with their own aims, looking for the best pillar to build upon."

Baksis was dangling bait—and there was both aggravation and determination in Kaveh's expression. "Omari will be destroyed."

Baksis's smile was a slash. "Putting Omari on the throne of Cuipsin was a move with great consequence and reward. Namir will kill me for it, should the consequence gain ground, but it was the only way to secure a position in a Nera-run empire. Should Aros fall to madness and death and Nera prevail as empress, Omari, Cuipsin, and all of eastern Ersine will fight against the other provinces for dominance, but Omari and Kush will be swallowed fully in Nera's world without that foothold to box Nera in. It was the only way to hedge against that outcome."

Nin understood fully in a way that someone born of Salare Carre could. "Nera will take up the throne when Aros succumbs to the scepter. That is her plan."

"Of course." Baksis tipped his head. "Aros can still be reasoned with, at the moment. It was against his wishes to have Omari in Cuipsin, but he has let it stand. I had to play a number of stones to make it happen. Aros knows his end. And so he plots, even now. Especially now, while he still possesses his faculties. He won't upset Cuipsin when there is nothing to be served by it and not when Omari and Namir pledge loyalty to Aros's throne. They both denounced you and swore to your killing of the emperor. They are not threats. But they will also not be allowed to survive. A few years, maybe."

"A small accident will befall Omari, then Kush will be enveloped within the empire and another put on the throne."

"And Namir will haunt me from the beyond."

"He will let Omari live, as long as she does not show as a threat."

"But soon there will be nothing left of Aros, and the empire will descend to chaos."

"Let it descend and begone," Rone spit.

Baksis smiled tightly. "You care not, Rone ul Valeran, but you do not comprehend how such a thing would effect even you—even should you flee to Helsgir."

The fighting for the throne would not only destroy the empire, but the territories within. A few dozen blessed children battling for a throne—or splitting away from one? Civil war would descend across the lands. And the blessed children were called that for a reason. Of the thousands of children bred specifically for power, they were the ones who had come out on top.

"Aros will destroy everything around him as he descends to madness. Nera might not even survive, but neither will many, many others. You care not, but your companions do not share this sentiment."

"The Summoras would find a wounded bird even in you, Baksis ul Fehl. I have no regard for their sentiment."

"No?" His gaze shifted to Taline, then back to Rone. "Then my words are not for you at all."

Rone sneered. "Your words serve no one."

"The empire will be destroyed unless someone who can strike true fear in the imperial children leashes them all." Baksis looked at Kaveh. So did Simin. "The emperor knew who could lead the rest."

"I have no power to lead through fear at the moment," Kaveh said harshly.

"No. And I will kill you, should I need to, in order to secure the lead for another to rise. I will kill you with some regret, as you were always a strong ally—but it will be without hesitation."

"A lovely family." Rone clapped his hands—a bold move in a tense atmosphere, and Nin could see the steel that slipped between his fingers. "Ninli, I see why you wanted to include the Shadow Prince in our club. Alas, I still vote no."

Simin tilted toward the threat of Rone, but Baksis surveyed Kaveh silently for long moments more. "Restore your powers, Imperator General, or I will kill you when you exit Darkness's lands." Baksis dropped two folded pieces of cloth to the ground, signaled to Simin, and water surrounded them. They rode out on a cresting wave, disappearing into the distance.

"What just happened?" Taline asked stiffly.

"We have a new glass of dripping sand," Nin answered, just as stiffly. She couldn't look at Kaveh. She could hear the sands of time falling.

"If they want him to succeed, they should help us travel the Land of Darkness. We could use their power in the forest," Taline said grimly.

"They have a game to play with Aros and the empire still. I am only one piece on the board. And," Kaveh murmured, kneeling down to open the cloth, "coming with us—would not be how a test for the throne works."

Baksis would follow Kaveh, should Kaveh regain his powers. Should he not... Kaveh's death would facilitate other plans—and Baksis would wield that knife easily as well.

Nin felt anxiety curl. There were so many ways that she might fix this—but none of the solutions were ones she could implement without betrayal or removing the agency of another.

The sands slipped, but there was still time. Everything could work out. Hard choices could be made. She had to believe that.

"What did he leave behind?" Rone indicated the dropped linens with a jerk of his hand.

"Cloth that will hide you both, should you drape yourself within. Baksis's mother..." Kaveh shook his head.

There was a story there, but Nin would hear it another time. She reached for the fabric.

Taline eyed it with distrust, but Nin, with Kaveh's help, made two scarves out of the cloth. She could feel the suppression spells in the fibers, and she felt a measure of hope. The threads would disallow blessed imperial children to see them.

They had given up on patching Taline's cloak—coaxing the small shadows to remain within.

"The spells in the cloth will only last for a few moons, at most," Kaveh said. "Then it will be back to the shadows."

"Better for the lesser one to be on me," Taline said when Nin offered to switch cloaks. "They have to pass me to feel my strings. Aros would find you from afar without that suppression."

Even with the new protections in place, it was with real weariness and tension that they entered Galit on foot.

Galit was a bustling trade town on the royal road—a stop for travelers far and wide. And, as expected, it was full of tales from the empire. The biggest inn was overflowing with travelers in the common room, where people went to exchange tales. Rumors swirled on broken tongues.

"The Shadow Prince killed the emperor. Did you hear? He is without power now."

"Good. He can't conquer us with his unnatural powers," a Scythian responded. "The royals are gathering forces in the northwest. Soon, we knock the Fehls back from the palace. They will regret ever stepping conquering foot in Tomyr."

"But it is whispered that Aros ul Fehl has the Scepter of Darkness. That he is a Carre."

"A Carre or a Fehl can try to conquer lower Scythia all they want. He won't succeed past the mid-gate. Only the Shadow Prince was a danger to upper Scythia."

"They say the Night Terror is back in her forest, where the shadows grow monstrous once more."

"Death begets anyone who travels the Land of Darkness."

"Like mother, like son."

Aros had attached all of Irsula's actions to Kaveh. The only variations that Nin had heard was that Irsula killed the emperor on Kaveh's command.

Nin placed herself between Kaveh and the rest of the room. Each day without his magic, he became tenser and shorter tempered. She was afraid that one of the days, he would snap.

Especially now that there was a time slip in place.

"I don't believe the Shadow Prince is without power. And if he is, it is temporary. Aros ul Fehl just released another bounty and this one hinted at an even greater reward. That reeks of desperation. He knows something and he's scared."

Nin pushed Kavel with her as the line moved.

"A room for four, please," Nin called to the innkeeper from her spot behind Kaveh, crowding him more toward the man seated behind the large table and away from the crowd behind her. She dipped into the heavy bag of gold Kaveh had taken from the tent.

It was more dangerous to stay in city establishments rather than camp in caves and forests, but this close to the Land of Darkness, serious agents would be searching the brush. They would not be expecting to find fugitives in an inn.

Taline had expressed no little relief at not sleeping in another cave. They were likely to have to go back to them—or camp in worse—in the Land of Darkness, though.

Ninli followed the innkeeper to their room and watched vaguely as the man pointed at the shared bathing rooms to the left and waste rooms to the right.

They were a day's ride from the Land of Darkness. They would find out then whether they would gain reprieve.

RONE

Shepherd's Inn in Galit

Stuck within the inn's walls and the room that they had reluctantly and acrimoniously agreed to share, Rone sat on his rolled-out pallet of erial bird feathers and sustern sheep wool with Taline's sleeping body on the pallet behind him. She was wrapped in that cursed cloak, and the even more accursed scarf that mirrored his own.

She had worn herself out redoing all the disguise boxes with new enchantments and features, ready at a touch, over and over again. Even with Ninli and Rone giving her a steady stream of magic to work with, Taline's pathways were still shredded from her battle with the scepter.

Rest and time would heal her, but both were things that might be ripped from them at any point.

He watched as Ninli failed yet again to heal the Shadow Prince's magic in the flickering torchlight. It was a nightly ritual for them. A nightly failed ritual.

He watched as she painted his body—from his temples and all the way around the blocked energy points of his body, draped only by a bathing sash across his lap.

Rone watched the magic swirling under the block of Fehl's magic. The ritual enchantment Ninli was attempting was for both energy and spiritual cleansing. For someone with full access to their magic, Ninli's ritual, with her power behind it, would heighten and brighten the inherent energy within.

Ninli herself was a beacon. Her own points shone with golden light. They always had.

Even when touched by a scepter, her light tried to overwhelm its darkness.

He watched Ninli work, but for all her abilities in healing and her outpouring of magical ability, she would never unlock the emperor's spell.

He could see exactly how the energy failed to connect to Fehl's magic, and how it didn't unlock the manacle containing it within. The ability to portion another's energy and lock it beneath was the cruelest of abilities.

Like what had happened to Taline, with Etelian's quartered ability to take away a portion of magic for a period of time, the body starved and scabbed the injury with thick, scarred ropes that never worked completely right again.

Rone pressed his lips together. Not even the emperor could have healed the injuries to Taline's magic. Not after they had scarred. Only during the process of scarring might he have been able to heal her.

Eventually, left to its locked state, Fehl's body would stop making magic at all. It would scab, then scar, then be a reminder only of what once was. Rone watched the scabs slowly form, regardless of how Ninli tried to halt them.

Fehl grabbed her fingers. "They won't heal." He closed his eyes. "You should stop trying."

Ninli freed her hand and ran her fingers down the muscles of Fehl's right arm. "We will keep trying. Perhaps in the cleansing waters, the magic will be able to connect. The renewal waters might be able to alleviate the blocks enough to dig beneath."

Fehl's gaze was intense on hers. His fingers brushed her cheek and he rose. Rone watched him coldly, but Fehl never looked his way as he exited the room to wash the ritual marks from his body.

Ninli extinguished the embers beneath the room's firepot and began scooping the crushed herb paste from the cauldron into a leaf pouch, leaving Rone to his silent brooding.

"Aren't you going to say it, Ninli? Ask your question."

Ninli scraped the cauldron then wiped the contents from the wooden spoon to the pouch. "You know I will not."

Rone flicked a piece of the wood he had been carving, watching the shaving fly in an arc, then slide on the floor. "Smart of you. I won't do it."

"I know." She didn't look up. "Choices cannot be made for others."

"You could force this choice on me," he said, voice rough.

She had always been his weak spot—the closest thing to family that he would ever claim. And now he had two weak spots—the second one even worse, for he felt none of the sisterly affection for Taline that he felt for Ninli.

Ninli could force this choice on him. He would hate her for it, and he would never forgive her the breech, but he would do it. In doing so, they would finally be equal. He could eject Ninli ul Summora from his life.

She looked up at him finally. "You don't want to become your parents, yet want me to become mine?"

He threw the carved block across the floor and stabbed his knife into the floor. "I don't understand you." Rage pulsed through him—a fury he couldn't stop. He didn't even know who he was angry with. Everyone. Life itself.

Ninli tilted her head in that calm way he hated—and in that way that he craved. Because it meant that she was trustworthy. Even when choice pitted one of her people against another, she never betrayed.

He hated her.

He hated that she was trustworthy—that she held a dependability that in anyone else he had say was in her bones, due to how deeply the quality was embedded. But nothing could be further from the truth. Ninli had birthed that trait all on her own by shedding her bloodline.

"You didn't understand me before." Her gaze shifted behind him. "But now, I think you begin to."

He followed the sweep of her gaze to Taline, who was sleeping peacefully for once. Rone's gaze drifted back to the door. "It's not the same. He's a monster, Ninli. We should be rid of him."

"Rone," Nin said tiredly.

"What if his mother can unlock his magic? Or if the spring works? What then? He takes down Aros, then continues the empire? He doesn't know how to rule, Ninli. He will continue flattening every country that he comes across without a single thought to any other way."

"He can be better. He can make the empire better. I know it. I know him."

"He's a monster, Ninli. Monsters can't make anything better. If he gets the scepter, we will all die."

She looked at him. "You aren't a monster, Rone."

The fury rolled through him in a chaotic wave. "Taking him with us puts you and Taline in greater danger."

"Wearing his cloaks was the only thing that was keeping us from it. And now that protection extends to the gifted cloth that you wear."

"Making friends with a monster doesn't keep you safe from one." He leaned forward, furious. "How many times have I betrayed you?"

Her eyes softened like the soft fool she was. "Never enough for me to fear the outcome; always with the knowledge that you did it for reasons that were good."

"No. No." He grabbed his cursed hair in his hands. "That is madness, Ninli. You are mad."

"I am begot of madness, Rone. Allow me to revel in my roots," she said, far too lightly.

"I won't—"

Any further conversation was obstructed as Fehl re-entered and sat on his pallet. Ninli immediately laid a warming charm upon him. Rone, happy to redirect his rage, watched with vicious satisfaction as Fehl's features tightened because Ninli needed to care for him again.

Fehl had nearly turned blue their first night running from the empire. Used to his shadows keeping him free from wind, threat, and danger, Fehl had obviously never even learned how to manipulate wind other than to bring shadows closer. He was unable to warm his bones without his powers. Useless.

Rone watched Fehl's seething magic swirl beneath its lock, and smiled. Irsula and the

Spring could be dealt with, as could Ninli's too-soft heart and earnest desire for a better imperial future. What was given back could be taken once more. In the trick of light and returned powers, Rone could make sure that any renewal of Kaveh ul Fehl's powers failed.

Sher Fehl had birthed more than one monster in this room. And of the thousands of them birthed, only Rone could return what the emperor had stolen—or steal it again.

The power burned within him, whispering to take, take, take. Forever wanting more—that was the monster within—the monster that the woman nestled behind him feared more than any other in the night.

Rone felt ice curl. He would never help Kaveh ul Fehl. And he would ensure that all plans otherwise failed. He would make sure that the girls were safe, and that the world would never see Kaveh ul Fehl with a scepter in hand.

The Shadow Prince would never get his powers back.

CHAPTER EIGHT

FOREST OF SHADOW

TALINE

(Approaching the Land of Darkness)

They bought new horses with Nin and Fehl's seemingly endless bag of gold and traveled for another long day—the Shadow Prince becoming more aggravated as he tried and failed to bring his magic back at two more spiritual sites between Galit and the southern border of the Land of Darkness.

Taline liked less the look of resignation and sadness on Nin's face than she cared for Fehl's anger.

Taline resolutely avoided looking at her sister and her pain, instead using every free moment as they rode to restock her boxes, containers, and vials, and to plan for the worst. She clutched at her stomach and head whenever a sick wave came, but she tried as much as she could to mentally ride past them.

She would overcome this dependence on the scepter that she had never asked to possess.

As opposed to past ventures, Rone didn't say a cutting word about her paranoia—he simply extended an arm and let her drag magic from his veins. He had never offered before, but now he was volunteering it before Nin could even roll up her sleeve.

His cutting tongue was instead spent on another entirely.

"Your shadows slip away from the cloaks the closer we get, Shadow Prince."

"Your tongue will be the first thing I slice free, Valeran spawn."

"The only thing sliced will be your limbs when there is nothing left to protect."

Taline gripped her satchel, boxes clinking inside, and touched the scarf at her neck. Rone pulled his horse closer in case he had to catch her—embarrassingly, he'd had to do so twice during their travels. He had done it each time without magic.

Nin and Taline had left most of the active magic to Rone in the days before, thinking they were the biggest beacons for Aros and not wanting anything to slip through. It had been an unpleasant shock to learn that the blessed children could find the others of their lines. Without the enchanted cloth that Baksis ul Fehl had given them, if a child of Nera found them...

If Etelian found them...

Taline shuddered. She didn't know Baksis ul Fehl's game, but she would wear this cloth until its fibers fell apart if it kept her from anyone with a sand grain of the emperor's powers.

"Empty," she murmured, looking at Kaveh ul Fehl and shuddering again at the utter nothing that emerged from him.

Next to her, Rone's horse whinnied and she looked over to see his face had gone grim and his grip tight.

They were all tense. They just needed to make it into the forest. Nin and Fehl were certain Aros would not hunt them there.

But everything else would.

She looked at the scarf wound around Rone's neck. He had been well hidden from all but the blessed children due to a shield that she could still not properly discern. It intrigued her, as all magic did. He had put off her attempts at inquiry, though, saying it was simply a relic's influence that could not be used again, so the secrets of its magic didn't matter.

She had not pushed, but she knew it was less a relic and more something to do with the secret that he and Nin shared—the secret that he kept locked tightly in self-loathing within his chest.

He should just tell them. Exasperation wound through her. How bad could it be? They were in one of the most terrifying parts of the layer—literally approaching a territory called the Land of Darkness. What could he possess that would be worse than shadows that could consume—screaming as they ate a person one bite at a time, or all in a single gulp? One moment there, then gone the next—there was nothing that he could possibly possess that would beat such nightmares.

It wasn't like he was the emperor.

Storm clouds circled insidiously around the immense treetops as they reached the border to the Land of Darkness. Nin let out an audible breath of relief at the first sight of the forest. Taline did not feel the same. Her sister was relying on the fact that should Aros locate them now, he would not chase them inside—that he would not enter Irsula's territory.

But Aros was not the worst thing that could happen to them. The worst thing was whatever first happened to them that they couldn't work their way out of.

Nin pulled magic into her palms as they stepped over the border, and Rone's palms glistened as well. Taline grappled with familiar, insidious feelings of uselessness. With her corrupted, small stores, she was not much of an asset on this journey.

You can call me. The lingering voice was easy to overcome, but that it was there at all was unsettling. Having something of evil mind with any control over her was not something she ever wished.

No, she would embrace her small stores and free will, and continue forward to assist.

She looked at the Shadow Prince. Unable to do magic, Fehl was having worse trouble with his reality. Letting the tasks of keeping them safe fall to Rone and Nin upset him greatly.

Though Rone and Nin made a quick combination and the three of them had the components for this type of quest already assembled—as they'd been planning to use similar items in the forest surrounding the scepter's temple, before the Shadow Prince had rendered that unnecessary—the opponents here were of much greater mass and variety.

Worse, Nin couldn't make ripgates, if things got out of hand. It was always their unspoken backup plan on dangerous quests. But Aros would appear if he had her exact coordinates. He would strike, take, and ripgate back out before disturbing the shadowy inhabitants of the land.

They turned the horses loose at the border of the barrier forest. The animals quickly scampered away from the trees, keeping to the dirt path they had just trod. They would make their way back down the road, seeking familiar stalls.

Even Fehl looked visibly uncertain about stepping inside with their current lineup of resources. But as much as Taline didn't want to go into the forest, she was willing to risk much to get to the spring that might set all of them free.

The smell of rotten death and new life rode the forest breeze. A continual turn of life and death clung to the edges of magic. Light, shadow, and darkness swirled through the trees in unnatural ways.

She looked back. Unbearable, full sunlight shone all around the edges of the barrier trees—glowing like a lifeline. So easy to turn back. Swallowing, she forced herself to take another step into darkness.

Here they would be hunted. By men, and by monsters, too.

The forests of Khursen in Tehrasi—two complete moon cycles ago when Kaveh ul Fehl had held off the monsters just by being the biggest monster on the path—seemed a distant memory.

"Are we sure about this?" Rone pushed aside a branch and watched the life-stealing insects crawling the tree it was attached to. "Fehl's moth—"

"If we keep to the northern spread of the forest," Nin said, "we won't even come near her territory."

A truly hope-based strategy. Irsula of Denz's territory was the entire forest, even if the greatest knot of shadows swirled southeast of dead center.

Taline exchanged a look with Rone. Rone and Taline didn't want to pass by Irsula, but there were four of them. "Nin—"

"We'll pass by with plenty of room to spare," she said. "There's a village that rides the northern ridge of the forest. We will skim through and maybe even restock our supplies. No worries."

"A fabled village," Rone stressed.

"We'll see when we get there," Nin said optimistically, looking to Rone. "We need to get through to the grove surrounded by mountains too high and stormy to breach."

Rone's lips pressed together. He knew as well as Taline did that Nin had ulterior motives for going through the forest that didn't completely encompass the desire to reach the fabled spring. Taline looked at the Shadow Prince, who was gazing off into the forested distance.

When Taline looked back at Rone, he was watching her, something unhappy but certain to his expression. Nin was determined to see the Shadow Prince's powers returned. Rone was determined to do the opposite.

Taline just wanted to get to the spring. Everything else would work its way out. When Nin was involved, things invariably did.

The Land of Darkness lived up to its name and reputation. They were attacked immediately—fiercely and with terrible zeal.

The attacks, once started, ceased only with the play of a predator backing off temporarily while searching for ability and weakness. They were being tested. Taline liked it not at all.

Within two days, though, they were making progress with the tools they had brought—with khursifas lifting them into the trees to sleep in strung, enchanted hammocks and with fire wards set at night. But that they were being hunted was without doubt, and the predators' numbers kept increasing. One predator turned into two, then three, then five.

A pack of inlari had been chasing them for a day and a half. An ogre had kept steady step, watching from the bushes. A swarm of pufilmare—magic-sucking flies—swept through in steady, diving swaths, losing hundreds of their numbers but gaining magic with every swipe.

Death by a thousand bites. The horror of the pufilmare swarms—one of the legendary nightmares of the Land of Darkness. New swarms hatched from the carcasses of their dead. Growing in number with every death, the pufilmare would overtake them eventually, then they would consume their own.

Taline grimly inspected the landscape ahead as she held up one of the boxes she had made to attack a similar swarm horde in Tehrasi. When the horde got big enough, there would be little that could stop it. It was what made fighting pufilmare less tenable the longer one spent in their habitat.

According to legend, the village should be within view soon. They just needed to hold out. The village would have wards against pufilmare. They just needed to get there.

They had resorted to their own forms within the forest—for ease of movement and avoiding missteps that could be caused by perceived differences in arm length and waist girth. Worried that they might mistake a companion's reach or actual form in a strike, they had tossed their disguises and planned to resume their altered forms as soon as the village was near. But at this point, Taline didn't care how they entered the village—just that they did.

Magic curled more furiously under her skin, pushing in painful ways. Taline looked to the sides of the forest, steadying herself. They had been lucky so far—the feel of the dwindling shadows in the cloaks had saved them from attack here inside Irsula's domain. But the shadows had dwindled and most had fled, and the predators grew bolder. They would wait no longer.

Nin signaled with her fingers and Taline signaled back. An inlari scout, two ogres, and a shirestan were tracking them and preparing to attack. The inlari, with its giant frame and tusked face, was not the stealthy predator that the other creatures waiting in the darkness were.

Taline slipped a second small box free and pushed it against the Shadow Prince's side.

His fingers flicked at her automatically—to rend and tear—then slowly lowered. Still thinking he had magic? She knew how long it took for the mind to resolve such a thing. She let the box fall into his hand with a grim press of her lips. She didn't want to feel sympathy for the Shadow Prince, and yet, she felt a kinship she could not deny. To be drained of power? A waking nightmare.

The ogres, with foaming fangs, roared and attacked from both sides, while the shirestan and inlari drove straight through. Attacking as a unit this time, to increase their success. Like the pufilmare, they would consume enemies, then turn on their allies.

Taline darted backward as she threw her own box at the inlari's feet. Twisting ropes of light ensnared its ankles and tripped it to land heavily on the ground.

The inlari pulsed with magic and the bindings burst like star showers.

Taline sprinted right, leaping up onto a tree branch and flipping up to the next while the feral shirestan clawed its way upward.

She managed heavy breaths and dropped a net box upon its head with a practiced flick. She jumped to another position and threw another net. It took time to get accustomed, but eventually one got used to having little or no magic.

One got used to it or one died.

Kaveh ul Fehl was staring at the box in his hand, brow creased, as the inlari lumbered up onto four hoofed feet again. Kaveh ul Fehl had someone else's magic in his hands, and he looked lost with what to do with it.

"Throw it!" Taline yelled and leaped from the branch to land and purposefully tumble past the ogre Nin was fighting, lightning zipping from her fingers as she shot them into the ogre's back.

It wasn't enough to do damage, but the ogre jerked and gave Nin the opportunity she needed to secure it. Nin was a creative fighter and runner, but she had also always known she could escape during fights if she had to, which usually increased her risk taking. Hampered by her inability to use ripgates even in emergencies here, Nin had to take greater care—she couldn't rely on her largest stone in the game.

And Rone—something had been off about him for days. He was using less and less magic, as if it mentally pained him to craft a spell.

As opposed to the others who were working at a disadvantage, Taline was used to uselessness. She was always at a disadvantage—and this was no less than that. Creativity and planning counted above all else when power was a disadvantage.

She dove, then leaped—using her khursifa and wind boxes to ferry her above sharp, tearing claws.

Movement was key. Moving and not allowing an opponent the opportunity to trap. She needed to be the trap, instead. Like Taline, Rone and Nin knew the advantage of moving.

Kaveh ul Fehl, on the other hand, was used to standing his ground. He was currently doing so, staring at the crater before him—he had thrown the box after all.

"Run!" she yelled at him as she swung by on her khursifa. She grabbed Rone's outstretched hand. "North, then east, quickly!"

Rone jumped onto the back of her khursifa. Fehl stared at them, and it was only Nin scooping him up on hers and blowing wind beneath that seemed to shake him free.

Taline threw a second wind box on top of their woven mat. It would power the khursifa a few hundred feet in five bursts. Nin was defending behind them, as was Rone, so it was left to Taline and Kaveh to steer and keep aloft. "Press down on the front cord each time you start to fall! Five presses only! Then Nin will have to take over!"

They soared and fought. One press, two presses, three...

Seven statues rose into view and a pulse of magic lit the air. The trees came to life—creaking and spreading hundreds of arms as they roared.

A dragon dove from the sky.

People appeared—so suddenly and out of position, that Taline slowed automatically.

"To the boundary points!" a booming woman's voice yelled. "Pufilmare! Shirestan! Inlari! Too many pufilmare for the wards! Increase them, now!"

Taline pinpointed the location of the voice and saw a woman looking down at them from the tops of the trees, a thousand tiny jaws descending behind her.

"Four magi of unknown status!" the woman shouted.

Taline launched a box upward and the woman's eyes narrowed violently as she pulled back her bowstring. The box burst and pulled the descending pufilmare into the swirling cloud before bursting into golden dust.

The woman's eyes narrowed further as the broken pufilmare surged around her, unnaturally disappearing into the cloud, but her bow changed directions and her arrow hit the inlari charging from the west.

"Status of four magi—temporary allies!" the woman shouted, then let off another arrow. The forest magi entered the fray.

The ogre made its move, launching itself at Taline and Rone, then Nin and Fehl. They dodged its strikes, moving around it as it swung, hitting it in the armpits and knees.

They pushed past the first village hut.

A dragon roared. Flame flashed from above.

The village lit on fire. The wards shuddered and fell.

"Wards, now!" someone yelled. "Keep them on the edges of the village!"

They tumbled from the khursifas, landing on their feet, and rolling them in. They would lose an open-air fight with dragons. Better to fight from shielded ground. Taline lost visual reference as she got caught up in the fray on the village's edge, darting between opponents and combatants and lending aid where needed or helpful.

They couldn't put these people—this village—in more peril.

Kaveh ul Fehl got in the way of the third strike and the fourth that Nin attempted, too concerned with trying to protect her and too used to having might.

Taline still wasn't particularly excited about the Shadow Prince, but she had seen him interact with Nin for nine days now. She had seen him put himself in the way of the hits meant for Nin—even when he would have been better served elsewhere in the fight.

Kaveh ul Fehl meant to keep Nin safe. And Taline would return that favor.

So when the third inlari charged him from the village's tree line, Taline swung forward and grabbed its left tusk, swinging up and around to momentarily ground it. It shook off the rough landing and charged after her as she darted through the tree line, using trunks and foliage to hamper the chase.

KAVEH

Kaveh watched the fleeing woman and the lumbering beast galloping behind her.

Taline ul Summora had saved him. Saved him from a strike that would probably not have killed him. Maimed him, caused him pain, sidelined him until Nin could heal him, but Taline had saved him from that pain. And it had not been the first time.

Kaveh ducked the flying crawpits and watched Taline circle back around the tree line and head for him again.

She tossed a box underhand as she ran toward him. She mimicked pressing a finger down and her fingers drew a harried spiral as she passed.

He thrust the box outward and pressed the spiral design on the side. Flames roared outward and the inlari flailed, trying to stop, its feet kicking up as it scraped against leaves and dirt. It fell to the ground in a lumbering crash and pained scream, then tripped heavily to its feet and galloped off.

Kaveh held out his hand to put out the flames—burning a forest down was only a good idea if one was able to leave it—but no shadows or water answered his automatic call. Stupid. He shook off his anger and looked at the box and pressed the spiral again. The fire continued to rage. They were all going to die.

He scrambled back to grab Nin and flee, then caught himself as his sight resolved with his change of position. Nothing was on fire. He stared at the box and pushed the button again. Flames shot upward and the crawpits screamed. But there was no heat. Kaveh slowly passed his hand through the flames.

Nothing.

Illusion.

"This is not the time to play! They learn fast!"

He looked up just in time to catch another box thrown his way, mimicking lightning.

"That one actually works!"

Crawpits lunged from three sides. He activated the box. It exploded, blasting combatants in a wide arc. Some of them rose almost immediately, though. Dissatisfaction wound through him. He had never had a foe rise again.

Taline threw another box to him.

He tried to get his mind around what was happening, even as he automatically caught what she threw. She was helping him defend the group. She was helping him. Like Nin's duckling—Akel—someone he had treated poorly before.

Why?

He grabbed the next one she tossed his way, too, but uncertainty and discomfort in her help turned to fury quickly—for he understood her role. She was useful, obviously, if the myriad numbers of opponents she was taking out was any indication. Useful, in that she was clearing the stragglers and outside forces from interfering with the main fray.

An assistant. A supporter. A subordinate.

Something disfigured curled inside him. He imagined the expression on the emperor's face, the disappointment as he looked upon his most powerful son and saw an assistant instead.

Was this what he was to be? Was that his fate now? The person on the sidelines supporting the main players in the fray?

He watched Taline dance around Nin and Valeran, graceful and sure. He remembered fighting her in the alley. She had been a better technical fighter than Nin—trained by someone in hand-to-hand combat. But without Nin's quickness and power, she had been just another combatant to crush.

He watched her now. She and Nin were creative in different ways. Nin was ingenious at turning anything that could be done into something more, but Taline lacked the power for that. Instead, she was confident, and she was prepared. She was creative in how she used what she had and how she prepared in advance. She understood exactly what each thing she made did and her gaze darted between opponents, locating openings and strikes for maximum impact.

She had likely made a good fit for the scepter—the scepter giving her the power she needed to make intricately laid plans come true. That, and madness, of course. Still, there were other scepters. Other relics of power that would make someone like her a threat. Taline had the potential to be more.

"Head it off! Don't let it into the main—"

There was a clash of magic, voice, and earth and half the village seemed to simultaneously curse the skies. The village was on fire. Kaveh could feel the heat of the flames from the dragon diving from above.

"Get it away from the center!" someone yelled.

Nin and Valeran tumbled in front, ripping Nin's bag wide. Nin grabbed a box—how many did they have?—and banged it against the ground. The four flaps of the top bloomed outward like a flower's petals and Valeran slapped his palm on top. When he ripped it away, a jet of sunlight blazed into the sky. Nin angled it.

The dragon screamed and pivoted into a snaking ascension. Long wings flapped against the treetops, shaking their boughs, and smoke bloomed from the wound in its belly.

Kaveh stared at the device. A sunlight device. Nin's eyes focused on him, and he could see the apology already forming. They had made that to work against him when he had chased them a lifetime ago.

He smiled and immediate relief swept her expression as she bundled up the ripped bag and dove from the path of the charging inlari.

Kaveh stabbed the one in front of him. But here on the edge of the village, even as the new wards were lighting to keep them out, there were dozens more. This was something shadow could end, but steel could not.

Ten inlari turned his way and bared their teeth.

He held up his weapon. He would do as he could. He would not be useless.

Air and branch cut against his arms and cheeks as a sweep of a wooden arm knocked the inlari back. The inlari howled, turned, and ran.

Two enormous isu lumbered past Kaveh behind him—their hundreds of branches swinging—and knocked the other inlari back with the force of their hundred-year-old blows.

With the entrance of the isu pair, the other monsters took off, darting and sprinting back into the forest's shadows.

Kaveh tensed, facing the isu. They had come from behind—from the village. He waited for them to crush everything else to paste.

But they settled, shaking their branches, leaves curling and standing upright as they peered into the trees, alert.

The last shirestan flew through the air on the end of a broom in Taline's hand—using it like she would a staff or scepter. It landed hard, shook its head, darted its feline gaze around, then took off into the brush.

Taline struck the branch against the ground. "And that's how you do it without using magic."

Valeran started laughing, a disjointed, horrible sound.

Taline frowned. "Did you suffer a head wound? Do I need to get Nin?"

Valeran's gaze was bleak. "Monsters make people prepare, narsumina. But preparation still requires deep fear to motivate." Kaveh followed his gaze to the village on fire and the villagers running forth with spells to mend and heal.

"What are you on about, Rone?"

"Living in fear of having your magic removed made you stronger, more prepared. You prepared for the day when you would have nothing. You lived in fear of it."

"Of the day when I would have to beat a shirestan with a broom?"

Valeran's unhappy gaze turned almost fond. "You truly are a marvel."

"Clear!" the woman who had been in charge at the barrier shouted. Kaveh could feel the wards reengaging—like a jolt of lightning over his skin.

"Good job, folks," a man shouted back. "Let's get the last of the fires out and the timbers together for repairs."

The villagers looked winded. Some clapped each other on the backs; others looked at ruined houses with slumped shoulders.

Kaveh wondered at the strange feeling in his chest.

Small signs with symbols ran the perimeter of the village on stakes. The pointed symbols told directions to all sorts of things outside the village's borders. Fate had decreed that the one closest to him contained a sign of which he was most familiar. Shadow. His cloak pulsed. More shadows fled.

Useless.

Nin was deep into the guts of an ogre, stitching it back together so it would survive another day. It was staring at her with white and green eyes inside the spell that held it immobile.

Another monster to be spared, to live again. But to what type of life? Kaveh stepped slowly backward, keeping her in sight. He would keep this last view of her as she reached for a jar of salve, coated her fingers, then pressed them on top of the wound, closing her eyes.

Valeran and Taline were still bickering. Valeran, usually quite aware of what was happening around him, was, for once, completely oblivious to Kaveh. Valeran had been eaten away slowly by something for the nine days they had traveled together, and his expression indicated he was in full grips of said ailment as he looked at Taline. Kaveh didn't care what was wrong with Valeran—only that it was distracting enough.

He stepped backward, into the trees, then into the darkness beyond.

He would fix his weakness, his uselessness.

Their bickering grew fainter as Kaveh took one last look at Nin, then carefully made his way toward the distant point where darkness knotted and pulsed with each breath.

CHAPTER NINE

PRINCE OF NOTHING

KAVEH

(The Land of Darkness)

He knew the way, even without shadow to guide him. He could read the shadows still. He could see how they curled and curved and pointed. They weren't his to command anymore, but he had spent his lifetime understanding them.

He watched the way they shifted in the breeze blowing through the trees, and he followed the shifting patterns that grew larger and sharper.

Kaveh walked through the darkness. The shadows pressed in against him—clinging to him in a way that produced a strange, unwanted feeling of consternation and disquiet instead of relief and comfort. These were shadows he could not control—and therefore, they were the enemy.

Was this how people felt who walked beside him? Did Nin feel this press? The thought was singularly unnerving.

Once he regained his powers, would it be better for her to stay far from his presence? Would it be better for the glimpse he had just taken of her to be his last?

He had never cared for the comfort of others. Not until Nin. Even the emperor, precious as he had been, would have thought it weakness to have had Kaveh care about his comfort. His security, yes; his comfort, no. The emperor had always seen to his own.

Kaveh intensely disliked the disquiet he felt.

The shadows pressed harder the farther in he traveled and beasts prowled beyond the darkness. He was a free meal, yet they didn't attack. This was a different type of waiting, now. The animals paused out of fear instead of uncertainty. He supposed this was what Irsula's curiosity bought him—the ability to at least sate her questions under the cover of her protection before he was consumed.

The minimal shadows remaining in his cloak gained sudden urgency. They connected to the others and ferried him forward on faster wings than he could have walked.

Kaveh stepped through shadow and forest and into the darkest knot. The knot uncoiled and spread great wings.

It was only the second time that he had seen Irsula uncaged and free, and he could feel her true power. It was strange to be in the presence of something so familiar, yet so much greater than he.

As her shadowed wings spread free, he felt the true weight and press of her. She had always been repressed and contained in the cage that had bound her. He had felt her beyond the walls of her gold cage—felt and marveled at the power within.

She had been a cautionary tale, captured in a cage, her power said to dwarf even his own.

"Spawn."

"Irsula."

Without magic, even the meanest of magi was more powerful than he was at this moment in time, but even at his greatest, could he have beaten the woman before him?

He observed the shadows roiling around her skin. He would like to find out.

She examined him coldly. "Look at you now—an insect without a speck of bite—neutered by your humanity. I could kill you where you stand."

"You can, and yet I made it here whole." He had made it there at her command, there was no doubt. She was curious about something—curious enough to let him live.

Golden eyes blinked open and peered from within Irsula's writhing wings. Ifret.

Kaveh touched his chest. He felt her loss like the loss of his magic. She had been his companion since birth.

Shadows shuddered around him and he refocused on Irsula, whose dark eyes were narrowed on him. Her expression had gone colder. "Why have you come, spawn?"

"To see if what was done can be undone."

"You wish to know if I can wipe free that man's spell? The spell that tears the shadows from your skin and locks away your reach?"

A hundred shadows just like Ifret twisted and curled in Irsula's wings, hissing. Their gazes were far more accusatory and hate-filled than the ambiguous expression of his old companion.

"You hated him," Kaveh said. "Undoing his last work—would it not please you?"

"Pleasure comes to me in ripped forms and last words."

"I had no last words to say." A regret that would never heal—those final moments with the emperor.

"He deserved his fate." She snarled. "And you should think so as well. He took your power. He sealed it away, like ripping the flesh from your form."

"He did." And it had felt that way—being taken and skinned. "But he was reaching out to unlock the spell when you came forth."

"I care not what he was about to do. It was not his to take in the first place." Darkness rippled around her. "I was not human enough for him to hold me under for long. But you are. He tested his powers upon you, did he not?"

"Yes."

"I cannot fix what has been done."

He watched her unnaturally beautiful and cruel face carefully, dealing with the shattering disappointment internally while digging beneath the way she had only said that she could not fix it. "I understand."

"Do you? Are you sad? Do you shed human tears? For the human who sired you?"

"I shed no tears." He had never had that particular curse of humanity. Had never understood it—either the mechanics or the emotion behind it.

"Humans and their tears," she sneered. "Something I'll never understand." There was a touch of something else to the words, though, as if the very nature of tears had caused her to wonder and been stymied. "Do you regret, spawn? Do you regret his loss? His empire?"

"Yes. I know regret."

"I regret only that his death was quick."

"He knew you would kill him." The emperor had been the furthest thing from stupid. "He knew if you were free of that cage, you would shepherd him to his death."

"And I did." Shadowed wings spread wide, snapping with thousands of teeth. "And I feel pleasure again."

"He should not have caged you." Kaveh could acknowledge it now—that the emperor had made poor choices to go with his grand ones. He had been fallible. He had caged her because he could not deal with the consequence of taking her in any other way. But to seek out an unwilling participant in his plans made him little better than Etelian.

The thing that separated the two was that Sher Fehl had learned from his mistake, and that he had felt regret. He had been very careful after Irsula only to deal with those who threw themselves at him, or those who could be compensated in direct exchange. Kush and the deal for a child of the queen's line—the emperor's best bet for a child or grandchild who might gain his powers—was Nera's least favorite example of such exchange. Etelian seemed incapable of learning at all.

That did not mean that Sher Fehl's regret in caging a magnificent being forevermore did not also secretly hide his pleasure at having her near. He had, indeed, been fallible.

"He could not have caged me on his own. Darkness helped him. That man would have been scattered to the sands long before, if he had not secured me in that cage with Darkness's help. He held me as laurel and prize." She looked at him coldly. "He would have bound you, too, if he had not found human ways to tie you to his side."

Darkness had helped bind Irsula? It was a piece of a puzzle that had always eluded him—how had the emperor overcome her?

"Why didn't you kill me? From the beginning, when you held me within you." It was something he had always wondered—what had made Irsula allow him life? There was nothing the emperor could have done to save him. Irsula's cage was as tight against outside influence as it was within.

Shadows snapped and rippled, writhing around her like a living cloak.

"Curiosity. Darkness's affliction, curiosity. What would a quarter of Darkness look like?
What part of humanity would remain in a being three-quarters human?" She shrugged a hundred shadows. "I cared nothing for you, but Darkness strongly encouraged the trial."

There was no surprise hearing about her own lack of care, but the latter part of her statement caused him to frown. "You said it helped bind you."

Blackness deeper than any ink found in nature billowed. "Darkness is always with me."

He looked at the endless surge blotting out everything around it. "Always? Why did it help bind you? Why didn't it release you? Why didn't it prevent you from being taken?"

"Darkness is a fickle and vile beast, and it found amusement to see me inside. Curiosity is the one trait shared across species. The bane of Darkness. As I was the product of Darkness's curiosity, my captivity was also a curiosity. Darkness found your sire's goals interesting—as it had once found its own—what would it mean to cross its shadows with the emperor's magic?" She smiled sharply. "My powers won out, though you reek of humanity."

"Darkness…chooses?" He carefully examined the unnatural cloud.

"Its curiosity is insatiable." She looked upon him, shadows writhing. "You think it can give you back your powers or supply you with new ones?"

Kaveh did not respond. He didn't need to.

A cold smile bloomed over sharp teeth. "You aren't mistaken. But are you willing to pay the price, spawn? For Darkness demands sacrifice."

"I can meet its demands."

She laughed—the sound of brittle and scraping branches with spindly thorns. "That is your humanity speaking, so greedy and misunderstanding of true cost."

"And you understand?"

"Darkness made me. Darkness flows through me." Inked shadow pulsed. "I understand its price."

"Then it flows in me as well."

She observed him. "At one time, I thought so. But the stink of humanity grows stronger upon you." She lifted a hand. "Darkness has always ridden my steps yet stayed outside of my desires. It laughed at my predicament and did nothing to aid me. It aided your sire because he gained its curiosity. It had a direct hand in my cage. It wanted to see what would happen to a piece of it, trapped." She looked at him. "Darkness demands deals from those who seek it, however. Deals of blood or power."

Aros. Kaveh remembered the emperor's words to Ifret when Ifret had first tried to strike the emperor down—that the cage could only be unlocked by a force equal or greater than the one used to lock it. Aros had made a deal with Darkness. He had made a deal with Darkness to undo Irsula's cage. He had sacrificed his own child for it. A blood deal.

"I can sacrifice a brother to Darkness—to satisfy shared blood?" Even Valeran would help him kill

Etelian. They could ripgate to him and back with him as Aros followed. Kaveh would regain his powers, then—

"The only shared blood it would accept from you would be mine. I am curious to see you try to kill me, spawn."

So no sacrifice of blood then. "A sacrifice of power?"

"It will take the power you value most."

"A time-based contract?" He thought on the possibility. He would regain his magic, then lose it again. He would have to be crafty.

The billowing cloud pulsed in something like cruel humor. It was reflected across Irsula's face. "A ripping-of-humanity contract, spawn. You interest Darkness. It will make a deal. But your humanity will weep at the cost." She tilted her head in a birdlike manner. "You would do better to seek help from the spawn of your sire."

"Impossible." He disregarded that entirely. No other had the emperor's power. The emperor had searched and tested. He had been extensively trying to duplicate his power for thirty years. Kaveh's gut turned. The emperor could try no more.

She smiled with glittering teeth. "You feel. You love. And you will lose that humanity. You will be unable to survive without it, I think."

Would Nin love the monster without the human inside?

"I will give power without sacrificing humanity." Nin's sister had dropped the Scepter of Darkness. Humanity could overcome power.

"Call upon Darkness at the set of the half-moon, when all split things are possible, and feed it your chosen sacrifice then. I will be here to celebrate your failure." She smiled—a jagged, eldritch stretch of lips.

Kaveh curled his nails into his palms. Was this hurt—this jagged feel in his chest? He had never liked visiting Irsula for complicated reasons he had never parsed. Why did it feel worse now? He looked at his powerless hands. Without power, perhaps his humanity was more affecting. There was no other reason he had feel this way.

"You are a curiosity with your humanity and feelings, but I desire to see what you are like without, as well, I think."

Kaveh, who had always had power, had always disdained, but never questioned the fear of others. Was this what those without power felt? A lack of choice and agency that fed into fear? That led to hurt?

Without power, he had no buffer. He curled his fingers tighter, splitting the skin. Weakness. Truly.

Irsula tilted her head, birdlike now only in the way that a raptor homes upon prey. "The others come for you, slipping through the forest on shadows in their hems, barely staying alive as they try to follow your path. Humans—so biddable and breakable. Their emotions are so fragile and weak."

He thought of Nin and her emotions—so strong and fierce.

"You stink even more of weakness, spawn, with whatever you contemplate now."

He looked at her without answer. What was weakness then?

"You won't survive the choice," she mused, tilting her head the other way. "You should make the humans fix you instead. You will make more of us, then. I find myself just as curious to see multiple beings made of an eighth Darkness as to see you without humanity."

Nin, Valeran, and Taline edged carefully into the grove.

Irsula waved a careless hand in their direction. "Use your cursed skill to release this wretched quartered beast I birthed."

"You cannot help him, mistress?" Nin asked carefully. Her eyes focused on Ifret, who was watching intently from Irsula's wings.

"It is not something I can unlock, wretch."

Nin nodded, her sure acceptance of others such an integral part of her. "Will you continue to defend him against those who seek his death?"

Irsula smiled unpleasantly. "You seek death."

"My apologies." Nin looked at Ifret, who had risen slightly, then back to Irsula. "Will you lend him aid?"

"I haven't killed him yet. Nor you."

"Aros ul Fehl seeks to rule the human lands."

"Human squabbles," she said dispassionately. "I care nothing for which of you humans rules."

"No?"

Irsula narrowed her eyes and shoved Ifret down, as though she were an unwanted emotion. "I didn't ask for the spawn, nor did I want him. He's not even worth the birth that was forced from me."

Kaveh looked at Ifret, who was staring intently back. Strange things—loose threads—dangled in his mind.

"Maternal sentiment is always such a pleasure to observe," Valeran said.

Taline breathed in sharply, expression going horrified. Kaveh tilted his head at his half-brother certain he was going to watch Valeran die.

Nestled in her shadows, a grim, mean smile formed on Irsula's mouth as she looked at Valeran. "Fehlspawn. I almost killed you upon your first step into my nest. Did you really think you would survive meeting me?"

Valeran's casual disregard turned sharp. "I think we would have an interesting match, mistress. And I wouldn't be so certain you'd be the victor. You haven't been before." His body tightened, ready.

Irsula's shadows whirled and Valeran was engulfed. "There were factors that one such as you couldn't bear to involve. And even now? You wouldn't. You can't." She laughed cruelly as her shadows read his thoughts. "Holding it in so hard it pains you. It drags at your human veins. Such feelings. Such pitiful emotions. The pain of your secret amuses me, Fehlspawn."

"I'll have you know, I'm the least emotional magi in the empire and twelve additional kingdoms," Rone said laconically, face blank.

Kaveh was reluctantly impressed. Surrounded by Irsula's shadows and mind, Valeran only looked five shades paler but his tongue was just as sharp.

"Humans are easy to read. I don't even have to rip open your mind. You smell of the others, but especially of the girl whose scent is entwined with yours. You want nestlings with her. You want to please her. You don't want to terrify her."

"Nestlings are not something I currently seek."

"No. Too terrified of your cursed power and what you might pass on. Fehlspawn."

Valeran took a step backward.

Irsula sneered. "Such ridiculous beings, humans."

"They will come for you," Kaveh said. "The humans. From fear, now that you are free."

She laughed, wings rippling. "Let them come. My shadows demand sustenance and blood." She smiled with sharp teeth. "It was one thing that man was good at. He fed his pet the choicest meats."

It had been one of the most feared execution tactics in the empire: the blood and meaty spread of Irsula's tower room floor.

One could enter Irsula's wall-less cage—or be shoved within—but the only way to leave had been in a bodily spray. Pieces of body hadn't been considered a person in the cage's magic.

The emperor had always kept himself and Kaveh behind a deeply gouged line of symbols.

"I am sorry," Nin said. "I am sorry that you were kept unwillingly, and for so long."

Irsula's shadows pulsed. "You risk being eaten, wretch."

"I know. Thank you for keeping Kaveh safe."

Irsula's shadows pulsed again, and Kaveh wondered at the unbroken gazes between them—as if this was not the first conversation they had had. But Kaveh had not taken Nin to see Irsula, so they couldn't have spoken before.

"I have done nothing for him."

Nin nodded in acceptance. "Will you enchant Kaveh's cloak while we continue on? His protection fades."

"I care not what eats any of you." But there was something strange in the way she didn't quite meet Nin's gaze.

"I know," Nin said gently. "But for Kaveh—"

Irsula growled. "You speak with the tongue of humans. Humans and their filthy promises."

"It doesn't make the words any less true." And Kaveh understood Nin's gentle meaning. Irsula was less human than any of them, but she was still born of woman.

"If I see you again, you will die."

"I understand."

Irsula growled again, then waved her hand. Shadows turned and dove within the cloaks en masse. Not just within Kaveh's cloak, either, but within all three. Kaveh could see Taline grimace as she was swallowed for a moment in their clutch.

"Do not return." Irsula narrowed her eyes at Nin, whose own gaze shifted slowly to Ifret before returning to Irsula.

"We understand, mistress."

Irsula bared her teeth—perfectly silver and with one too many rows. "I've been motivated to kill you five times in the last two moon cycles. Don't make it six. I will eat you, girl."

Kaveh frowned. Why would she have been motivated to kill Nin? How had she even known about her? The emperor?

"I am told that I make a poor meal. Good night, mistress, and thank you. May Darkness ever be your guide."

The rage within Irsula grew monstrous for a moment before settling. "May Darkness not be yours, wretch."

Nin dipped her head in acknowledgment and turned. She motioned to Valeran and Taline, and they retreated to the edge of the shadowed grove.

"You have chosen poorly, as all your species," Irsula said to Kaveh, looking at Nin's figure coldly. But there was something else there, too, some vicious blessing. "Humans are a pitiful species, and you, now—you are just as pitiful as the rest. The girl will get herself killed before I see one-eighth darklings. You won't be able to protect her."

It hit at the point of him that her other jabs could no longer touch. "I will protect her."

Irsula smiled—a too-full smile. "You will all die, all you humans, pitiful species that you are."

"And you, half that you are?" He felt...removed. "What will you become other than lonely?"

She barked a laugh that screeched along branch and brush. "I wonder what you would taste like, spawn?"

He absently touched the broken oath band tucked into the sash at his waist. "The same as you, I think. Of isolation and regret."

She bared her teeth again. "Leave."

He turned but before he took three steps, a shadow coiled in his path—raising up on a viper's tail. He looked down to see Ifret looking back. He looked back at Irsula, within whose wings Ifret had been at rest.

Irsula waved a sharp hand. "I want it not. Like you, it is damaged."

He bent down and let the shadow wrap around his wrist. Piercing gold eyes looked back. He felt something in him settle—something that he had pushed away in fear. He had thought Ifret gone.

"Farewell, Irsula," he said softly. "I hope you find happiness in your freedom."

"Spawn. I hope you find misery in yours."

He walked to the others.

"Lovely woman, your mother," Valeran said, almost cheerfully as they made their way back to the village, ferried by the same shadows in reverse. No predators lurked in the shadows. All that were left were those within.

Kaveh looked at Ifret, wrapped tightly around his wrist. "Cages make for bad temperaments."

"As does a lack of humanity, I would think. Or perhaps it is simply broken maternal wanderings. A price paid by those who the emperor bought to birth. Monsters beget by monsters."

Nin's small hand slipped into his. He looked at her and saw her eyes shining with unshed tears. He tipped his head and brushed one away. Ifret oddly leaned forward to taste the moisture on his thumb.

"Why do you cry?" he asked.

"You are worth your birth."

A throwaway, cutting statement from Irsula? Was this why one cried?

"Irsula has never held any affection for me, Nin. I have always known this." He had grown up isolated from all but those who lived in complete terror of him. The only exception had been the emperor, always doting, always approving. "The emperor dismissed her lack of affection as completely normal. I never needed or noticed its lack."

He'd had no notion that something might be missing. He still did not completely understand. The shadows had always been there, filling any void. Ifret had been a vicious maternal figure in many ways, once they'd come to an accord. Of course, he had seen enough in the majex courts to know most wouldn't see Ifret's care as anything approaching maternal, but he knew little else.

Nin looked at his wrapped wrist, then back at him. "Because of Ifret?"

He frowned, looking down at the shadow who stared unblinkingly back. "Because of Ifret what?"

"You never noticed a lack of Irsula because of Ifret. You care for Ifret. Deeply. And she for you."

Kaveh stared at her, slowing their steps. "I do." It was strange still, admitting such things. He wondered whether it would become easier. He wondered whether this was the state of things for people who had to ask things of others—did they have to sacrifice pieces of themselves so often?

Ifret stared at Nin, issuing a low, rumbling hiss.

Nin stared solemnly back at Ifret.

Maybe it was because he had just come from seeing Irsula without magic, but without his magic to parse the difference between Irsula's magic and Ifret's, they felt surprisingly similar. The nuances were gone. Missing. Did all non-shadowshapers feel them as the same? He wondered whether he had also felt similar.

"Did I magically feel the same to you as Ifret does?"

Nin cocked her head. "You feel like you, and Ifret feels like Ifret."

"And Ifret and Irsula?"

Nin looked steadily at him—staring at him as if she expected him to answer his own question.

"Do they feel the same?" he prompted.

"Ifret and Irsula feel similar," she said slowly.

He wondered whether it had something to do with being born as shadow. He looked down at Ifret. She was the same as he remembered, but it was as if being in the presence of Irsula, she had taken on a feel of the Mistress of Shadows. It was strange.

Nin seemed to have some opinion on the matter, but where Ifret had bonded to Nin before, there was a standoffish element between them again—as if they were relearning each other after a long period of time apart.

It had only been nine days since he had lost Ifret and his magic, though, and only a few moments of time since she had been returned to him. The strangeness was simply his magicless state feeling everything as off. Everything would settle again after he had his powers back.

"I need you to promise me that you will not do that again," Nin said.

He looked at her. "Do what?" Be powerless? Be a burden?

"That you will not go off on your own."

280

He blinked. "I—"

"Don't go off on your own," Nin said softly. "Don't go where I cannot help."

He stared at her for long moments. "If something comes that will hurt or aid you, I will meet it in battle without a thought otherwise."

And to regain his power—the power to protect her—he would do whatever it took.

"Look, Ninli, a man after your own heart." Valeran swanned by, touching his chest.

Taline looked sharply at Valeran. "Nin isn't going to leave."

Valeran looked steadily back. "For the price of your life, she will lay down hers."

"No," Kaveh said. That was a sacrifice that would not be made.

Valeran laughed without humor. "Tell me that Aros did not see her give something up for you, Fehl. Tell me the tale. Tell me that he did not see her sacrifice for you already?" Valeran smiled coldly when Kaveh hesitated. "Yes, and now you begin to see. To know Ninli is to know sacrifice.

And when next we see him, Aros won't be aiming at Ninli. He won't have to."

"Stop," Nin said sharply. She turned to Kaveh. "We will find the spring. We will do whatever is needed. Promise me. Promise not to go off on your own."

He looked at her. "I will seek the spring with you."

"Yes." She looked far too relieved. "Yes."

With unlimited power came candor. Kaveh had always been one for direct talk and action. He had had no need to play games, and he had disdained the matches of speech that Aros loved. But he hadn't ignored the rules—he just had never played by them.

Nin's relieved expression told him that she thought he still eschewed such games—that he was thinking along the same paths he had always traveled.

But he was without the power that had given him the ability not to play.

He would give her this day and the next. Then, when the half-moon bled...he would give up his humanity for her. He touched her cheek. He would strike a deal with Darkness, rid the world of Aros, then let Darkness take him. He would leave the world safe for Nin.

CHAPTER TEN

FABLED CONSTRUCTION

KAVEH

(The Village of Myth in the Land of Darkness)

They headed back to the village because Nin was determined to do so. Kaveh followed docilely in her path. He had promised to search for the spring with her and he would keep his promise. Then he would face his destiny.

The village was no longer on fire. Kaveh hadn't cared to catalog it during the fight or after, but as they walked through the perimeter wards to the small valley below that contained the settlement, he could see that there were at least a hundred buildings in the inner circle, while thatched and mud houses spoked outward on all sides to form a series of repeated ward circles ten deep.

He wondered how the village sorted itself—if newcomers were relegated to the lesser warded housing circles around the perimeter or if the greatest fighters lived nearest the perimeter. The first option was the easiest, as the village would naturally gain more circles as more people joined. In that option, the oldest members would remain in the most interior and protected areas. The second option meant shuffling, depending on sliding strengths and weaknesses of the members, in order to keep the more vulnerable in the center.

Two different ways to approach such a thing. How they did it would show what this village valued.

The wards let them through, and although the four of them were watched all the way from the outskirts into the main village proper, no one stopped them. Ifret hissed from his wrist and gazes widened on her the farther they went, but still, no one stopped their advance. Kaveh questioned their sense.

The Village of Myth. Perhaps it was a myth because it was repeatedly destroyed—rather than the legend of strength and fortitude usually associated with such a word.

Kaveh's gaze narrowed in on the man who was directing the chaos. He was easily spotted as villagers ran in continuous streams toward and away from him.

Nin joined the flow walking toward the man in charge. Valeran's expression tightened while Taline's was as determined as her adopted sister's.

As they approached, the man's middle-aged gaze rested briefly on their cloaks, on Ifret, then on Kaveh, where it stayed.

Kaveh narrowed his gaze in return. Irsula had been imprisoned for twenty-three years, but in an area so close to the den of the Mistress of Shadows, there would still be those who would remember the feel of her—magi who would recognize the feel of her spawn.

The man held his gaze, eyes seeking something. Kaveh had no idea whether the man found it, but his gaze slid back to Ifret, then the shadows swirling thickly around the bottoms of their cloaks. "You've picked up passengers in the time you left and returned. Dangerous things in these parts, passengers."

Nin stepped forward, bowing. "We did you a disservice, by bringing our fight so close to your village and involving you in it. I apologize for that."

"We are used to the forest having teeth." The man's gaze slid back to Ifret.

"Still, you fought with us, you helped us," she said, spreading her fingers. "We must recompense your aid."

"It is unnecessary." The man's gaze turned shrewd, though. "We aid all those who cross our boundaries. And we use every threat as a means to improve our wards and growth."

They could be going then. Excellent. Kaveh began to pivot along with Valeran.

Nin wound her arm through Kaveh's, pulling his pivot to an abrupt stop. Her arm slipped fully through his, and his feet moved automatically where she directed—forward.

She squeezed his arm lightly, in the way she did when she was pleased. It made pleasure rise in him, mixing with confusion. He realized too late that he was standing before the man and that Nin had bowed in a stance of supplication beside him.

"We must recompense your aid," she repeated softly.

Kaveh did not bow.

The man looked between them, expression controlled, but eyes narrowed in inquiry. In his position, Kaveh would be wondering how she meant to take advantage. He would have already sliced the legs or throat of someone making such a move.

"Master Ishum!" A boy ran up to the man, ignoring the four of them. "The boughs are ready."

The man—Ishum—nodded, then turned back to them. "Blessings on wherever the forest takes you. If you would like to trade with the village before you leave, stalls will be setting up soon to support the rebuilding efforts. If you'll pardon me, I must return to the repairs. We must rebuild rapidly before the forest finds us vulnerable."

"May we help you with your repairs?" Nin asked quickly. Kaveh narrowed his eyes at her. "Construction, lifting, fastening spells? We can help you rebuild that which was lost," Nin said, earnest smile turning to Kaveh before setting on the man again.

Kaveh stared at her. He was a killer. Not a builder.

Kaveh heard Valeran audibly sigh behind him. "On the breath of fools, we ride to folly once more."

"We have no need of your coin, but offers of physical assistance are never turned down," Ishum said slowly. "If you desire—"

"Master Ishum!" A reedy, young man sprinted, sliding to a stop in front of the leader. "Mayrie is in labor."

Ishum pulled his fingers inwardly across his eyes to pinch the bridge of his nose. "Of course she is." He shook his head and let go. "But this is news to be celebrated, not feared, no matter her previous troubles. Corrin and Yasli will know what to do."

The younger man shifted.

Ishum sighed at the non-response. "What is it?"

"Well, sir, Corrin's wrist was hurt in the fight and she ingested a firt tonic. It will be an hour before she is able to work without the tonic's influence. Yasli left ten minutes past to gather herbs to aid the wounded. She...she won't be back for an hour."

Nin and Taline's gazes slid together then apart. Unease, a newly constant companion, oozed through Kaveh.

"Well, Barnit, it's a good thing babies take awhile." Ishum clapped the young man on the shoulder. "In an hour—"

"But it's her third, sir, and it is going fast, and we almost lost her last—"

"I can do it." Nin stepped forward. "I am a healer who specializes in births. Allow me to help."

Kaveh looked at Nin's earnest face and his unease doubled. Divide and conquer was one of the easiest ways to rip enemies apart. Kaveh had used it countless times. Kaveh gave a small shake of his head and saw Valeran do the same. They narrowed eyes at each other, disgruntled.

Ishum looked Nin over, sizing her up. "Mayrie had bleeding trouble last time."

Nin's expression remained calm. "I've never lost a mother, nor a babe."

Ishum tipped his head and his eyes narrowed. Kaveh realized quite suddenly that they were wearing their own faces. They had been without disguise before the villagers had seen them, and it had been too late to change thereafter.

Kaveh shifted on his feet, fingers curling, as Ishum nodded slowly. "We trust our most precious to you then, mistress."

Nin smiled, a fleeting, lovely thing. She looked at Kaveh then, expression questioning—as if asking permission to leave him, magicless and useless, alone in an unfamiliar village. The lovely, fleeting edge of a smile remained, hoping, seeking, looking for something desperately that had been denied.

That he had denied her for weeks, dragging her around battlefields and death.

His head stiltedly dipped.

Her smile bloomed true. Radiance and light. Happiness. She touched his hand. Warmth cascaded through him like blistering water falling into a hot spring.

She turned to the thin man, Barnit, who had delivered the news. "Take me to her quickly."

Barnit turned and ran, Nin at his heels, Taline at hers.

Kaveh watched her disappear. He felt unease at her leaving his view now that he knew so little time remained, but her smile—her warmth—stayed with him, strangely overwhelming all else. She had looked aglow. Radiant. Purposeful.

He thought of the overpoweringly positive numbers in Tehras's birth records. Of the overwhelming success that reeked of hubris.

He thought of passion.

Five weeks ago, he would have called delivering a baby mundane. The most ordinary of tasks. Utilitarian need masquerading as passion. And now...

He looked at the older man, who was watching him with a raised brow.

"You look as if you've had an epiphany," Ishum said bluntly. "Good for you. Too few or too many of those to go round these days in such times of overwhelming progress. You willing to help with the repairs the girl was volunteering you for, or do you want to sit outside Mayrie's hut and wait?"

There was something watchful, but not judgmental, in the man's gaze, and there was something very Nin-like about his expression. This man, Ishum, head of the village, was someone who held no expectations, but still extended a hand.

And as much as Kaveh did want to go where Nin was, she had left him with her purpose.

"I'm not a builder," Kaveh said gruffly. He looked at his cloak, teeming with shadowed life he could not reach. "And I have no power to aid you."

No power now. But as the half-moon broke...

"Power is not what we seek. Are you willing to help?"

Kaveh's eyes narrowed. What was this game? Why would someone want help from someone who could offer so little? It seemed that he still didn't understand these games, though he had successfully used subterfuge against Nin with the non-promise he had made. How many times had Aros told him he didn't understand people, and that it would cost him?

"Yes," he answered. He would learn this game.

"Excellent." The man nodded, and his watchful expression turned thoughtful. "And you, sir?"

Kaveh realized Valeran still stood a few paces to the side and that he hadn't followed Nin and Taline.

"He will be useless to you." Valeran shrugged. "He has no magic anymore."

Kaveh's fingers pulsed in a familiar—and now useless—gesture of death.

The man raised a brow. "The magicless are not useless, and neither are those with less power." Ishum's eyes narrowed. "And I already have his answer. I was asking after yours."

Valeran's eyes narrowed in kind. Kaveh recognized fury easily, but there was something else underlying Valeran's anger. How could Kaveh understand what it was? He cocked his head and thought of Nin, whose emotions had run through his mind like the best smelling shadowsmoke for the loveliness of a moon cycle. Valeran's held the same underpinning expression as Nin's face did when she thought of her family and beloved servants. Quiet sadness and grief always galloped through her thoughts of them, nearly drowning all else, but underneath... Underneath lay a giant well of guilt that she had survived and they had not.

Self-loathing.

He looked back to Valeran. What did he hate with such self-loathing thoughts?

"Those with less power who choose to do more are never useless," Valeran spit, chin tilted up so that his eyelids half-covered his eyes as he looked down upon the other man.

Conceit was easy to surmise. Valeran was ever so sure of his own power, however pitiful Kaveh found it to be. But there, again, was that strange underpinning to his expression. Determined to understand, now that he couldn't simply overpower something and make it do his bidding, Kaveh tried to fit this expression into Nin's mold. Nin held very little conceit, but when they'd been in Tehras, stealing from the palace, or at the gates—silently and secretly renewing them—she had been certain of her craft.

Strip that away and look beneath... Ah, this was guilt and self-loathing, again. Why—?

It came to him, as all things that concerned Valeran did—to Taline—the girl who lacked real power and had to compensate in unusual ways. Taline ul Summora was the pole around which Rone ul Valeran wound. What a strange weave Valeran was caught within.

"You are concerned with uselessness," the man said to Valeran, gaze calm.

"Master Ishum! Master Ishum!" A boy and girl ran toward the man.

"I didn't ruin your village," Valeran said coldly.

Ishum knelt and softly dealt with the children's issue, then stood and turned back to Valeran. "No. And you don't have to fix it."

Ishum's gaze slid to Kaveh in question. Kaveh stared blankly back. What—? Oh. Would he still help? He nodded shortly.

Ishum nodded back and gestured for Kaveh to follow as he turned to follow in the children's path. Kaveh stepped after, feeling as if his legs were separate from the rest of him, following a man twice his age who had asked nothing of him, but had taken up his offer of help—Nin's offer of help—even though Kaveh was powerless.

Age had never mattered in the empire, so Kaveh was unused to taking orders from anyone other than the emperor. Even Carsue, when he had been head of the imperial forces, had simply pointed Kaveh in a direction and let him go.

They caught up to the children, who chattered about something, pointing and gesturing. Ishum directed them calmly. Kaveh processed none of the details, mind swirling strangely.

Ishum turned back to him, seemingly unsurprised to find that he had followed. It seemed only Kaveh would be possessed of that emotion here. "Always something to be done or solved. Building requires continual checks." The man shook his head, but his expression stayed firm and positive. "Let's get to the front."

Kaveh blinked, feeling increasingly wrong-footed.

As it turned out, the front meant the front line of construction, not warfare. But it held the same sort of energy, if not the same sort of company.

It wasn't only magi helping to rebuild. The two isu—the fabled talking trees, with their hundred-arm branches and thousand-spindled fingers—shook in heavy harmony with each other. Wind rustled their leafy manes as they helped villagers clear, lift, and place. Dryads and half-dryads wound their way over the earth—feet barely touching the ground.

Human villagers overwhelmed their numbers, but the presence of such creatures and beings...

Kaveh was strangely surprised to find Valeran following behind as well, lips tightly pressed together as he watched the strangely harmonious activity between humans, creatures, and magical beings—his gaze weirdly tracking the humans more than the others.

"The bundling spells could use another spellcaster," Ishum said to Valeran. He seemed willing to treat Valeran as a willing participant and ignore his attitude completely.

Valeran picked up a bundle, turned it in examination, and threw it back on the pile, but he surprisingly started duplicating the spells.

Kaveh hadn't thought Valeran would help after what he had said. But then, Valeran never seemed to say or show what he truly felt. A notion held true by the way Valeran watched the villagers through narrowed eyes. Kaveh looked out at the villagers, but he could see nothing noteworthy about them—no exceptional magical skills were on display. Humans had never held much interest for Kaveh, though, in opposition to Valeran.

Ishum examined Kaveh. "You aren't heavy of frame, but you look like you could lift a horse without a single spell."

Kaveh stared at him. Why would someone lift a horse without magic?

The man cocked his head. "Do you practice manual rituals?"

"No." Kaveh had a feeling that he didn't mean the rituals Kaveh performed to keep his magic flowing sharply.

The man's eyes slid to Ifret, who was staring coldly from where she had coiled in Kaveh's cloak. "Ah, other things kept you fit then."

Magic allowed a good amount of physical sloth for many types of magi, but the shadows had never allowed Kaveh laziness. They were living things waiting to gobble everything in their path. And Kaveh had learned early from the emperor that if he simply laid waste to all around him, there would be nothing to conquer or collect. So Kaveh had reined in shadows and demons for twenty-two years with tightened muscle and corded effort while walking over body-filled fields.

"Once, they did." Soon, they would again.

The man's gaze was piercing. "Start here and let us see what you can carry and load."

Kaveh was shown what to do—lifting and laying wood and stone. He had no trouble lifting the heaviest of stone nor keeping up.

It became tedious quickly, but then he fell into a rhythm—like shadows that needed to be layered and placed, wood and stone were fitted into a pattern and mold.

The sun lifted into the sky along with his labors. This was easy, rhythmic. Lift, place, lift again. Thought drained to the background in the way it did when he was especially deadly on a battlefield.

Fruit vendors were busy as the sun rose toward its peak. Though in this village, there appeared to be more of a shared wealth and experience than an economic collective—people were being thrown a fig or pomegranate as they ran past, and the bowls of stew and mosof bread were being scooped up by workers who weren't paying a thing in exchange.

"If you want a bowl, grab one," Ishum said, following his gaze. "When they run out, you'll have to wait for the second cooking and serving to get a portion."

Kaveh's stomach growled. "No, thank you."

Ishum shook his head and a hand gesture brought a man hurrying over with two bowls.

Kaveh knew better than to disregard food that was placed before him—even without being able to form poison detection spells. They wouldn't be able to hide his body from Nin, and a live body didn't perform without energy.

The vegetable and meat stew was filling. He thought Nin would like its flavor. He wondered whether she had gotten something to eat. He frowned at the nearly empty bowl and asked.

Ishum laughed lightly. "They will have been taken care of first. Workers of all type forget to eat, so healers are the ones we make sure to feed first, as they care for all others."

Satisfied, Kaveh returned the emptied bowl and went back to his stones.

"You are good at this," Ishum commented as the sun approached its zenith. He had given enough commands to get everyone settled and, like a good field general, he was now helping the campaign by breaking large, uneven rocks into small, uniform stones. "For someone who has never built."

Kaveh grunted, lifting a large rock that had already been squared into its designated pillar spot. "I'm a destroyer."

The man smiled. He had received some piece of news halfway through the morning that had made his shoulders ease and Kaveh knew the pregnant woman had survived. Of course she had. Kaveh could have told him she would when Nin had gone to care for her.

"Destruction and creation. It's like this rock." Ishum touched one of the jagged ones that held a thinning center line in the large pile. He broke the rock along its thinning center to separate it into two more viable pieces. "I need to destroy its original grandeur in order to make something that will handle more support for the entire structure. Sometimes destruction aids in creation."

Kaveh eyed him dubiously.

"You don't—boy, seek help!" Ishum cut off to yell at a boy wobbling beneath a too-heavy pole fifteen paces away as the boy tied a crisscross knot to secure it.

"Why does he not use magic?" Kaveh eyed the boy as another ran over to aid him. Other villagers were using magic—some lifting stones easily while Kaveh heaved them manually.

The wobbling boy reminded him of Akel, for some unknown reason—maybe the way that he was trying so hard in a frame far too thin—an underpowered human trying to do a feat too strong.

"We use magic for some things, but stonemasons and those who work with the earth"—Ishum thumped the wall—"their trades will continue long into the future. Everyone wants a house that is solidly built, and sometimes magic is a fey and mercurial force."

Kaveh frowned. "That boy could hold the pole with magic. He doesn't have to secure the binding with it."

The man shrugged, but there was something strange in his gaze for a moment before he shook it away. "He does no magic yet of his own, but he could ask for another to do it. However, even with the strongest magic, it is too easy to be weakened. Too easy to use too much magic in place of good sense. It is good practice, I find, to be without."

"Without sense?"

Ishum laughed and Kaveh felt a weird feeling of pleasure. "That too. But when one relies on a single skill or talent, what happens when that is taken away?" The man didn't look at him, which was good, because Kaveh's humor fell from him completely. He might use the next rock he lifted to bash the man's skull. "Magic has its limitations. This house"—Ishum indicated the plot they were building upon—"it was an experiment to see how far progress carried."

Kaveh looked at the pillar he was constructing. It was strange to think that he was helping build a house—a place where someone would live. Would this be his fate should he stay by Nin's side and not seek Darkness? He grappled with the strange gut churning and pushed the feelings inward. No.

"It was built with magic?"

Ishum nodded. "And its foundations lessened and were weakened when the inlari and its magic draining abilities hit it."

Kaveh eyed the rest of the village. "You built the rest without magic?"

"Some with, some without, most with a little bit. We build without magic in the gaps usually, because magic needs to be renewed. You can lift stones with magic—no problem—but you can't support stones with magic unless you are going to renew it on a regular basis. Once you start building a village, renewal becomes a lot more complicated. Sometimes doing things by hand makes the interim challenges easier. A...flexibility of mind is ever desired in a village such as this."

There seemed to be a joke, hidden within his words.

Kaveh grunted, lifting another pillar stone. "You need a guild."

The man shrugged. "Another interim solution. I like to think further. Maybe in the future, we will exist in cities that regulate all the magic themselves. Where we won't need to think about how to enchant stone to last more than a year."

"Progress." The prime aim of the empire.

"Progress comes for all of us, and with it our older ways. It is why we continually challenge ourselves to more."

Kaveh eyed the isu swinging their hundred branches and gripping with their thousand hands. "Except when the monsters come."

"We are used to monsters." The man shrugged. "And we are used to coming together to fight and continue."

"Don't you get tired of the monsters?" a strident voice asked.

Kaveh looked to see Valeran watching them with narrowed eyes. He hadn't realized the other man had worked his way closer—too used to the shadows feeding his senses to rely so extensively on human ones.

"One can only control that which is within oneself," Ishum said. "I can be angry at the monsters, or I can focus on making something new."

"You can kill the monsters."

"We used to kill the monsters. Yet we found another monster always takes its place."

"So you just...live in fear? Live as prey?" Kaveh felt his stomach turn in the same way it had when Aros had put the crown upon his head.

The man tilted his head. "We build in ways that make it so that we can weather whatever comes."

"They destroy your village," Valeran said, imposing himself fully in the conversation.

How many cities had Kaveh wiped clean—flattening those that did not immediately cede to the empire? He had lost count by the time he had turned thirteen.

Ishum smiled. "Another monster always comes. Better to teach our people how to recognize and deal with threats. Teach them how to be open to what comes and to take each threat individually."

Kaveh thought of Valeran's words to Taline ul Summora. Monsters make people prepare.

"Sometimes a monster is only an animal hurt and afraid," Ishum said. "And sometimes a monster comes from within."

Kaveh looked at his hands and said nothing. He lifted another stone.

"And sometimes, when you show a monster kindness and truth, the monster becomes your ally. Not always. But the monsters who can see the results of their actions often become the staunchest defenders of the village."

Kaveh followed Ishum's gaze to the sylvan oaks and the isu rumbling and casting their boughs forward. Fierce opponents, isu—known to decimate all in their path when riled.

"They fight with you," Kaveh said.

Ishum smiled. "Some who sought our destruction now seek our company. And it is always within us, as well, to guard those who choose harmony, and yet never to close ourselves off to new elements seeking harmony."

"Harmony?" Kaveh thought of Nin and her bright smile, given freely to him instead of hoarded like the prize it was. "Is that what this is?"

"Harmony is what you make of it. It isn't something you are granted. It is something that must actively be worked for. If we become too protectionist, we limit the concordance of nature. If we become too open, we forget our own safety. We try to take our piece without destroying all else, instead. Monsters make choices, too."

One isu shook old branches free as it harvested fallen trunks from the forest. The other lumbered into the village center, sunk its roots into the sunlit ground, and pulled. New branches grew all along its massive frame from the places where thick branches had been shed. Thicker, stronger new growth appeared. The shed old limbs littered the ground for the villagers to gather and use.

Commotion clamored suddenly and the village moved, almost as one, pausing in its labors. Even the isu lifted its leaf-crowned head. Kaveh looked over with Valeran, wondering what was going on—the rock he had just lifted still in his hand.

Nin and Taline stood next to a woman swathed in blankets, who was holding a bundle in her arms. She glowed as a man joined her, and Ishum raised a hand to give a blessing as he strode their way.

Kaveh's eyes slid to the woman who glowed far brighter than all the others. Nin turned to him and smiled like a sunbeam come to life.

He dropped the rock on his foot.

Valeran sneered, but his eyes, too, slid like magnets back to the scene.

Nin touched the babe's forehead, then the hand of the mother cradling the infant's cheek.

Awe and humility. Desire.

This woman, who was capable of as much death and destruction as he was if she wished, looked upon the babe and mother—the community of magi around them—with a warm smile on her face. A warm smile from a warm heart born into the coldest of families.

He would protect this.

He looked at his hands. He looked at the sky. The half-moon pulled.

"A good day, indeed," Ishum said, lifting another rock.

"Half your village was destroyed," Valeran said gruffly.

"But we lost no lives. We rebuilt. We made the village stronger today."

Kaveh curled his fingers into his palm. "If a monster wanted you gone, you would fall."

"Perhaps." The man nodded. "If the monster was especially fierce. Or perhaps we would triumph. Perhaps we would learn something that would help us against our next obstacle. Perhaps we would be lost to time and circumstance. But our people would have spent their days secure in the knowledge that they were always growing. With hope, not fear. And that is something precious."

"You risk the lives of your village." What could Kaveh do to protect Nin?

"But not their souls."

Kaveh stared at him.

"You misunderstand if you think we do not protect." Ishum pointed to the defenses. "For we consider life precious and we love each other, even with our many individual differences. But we also consider differences essential in how we move forward. What makes people think differently? What informs their views? Why does one want to keep others out and another wants to welcome them in?"

"You speak in riddles. And what happens when a decision is made? If someone doesn't agree? If a child rebels?"

"Then they bring new questions, new possible truths. If one is open to other viewpoints, one doesn't need to zealously guard one's own. It is not a threat to recognize new information and to change one's mind. Even from one year to the next. If famine were to hit, if fire were to encase us, then we would need to change. Change is inevitable. It is the fear of change that causes downfall and perpetuates itself. Moving with new information with new changes in circumstance to the best of our abilities with the best of communal intentions—we will make mistakes, but we will grow and we will continue."

"Foolishness. I could have—"

"Wiped us out with a flick of your fingers?"

Kaveh stared at the man, cold running through him. Was this fear? This feeling? Dread? He had only experienced anything akin to it since Nin had come into his life.

"Yes," Kaveh answered—for he had never run. And he had only apologized twice.

The man smiled. "It is good, to own one's actions. Do you feel regret?"

Valeran's gaze slid to him.

"I know regret," Kaveh said. Pain struck memory. The emperor had been about to reinstate Kaveh's magic, but they hadn't resolved anything...the emperor had died disappointed in him.

There was no way now to make amends with his father. That choice and outcome had been taken away. Forgiveness, or understanding, would never come.

"A monster does not regret," Ishum said.

"A monster cannot cry," Kaveh murmured.

"What is a monster, Shadow Prince?"

Kaveh had known the man knew who he was by the way he had phrased his comments before—by the way he had looked at Ifret—but it still made that cold thing in his chest shrivel further. Was this, too, regret?

"I am," Kaveh said.

Valeran looked sharply at him.

Ishum cocked his head. "Only if you want to be."

"A monster is always a monster," Valeran said harshly.

Ishum didn't look at Valeran, pinning Kaveh, instead, with his gaze. "You are human. And humans can be monsters. But the thing about humans is—they can be anything they want. What do you want?"

Kaveh looked at Nin. What did he want? To be worthy of her?

The man followed his gaze. "Such power," Ishum murmured. "A good example, as some feel they are monsters when others see them quite differently."

"She's no monster," Kaveh said harshly.

"No. She appears quite far from one. But the way we feel about ourselves can differ greatly from the way others feel about us. And when it comes to others, actions are what matter most. She might see herself as a monster, but her actions say otherwise."

"Would you still think that if she were a Fehl?"

The man looked at him. "I would still think that if she were descended from the bloodiest of kings."

Kaveh's fingers inched toward the knife at his belt. Ishum knew Nin was a Carre.

Ishum shook his head. "You can be born of anything. No man or woman gets to choose their birth. The only thing we can do is live our lives as they spread before us, one step at a time. The only thing we can do is make choices when they come before us. To spread kindness when we are able and to do no additional harm when we aren't."

"Weakness." Kaveh let his fingers fall.

"Yes." The man smiled. "And strength. Like a knot in a rope. It can be weak or strong. The experience of the one tying it, and the purpose of the knot itself, make all the difference."

The man looked to his kinsman rebuilding the structure. "Continual choices. Continual knots. Choose your path, Shadow Prince."

"I'm no longer worthy of that name."

"No?" The man cocked his head. "But perhaps one day you will be again. Power lost through magic strains to be regained." His gaze slid to the same boy who had struggled under the weight of the bough, a boy who even now, as underpowered of frame, came up with an interesting solution to the problem in front of him—a creative, odd solution that solved multiple issues. Ishum praised the boy, but Kaveh watched as some of the other villagers kept a closer watch.

Kaveh frowned. He wished he had his shadows to discern what the village had to be watchful about. Ifret would know, but she was now fast asleep in her pouch, having found nothing to interest her in Kaveh's tasks.

Ishum's gaze was a mixture of fondness, resignation, and remorse as he watched the boy. Odd. "Or perhaps you will not, but you still have paths within your grasp." He shook his head, turning back to Kaveh. "You can be what you want. Look within yourself for what you want, and without yourself for what you can learn and add."

Valeran's fists were gripped so tightly that Kaveh wondered whether he was going to explode. Kaveh cared not.

Ishum looked between Valeran and Kaveh, gaze sticking to Kaveh once more. "Do not allow yourself to think you ever have all the answers. You might for a moment in time. But time is swift and ever-changing. And the world changes itself around you. No man has the answers for all time. Truth, once sought, can become lies if one isn't continually seeking further truth."

Kaveh frowned. "That makes no sense. Truth is truth."

"Is it?" The man tilted his head. "And what then is your truth?"

"That the—" Kaveh's stomach turned unpleasantly and he touched it with unsteady fingers. Would he ever get used to this feeling? It was part of his very being. The empire, the emperor, the knowledge that might was right. That might was always in his hand.

He struggled.

The man put a hand on his shoulder. Kaveh looked at it like the alien motion that it was.

Only Nin touched him. The man squeezed his shoulder and Kaveh looked up at him, thoroughly bewildered.

"Truth can change," the man said with another squeeze. "The qualities of a man who seeks truth, though, those are ones to guard and nurture."

"Might triumphs over truth."

The man nodded. "This is indeed a truth. However"—he passed a sweeping hand along the village—"might is also something that can be nurtured and can evolve into other aspects. Community, building, creation."

He looked at Nin, who was helping with the healing supplies now—her gentle smile making the other healers smile in return.

He looked at Taline ul Summora, helping as well, using her boxes to aid others—as she had aided him.

The man's hand squeezed again, then dropped. "Decide what you seek." He moved away to help with a cohort of villagers who were arguing over covering a well.

Valeran was looking at the man's back with a mixed expression—tight with things Kaveh didn't care about at the moment.

What did Kaveh seek? He sought a return of his power. It would make everything right again.

Kaveh's attention was grabbed by jerking movement to his right.

The same boy was having trouble with a new section of lumber, painstakingly continuing with a fierce look upon his face. He was tying a complicated magicless knot in a rope connecting two sections.

The boy reminded him of Nin's duckling Akel even more strongly, with his fierce expression on a thin body. He looked as if he would blow away in a stiff breeze.

Kaveh walked over and knelt, taking the rope ends and giving them a securing tug. "You have made a strong tie," he said to him. Stronger than it had been before—even in the span of an hour.

"I will protect my village," the boy said fiercely.

Kaveh handed the ends back so the boy could tuck them into place. "From monsters?"

"From everything." The boy handed him the next set. "Even without magic."

Kaveh looked at the knotted rope held out to him for a long moment, then took it to give it the same hard yank. "You don't mind me helping?" he asked gruffly, giving it a final hard tug.

"I want my village to be strong. Asking for help in making my village strong does not show weakness. I offer solutions that help the others go faster and build stronger." The boy's gaze was challenging. But uncertainty underlay it. He had tried to do things himself then been told to seek help, and he had. A precipice.

Kaveh looked at the boy, once again strongly reminded of Akel and the help he had received from a person who had previously considered him monster, colossus, and myth.

"I will help." Kaveh handed the knotted rope back.

The boy looked relieved—and resolved. He nodded fiercely and began the next knot. They were intricate and strong. Kaveh only helped in setting them, as the designs were all the boy's own.

They worked that way through the rest of the rope knots, the sun descending overhead.

"That's it, sir. The final one. Thank you for your help. May Akkan bless your steps."

The god of travelers. Kaveh was used to being invoked to Marsk, the god of war.

"You are welcome," Kaveh said. "May Verdis bless yours."

The boy nodded seriously, then brushed himself off and ran over to where the stalls were reloading for dusk.

Valeran was walking away, easy loping steps, but with too much tension in his shoulders.

Valeran, like the villagers, looked at the boy with a strange look, as if he found something off about him. Perhaps because of the lack of magic at his age—the boy should have already Awakened at, what, fifteen, sixteen? Kaveh had never paid much attention to the ages of others. He had come into most of his powers from birth due to his mother's blood. But magi normally Awakened at, what, ten to fifteen?

Valeran's eyes narrowed on Kaveh, examining him as they fell into step. "Finally chased him off? Away from the monsters in the night?"

"The monsters here seem to don masks." Kaveh looked at the isu, weaving gently at the edges of the village, and the dryads braiding twine. "Perhaps a monster can learn to wear one that is human."

Valeran crossed his arms. "Still a monster underneath. Still the same bones beneath."

Kaveh looked at his hands, turning them, still marveling at their lack of shadowed wisp. Even Ifret was still asleep in her pouch. "But the monster decides the skin to wear. Decides whether its arms hurt or help."

"A monster can never be rid of what's inside him," Valeran said tightly.

Kaveh looked up. "Is nothing left then when the monster is removed? Is it all there ever is?" What sort of sacrifice would his humanity take? What kind of man would he be?

Valeran's fists clenched. "It's all that matters, in the end."

Kaveh looked back at his hands. "I don't think so. For I am nothing but the memory of a monster. But in that memory, I still exist." He touched the wall of stone they'd built as they passed. "I still exist."

And for the first time, he was not struggling with the power within him. Shadows weren't speaking to him from every direction. There was no shadow shading his sight. No shadow lingering in his mouth, consuming taste.

He looked at his fingers, flexing them slowly around the stone. He had no control, and yet full control. He was only in control of himself and not also the force that wrapped and choked itself around him—always having to keep it chained and gripped unless he was on a battlefield.

He had forgotten what it was like to just...exist. He wasn't sure he had ever known.

He thought of Ishum's words.

What did he want?

He had embraced his father's aims as his own. For as long as he could remember, the emperor's aims had been his creed. They had been aims that he understood because he was good at it, and so they had never caused him to question. He was good at death and destruction. He was good at conquest.

But at ruling? At making decisions that would benefit others?

He had only ever been concerned with benefiting the emperor, the empire. It had satisfied his bloodlust and the monster within.

He stared at the lines streaking his palms. But now? There was no magic to rigidly control, no meditation to undertake, no plans to make. There was...nothing.

It was as disturbing a revelation as the strange coil of freedom unfurling in his belly. What did he seek?

He blindly followed Valeran back to where Nin and Taline were speaking to Ishum and picking out food from the large spread that had been laid. Whispers followed as they drew closer.

"The news from Tehrasi. Did you hear?"

Kaveh looked up—the country's name sharpening his attention back to present matters.

"The Festival of Blood," a woman in a gathered group said. "They are reinstating it."

Kaveh went cold, gaze jerking to Nin. No.

CHAPTER ELEVEN
TIDINGS OF BLOOD

RONE

(The Village of Myth)

Rone looked sharply away from the Shadow Prince, who had been having some sort of inner epiphany, and focused on the women speaking.

"The Feast of Sustenance and Renewal?" A woman touched her creaseless forehead. "They cannot restart it."

"Why not? There's a Carre on the throne again, isn't there?"

Rone's hard gaze flew to Ninli, whose face was drained of color. He then took stock of the villagers, cataloging the potential danger posed by each threat. They had all been threats since the foursome had set foot in this cursed village.

Ishum stared at him with a knowing, sad gaze from his place next to Ninli. Rone's eyes tightened. He didn't like this man and he wanted out of this village. There were too many questions, too many informed looks. And Fehl, pretending at epiphany in their midst.

Ninli shook her head as she stepped toward the women, hand extended in some parody of calm comfort. "You must be mistaken. The activation of the Feast of Sustenance and Renewal requires specific parameters."

It was one of the reasons Ninli used as a rationale for being pro-empire—that the common people of Tehrasi accepted the empire so readily because the emperor had removed so many of the harshest rituals that only benefited the ruling elite while leaving the people free to their individual worship and religious activities. The Feast of Sustenance and Renewal—the Festival of Blood—had been her cornerstone point, because she had known that sometimes the empire paid no attention to the festivals of some of the other provinces and territories. Like the Festival of Marsk or the Spread of Verdis. Ninli had gotten directly involved in dismantling those when the empire moved on in their conquest.

That the empire had gotten rid of her family's slaughter rites had secured her loyalty in part.

"And now those parameters have been met," the village woman said bitterly. "We were given only ten years without a Carre."

"There are other param—"

"I know of what I speak!" Anger suffused the woman's face, stretching too-smooth skin. "I am of Tehrasi! The rituals have not been held for ten years, but I know them as if they happened yesterday. I lived through them for forty years. I can see it. I can feel it. Even with the wa..." She shook her head, not completing the word.

Rone's eyes narrowed. Waters?

The woman ran a shaking hand over her wrinkle-free forehead and Rone's gaze narrowed. Forty years of festivals plus ten years of rest after? This woman, who looked to be no more than twenty, was proclaiming intimate memory of forty years of the bloodiest of rites. Rone watched the villagers' gazes shift to the four of them—the outsiders—then back to the woman who had opened her mouth to speak again.

"I buried five chil—"

Another woman hushed her, but Rone knew how she was going to finish her sentence. He had noticed it before—most of the villagers appeared to be in their twenties and thirties. There were only a few outliers, like Ishum, who appeared to be in their forties. None appeared older. It was part of what itched under his skin, making him want to leave. Everything felt off, and he already had a good guess as to why.

"Sela, maybe it was—"

"I saw. I witnessed the celebration by those who have been campaigning to bring them back, Doni! There are those of us who keep track of those who want the rituals returned to the old ways!"

There were still some in the Tehrasian aristocracy who believed in the Feast of Sustenance and Renewal. The festival filled the streets with blood and the pillars with magic. It filled their coffers with power and their bones with energy. The elites must be excited beyond belief to have it restart.

Rone's gaze slid back to Ninli. He knew she had been trying to eradicate the belief, working to instill the idea that the population didn't need culling or churning to prosper—that there need be no sacrifice to the gods or to magic or to the gates in order to thrive.

Tehrasi had ritually sacrificed segments of its own populace for two hundred years. Embedded in the very bones of Tehrasians was the idea that sacrifice to those above was necessary for society to flourish.

Ninli had never accepted the notion of sacrificing her people—she had embraced sacrificing herself instead.

"Will they call you back, Sela?"

The woman who had called herself Tehrasian looked at her wrists. "They vowed that the oath was removed. Changed. By the empire. And even with..." She held out her wrists, unable to look away from her youthful skin. "But it is inevitable, is it not? The blood rituals were always inevitable," she whispered.

"How do you—?" Ninli's hands clenched into fists. "Why do you say this? Where are you hearing of the Feast of Sustenance and Renewal?"

They looked at each other, then down at something in the first's hands. "An imperial message was sent." The woman stuffed the enchanted papyrus into a pocket, looking guilty at having it. "And I used my powers to check by sight."

Ninli pulled the sand orb from her pack with frantic hands.

"You are allowed to seek news of home, Sela," Ishum said with a frown.

"I know." Sela looked down. "But I am a citizen here now. I escaped from the Carres and all that they—"

"Ninli—" Rone moved to stop her—they had way too many problems at the moment to add this one to the mix—but she had already activated the orb.

Unlike papyrus missives that delivered old news, the sand orb was fully realized and actuated. Sand and crushed gemstones coalesced and shifted into the shape of Aros, the new emperor, crown upon his head. A few in the village gasped.

Aros put a hand to his sand chest. "I harbor ill news on the eve of the blood rituals that swept Tehrasi throughout the Carres' reign. The Feast of Sustenance and Renewal has begun again—a festival that was abolished by the empire. An abominable festival that few want reinstated." He bowed his head. "Alas, the blood of a Carre has graced the halls of Tehras and the festival has reactivated. Zehra Amanan Carre is alive."

Rone swore softly and did not look at Ninli. Here, then, was the path of doom's beginning.

Aros pointed to the scepters along the curved walls, all lit and strumming with life along the edges of the orb.

"He lit them," Ninli whispered. "He lit them all with the Scepter of Darkness."

Gasps and alarm rang through the village center at Ninli's words. Ishum's lips pressed together. Rone couldn't care less what the man thought, but he kept him in view as Ishum's concentration narrowed in on Ninli and Taline.

Aros held his hand to his heart. "Zehra Amanan Carre activated her scepter in an attempt to renew the gates, but such backlash reinvigorated the ritual spells locked within the palace."

"Lies," Ninli whispered.

"Zehra Amanan Carre has been living under this assumed face and name."

Ninli's fingers whitened against the orb as her face appeared, recreated in crushed gem and sand. A glyph of her full imperial designation appeared alongside it. It was a designation she could not read, but the haste of the villagers as they scrambled back from her made the whole scene comically tragic. The woman, Sela, dropped, prostrate and shaking, seemingly unable to stop terrified, ingrained obedience when a Carre stood before her.

Fehl stepped forward to grab the orb, but Ninli put a hand on his wrist and shook her head, eyes brimming with tears and mouth pressed tight.

"Zehra Amanan Carre, an oathbreaker who knew her family's magic enough to hide her crimes under the name Ninli ul Summora, has

334

been living in Tehras as a healer, helping the citizenry there."

The villagers shouted and a few hustled the birth mother and baby away.

Fehl looked ready to kill. Rone cocked his head and considered returning Fehl's powers for the first time. If the Shadow Prince's powers were released, he would wipe the entire village. Wipe this entire farce from the land. The Summoras would disapprove, but—

"I urge Zehra to return"—Aros entreated, voice both appealing and provoking—"so that we might stop this action before it goes further—before the festival has to take place, before we rise with the growing moon to full bloodshed—so that we may save the City of a Hundred Gates. Every oathbound citizen will be affected, no matter how far they are from Tehrasi."

"Save them!" a villager yelled at Ninli.

"Yes! Why are you just standing there?"

"A Carre. Terror—"

"Silence," the Shadow Prince said. His voice carried coldly and with command. His shadow companion curled around his neck, hissing.

Ninli turned to Fehl with big, wet eyes. "He wouldn't." Brown speckled with red tears. "He wouldn't."

"He will," Fehl said grimly.

Within the orb, Aros lifted another—thousands of pieces of crystals glittered inside. "It has already begun. The citizenry will develop the sickness, and only bloodletting and sacrifice will stave off the curse."

The orb fell from Ninli's slack fingers and Taline lunged forward to catch it. "He initiated it," Ninli whispered. "He activated the festival. How could he? How could he?"

"The scepter has fully possessed him now," Fehl said grimly. "He seeks your return. And Aros has never been one to set small goals."

Taline had the orb in her hand now, listening as Aros continued speaking. "Zehra Amanan Carre has been taken by Kaveh ul Fehl and Rone ul Valeran to secure their plans for the destruction of the empire."

Rone looked skyward, then back to Aros's orb-enchanted eyes. There were more flecks of amber, jasper, and carnelian there now. A color-changing diaspora, they echoed the feverish look of his sand-displayed skin.

"The scepter…" Ninli shakily took the orb back from Taline. "The festivals increased control over the scepters. He might think this will separate him from the Scepter of Darkness."

Again, there was muffled shock and panic from the people around them, but Ninli only had eyes for the orb.

She looked straight at the orb, and Rone swore. The orb's effect made it appear as if Aros were staring straight at the viewer. When Rone looked at the orb, it appeared as if Aros was entreating him alone. However, Rone could never be compelled, but Ninli…

He heard Ninli's caught breath. It would be as if Aros were peering into her heart through the glass—with compassion and entreaty.

He snatched the orb from her fingers. Aros continued to speak. "Together, we can stop the festival from taking place. Break free of Valeran and Fehl. Turn yourself in, Zehra, and save the people you profess to love. Only you can—"

Rone crushed the orb with a push of power, and sand streamed through his fingers. He felt inevitability.

Fehl gripped Rone's wrist painfully, and Rone powered up a spell to sear him. But there was only a strange desperation riding Fehl's face.

"You...you were right," Fehl said, not looking away from Ninli. "She will..." His throat spasmed.

Rone shook himself free. "She will turn herself over to him to stop this? She will flee from us in the night in order to do so?" He looked at Fehl in grim resignation and resolve. "Yes. You are staring at the end of Ninli ul Summora."

Fehl stared at Ninli in some strange sort of incomprehension, then at his own hands. His face contorted and Rone stepped quickly back.

Fehl leaned over and vomited.

"Weakness," Fehl whispered. "Weakness."

Rone felt something odd rise within him amid the fury and disgust. He looked away. "Get used to it, Kaveh ul Fehl."

But Rone felt a strange feeling within himself as he looked at Ninli's expression. He didn't need to see her resolve form. He knew it already. He had known since Taline had shown up in his home in Tehras with an endgame plan. He had known then it would be the end of Ninli ul Summora. Why feel any differently now? Because he was actually looking at the end, seeing it form in clear marks?

"I will not get used to it, Rone ul Valeran." Fehl looked up. "I will stop this."

"Without magic?" Rone laughed unpleasantly. "You will be destroyed."

Fehl's gaze slid to the boy who he had helped, then back at his hands, an odd resolve in his eyes. "Then my humanity will be the first to go. I will protect her."

Rone felt that same strange feeling flow through him. Could Fehl not be pretending? Could someone change in so little time?

Fehl was oddly protective of Ninli. And when looked at without bias, it seemed he might actually love her. He had saved her from the emperor—done enough to get the emperor angry enough to punish him in front of the others. Could a person change their personality, their demeanor, their beliefs in two full moon cycles? It had been less than that since the Shadow Prince had held them in his grasp with the intent to kill. Could someone change so much in so little time? Someone who held so little soul in the first place? Who spoke of humanity as something he could rid himself of?

Monster.

If Fehl's powers were restored, would he prioritize Ninli's safety or his revenge? No one else would be able to stop her from sacrificing herself for her bloody country—not even Taline. Hell, Rone had never even tried to dissuade Ninli from that path. He could tell a losing cause from the outset. What chance did Fehl have when all he seemed driven by was taking Aros's blood and head?

If he got his powers back, what would Fehl do?

What would happen when Fehl lifted the scepter from Aros's dead hand? What worse could come from a spawn of Darkness gripping an object of madness and power?

Rone gripped his fingers together tightly.

Taline turned to look at him, gaze beseeching him to save Ninli, eyes gone glossy to the beginnings of sickness once more.

He shuddered.

Taline's expression turned questioning, concern suddenly showing for him as well. He shut his eyes against her regard.

Monsters did not deserve compassion.

"An unfortunate bit of damage, having a Carre acknowledged by the scepters," Ishum murmured. Rone considered putting a knife through his throat.

"The festival must take place. Only the return of Zehra Amanan Carre will stop the call." Sela had pulled herself from the ground and now looked furious in only the way that one angry and embarrassed could. She stared furiously at the woman who she had automatically prostrated herself to. "You owe it to—"

Ishum held up a hand. "Sela."

"He will call all to him with the scepter! Ishum—"

"I know." Ishum's calmness seemed to deflate her hostility.

"I don't—"

"I know, Sela. Be at ease. Go with the others."

A few villagers formed a comforting circle around her and led her off.

Her words lingered, though. Aros would call them as citizens of Tehrasi. It would not be long before Aros figured out how to activate every scepter's properties. The prime scepters could call citizens within Tehras's boundaries, and Aros would already know how to do that from watching Etelian and Osni, but outside of them? With the festival begun? The Scepter of Darkness only had to be aimed correctly, and to find the right strings.

Ninli would be the first called. Rone would be the second.

Ninli did not look at Rone. She didn't have to. Aros would be able to target anyone. It was what Rone had been most afraid of. It had been the reason he had wanted to break the scepter.

Villagers were staring fearfully at Ninli. Staring at all of them, piecing together who was who in Aros's recitation and bounty.

A villager stepped forward and placed a hand upon Taline's arm, pulling her away from Ninli and Rone. Rone thought of inevitability.

Taline turned to the woman who had grabbed her. "Is something wrong with Mayrie?" Her gaze darted between the woman and Ninli. "The baby? The afterbirth care?" Taline's gaze moved from the woman to Ninli and back, keeping track of both.

The overwhelming empathy within this woman who had been so hurt filled the same pit within his stomach that it always did. Rone hated this press of feelings as much as he craved it. She would turn from him, soon, and it would rip away a part of him he had hoarded for so long. A part that she had reached in and claimed as easily as she stood tall in the face of danger.

Inevitability. How long did he have? A day? Two?

"No, you did well. Better than I could have, had I not been out." This must be the healer who had been gathering herbs. "You will stay here, with us."

Taline blinked slowly at her. "Stay here?"

"There is a place for you here. And"—her gaze slid to Ninli—"you can support her from afar."

She was not saying that Ninli shouldn't go, that Ninli should also hide away within the forest. Taline would never accept that.

The expression twisting Taline's face was easily understood and the other woman shook her head at it. "Do not mistake us. We understand sacrifice. We are from places far and wide, but we know people and their hearts. She helped Mayrie without thought. Her heart is good. But she needs to help Tehrasi now. It is her duty. There is nothing we can do for her."

Taline's mouth worked. "So you propose to...what...assist the three of us while sacrificing Nin?"

"No." The woman's eyes slid sideways, touching on Rone. "Just you and the Shadow Prince."

"What do you mean?" Taline demanded. Her fury at their sacrifice of Ninli was automatically reaching out to encompass him as well. "Why do you separate Rone out as well?"

"Ishum has placed Kaveh ul Fehl under his care and vouched for him. We have lived with the shadows here for a long time."

For a land lived in the shade of the Mistress of Shadows, they would not fear Fehl the same way sensible people did. And Fehl was neutered of his power. He wasn't a threat. He was likely an asset, even, if he had survived Irsula and come back with her blessing of shadows in his cloak.

Rone, on the other hand, had not helped the village in the same way that Fehl had. Instead, he had chosen to keep most of his attention fixed on the hut the girls had been inside. A useful watch, but not one to endear him to the villagers. And he cared not at all about their regard. He had learned long ago that regard was only worth its weight in what could be used to deceive and what could be gained.

"We can keep him safe from his kin. And you safe from them as well. Etelian ul Fehl seeks you."

"Etelian ul Fehl's powers are too weak to help or hinder." She wet her lips and shuddered involuntarily. "Though they are horrible even so weak."

Rone's eyes slid shut. He was going to lose her. A day, two days, or one moment more.

"So many monsters in the Fehl family," the woman murmured. She looked at him, knowing full well he was listening. "We will make certain they never enter this forest again. You will be safe."

Shock visibly stole over Taline's face. "Rone is not a monster," she said sharply.

Inevitability. His loss of her was inevitable.

"He's a Valeran and a Fehl. Nothing to trust there, Mistress Summora, on either side." The woman shook her head. "And he has the new emperor as an enemy."

"He's not allied with either side. He's a citizen of Tehras," Taline said harshly. "He will be on the rolls as well, called for sacrifice."

"Only by accident. Only by trickery." The woman leaned in. "The Valerans are terrible people. That they don't even want one of their own to play as a piece against the empire?" She shook her head. "There is something wrong with him—and his magic. He feels empty, like a revenant drained of life."

Rone looked at the woman's light hair and eyes. He had a guess at what this was about, but he didn't care to find out. Rone started to move away, but Taline's hand reached out and snagged his wrist.

She was looking at the woman carefully, looking at her hair and eyes. "You are from Denma."

The woman looked grim. "I know the Valerans well."

The humor of the situation almost made Rone laugh. Kaveh ul Fehl, the nightmare people told their children to keep them in line—the Shadow Prince will come for you, in the darkness, with his cleavers of shadow, if you don't behave—was being given safe haven while Rone was to be ostracized because of his maternal ancestry.

Rone found bitter humor in the thought that he had finally beaten Kaveh ul Fehl, without even using his power. Ninli and Rone truly were the damnation of their birth.

"Rone ul Valeran is trustworthy, loyal, and good," Taline said stiffly. "And I will hear none of your talk."

Rone let his smile reflect his feelings—a chilly, dispossessed thing to hide his flinch.

The woman looked between them. "Tricked you, has he?"

"No," Taline said coldly. "I believed exactly as you did. Then I saw otherwise. Can you say the same?"

The woman said nothing for long moments. "Very well, Mistress Summora. I will see for myself."

"You do that," she said coolly. Then Taline looked at Rone. Her expression softened. She squeezed his wrist. "We will stay together. You promised."

He had, and he nodded. But she would run soon. She would run far, and fast. Rone didn't know how he would stand it. He didn't know how he would survive watching her expression turn to terror as the knife of comprehension slid inside.

"Time slips past." Ninli pocketed the orb and looked at each of them, expression solemn. I must make haste in returning to Tehrasi, she didn't say, but everyone could hear it.

She turned to Ishum. "Thank you for your aid and supplies. We are sorry for the trouble we have caused. May Sehk-Ra bless your village."

Ishum stared at her for a prolonged moment, sizing up everything that was and would be.

"You seek the waters," Ishum said to Ninli. It wasn't a question.

"Sehk-Ra's headdress, how did you ever guess?" Rone muttered. This village was a veritable signpost to the Eternal Spring—if you could make it here alive. There was an actual signpost with a pitcher on it.

The man turned to him, gaze calm. Rone's fists tightened. He couldn't wait to be free of this village.

"We do," Ninli said. "We need to be cleansed in order to hide my sister—sister in heart, not blood," she stressed. "To keep her safe. Especially now, before... She is innocent in all of this."

"We will keep her safe here." The woman from Denma eagerly restated.

"I will make certain she visits the spring first." Ninli would see the scepter taint removed before sacrificing herself. Rone felt no surprise.

"And even after, I will go with Nin," Taline said tensely.

A charged silence fell. The leader turned to Ninli. "Travelers haven't come in many a moon. Usually we trade by sending our best negotiators into the world outside Darkness's borders. Occasionally, they will bring someone back to join us and live here. But rarely do humans arrive here on their own, and alive. When they do, they are always interesting." Ishum tilted his head. "Stay the night. Rest and find the spring tomorrow with clearer heads."

Stay the night—forget—stay here in the village. Rone let his gaze slide, looking for the villager whose magic would wipe them free of their will to leave.

"You know where the spring is," Ninli said, examining Ishum.

"We are the stop before Glory and Despair. The stop before all is lost within."

Ninli looked around, gaze stopping on each face—seeing exactly what Rone had seen—the too-young faces with eyes either far too old or far too free of concern. "You know the way."

Ishum shook his head. "No one born without creation knows the way."

"You've been there, though," Rone said tightly. "Everyone in this village has been."

Ishum smiled. "So full of distrust, Rone ul Valeran. It is your weakest element."

"Don't worry." Rone let a cold smile slip through. "I have weaker ones still."

The village leader stared at him with old eyes. "All require a guide."

"Doubtful. We will go in that direction"—Rone pointed to the signpost with the pitcher glyph—"and we will be fine."

Ishum examined him in the way that made Rone want to turn on his heel immediately and head into the forest. He wanted out of this village, this forest, this reminder of everything that was inside him.

"The spring doesn't reside within any layer, Rone ul Valeran. It is outside of them, always floating between. Even a gatemaker will pass it by."

"Please." All eyes turned to Fehl. Even Rone took the moment to check to see whether someone had replaced the Shadow Prince while he was looking away. But the same locks were on his magic, the same shadows swirled inside. Fehl had just said please.

"Please," Fehl said again in his deep voice, gaze locked on the leader. "You have someone who can guide us?"

Ishum waffled, expression conflicted. "We do." As soon as he said it, decision made, he seemed to find peace with it. "Eat, stay the night here, and we will take you in the morning."

Eat our poisoned food, stay the night in our silken lair, and we will change your hearts and mind.

Sehk, no.

"No," Rone said.

Taline looked at him as if he had grown another head. "We—"

"Can stay so that they can bury us in wards?" he demanded. "So they can change our minds?"

"Rone!" Taline looked at him as if he had gone mad. But her skin was starting to sweat and she was weaving on her feet. He could see the sickness taking hold. Ninli touched her arm, sending a wave of healing magic.

Ninli looked exhausted—purple crescents underscoring brown eyes—the eye color spell the only one she had renewed. Taline looked at her, then back at him. "Rone, we need—"

"Not here. We will rest after the spring."

"Nin needs to—"

Rone passed a hand around, willing Taline to look. Willing Taline to see what she would normally see if not for the absurdity of their situation. To see past the alarmed and horrified expressions and beneath to the skin of the villagers.

It wasn't something he thought Fehl had noticed, as distracted as he had been all day, making nice with the locals, but there was something off with this village. Something was off with the people.

And it wasn't just making friends with monsters, though that was its own problem.

No, it was how everyone looked.

It was in the disparate groups in the village and the differences between them.

"We will not change your thoughts, Rone ul Valeran." Ishum stared at him. "I think only you can change your mind."

Rone focused on the linchipin. "We go now, Ninli, with or without them."

The villagers started to murmur. Ishum held up his hand.

"Valeran—" Fehl started to say.

"Do as you want, Fehl. Ninli?" He looked deliberately at Taline. "Do you plan to wait another day?" To relieve Taline of her suffering—to relieve her of the addiction that lessened by the day, but that caused her pain and trauma?

"No," she murmured.

The villagers started to disperse under Ishum's command. Each began to load a plate of food to eat. Rone didn't like the coordinated efforts, the signals, the too-young and content expressions, or the way they ate. He would be happy to see their backs. He would be happier when they were gone from this cursed place completely.

"We will take you after we eat," Ishum said.

"I don't trust you and I don't trust your food." This man who spoke of monsters who could become more.

"I know. But you will not find the spring on your own. Festival sacrifices do not begin until the half-moon rests." Ishum smiled gently. "Then they gather to high bloodshed on the full moon. Tomorrow's night through dawn is the celebration of half. Will you find it by then, Rone ul Valeran?"

Taline touched his arm, then she and Ninli took a few more nuts, berries, and meat.

"At moonset, we will go," Ishum said. "Near the half-moon—in the change between states, there is an opening between worlds."

Fehl stiffened. Rone didn't care why. They would be leaving here tonight, no matter what.

Fehl grabbed food and pointedly ate while staring at Rone, who took nothing. Someone had to maintain sense. Ninli and Taline were eating and speaking with the villagers like the kind idiots they were.

"You have imbibed the waters?" Ninli asked Ishum.

"Yes."

"Can you tell what is involved?"

"No." Ishum shook his head. "Better to be cleansed in the moment of choice. One chance."

"One chance?" Rone looked at him, eyes sharpening.

"It is a trip that we make once in our lifetime. A single choice to make."

"You can only visit once?" Rone demanded, looking at the village full of young people. Lies.

"You can visit as many times as you wish." Ishum spread his hands. "But the eternal waters only work for the single visit that is made."

Rone frowned. He hated riddles when he was already feeling uneasy.

The man smiled. "A decision for each to make on their own, once they understand."

"We could understand right now."

"I will say no more. You will be shown to the spring. Your choices thereafter are yours. My choice not to tell you is mine."

Rone really hated this village. He kept close eyes on Taline and Ninli, and even the Shadow Prince, who had taken to making rope knots with the boy again once they had both finished eating.

Rone felt weirdly uneasy about the Shadow Prince's normality. It was too surreal. He had to get out of here. Everything would be back to normal once they left this accursed place.

Moonset was just under two ticks of the sand dial as one day folded into another.

Ishum signaled to the boy—the one Fehl had been helping. "Are you ready?"

The boy nodded.

Unease ran through Rone. This was not a coincidence. He looked at the boy with new eyes. Rone had been paying more attention to the hut that had contained the girls than to Fehl's ridiculous construction efforts, but he had overheard the boy talk about his "protection" goals. Rone had dismissed him as useless.

He reached out for the boy's magic and jerked back a moment later. Unawakened, but teeming with life.

"How old are you?" he asked harshly.

The boy tilted his head. "Sixteen."

Sixteen was far too old even for a late-blooming magi. Unease turned into intense disquiet. The earliest and latest bloomers were always the magi to fear: those born to their powers, those who developed them devastatingly early—and those who developed them far too late.

"Will you turn the offer of a guide down then?" Ishum regarded him.

Taline looked at Rone as if he were crazy. Rone truly hated the man.

The food had bolstered her, but he could still see the tired lines stretching her face. Rone would face down a worldbreaker for her. "No."

Ishum nodded, as if it were the expected response and Rone hated him just a little bit more.

They left the village and its wards as one day became the next.

Standing outside the wards, the boy cocked his head, and the magic that had not yet filled him reached tentative fingers forward.

Rone put himself in between the boy and Taline and Ninli.

The boy's magic was on the edge, waiting—and it was the form of magic that made up the layers themselves. Ninli had a bit of that feel, gatemaker that she was. But locked inside this boy was...more. A worldbreaker had been born to this age, and he was standing before them.

Could he fix Fehl's magic? Was Ishum simply waiting until Rone was gone before fixing Fehl and letting him loose on the world? Was he planning to hook Fehl to a worldbreaker in order to end the world?

Worldbreakers were magi of myth—spoken of in harsh whispers, for there was as much death in their paths as creation. Worldbreakers had created the five layers of the earth. And because their magic ran through the layers, the worlds within each, in which everything lived, were vulnerable to them.

Explosions that had taken down cities and broken civilizations were almost always caused by a worldbreaker.

If Rone didn't already know that he himself was a monster, then being surrounded by yet another example would have certainly cemented it. Monsters attracted their own.

He looked at Taline, who was paying attention to whatever Ishum was saying. Then to Fehl, who also was looking at the village leader. But Ninli...she met his gaze and nodded, solemn knowledge there.

She knew the boy was a worldbreaker, on the verge of Awakening.

What would stop them from using a worldbreaker. The Scepter of Darkness had been created by a worldbreaker tortured to madness. They could take this one and capture Aros within.

Ninli shook her head faintly. Rone frowned and curled his pinky. Ninli shook her head again under the cover of moving her hair.

Taline jabbed Rone in the side. "Stop being secretive together," she hissed under her breath.

But Rone eyed the boy, wondering.

Because there was that strange, ageless look to the boy as well. The same look the woman from Tehrasi, Sela, had, as did so many of the others. A strange newness to the skin. That this boy had it, too… Rone felt his unease triple.

The worldbreaker had been through the spring, and yet he was still unawakened to magic. What did that mean?

They stopped as the edge of forest thicket gave way to the mountains beyond.

"Here," the boy said quietly. "We must wait for the moon to pass. The threshold. Two of them to open."

Ishum nodded. "Well done, Teir. Rest."

Rone exchanged another look with Ninli. Time would tell what sort of benefit or curse finding the village had been.

The boy sat on a large stone. Fehl knelt and said something to him. Taline and Ninli conversed quietly to the side.

Rone locked gazes with Ishum. "This is an easily attainable location once found. Why do you require him to return?"

Ishum shook his head. "There are plenty of places in the Land of Darkness where thresholds exist. Too many to station or sustain. The opening to the spring is never the same twice in a row. To locate the Eternal Spring without simple luck requires a guide."

The legends said so, but Rone had concocted enough of his own legends never to put full faith within any that he was told.

"What will you do when his powers Awaken?"

"That is not something for you to worry about, Rone ul Valeran." Ishum looked at the boy and Fehl. "Your own travails fill too much of your mind. Seek your peace within. Many who seek the spring are not given encouragement to find it."

"We should feel fortunate, then." Rone's smile was cutting.

Ishum looked at him. "Do you feel fortunate, Rone ul Valeran?"

Rone narrowed his eyes. "Why did you accompany us? Why show us the way?"

"It was not for you, Rone ul Valeran, though your choice will be influenced by who it was for, I think."

"The Shadow Prince?" Rone was amused. "You think the spring will return his powers?"

"No. The spring is not what will heal Kaveh ul Fehl. The spring is for the two touched by the Scepter of Darkness."

Rone's amusement dropped completely and a knife blade dropped from his sleeve to touch his palm. "How did you know?"

Ishum shook his head but didn't call forth defenses of his own. "It is an old gift, to know the feeling of power, acquisition, and talent."

Rone looked sharply at him. "You are a mūdû."

"That is one name, yes."

No wonder he was the leader. Though Rone supposed it was more than just knowing what others' talents were—a leader had to be able to use and direct those talents.

Rone looked at the Shadow Prince. It was one of the things that had made Kaveh ul Fehl a conqueror, but not a true leader. For he used his people as the things that they were but disdained them for all being less. He used his own gifts to do everything, instead of seeking the best way to use all his resources. It was the downfall of those with too much power or intellect—that they took too much upon themselves and refused to learn how to delegate, how to spread a burden, how to allow others to do more, how to extend a sense of pride and ownership for the tasks.

Fehl would make a disastrous emperor.

Rone couldn't say that he would make a better one. He hated humanity, too. And he was quite happy in his silo of solitary life.

His gaze slid to Taline unwillingly. Had been quite happy.

"You are at a crossroads," the mūdû said.

And it struck Rone with a cold suddenness that the man could see his powers. He knew.

The blade curled into his palm.

"You are filled with conflict, Rone ul Valeran."

"Not as such, no." He was not going to lift a finger to help Kaveh ul Fehl, no less extend a hand.

"You are a conflicted soul. How long has it been since you've hidden yourself from the world?"

When Rone had been tested, the emperor had been without such aid as having a mūdû at hand. It had been the only blessing besides Ninli that Rone had ever had. The only blessing before—

"Pain. Uncertainty. Desire." Ishum tipped his head. "Conflict."

"Don't worry, old man. I feel no conflict in this."

"Master Ishum." The boy stood and looked to where the forest became mountain with his strange gaze. "The light. It opens."

Ishum stepped forward and put a hand on the boy's shoulder. "Good job, Teir. Step back, now."

The boy shook his head slowly, gaze intent on something only he could see. "It is like something…" His fingers stretched.

"Teir," Ishum said softly, stepping in front of his gaze and taking his hand.

Teir shook his head and swallowed. He looked at the man, then stepped back.

"What?" Ninli asked, voice strangely insistent. "What is it like?"

The boy looked at her. "Like something out of a dream," he murmured. Then he shook his head and looked at Ishum. "I'm tired, Master Ishum."

"Yes." Ishum smiled and turned the boy to face in the opposite direction. He looked at the four of them over his shoulder. "Blessings upon you."

Lovely. Not concerning at all.

Taline gave her own blessing, eyes shining with anticipation. She saw the goal, not the trap.

Ninli bowed. "Thank you for your accompaniment, your guidance, and your aid."

Ishum bowed back. "It has been my pleasure." His eyes slid to Fehl. "And you will be welcome in the village, should you ever seek to return."

Rone would make certain Fehl never returned.

Fehl looked at Ishum, though, with that same strange look in his eyes. And Rone recognized it finally—Fehl wondered why this man, like Ninli, cared.

The mūdû nodded, as if he had received a response. "There are costs to the spring, so weigh your choices well. And take care in your home territory—with the choices that fall before you now and in the near future."

Ishum looked at Rone. "I hope you discover what your choice is worth."

Cold slithered down his spine.

CHAPTER TWELVE

ETERNAL SPRING OF DESPAIR

TALINE

(The Eternal Spring, the Land of Darkness)

Taline felt more conflicted than ever as she looked at the entrance to the spring and back to her sister. For this was the end of their journey. "Nin—"

"Do not despair, Tali. For we are here."

Despair took her anyway. Taline wanted to fix Nin's quiet acceptance of fate. The Festival of Blood had begun, and Nin was the only Carre who could stop it, for Aros never would. The look in her sister's eyes made Taline want to sob. For Nin truly had not believed the festival would ever begin again.

"It was your promise, to get me here. That means you might be gone when I blink free."

Nin looked sad. "I will not leave yet."

But she would leave, and they all knew it. Taline had seen the veil fall across her eyes when the women of the village had spoken of the festival's renewal. The village had brought them both hope and despair. Rone's eyes looked almost feral as he gazed at the backs of the two villagers as they walked away.

But then he blinked, and his gaze was calm again, one brow raised at her in question.

No, it had been even before the village that he had started acting strangely. It had been ever since being forced to play companion to Kaveh ul Fehl. Rone looked at Taline now with a sort of distance in his eyes—as though he was already leaving as well, even though he had promised to stay.

Taline wanted to fix his look, she wanted to fix Nin's despair, but she hadn't even been able to fix herself.

They waved a final farewell to Ishum and Teir.

The lingering traces of the scepter reached for the strange boy and his undeveloped magic. Taline shook the feeling away, used to magi far more powerful than she, and turned to the air behind them as it rippled. Like a ripgate opening between two worlds, an arch of turquoise drew itself into the air.

This was her opportunity. She would fix herself and be a true asset for the group in the shared pain to come.

The arch gave way to a waterfall of greenery—vines and dripping, colorfully petaled plants—a lush growth that gave way to the sound of falling water behind. A protected space between layers opening as one day turned to the next in the half-moon's light.

Nin stepped inside first. Of course she did. Taline could not fault her for it, for wanting to protect, and she quickly stepped behind her and into a tunnel of green.

At the end of the tunnel there was a light, strange and brightly glowing, and the tunnel opened into a glade of inordinate beauty, in this place out of time. A pristine pool of blue crystal water glistened in a false light between worlds.

Blue and silver fish slipped through the waters, their scales shining, then slipped into the softly dripping waterfall begat of nothing—figments of an imagination and scene.

Like a fragment of a glade snipped from its place and deposited elsewhere, this was a never ending, never beginning spot.

A nymph stood with a large pitcher in her webbed hands, staring solemnly at them as they progressed into the cut glade.

Unlike the tall dryads, with their spindly fingers and leafy nails, the nymph was short of body, with webbed feet and hands. Small fins encapsulated her ears and larger ones attached to the backs of her arms, legs, and back. Scales glittered across every bit of her—silver, blue, and green—and her entire body lit with changing patterns. Her scales caught the reflection of the lights, urging Taline closer to peer at the beauty of the sea.

Dangerous beings—those of the sea—with their ever-changing camouflage and taunting baits of light. The beings of the forests, mountains, and deserts were charismatic in their own ways, but something about the sea had always called to

Taline. The wind on the waves, the way light hit water—all of that deadly power and natural triumph. It called to her in a way that made the beings of water—the sirens, and the nerens, and the potamens—so much more hazardous.

Taline stepped forward—for it was because of her that this quest had commenced, and she would drown in guilt if anything happened to Nin or Rone. The village had felt like new life—from the actual birth of it to a rebirth of spirit—it had been invigorating after going so long without seeing Nin, to return to her side. To return to a more normal world—seeing that which she loved and had missed. Seeing Nin's eyes light with the inner peace she always found in the skill she had embraced as her own—bringing new life into the world instead of extinguishing it.

Taline stepped forward until she stood before the nymph. The tales regarding the Eternal Spring were vague, but Taline wasn't as unaware as Rone seemed to think she was. She had seen him chewing over the questions of the village. She had seen him look at her in frustration, as if she hadn't noticed. If he had thought she was immune to the questions raised by the village itself, as well as queries concerning the boy who had brought them here, he had forgotten her own well-developed observational skills went along with a practiced mien at pretending nothing was wrong.

But whatever had been eating at Rone, had obscured his view of all else. He wanted her to remain unaware, because it meant she might not notice whatever had been wearing at him.

She would pin him down about it tonight. It was time. But for now...

Taline made the sign of a peaceful visit—fingers interwoven, palms touching, the thumb edges of her bound together hands touching her forehead. Most magi used their hands extensively to cast spells, and though it was not necessary—especially for the gifted and clever—magi seemed to default to it. There was something about the accuracy and general nature of pointing that engendered it. It was a sign of peace and goodwill to wrap one's fingers together and prevent them from being used as weapons—to offer oneself up for attack in tying their main weapons together.

The nymph examined her with large multicolored eyes that pierced her soul. "Greetings, traveler. What is it that you seek?"

"I seek the Eternal Spring. To be cleansed of the spells placed upon me, depending on the price."

The nymph looked her over in distant examination. "To bathe? You have many spells upon you. But I see the one that you seek to remove. A potent veil of malice that doesn't match the light shining inside you."

Taline swallowed heavily. She desperately wanted that to be true. The desire for revenge against Etelian was something that had required immense effort over many years to stop from devouring her. And yet, like everything else associated with him, his foulness remained in some small measure.

"Yes. I seek the waters of the spring to remove that veil."

"Is that all you seek?" The nymph's ageless eyes examined her. "To bathe? The veil spells themselves are the price for bathing, for they feed other things that the spring relies upon."

Taline nodded sharply. She and Nin had talked about what the price would likely be, and this was far less than assumed.

The nymph's silvered head tilted. "Do you not seek more, damaged one?"

Behind her, she felt Rone take a step closer—she knew the sound of his footsteps and the presence that he exuded. She felt Nin reach out a hand to stop him.

"What else might I seek, spring protector?" Taline asked.

"The damage inside you...there is so much." The nymph peered at her with large, sad eyes. Taline inwardly cringed, but outwardly raised her chin as the nymph continued. "You say you want the veil removed, but the damage inside you can be healed as well. Your body can be renewed. You have but to choose to drink."

"Renewed?" Rone asked sharply, his voice cutting through the sudden buzzing in Taline's head.

The nymph looked over Taline's shoulder. "Yes, empty one. Her body and mind would return to the way they were. Before the wounds were set inside."

"The damage to my magic can be healed?" The damage done by Etelian? Taline's heart picked up speed. Rone stepped to her left side.

The nymph spread shimmering, blue-green, webbed hands over the pitcher's side, stroking the vessel with the motions. "You have not just to bathe, but to drink."

Taline clutched at her chest. To be whole again—

Fehl and Nin stepped forward on her right. Fehl's eyes were fierce. "Then the spring can heal a nullification of power?"

Rone stiffened. He was still not in agreement with the Shadow Prince regaining his power, but his eyes were fierce.

But Taline didn't care at the moment about the Shadow Prince recouping his powers—she was caught in the staggering possibility of regaining her youth's power.

The nymph tipped her head in question. "A nullification?"

"His powers are bound," Nin said, indicating Fehl.

Rone's sharp gaze switched to Nin, and something complicated passed between them again. But in Taline's shock, understanding was far from her reach.

"Can the waters undo the binding?" Nin asked.

The nymph's multicolored eyes slid to Fehl. "But there is no damage, nothing to undo. His magic is fine, locked within."

"The lock, can you undo the lock?" Rone asked sharply.

"Of course not." The nymph spread her webs. "That is not within the spring's renewal. The spring doesn't make that which is not natural to the magi suddenly grow."

"But it's not natural to the magi."

"It is. This lock, it is done with his own magic." She tilted her head at Fehl. "Can you not rid yourself of it, shadowed one?"

Fehl looked at his hands, his waist. "No," he said grimly.

Taline frowned. If the emperor's ultimate power had been using a magi's power against the magi...could she only regain hers because of the temporary nature of Etelian's powers?

The nymph shook her head. "You would have to undo your body to before such a lock was ever initiated, or it would simply keep existing. Renewal comes from wear, from tear, from distress. Spells and enchantments are washed free by the waters. All spells upon you will be wiped away and all imperfections healed. But such a lock..." She cocked her head. "It is beyond the natural order. Not found in nature. And therefore you would have to undo the body and mind to before a time the body knew the lock."

Rone stiffened next to her. Taline touched his shoulder. He was always so worried about Etelian and unnatural powers and monsters. She smiled, wanting to reassure him that all would be well.

Horror briefly crossed Rone's expression, followed by pain, and despair. Concerned, she leaned closer. He scuttled away.

"Rone?" She reached out a hand, hurt.

His gaze whipped away from Taline, as if desperate, and focused narrowly on the nymph. "You said...the body and mind."

"There are two aspects to the spring, and it is each traveler's choice, whether to drink." Lidded eyes blinked and webbed hands clasped the pitcher tight. "As stated, drinking will reverse your body and mind and all that is inside. Bathing will clear you of all that is without."

Nin put a closed fist to her chest. "So if this man wanted to be in the body he had ten days' past?"

The nymph nodded. "Of course. An easy youthening."

Nin's body sagged against the Shadow Prince, true relief visible.

It unnerved Taline how much Nin had come to put faith in the man. But Taline had always had faith in Nin, and in the past few days, she had seen nuggets of what might have drawn her sister to him. If the Shadow Prince was to regain his powers here, she would put faith in that, too.

"I will..." The Shadow Prince let out a long breath. "This will work then."

The nymph tipped her scaled head, as if trying to understand the undercurrents. "Any external damage will be undone. Your lock is not ten days' old, however."

Relief froze on Fehl's face, creating a rictus of dawning horror.

"You were five," Nin murmured, resignation overtaking her expression. "When the emperor locked your magic in test."

The glade was silent but for the fall of the water into the pond. Taline stared at the Shadow Prince. His body would turn...five, if he drank?

Nin closed her eyes. "How many times can the spring be bathed within?"

"As many times as there are days."

Taline knew what Nin was trying to divine—if there was a loophole that would allow the lock to be worn down without making the Shadow Prince a child.

"But beware, rending one, if you leave, the spring will not be in the same place you arrived or with any markers you seek. Knowledge of the spring becomes harder each time it is sought."

That was why the village had sent the boy as guide. Taline thought of how Rone and Nin had cautiously watched him. How the village leader had. She remembered what the boy had said. What Nin has asked. He had said it seemed like something out of a dream.

The boy had been here but did not remember it.

But many of the others in the village did.

Taline squinted at the blue crystal waters. "Mayrie could have visited the spring and been fixed after the birth of her second child."

Nin frowned and turned to the nymph. "There is a price. But only to drink from it?"

The nymph's head tilted. "You will be renewed." She looked directly at Taline. "You can live renewed without price of power."

It was like a hope that had been dashed years ago, existing only in embers burning out upon the ground, and then a magi came along with the ability to ignite those embers back into a blaze.

She thought of the village and the ageless faces that had scattered the landscape. The legends were true. She had never held hope of something that could erase the pain of her past.

Taline looked at Rone, who had gone beyond tense, then to Nin, who had become sad.

"Without price of power. But what is the price then?" Nin asked. Some of Taline's hope turned to tension. She looked back at the nymph.

"The price of memory."

What did that mean? She wouldn't remember the pain?

Rone's eyes slid shut. Pain and resignation etched themselves into the skin around his eyes and mouth. Nin's eyes were full of sorrow.

Taline didn't understand their reactions. To be without scars and memories, to erase that which had been a burden, a wound, a chasm, a pain so deep that she hadn't thought herself capable of surmounting it, of clawing her way without, would be a blessing. Her escape had made the wounds fester, then close. Scar tissue had formed.

She looked at her hands. Hands that had seen and done so much since she had been thirteen and under Etelian's charge. Taline's brows creased. She would be well rid of such memories. Would not the Shadow Prince want to get rid of those of his father taking his magic, as well?

"You are of the spring," Nin was saying to the nymph. "You have drunk the waters."

"It is possible, rending one."

Taline looked sharply at the nymph. It was possible?

"I can see your lip prints upon the pitcher in your grasp," Nin said softly. Her gaze was resigned and distant. "But you cannot remember drinking."

The nymph extended one webbed hand in acknowledgment, untroubled by this. "Then I will have performed my task. When nightfall comes, from the pitcher I will drink."

"No matter what, tonight you will drink?"

"It is a task of the spring. To offer each anew. To be renewed."

To be renewed. Taline wanted.

"Every night. Every night, you drink," Nin said, voice strange.

"Nin," Taline urged. What if the nymph wearied of their questions? What if she disallowed them from the spring? Taline felt an urge—like the urge to lift the scepter—snake over her.

But Nin wasn't looking at her—she was looking at the strange eyeglass she turned between her fingers when she thought no one was watching. A wisp of shadow snaked through the glass.

"Nin—"

"The day," Nin said. "Each person chooses the day?"

"The day is chosen by the one who drinks." The nymph dipped her head. "Depending on what needs renewal."

Great hope rose within Taline. "Nin. You can—"

"Tali." She looked up at her, gaze beyond sad. "Think of the price."

"The price? Nin, your mind. You will be able to read again."

It was a moment of surreal absurdity. Nin and she stood on opposite squares from their usual positions—with Taline ready to jump and Nin urging caution. Taline was ready to jump now. Everything in her ached for it. To be renewed. The promise of it. Her magic back. Her scars gone. Etelian not even a distant memory. It was an all-encompassing urge to jump in and start swallowing.

And Nin was the one standing back, questioning, hand upon Taline's wrist.

"Your mind, Nin," Taline whispered.

Nin looked at the glass, then up at her. "I have you for that, Tali."

"You won't need me. You'll have everything. And you can forget falling and being in pain. And the Shadow Prince can forget his father taking his magic."

Sadness encompassed Nin's expression, something Taline wanted to wipe away. Nin squeezed her hand. "You are renewed to the same moment, Tali. Do not feel distress. I will look after you. And Kaveh, too, should he choose."

Taline looked at Nin, and for the first time in the conversation, she felt distinct unease. This is what Nin did when she was sacrificing—when she was giving up something she wanted, so that someone else could have what they desired.

"No," Fehl said.

"Kaveh—"

"No." Fehl's voice was implacable. He looked to the waters. "I refuse. I will find another way. There are other ways."

"But you are renewed when you drink?" Taline asked the nymph, a thread of desperation creeping in.

The nymph cocked her head. "I am forever renewed to the state of my mind and body at the start of my journey. It is part of my vow. To return to a singular point and state in time."

"The start of...at that singular point in time..." There was something wrong with Taline's chest. Her heart wasn't beating correctly.

The nymph nodded. "To the exact time and day of the form you choose."

Sehk. No.

Nin looked at Taline, expression solemn. "To fix the damage, I'd have to go back to the age of the trauma. I would be nine again, in body and mind. And Kaveh, he would be five. Neither of us would have memories beyond."

"Yes," the nymph answered.

Sound retreated to the edges of Taline's consciousness. And Taline...she would be...

Taline's hand went limp under Nin's. Nin's fingers turned soft, but the crumbling of hope was hard. Understanding didn't want to come.

"It was Mayrie's first birth that caused her issue," Taline said. Her own voice sounded like it came from a great distance. Nin looked at Taline, sadness and sympathy mixing. "But it was her second birth that exacerbated the problem. She barely survived."

Understanding didn't want to come, but it was forced upon her all the same. The spring would have taken from Mayrie more than she would be willing to give. To remove the damage would have meant to unwind her mind and body before the first birth. To remove the memories of her children.

Mayrie could return right now to the body and mind of a woman who had never given birth, but she would forget her children—children ages three and five—she would have no memory of them.

"After the second birth—" But Taline knew the answer before Nin gave it.

"She could have come then, but she would have lost the first two years of her first child's life. She chose."

Taline looked back at the waters. This was the cost of the spring.

"A cost." Taline murmured her thought aloud. "And a reward. Eternal youth and life for those who know how to use it."

"The spring becomes harder to find—each time becomes more difficult. Unless you have a magi you renew repeatedly to stay the age before they Awaken."

But of course. A worldbreaker. Nin would know the feel of one, so much more dangerous than a gatemaker. Continuously renewed to a younger state in order to stay out of the eyes of the world. Did he have the choice? Did they make the choice for him?

"There is always the choice to remain here," the nymph said. "If you stay here, you will remain forever in your prime."

Taline looked around. There was no one else in the glade. Tense, she looked back. "Where are the others, then?" For surely some had chosen.

The nymph's large eyes blinked. "I only know that the option exists."

"You have no knowledge of when you arrived," Nin said. "Of whether this is your first day or one thousandth."

The nymph eyed Nin. "Yes."

"It is your first day. Eternally."

"It is, rending one."

"Eternally." Nin eyed the arch behind them that glimmered with a world beyond, then narrowed back on the nymph. "You have never met a traveler. We are your first."

Taline understood what Nin was getting at. Of course the villagers had been here. Too many held that ageless look that spoke of old eyes in fresh skin.

"You are the first of my memory."

Nin nodded. "And yet we are not."

"As you say, rending one." The nymph looked unmoved and unconcerned.

"You will meet another traveler—tomorrow perhaps—and never remember the experience of meeting us."

The nymph smiled. "I will follow the instructions I received this morning—or a morning many moons ago—with the rules of the eternal waters. And I will welcome each traveler who comes forth."

"Are you...trapped here?"

The nymph's eyes narrowed. "It is my duty. My eternal duty to put forth the spring, but not to have a say in the matters of human, creature, and beast. All who come are welcome to partake. All who partake are welcome to stay as long as they continue to drink."

Taline understood. A being who spent dozens—hundreds, thousands—of years meeting people would assuredly form opinions on their task. Would form an opinion on whether the spring should be used at all. Or on who should use it.

To keep the spring eternal and without judgment, the keeper was ever the former and never the latter. Eternally new and exhilarated at their task.

"What was happening in the world on the day you arrived?" She tried to pinpoint the year—for how else could you calculate the age of someone who forever drank the waters of a same day?

"I do not know anything of the 'world,' as you say. I know my teachers and my guides." The nymph looked at them, calm and relaxed. "I was taught by Ferrengala and Abserti."

Exchanged looks said that none of them knew enough about nymph history to take a stab at a guess.

"I do not know if this is my first day, or my ten thousandth, as your companion has said." There was something strained in that statement—the only tension the nymph had shown thus far. "But I am two and ten."

Twelve. And isolated. The powers to be had isolated her from everything. Taline bet they would never find those names in lore. They had deliberately kept their chosen keeper from layer affairs, so she would have no answer to anyone asking about them. There was no other curiosity to be had, either, for this was her first day in her new position and would provide its own eternal excitement. Her first day for eternity.

It was ingenious, really. For who would stray from the path set out for them on a day that was their first? The nymph might question—for all that Nin was battering her with truth—but it would not sway her. Not in a span of time that would see the spring's attendant renewed.

"You do not age. You do not gain experience."

"I am but a tool of the world, rending one. A perfect tool of unending state."

The men remained silent and still in their understanding.

"You have no wish to leave?"

"It is my duty, rending one."

There was no real rescuing of her. The nymph was perfectly satisfied at this exact moment in time. She was looking forward to her duty—eternally—for she would "renew" again and look forward to her first day on task the next day. And the next.

What did rescue even mean, in this? For in the nymph's mind, it would not be rescue. It would be kidnapping and torture. And what did anything mean, except that which occurred within one's own mind and reality?

"I will go first." Nin stepped forward.

Activity came back to the glade, breaking the stillness.

"No."

"No."

Both men surged in front, eyeing each other in displeasure over their shared concern.

"I will go first," Fehl said. "It will do nothing to me that isn't worse than what has already been done."

Fehl and Nin held a brief staring contest. It was unnerving. Taline knew they could no longer mind speak, but it was like watching two people who knew each other well enough that they didn't need to. Taline and Nin had that. And now Nin had it with Fehl...

Taline stood numbly, gazing at the waters and the choice before her.

Nin pushed gently past Fehl.

"I will choose to bathe, but not to drink," Nin said to the nymph.

The nymph nodded easily and extended a hand.

Nin shed her garments with three twists of the pins holding them in place and entered the waters.

She paused as the water reached her waist. "If I go beneath?"

"Only water taken from the spring by the pitcher gives internal renewal of a past state."

Nin nodded and slipped fully beneath the waters.

Taline felt a thousand thoughts scraping her mind, her scars itching against her skin and against the interior of her head.

Nin emerged upward, eyes bleeding red, the waters washing away the spell like water sliding down a rock already worn a thousand years in the same stream.

But when she stood up, she was still Nin. Nineteen years in body and ancient in mind.

Not nine.

"Well?" Rone asked tightly, eyes drifting to Taline before looking back at Nin.

Nin closed her red eyes. "No chunks of memory gone. Nothing internally different." She looked up and smiled wanly. "No falling into the sleep of beauty and waking up ten years in the future."

Taline shivered. For that was what it would be—going back to a past version of oneself. She would wake up and look around and know no one in this glade.

She would know...no one...in this glade.

She would wake whole—her magic would once more be hers—and she would be alone.

"No ill effects?" Rone asked.

Nin shook her head and emerged from the waters, drying herself as she did. "External spells are...muted. Like they have been encased in the waters themselves."

"Imperial spells?"

Nin tilted her head. "Some are still there—those that I have accepted as part of me." She looked to Taline as Taline mechanically handed over her garments and helped her reclasp them. "But others are gone. I wonder...?" Nin shook her head and clasped the shadow cloak back around her throat.

"You don't need it anymore," Taline heard herself say.

Nin's gaze drifted behind Taline. "I will continue to wear it because I wish it."

Fehl looked at Nin, then he divested himself of his cloak and clothing and stepped into the spring. Ifret wound herself around Nin.

"Do you wish to drink, shadowed one?" the nymph asked.

There was something cold and set in Fehl's expression. It unnerved Taline, what he could be thinking, but she was too consumed by her own choices rising up again in the miasma of her mind. Did she wish to drink?

"No." Fehl ducked beneath the water—as large a force of nature outside his clothing and without power as he had been while cloaked and within. When he emerged, water streaming down his face and not an ounce of his power renewed, Taline felt something crawl down her spine at the determined look that settled upon his face.

Foul choices were being made in that look—old and set. Ifret wound around his wrist once more and he touched the shadow's head. "It matters not. I will rise another way."

Rone's lips twisted in some glittering, mean pleasure, but he, too, shed his garments and stepped quickly into the waters. He was squeezing something in his hand as he entered. She had seen him palm too many things before to miss the way his palms clenched and fingers curled. She could barely concentrate on the strength of the vision of him, though.

The question that stood before her was too all-consuming.

It was not a question of whether she would enter the waters. The anxiety, sweating, irritability, fatigue, the abdominal cramps...she wanted all of the scepter withdrawal gone.

The question was...would she drink?

To be thirteen again? Did she want to be thirteen again? To start over and live anew? To live her dreams of being a windchaser?

She would have the power. And memories of her time with Etelian would be stripped—gone. They would not exist for the Taline she would be again.

Nin and Rone had not existed for Taline at thirteen either.

To be kept eternally young and perfect without gaining experience or new memories... Taline looked at the nymph. This was the cost.

Rone stepped free of the waters, drying and dressing himself with quick motions of long, perfect hands. His lips were pursed specifically—as if he had asked a question of the spring and been given a poor response.

Nin and Fehl were both looking at Rone with different, narrowed expressions. Fehl's looked about the same as normal, but Nin's... Taline wished she had been paying more attention with an unscrambled mind.

The nymph looked at Taline. "Your companions chose not to unwind the past. But for others"—for you, the breeze whispered—"to drink is a freedom they can find, for memories and wounds so deep that they are a burden to hold. In that, the spring offers chance."

The nymph looked back without regret or knowledge. For the cost in this choice would be to the others. They would remember the parts of the last four years they had spent with Taline. She would remember none of the last seven. And she would have no regret, for knowledge caused regret, and she would have none.

Her gaze slid to Nin, and emotion rose to choke her. She would not know Nin. And she would not know to feel regret. She would not know Nin to regret.

She closed her eyes, emotion pushing her to numbness—too overwhelming to deal with. In this moment, she would regret. But after drinking from the cup—she would have none. She would be thirteen. Perfect again. All terrible memories wiped free. All experiences to her body wiped free.

Etelian would not be hunting her—for he would be hunting a twenty-year-old woman, and Taline would show as a completely different age under any scan that could not be faked.

Taline swallowed.

Nin touched her shoulder. "Whatever you choose, I will be with you. We shall meet as many times as you need, and I will be your comfort in all uncertain times."

And Taline knew that Nin spoke true. Nin wanted for her whatever Taline wanted. And it was that strength of kinship that had held her to Nin. Always. For Nin wanted for Taline only what Taline wanted for herself. Constant consent for her own choices, without pressure to follow Nin's.

Nin's hand slipped into hers. "You will have me, no matter what."

"I won't know you."

"But I will know you."

But Nin...Nin wouldn't know her. For what was Taline but the sum of her experiences? What was she but all that she had loved and suffered?

Nin stepped forward, as if reading her mind. "You are more than the sum of your experiences."

And Taline felt herself settling. For it was true. She was more than the sum of her experiences. And it was also true that her experiences defined her.

She could start anew. She could be the person she had dreamed of at thirteen.

Or she could be the person she was now.

"I will know you. Always," Nin said.

Relief flowed through Taline's veins—like the hardest aspect of the choice had been removed, and a path opened before her.

Taline let her clothing slip to the grass and stepped forth.

She heard the sad sounds from the nymph, and curses from the men.

Unlike Nin, who had no qualms about undressing in front of others, Taline was always careful to remain covered. Both had been raised surrounded by many—modesty an unknowable luxury. Nin had known no privacy in the palace—surrounded by servants at all times—and had experienced a different lack of privacy on the streets. She cared little for her state of clothing, only her state of mind. But for Taline, after Etelian...

She knew what her form showed without the spells she usually cloaked herself within. She knew whose name had been carved forevermore across her skin. Brands, reminders, ownership marks.

But forevermore had a different meaning when standing before the Eternal Spring.

Taline felt the waters surround and envelop her as she stepped down. She felt them ease her temporarily from the scepter's grasp—a spell she had never wanted and never accepted—a spell she had actively rejected, and her body and mind knew it. She felt them peel away the pain of the past—smoothing the marks upon her skin, carved and scarred—and she felt the waters seep inside, whispering of a promise to take it all away.

To take all of the memories as well.

The nymph extended the pitcher.

Her magic, broken by Etelian so long ago, would form back together. Just like the marks on her skin, the marks on her soul would be gone.

She would be who she had once been. Siran.

No longer Taline.

She closed her eyes, held her breath, and slid into the depths, letting the water wash away the tears spilling down her cheeks. She folded her legs and sat upon the sand. She would take a moment—a moment to mourn this loss.

For this was a choice, and she would make it without regret. But it was also a loss. A loss of much that would never fully heal, for all that it had scabbed over and faded. Taline's memory had ever been keen.

She let her sorrows slip out with the scepter's oil.

The fingers of her right hand grazed pebbles in the sand and one sparked her curiosity with its familiar feel. She curved her fingers around it. There was something alive about it. About everything in the spring. But this one...the familiarity...

It reached toward her, questioning.

And there was... She could feel something—like some outside bit of magic was reaching upward and through the pebble toward her.

It felt like Etelian, but stronger. Far stronger. She recoiled and struggled against its touch and it eased back immediately. And that was what made her pause. For Etelian never paused, never waited, never asked whether something was wrong or took care in any way not to hurt her.

And this magic...it felt as if it cared. As though it wanted to please her. Something in the magic felt like the spell papers. Like Rone and Nin.

Perhaps this was part of the spring? A therapy of mind? A way to mute the damage?

The spell papers were a magic she associated with Rone mostly, in part because of the time spent together using them.

She let the magic curl over her fingers and absorb inside her skin.

She felt the damage inside her ease—felt a tiny bit of her power heal. She immediately sought her mind for holes, but all her memories were intact. The nymph had said that her internal damage would remain untouched without drinking, but...

She filtered air through the water and into her mouth with a small spell, allowing her to stay at the bottom. She hadn't healed all the way, but she hadn't felt this good in ages. She could not remember the last time she had felt her magic swirl without the ache that accompanied it—like a worn joint that would never heal.

The scepter had overwritten those pains—making the ecstasy burn brighter than the pain—but it had not erased them. It had just overtaken them, hidden them beneath its bright, addictive burn.

Taline surfaced and opened her eyes to see four faces peering back—two anxious and dear, two curious and examining.

Taline lifted her arms and looked at them. She choked on a sob. Free of the damage, her skin was whole and smooth—the strange ageless look of it held the same endless glow that the villagers had. It was the absence of damage, the perfection of what was possible in this time of her body's life. The elders in the village had wrinkles, but not deep lines.

She wondered how old Ishum truly was.

"Tali?"

She felt no more of the scepter's grip. All of her memories were still inside, still there, but lessened—for the moment, eased.

She looked at her skin, then she looked at Nin, who looked anxious, and at Rone, who looked tense.

Taline looked at her hands, let out a little sob, and felt a small sliver of hope return.

CHAPTER THIRTEEN

ETERNAL FALL OF GLORY

RONE

(The southern border of the Land of Darkness)

"That a worldbreaker has been born gives us another option." Rone poked the fire in the middle of their newest camp, at the southern border of the Land of Darkness. He couldn't watch Taline stare at the glowing skin of her bare arms for the hundredth time. It made him feel too many things. "Fight a force with a force."

Fehl wouldn't even be needed.

"The boy isn't yet Awakened," Ninli murmured. "He might remain that way."

"He has been unmade at least once." Rone poked his stick in her direction. "How many times do you think they have reversed that boy?"

Ninli looked uncomfortable. "I don't know."

He regarded her for a moment, then went back to tending the fire. "You want to save him. Like you wanted to save the nymph."

"Maybe they are saving him," she murmured. "By keeping him unmade right now."

"So he can't break the world?" Rone jabbed the fire and flipped four strips of meat. "We know more than most that some powers should never be realized."

"That's not what I meant," she chided. "The Scepter of Darkness contains the agony of a worldbreaker—the lingering madness of one. In the hands of another worldbreaker…"

Ninli's ancestors really had been horrible people. Rone was a scepter scholar. He knew the tales of how they had made the scepter—and the torture involved.

"A different worldbreaker."

Ninli shook her head. "It might make things worse."

She was right. He knew that. "It is a possibility, though." Especially when other options dwindled. Especially when fate was staring at him and telling him he had nowhere else to run.

Sitting around the fire, cooking, Rone tried to keep his words light and his subdued thoughts from showing. An ebullient Taline deserved that he keep his self-loathing inside.

When they had exited the spring, Ninli had been first in line again. He wondered whether her thoughts had made an impact on their exit point. They had ended up as close to Tehrasi as they could get while still being in Darkness's borders.

The villagers had given them small illuminates for camping that also served to warn off predators. This far from the interior of the forest, and with Ninli and his powers renewed, as well as Taline's, they were better protected than they had been before.

Quite a bit of map still existed between their present position and Tehrasi. They could make it in a week with a bit of maneuvering through some of the old, enchanted paths, if they chose not to use a temple or gate.

He doubted Ninli would allow such a wait. She would want to be in Tehras tomorrow. She would make it so, to try to stop the opening sacrifices.

Rone had no more time. And yet he couldn't bear thinking of what he would have to do.

Taline looked better—lighter, but contemplative—but there was a sadness in her face. A sadness beneath the resolve. Rone lamented the timing—that Ninli could not have taken her to the spring after freeing her from that burning chariot years ago. Taline would have chosen to rid herself of her trauma had the price not been what she had worked for—and scraped to make for and of herself—in the past four years.

She was exceptional, whether she chose to go back to age thirteen, chose anytime between, or stayed as she was now. The spring could not erase her core, her very essence. Her strength just highlighted that.

She was special in all ways. As she sat now. Just as she was. In all the parts that made her Taline.

He loved her and he would lose her—this night or the next.

Taline rolled her hands into fists, then let them curl back out into the long, graceful fingers that had been the only part of her body below her neck that she had willingly shown before today. He had seen the edges of the scars while tending her—in wrapping her wounds in the non-magic lands. It couldn't be avoided, but he had not mentioned them and tried not to dwell upon them, knowing that they haunted her.

Rone's part in this mad farce would soon be over, and it would end in his doom. It would end as soon as Aros opened his mouth in front of Taline, or if he finally let Kaveh ul Fehl loose upon the world. But Rone vowed that even as he fell, Etelian ul Fehl would die.

"How do you feel?" Ninli asked Taline, checking her over.

"I...my power has...some of the damage was healed." She looked at her hands in thought. "The scepter must have healed some of it while I held it, then when its influence was removed..." She frowned.

Ninli looked at Rone, whose eyes slid toward the tree line.

"Well, I'm glad you are feeling well," he heard Ninli say.

"I feel...better than well. Still..." He could feel her frown. "It is strange. The nymph said—"

"The nymph knew as little as the day she arrived," Rone said dismissively, eager to move her away from the subject. "How could she? Resetting herself every day like that."

"I'm sure she had rigorous training beforehand," Ninli said, challenge in her voice. "She knew the spring."

"I thought you were trying to change the nymph's mind for a moment there, Nin," Taline said. "To work a Tehras gambit. To convince her not to bear the pitcher any longer."

Rone looked back to see Ninli staring at the fire.

"She was in no state to be swayed. A single day will not reverse the disciplinary measures her handlers used before putting her in that position. The disciplinary measures were likely even positive—a far harder command regimentation to break. It would take a far more concerted effort and emotion to sway such a mind."

"Falling in love?" Taline asked lightly.

Ninli smiled at her. "Ever our favorite tales."

Rone curled his fingers into fists. "A tale of horror. Falling in love over and over again with the same person on the same day, only to have that person not remember you the next? Madness."

Taline grimaced and Ninli's expression saddened again.

Kaveh ul Fehl looked into the distance. "I think it would be okay. If it was the one person you could fall in love with over and again."

Ninli looked at him, and for a moment, eternal stars shone in her eyes. Then they turned sad once more.

Rone clenched his fists. Anger burbled within.

Taline looked at her hands. "The spring felt like the seals—a combination of Nin and Rone's magic."

Rone's gaze slid away with his anger—discomfort swiftly drowning all else.

"Confusing," Ninli agreed evenly, not taking her eyes off the Shadow Prince.

But Rone felt the tightening in his gut all the same. "The nymph only knows what she knows. The Shadow Prince didn't heal." Rone waved a careless hand his way.

But Kaveh ul Fehl looked stuck on whatever his mind was dwelling upon, and he didn't rise to the taunt. Unease curled in Rone, and with it, anger. Why was he sitting with Fehl, sharing food? Like a family unit?

He knew where the blame for it lay.

He had not liked the way the Shadow Prince had been looking or acting. As though he had decided upon a course of action and had made some sort of peace with it. As if he knew he was on the precipice of some forfeiture and had come to some form of acceptance.

Like he had an epiphany and was somehow the better for it—less a monster.

As Rone toasted the last of the night's meat and vegetables, and as the fallen prince turned to stare at him in contemplation, Rone was even more certain he hated whatever this was—whatever was happening in Fehl's brain. Rone didn't want to know, especially since Fehl was prone to—

"You were a mistake."

—say things like that.

Rone looked northward, invoking a prayer for patience. "Thank you for that delightful reminder." Rone looked at Ninli so that he could non-verbally let her know that she was fully to blame for this, but she was staring off into space, eyes still blown from whatever had occurred between her and the stupid prince. Taline, however, began sharpening a dagger, eyes narrowing on Fehl.

Fehl didn't seem to detect the threat. "Your mother left you because you were a mistake. And the emperor should never have had me." The prince cocked his head. "The emperor took that which was not his to take."

Rone clapped slowly. "Sehk-Ra's hat, good for you. A revelation about taking that which is not yours to take. And having it in the midst of a gathering of professional thieves—truly exceptional."

"You jest." Fehl cocked his head the other way. "And yet you are a mistake."

Rone's stomach churned unpleasantly. He had never quite been able to rid himself of the reaction. He smiled tightly. "I am the bad seed, the leftover component, the hundredth mistake in a thou—"

"You are not," Taline said furiously.

"I am ever a mistake, narsumina."

"Don't, don't," she begged.

Ninli looked at them finally, gaze sad, but said nothing.

Rone opened his mouth to make it all worse. "I—"

"He made many. Mistakes." Fehl looked at the back of his hands, turning them slowly to the palms, and gazing deeply at them as if looking inward through their seams. "His empire... How he decided to build it... He took the choice from my mother."

Rone felt a strange curl of sympathy that he squashed ruthlessly. "He didn't take the choice from mine. Oralia was quite happy to bear an opportunity for the throne. She was too quick in her decision, alas. All her decisions. She ran with him before it was a notion for praise. She left me before it would have gained them power."

Power beyond, for the Valerans would have figured out Rone's power had he been encompassed within their care. They could have sold him to the emperor for any price. The emperor would have paid it.

Fehl frowned. "He was ever looking for children to strengthen the realms."

"He sought a stronger Etelian," Taline agreed softly, making Rone's gut tighten harder.

Fehl nodded distantly. "Nera tried. As did many others. Some without..." Fehl shook his head. "He was ever looking for children to strengthen his empire, but those without choice..."

"Fehl monsters. The woman from Denma was not wrong." Rone shut his eyes. "All of us are monsters."

Taline had been abused by a Fehl—a lesser monstered Fehl, even. And Rone had always known what he was. Sehk. She could never be his. Why had he allowed himself to climb to this peak?

He had known. He had always known the end would be a fall.

A palm touched his cheek. "Some are saviors."

Without opening his eyes, he put his hand upon the one against his cheek, rejecting the notion of it while greedily clasping it to him. "Why do you defend me?"

"Because you are nothing like them."

"I am just like them." More than she would ever know. "Fehl monsters. A truth beyond verity."

"You are nothing like them. You are kind, even when you refuse to be a man strapped by such weakness."

Rone opened his eyes. "I am strapped by far worse."

Taline smiled at him, soft, as if he had made a joke. Her smile was as sweet as sunrise speckled in pinks and yellows and browns. "Then it is a good thing I trust you."

He rose abruptly, scattering the remaining two meat sticks.

Trust. Lies. Damnation.

He strode from camp on legs that felt too long and a body that was jerking. Taline rose to follow, making a dismayed sound. He increased his pace.

"Leave him," he could hear Ninli say. "He needs to sort this out himself."

Sehk-be-damned Ninli. Sehk-be-damned Summoras. And the Sehk-be-damned useless prince.

Ninli would give herself up for the festival. It was without doubt. And Taline would follow her to her death or imprisonment.

Without the Shadow Prince, they would have little chance. Without any help that could remove Aros, they would suffer and be taken.

He gripped his hair in his hands. If... When Taline found out....

Why hadn't he ever said something? It would have been the one thing that he could have used as a shield—impenetrable between them. She would have looked at him in repulsion and disgust and never wavered. Looked at him in a way that could not be denied—the monster that he was inside.

He had already used his power on her today.

After watching Ninli and the Shadow Prince night after night and thinking about scarred magic, and how the scarring had stopped Taline's powers from returning to their full state—when the scars had peeled away from the Ninli and Fehl, Rone had grasped hope with both hands that while Taline's scars were turning back, some of the damage could be undone.

So he had laced a pebble with layer upon layer of his power and dropped it when he had stood in the center of the spring pool. She had sat right upon it, then sought its familiarity, as he knew she would, as the spring dispersed each layer of the pebble's magic in order to cleanse it.

The power rose within him even now. He had used it before. He had been nearly helpless not to. And it was so hard to keep it buttoned up. It wanted to be used. It wanted to be free. And it would be so easy—using it to do whatever he wished. It was so easy to take and push down all those who his power said were beneath him.

The Valerans, dancing and imbibing and celebrating the marriage of their princess, free of the imperial spawn. How he could have taken everything from them in that moment.

He crushed his eyes closed and felt the tearing pain at his scalp as he pulled.

But his hair, torn free, would just grow back in the morning. He had tried, long ago, to rid himself of the stigma. A curse all its own.

The way his mother had looked, whirling free, without him weighing her down.

The way Taline looked at him, as if he were something special...

He had allowed this. He had greedily taken admiration and affection when it had been offered. And now...

And now he would pay for that greed.

Before, he could have handled Taline's fear and disgust. What mattered in such hate when one's heart was guarded? He had handled her revulsion of his lifestyle before. Easily.

But now? Now that he had engendered some affection within her? Some measly piece of Rone ul Valeran slipping between her ribs?

She would hate him. She would hate him in a way that she had never truly hated him before.

Everything would be even worse now—for before, before they had become a unit, he had kept himself apart from her. He had known that she was trouble, and he had kept his feelings separate. But somewhere in the midst of their muddle in the non-magic lands, he had let her in. More, he had enveloped her.

When she turned her back on him, it would be devastating.

The image of his mother twirling, free, was a wraith in his mind. He wanted to bury it deep, like he had always done, and pretend at normality. But it kept bubbling up. Whether from exposure or his continued near use of the emperor's power, whether he was just masochistic enough to want to use it so she would push away from him in horror sooner than later, or whether his subconscious was telling him to get it over with, his body was pushing for him to use it.

When he did, she would recoil, and he wanted to prolong the moments before that happened for as long as possible.

She would hate him not just for the power, but also for the secrecy of it now.

He clutched his cursed hair in both hands.

"They want you to return."

Rone's fingers tightened painfully as his half-brother stepped onto the ledge.

"You worry them with your tantrum."

Rone did not have to look up to view the dispassion in his gaze or the censure in his voice. "Should I have done this there instead?"

"You are behaving like a child."

"And you aren't even as useful as one." Rone looked up, lashing out. "You won't get your powers back tomorrow. And you won't get them back the next day," Rone said savagely. "You will be without them forevermore."

Fehl looked out into the forest of his mother's birth. "Then I will be without them." Only the curling of his fingers into his palms belied the forced calm of his voice. "What difference does it make to you?"

"None. I hope you live without them for the rest of your days."

"Then it is a good thing that you seemingly live without much hope, Valeran. Now, if you are done with your tantrum?"

Rone thought about striking him—about reaching out with his power and squeezing Fehl until there was nothing left to squeeze. Only the image of Fehl's face would remain—his expression as he realized he was doomed.

Rone could see his magic seething beneath the lock the emperor had placed. Rone touched his fingers together then reached his fingers out, palm flat to the sky. A simple curl upward with his fingers, a simple yank...

His expression caught on the blade of the knife strapped to the underside of his wrist, reflecting his image back in the falling moon's half-light.

He was far more like his parents than he would ever claim.

He curled his fingers in, turning the reflection inward to his sleeve, and let the power drop. Another stepped into the clearing. There was a soft murmur, then the retreat of heavier steps. Rone never looked away from his sleeve.

"Aren't you going to ask, Ninli?" he asked, voice remote and unrecognizable. "Finally?"

"No."

"It will solve many of your problems."

"Yes."

He smiled without humor, refusing to look up. "And you are going to let that opportunity pass?"

"I told you I would say nothing," she said simply. "I will not endanger or expose your secret."

"I would do it, if you asked me to," he said, with an effort that was crushing—squeezing at his insides to admit aloud. Taline ul Summora had cursed him.

"I know." Ninli touched his shoulder—a fleeting thing. "I will find another way."

But finding "ways" dwindled with each trip of the moon across the sky and each step Aros played in this game. Ninli started to walk away.

"I hated him," he called.

She stopped and turned. "I know," she said quietly, knowing who he meant—the man who he had always hidden from and taken cold pleasure in that hiding.

Rone looked at his hands and folded them into themselves. "My life is a curse."

"Your life is yours," she said. "You make it what you will."

"Like you," he said.

"Better than me," she said softly.

"She will never..." He struggled with getting the words out, the fear.

Ninli did not respond for long moments. "Fear is a funny thing. Irrational. Overwhelming. But so, too, are other emotions. Love. Belonging."

"Fear keeps us alive. She is right to fear."

"Yes. She has been mistreated in terrible ways. But she is strong. And she gets to make her own decisions." The last was said without judgment.

"That decision is obvious, Ninli." He looked up to see that damned calm expression on her face.

"You are a gambler. Will you not take the chance?"

"I gamble for things that have no meaning."

Her eyes softened. "Not a gamble, then. A risk. For a reward greater than anything." She held his eyes for another moment. "For you, too, get to make your own decision. No one else."

And it was implicit in that statement that Ninli would abide by that choice.

"Overcoming the past is never easy." She laughed sadly. "A never-ending process, even, maybe. We all have to overcome something. But"—she looked at him—"some things are easier, when done together."

She stepped away, leaving him in the moonlight with only his chaotic thoughts and choices, and his desires.

It was always where he lost. Where he lost the bet. Where he lost the game. When he sought to want.

He stared at the half-moon as it slid lower, but it held no answers. Those answers were all inside him and her.

And he had no notion what to choose.

❧

KAVEH

There was something wrong with Valeran. Something wrong with the way that he perceived things.

Kaveh didn't have many answers in this new world he found himself in, but he knew that Valeran had done something that was beyond the man's own reach now—poisoned by something in the past.

Kaveh looked at Nin and thought of the exhaustive efforts she had made to allow him to see the empire from another angle. From her passion. From her desire. From his.

He saw it every time he saw her eyes bleed to beautiful red.

He felt it in his bones whenever she looked at him. A weakness, an imperfection in the structure of the connective tissues that held him together when all seemed to sag and weaken and break him.

Weakness.

And yet—he looked at his hands—and yet, she sat here with him, while he was without powers, and looked at him as if he were the same man. A man whose weakness was an essential part of him, and that part of him she accepted along with all the rest.

"How did you deal with it?" he asked, as she caught up to him, too slow in his return to the campfire. "When you were first on the streets?" She'd had all that power and protection, then...nothing. No ability to read, little ability to fend for herself.

"I clasped vengeance to me, for a while." She stopped with him, staring at the fire burning just beyond the trees, and at her sister who was frowning as she worked with one of her enchanted boxes. "A burning desire to destroy all who had killed my family."

He knew by family she meant her handmaidens more than her blood kin.

She sighed. "That kept me alive for a while. But it is an empty flame—for once it is burned, it leaves nothing behind." She looked at him. "I concentrated on other things—helping the people, extracting bits of vengeance, yes, but with the focus to aid others rather than secure my own bloodletting desire."

"The flame continued to burn. You got vengeance."

"Yes. Crushing the vials Osni had been using to keep the gates running was vengeance. And it did not help the people. But the vials were only ever a stopgap for Tehras. In my vengeance, I thought it better to have the population source solutions while I was still alive and able to patch the gates, than to wait until death took me and the gates fell."

Always the gates. Always the people. Always Tehrasi.

"You are still here, with me, even though you think, at this point, that a solution will not be found in time to help you with Tehrasi."

She looked at him. "I am with you for this time before the end because I want to be, not because you can help me save Tehrasi."

"I will." He touched his chest. "I will help you save Tehrasi and the empire."

She smiled and put her hand over his. "You have already helped me, Kaveh. Just being here helps me."

"You are going to turn yourself in."

She looked through the trees to the fire beyond. "There is time still. A little time. But in the end, I will do as I must." Her fingers slipped through his.

"What if I don't want you to?"

She turned to him, ageless eyes examining. "You would find me far less of interest if I turned my back. I would not be the same person that I am. I would not be a person you would desire."

"I think that in no world could that be true."

Her face softened.

He reached out slowly and touched her cheek, stretching a fingertip to draw a careful line beneath one eye. "How do you control it? The monster within?"

The loss of his humanity loomed—the price of sacrifice.

She smiled and lightly touched his finger with hers. "I think of those I love. And I ask myself, what do I want for them?"

He looked at her and saw her already fighting her need to go to Aros. To turn herself in. To sacrifice herself for the people of Tehrasi. He saw the quiet acceptance of her own fate.

He had been weak when he had not struck the emperor down before his powers had been taken. He had been weak when he had succumbed to Nin's song. He had been weak when he had not fought against his mother.

Love was weakness.

He looked at her.

But he had been strong to believe in the emperor. He had been strong to give himself to Nin's quest. He had been strong when ....

He drew his finger along her skin.

Love was strength.

To Nin, love was sacrifice.

He let his fingers drop. Let his nails bite into his palms. He would not let her sacrifice herself. He would make a deal and let Darkness claim its prize from him.

"Should we rest for tomorrow?" Taline asked from the tree line, tense gaze moving from Nin to Kaveh, then to where Valeran was walking back to rejoin them, lifelessness in his gaze.

Kaveh watched Nin as she tended to everyone, her soft smile hiding sadness beneath.

Perhaps he could swap his humanity for something else—perhaps he could get Darkness to take part of his life instead—shortening it to a few years.

He could live with that. He could live with that as long as he killed Aros. As long as he freed Nin from the empire's grasp.

He would regain his powers, then he would unleash and save that which he could not let go.

He waited for the others to slip into sleep. He curled Ifret around Nin's wrist. He waited for the breaths before moonset, then he stepped into the darkness.

CHAPTER FOURTEEN

DARK CHOICES

KAVEH

(The Land of Darkness)

Shadows receded as the half-moon clung to its last perch in the sky. Darkness rippled over the grove he had chosen—far enough from camp to keep those there unaware, but near enough to travel quickly by foot before his opportunity disappeared.

He was unable to wield regular power anymore, but oaths and bindings were a different type of magic. They tied the life-force of a being to a promise made. They could touch his magic locked inside.

With his blood, he drew the forbidden glyph of Darkness upon a rock. It was a forbidden glyph for good reason—it would rip apart any who drew it incorrectly.

Kaveh had never feared death. He had never had reason to. He went to each battlefield as a mythic figure and monster. He was the terror in the night.

He was the terror that regular people experienced, but he was but a branch on the tree. Few had experienced Darkness at its root.

Kaveh breathed deeply and finished the glyph, internally repeating the desire of his mind. The last drop of blood curled.

Darkness started as an absence—an absence of light and emotion. It started as the feeling of being sucked into a vortex of nothingness—of existence without meaning or comprehension. It was a hunger for all the things it lacked—knowledge of everything absent within it.

It connected to the place within him that was the birthplace of such things. He felt the connection of his past, the reality of his present, and the question of his future.

Darkness formed from a swirl of nothing into a great whorl of shadow and decay. Fungi and lorasis grew to full, vibrant life and wilted to curled, broken death. Life and decay burst repeatedly in endless cycles as insects were born and desiccated. The shadow spread and grew—an ever living and dying thing that was both separate from the natural order and an integral part of it.

A paradox of its own making.

Darkness pulsed. "The mostly human child." Its voice was that of broken branches pulled across stone. "The child without power to claim any more—an empty vessel of human flesh. You call me here with an offer of sacrifice, here upon the moon's most potent fade."

"I offer a sacrifice of my own for the reinstatement of those powers you see empty."

"What does a child of Darkness know of sacrifice?"

"Life and destiny, both of which are thought to be long in your shadow."

It was one of the things his father had always said about Irsula—that she would outlive the emperor by entire lifetimes—that trapping her within a cage was a mere blink to a being who would see the rise and fall of civilizations far beyond understanding or reach.

It was the rationale used by his father, to convince Kaveh that it wasn't a cruelty to trap her, for it was only a blink in time for her. Kaveh understood differently now.

Darkness pulsed. "I am immortal and those of my making live the span I deem worthy."

Kaveh understood why the emperor had caged her. Irsula had shown without a doubt that she would kill him if she were free. Kaveh understood self-preservation—he had seen it in every face he had choked free of life. He had put detection spells on his food, and he had shadows check constantly in the night, knowing that there were still things that could kill him.

It was automatic to life to try to guard it.

That the emperor had created the circumstances so that Irsula wanted to kill him...was something that could have been avoided. The emperor's need to see what he could create had ridden over all else—including Irsula's say in the matter.

It was a strange thing to contemplate as the child in the matter. If the emperor had not done so, Kaveh would not be here—but he did not think that the world would be worse without him. His fingers curled.

It was one of the reasons he was here. He could give back, for once. He could be like Nin. Be worthy of her. Love was sacrifice. Nin believed it to be so, and he believed in Nin. He could sacrifice some of himself and his remaining existence to save all that was important to her.

And—to all that was important to his father. He could honor his legacy, tarnished as it might currently be in the landscape of Kaveh's changing understanding. The notions that the emperor had sought were not without merit—the goals of the empire that he had created remained something worthy of safeguarding.

He looked at Darkness. "You are immortal, but I have life and perception within me to give."

"Perception?" Darkness pulsed and Kaveh nodded.

And this was something Irsula had given to him, this understanding. For Darkness had not rescued her. Not from Sher Fehl's manipulations to overcome and impregnate her. Not from the resulting cage she had been placed within. Darkness had been too curious about the experiments. Darkness had created Irsula from its own experiment into human life and humanity.

Its curiosity is insatiable.

Darkness crafts deals with those it seeks for answers.

"Are you not curious, what might happen to a being of your line, a mix of your line with human seed twice over—what might happen to it if you remove some of its life?"

He could see curiosity spike within the swirling mass. It was in the way that the swirls grew tighter, as if more interested and excited. It was how the shadows themselves showed their urgency and excitement.

He knew this monster.

His shoulders relaxed. He knew this foe. He would win this fight.

"Why would you bargain with your life, quarter spawn?" The branches scratched. "There are so many other things to bargain with."

He thought of the other things he could bargain with—lives that were not his. Two full moons ago, his answer might have been different.

"My lifespan and magic are what set me apart from others. Are those not the things you wish to test?"

Darkness pulsed and swirled, and cut branch pulled across stone. "There are many things I wish to test and see. Rend and rent. I will bury a hole inside your humanity. I will know how it works."

Kaveh braced himself. "It will be yours then, to understand."

"You would so easily give up that which you hold in your heart?" It swirled.

Unease crawled down his spine at the wording. "I will give my lifeblood."

It shifted in irritation—like shadows denied their prey. "Why do you seek the return of your power, quarter spawn? For revenge?"

"For revenge, and to protect."

It swirled faster, more eagerly—darkness scraping branches in urgency. "Yes. This. Humanity. Even the half-spawn has it, though in single quantity. You are human. You love." It pulsed with curiosity, hungry. "What is this emotion that drives humans to make bargains?"

"The same thing that drives all creatures."

"All others have been lackluster." Dissatisfaction grew in bristling, stringent tones. "Perhaps they have been too simple, the other creatures I've joined with and created. The creatures I've made, lack this, this heart thorn. I was unable to replicate that until Irsula... There is some of it within her, but more within you. She separated that piece of her. You have yours just burgeoning within. The light of it is growing. And I am hungry for it."

Unease grew.

Darkness swirled. "I want to know this emotion. And I will have it from your heart. I will know it from your pain and loss—you who are connected to me by shadows and threads. I will feel this emotion as I take your love."

Kaveh's stomach turned—but he stopped its upheaval and emptying in time, grown used to the feeling of imminence. "What?"

"The bargain. Your powers for the girl's soul—the human who burgeons within your heart. I will take it and consume it and understand what you feel. I will know this thing called love, finally, from the quarter spawn I helped create."

"No." Repulsion rose within him. "I decline this bargain."

But Darkness pulsed hungrily. "I will know. I will know, finally, what it is to feel love, to feel hunger not just for blood, but for soul. As I return your powers, I will consume her. As we become one in order for the pact to complete, I will eat her and digest her until I understand."

Kaveh's stomach-turning became a plunged weight so heavy that he stumbled with it. Everything pulled him down toward the earth.

He fell to his knees. Emotion overcame him to such an extent that he could only stare forward.

It was like looking into a reflection that was entirely backward. This was how he had seen all others in the past, kneeling or prostrate before him on a battlefield, frozen with... Was this...horror that he was feeling? Terror so heavy and oppressive that it made him want to deny the very existence of reality?

Hubris.

Here again, his undoing. He had thought...he had been so certain... When Irsula had said Darkness would seek his humanity, he had thought that would be something he was willing to pay. He hadn't understood what humanity meant. That it meant Nin. His fingers curled into his palm.

Irsula had been right. Kaveh was unable to pay the sacrifice. He would never pay with Nin.

"I decline this bargain." Never would he accept. He was too...human to pay.

Darkness pulsed. "I will know and rend this love."

Kaveh stared within the pulsing mass, pulling all the parameters of the glyph to the forefront of his mind. "You will not. Not from me." He looked at his hands and nodded sharply. "I will live without my power. I will keep my heart instead."

He would keep the weakness of his humanity, for in it was a different kind of strength. He would be without power, but powered elsewise all the same. He would find another way.

Darkness laughed.

Kaveh started carving into the rock the symbol to banish Darkness, but Darkness swept it away like ash, bitterly clumped and corrupted by rain before torrential winds forced its dispersal.

Kaveh's breath caught in his chest, but he made himself show no fear. He understood predator and prey. "I decline."

"I don't need your permission, human. The bargain was formed by you calling me here."

Terror.

Kaveh knew grief. He knew panic. He knew pain. And now he knew terror.

Preservation focused into a narrow line. Like a battle being drawn moments before action, he focused on the key areas he had to obliterate first. "You may not need my permission, but you need my blood, freely given, to take my body as you've specified in your desires."

Darkness paused and Kaveh felt grim pleasure.

"You cannot form a specific bargain without my blood, for it is partly yours as well. You are constrained, Darkness. You cannot envelop me and feel without my consent of it."

"I was promised blood and sacrifice with this glyph," Darkness hissed. "And both I shall take."

"I don't consent to the ritual. This bargain is declined."

"Stupid human, I don't need consent. You called me here. It is your choice if you do not want your powers restored for a simple blood sacrifice."

"You aren't asking for a simple blood sacrifice." Kaveh could sacrifice any one of Nera's children right this moment and not lose sleep. "You are asking for a specific one."

"I will have this, quarter spawn." Darkness dove.

Kaveh sliced his finger. "You will not." He drew one line of Darkness's glyph upon his palm. It halted in its dive.

Hubris, yes—Kaveh had entered into a situation where he had been sure he would succeed, but Kaveh hadn't done so stupidly. He had studied Darkness's glyph. He knew what the different parts meant.

It laughed, high and eerie, low and horrible. Seething dark spokes struck outward and attached to the blood on his palm. Darkness wrapped shadows around him, flaying at skin and flesh.

"I will tear all from you, if you don't stop this defiance, quarter spawn."

"You will not have her." Kaveh mentally pressed against the blood glyph, holding it in place.

"I will know a heart. I will know this thing."

It began to pull him along. It was all he could do to hold the glyph in place as it dragged him in retracing steps...back to the campfire. Darkness wanted its curiosity satisfied. Needed it.

And Darkness was not quiet as it let out a roar worse than any thunder, pitched higher than any shrieking coriolen.

The others sprung from their blankets with the panicked reaction of those used to light sleep and quick retreat. Ifret rose, wide-eyed with a hiss caught in the shadow's throat.

Darkness headed straight for Nin.

Grief. Panic. Pain.

Kaveh sliced his knife, blood pouring as he carved Darkness's symbol into his flesh over the glyph drawn in blood. The monster halted in its dive—straining against invisible bonds like a fish against an invisible line.

Kaveh wrapped his fingers around the dark lines connected to his mangled palm.

"Spawn!" Darkness whirled. "What do you think you do?"

"You will not! Your bargain is with me! You will fulfill the terms." New terms, terms embedded now within Kaveh.

"I will have my sacrifice!"

"You will not have her!" His flesh rent and his skin flayed, but Kaveh stayed upright with his fingers pressed upon the straining glyph carved into his palm. "You will not have her. This will not be your sacrifice."

Darkness twitched. "Stupid human, I do not want sixty years of life from y—"

"You will not have her." Kaveh held tightly to the glyph. Ifret slithered over the ground and up his body. She wrapped around his waist, eyes more serious than he had ever seen as she looked between Darkness and Kaveh. "As holder of the oath, I swear upon it. You can't touch her."

Darkness pulsed in fury. It looked down at Ifret, fury growing worse, then abruptly settling.

"No?" Darkness looked at Nin, its dozen shadowed eyes hungry and furious, then slid to the others. Darkness laughed. Curiosity whirled once more, more terrifying than before. "No. But my hunger can still be satisfied."

Kaveh held firm even as terror edged again.

"I have not to consume her to consume your response." Darkness clasped onto Kaveh's palm.

Ifret reared back.

"Fehl, what is this?" Valeran asked, hands aflame and half his face beyond firelight. "What is this you have brought upon us?"

But Kaveh didn't have time for Valeran, nor Taline, and he couldn't spare a thought or look in their direction, though he could feel Darkness swat against their incoming magic, as a human would an insect. Kaveh pulled and strained as Darkness stalked Nin. "Your deal is with me."

And Nin...Nin stood firm, watching Darkness jerk toward her with one wrench of Kaveh's body at a time. "Kaveh?"

A garbled sound burbled up his throat because he could see it in her—that she was assessing whether she needed to make this her end. For him.

"No." Kaveh pulled at the entity attached to his palm. "Your deal is with me."

Darkness pulsed. "My deal is with you. Oh, yes, spawn of spawn, with your stink of humanity. It is through you that I will know love, I will know loss, I will see the depths of this despair." It stretched its fingers toward Nin.

"You cannot have her."

"Foolish human." Darkness gripped the air around Nin, and Nin stood still, waiting. "The webs you make are far more than just between two. And this one you love has far more upon her." Darkness stroked the air around Nin as useless spells flew around them cast by Taline and Rone. "Webs and webs of undying promises. Wrenching webs that I will yank and strain and tear." Darkness pulled Kaveh forward another step. "And through you, I will know her pain and yours."

Confusion took him but did not stop him from yanking backward, holding Darkness.

"You will not have her."

"No." Darkness...smiled. An evil curving of shadow. "I will have the other with the cord so fat."

And finally, finally panic and terror lit Nin's eyes. Her horrified gaze traveled to Taline. "No," she whispered.

"I will take the other, and I will envelop you when I do, human. You have been touched by the quarter spawn. There are threads of shadow upon you. They cling to you."

The cloak. His throat closed. Nin had put his cloak back on after the spring.

"You love even more. I will know your pain and his."

"No," Kaveh said.

"Oh, yes. By the oath, I cannot consume and digest her, but I can know her pain, as I can know yours. And I can eat of another all I want. A sacrifice of and from the caster."

And Kaveh could not verbalize the wrongness of any of it. For Taline was special to Nin—as Darkness had identified. And that meant she was special to Kaveh. For part of Nin's very being was in the bonds she effortlessly formed.

And Taline...she had helped him when she had not needed to. Even struck by scepter sickness, she had made certain to fight alongside him when he was without power. He had seen her scars that had been deeply embedded by a Fehl. He had watched the pain lighten on her face when she had emerged without them. Had seen her smile freely at camp.

Taline was innocent. Like Akel, like Teir, like a thousand faces he had never given heed to. Innocent.

He knew grief. He knew panic. He knew pain. He knew terror. All emotions he had never experienced before Nin. It was terrifying to care.

It was terrifying to love.

Darkness smiled eagerly—shadows stretching around him and reaching for Nin. "Yes. This is the thing, the emotion, I need to know. You are distressed. You stink of animal fear. You care about the girl's feelings, about how she will react to losing these others. Especially the other girl who shares strong ties. I will consume her while they are attached. I will know. And I will not need you to allow it. I have the bargain. Sacrifice. I do not need your sacrifice; I can get it through hers. A death sacrifice."

Darkness struck outward toward Taline.

Taline, Nin's sister, who bled for her, who looked upon Nin with an expression as fierce as Kaveh's own. Who Nin loved. Who had just been renewed by the spring. Darkness was going to take her. Darkness was going to take her because Kaveh had lost his powers and tried to get them back. And that action would be at the expense of someone else.

His actions had consequence to others. Consequences he had never cared about before. Like Irsula and Darkness before her, he had not cared what he wrought—only that it satisfied his, or the emperor's, goals.

He had not cared until he had been attached emotionally to the girl who had sparked his curiosity. Thrice damned curiosity—Darkness's curse. Not until he had felt Nin's emotions, and consumed her as his own, had he understood. And he would be damned if he felt kinship with Darkness at this moment, but he understood.

Nin formed a ripgate—way past caring about being found—and Darkness ripped it from her, continuing its dive toward Taline. Valeran leaped in front and was violently cast to the side.

Nin sprung after it, trying to catch it in another ripgate, then another—for Nin would never let her sister be sacrificed. Kaveh pulled at Darkness's leash as he watched Darkness dodge, break another ripgate, then dodge again. Long years of warfare and training narrowed Kaveh's vision. Strikes became pre-designed. Movements settled into pattern. He could see where Darkness would shift next. He could feel it in his soul, in the place where Darkness lay within. Where it had always bred and spawn and grown inside of him.

He knew this darkness. It had always been with him. And it would always be with him.

What he chose to do with it...

Nin formed another ripgate and Darkness dodged and shattered it. Shattered it like Kaveh had always shattered his opponents.

He thought of his own hubris, still such a vital component to his very core, even after everything.

He thought of the boy—Akel—and his sacrifice, his belief. He thought of the man in the village—Ishum—and his words. He thought of Teir and his desire to protect his people. He thought of Nin...

He thought of her face in the moonlight. "I think of those I love. And I ask myself, what do I want for them?"

Moisture slid to the edge of his eye, curling around and hanging, before slipping down his cheek. He touched the drop with his unbloodied hand.

He looked at her sister and death flinging its way toward her.

What did he want for Nin?

He felt the way the cords attached to Darkness flexed and he saw where Nin's last ripgate formed and knew where Darkness would shift to avoid and extinguish it.

Kaveh dove between them and flung the blood from one palm, curling the tear into his other. Ifret brushed against his curling palm, sticking her nose in the water drop, then wailing with pained noise. But he couldn't take his eyes away from Darkness as his blood splattered on its eldritch wings.

"A death sacrifice. Made of love. I accept."

CHAPTER FIFTEEN

WHEN ALL IS LOST WITHIN

RONE

(The Land of Darkness)

Rone reached—a bloodied hand extended, a bloodied power that could do nothing against this foe. His power simply slipped through it and became nothing—like all that Rone was. Thrown to the side, he would never reach Taline in time. And this was not a foe that could be fought, even by moving it somewhere else as Ninli was attempting. Darkness was...not human. It was a force and magic all its own. It was a curiosity wrapped within a desire for bloodshed and destruction.

Rone ran for Taline, anyway, arms outstretched and every bit of terrifying magic within his palms. Darkness had nothing for him to attach his power to, but he had to try. Darkness dodged Ninli's ripgate—and Rone's power hit Taline instead. Frozen in terror, Taline's magic stuttered and disappeared completely beneath his hand. Rone tried to pull his magic back as he stumbled, but it was too late—too Sehk-Ra-be-dammed late—and he had done more damage in his own panicked, excruciating cast than if he had done nothing. And Darkness was diving, eldritch fingers outstretched, and there was nothing left to protect her with. Nothing to limit whatever that thing was going to do—monster teeth of darkness outlined by horrid, piercing light.

She was going to die without a single protection—for he had just stripped them from her. She was looking at her hands in terror and disbelief—power stripped.

Rone was going to lose her. He had always known he would lose her, but, Sehk, not to death. He was going to lose her, and he had done worse to her in her last moments than anything else could. He put all his power into his feet.

Ninli's ripgate shattered and Darkness dodged, but Darkness was too close and Ninli wasn't going to be able to make another—and this was it, and Rone wasn't going to make it in time. He wasn't going to make it.

Sehk, no.

Then something else was suddenly in front of Taline.

"A death sacrifice." Blood arced from the Shadow Prince's palm. "Made of love. I accept."

Darkness screamed and Rone's inner ears shattered. He was blown back and his body snapped against the trunk of a tree. Darkness dove at the Shadow Prince's heart with single-minded fury to rip him asunder.

Standing in front of Taline, the Shadow Prince was dripping with blood, and Rone was simply reaching out. Rone's chest felt strange. Tight. Uncomfortable. Disbelieving.

He clasped to the feeling of crushing relief that Taline was to be spared, but a staggering, patent disbelief overtook all else, because the Shadow Prince had stepped in front of her to sacrifice himself.

Rone was going to watch the Shadow Prince die—for the Shadow Prince had no power. No shadows, no magic, nothing but his body as a shield in front of a woman he barely knew.

The Shadow Prince was in front of Taline, and Rone was simply reaching out.

Kaveh ul Fehl, massive and unkillable, the horror that haunted the night, was going to die a man without power—ripped apart by the Darkness that had created him. The end of Kaveh ul Fehl.

Darkness dove and the dark shadow creature that always accompanied the Shadow Prince launched itself upward, maw open. Its mouth widened strangely, horribly cracking and chasm-wide. It launched itself and a water drop like dew dripped from one eye as it became the dawn, enveloping the night—enveloping the night and eating Darkness.

Darkness exploded, and the shadow along with it. A thousand shards of night rained down upon them.

Rone's outstretched, useless hand dropped. Sehk, what...?

Then Darkness reformed and Rone scrambled forward, hand out once more. Never again, never again.

But before he could reach the girls, Darkness pulsed—sending Rone flying backward again—then it screamed, shattering bones, and soared furiously into the forest.

Rone pushed heavily to his knees—world tilting around him, sound a strange thumping, broken beat. Leaves were falling, rising, swirling in the absence left behind.

The campsite was a mess. Greenery, debris, and belonging were strewn everywhere. Only Fehl remained upright, protected by his familiar's sacrifice.

Panting on his knees, Rone stared disbelievingly at Kaveh ul Fehl, who was kneeling and gathering the pieces of his fallen familiar—staring blankly at the place where it had exploded into a thousand shadows.

Rone looked away from Fehl's face—for it held an expression that Rone was uncomfortable with. An expression that did not belong to a monster.

Fehl gathered the pieces with shaking hands. The girls rose, helping each other stand. Hurt, but whole, undamaged. Alive.

"You saved her." Rone stared at Kaveh ul Fehl, who was staring at the shadowed remnants curled and bleeding out darkness in his hands. Rone's words were garbled by the bleeding of his ears and his broken jaw.

Rone wrenched a healing spell sloppily over his skull, only caring to fix enough so that he could know, so that he could understand. "You saved her," he repeated, blood still thick in his mouth.

"She's gone." Fehl's fingers pulled at the embers of shadow, slipping away into the wind, even now. "And I didn't even... Why...? Why did she—?"

"Taline. You saved Taline. You stepped in front of her."

But Kaveh ul Fehl stared silently down at the remnants of his shadow demon.

"Why? Why did you save her?" Rone pushed to his feet, stumbling forward to force Fehl's head up with his hands so that the former Shadow Prince was looking directly up at him. "Why did you save Taline?"

"She was innocent." Kaveh's gaze was almost childlike in the way he said it—like this was a recent realization for him—that the innocent needed saving, or perhaps, weren't acceptable collateral damage.

"You could have had your powers back. Darkness agreed." Terror rolled through Rone again at the memory of Darkness and its words. "You had to have made that bargain for your powers to be restored."

"I did. I offered myself—my life-force."

Rone shook him, fingers clasped around his skull. The Shadow Prince allowed it, drained of everything, staring at him mutely.

"You could have had your powers returned."

Bleakness filled the other's dark eyes. "It wanted Nin."

Rone shook him—he seemed unable to do anything else. "But you said no."

"Yes. It wanted to know... It wanted to know... I said no. I used the one power I had in the invocation—to save Nin. Then it chose Taline as its target instead."

"Why?" He hadn't meant to ask that. He didn't care why Darkness had chosen, only that it was thwarted, and yet, something in his half-brother's expression was familiar, a reflection of—

"It could still get what it wanted from her death."

"Why not let it? You don't need Taline alive to accomplish anything. You don't need her alive to get your revenge."

Kaveh ul Fehl's gaze was remote and unfocused. "No. But she... Nin loves her. And she is innocent. Taline ul Summora is...a good person. I would see her live. She will not be a sacrifice. I will not regain my power through the loss of her." Kaveh ul Fehl's gaze sharpened on something distant within his mind. "I will go out as I am, and I will have chosen well."

Rone gripped the Shadow Prince's head and a sound so animalistic that he could not identify it emerged from his own throat.

The Shadow Prince's gaze focused on Rone then, reacting to the animal sound—sharpening and narrowing on it.

"I hate you," Rone whispered. "I wish you were dead."

He wished he had never crossed paths with the Shadow Prince. Wished he had never crossed paths with the Summoras. Wished that he had never been ungodly born.

"Soon you will have your wish." The Shadow Prince's voice was weary. "Let me go, Valeran. I know they are alive, but I need to make sure they—"

"I hate you," Rone said, gripping tightly.

He hated this man who had been born of hatred and Darkness, and had become something more. Who had made a deal with Darkness, then given himself to it instead of the one he loved—or a love of his love, even more self-sacrificial. He hated this man who embodied everything Rone had been unwilling to grab. The man who had protected that which Rone loved.

"Yes," Fehl said. "I'm neither fond of y—"

Rone shook him again, still by the head, jarring all the stupid bits inside. He hated this man who could destroy the threat to his beloved one if he just had his powers back. Who had been trying to do so repeatedly for his own gains at the beginning of this ungodly journey, but who was now doing it for others. A metamorphosis—and like the ocean tides changing, the moment of the convergence from flowing in to flowing out, the end of one and the beginning of the new—Rone had pushed violently against believing it.

But it was there. And it was undeniable. And there was only one person who could reward the choices Kaveh ul Fehl had made.

Rone shut his eyes. The end of all.

But Taline was alive. And in the end...could he claim anything unselfish in himself for not making his own sacrifice?

The air pulsed around them and Aros ul Fehl appeared—suddenly and unwanted, a new and old threat wrapped into a space that had just existed in Darkness—called to the clearing by Ninli's ripgates.

A smirking smile pulled across Aros's mouth. "What a pleasant sc—"

"No," Rone said without inflection.

It was simply another reason in an endless line of them. Rone harshly pressed the Shadow Prince's head between his palms and he let his magic out—released the raging torrent from where it had been bound and chained for years.

Aros's smile dropped. "No!"

But Aros had no time to stop him—not when Rone had already committed to his sacrifice. Rone's magic burst free and wrapped around the man he held, rushing through him and burrowing beneath his skin, beneath the blood of his cheeks, down beneath his organs, in to his brain and the cold lock that was there, holding all the rest in place.

Rone knew how to use this accursed power—it was like knowing how to breathe—the knowledge encoded into his cells. He fit the key into the lock and let it explode.

In the timeless moment, all he could see was the deep brown of the Shadow Prince's gaze attached to his as everything burst free, shadows pouring from Kaveh ul Fehl and reaching out, pulling all the fleeing darkness toward them like a hole freed of light.

And all the darkness that was gathering swarmed over the Shadow Prince, winding around him—and around Rone, who still held the Shadow Prince's face in his palms.

As the last of it pulled, Rone could bear it no more, and he wrenched his hands free, breathing hard. Shadows swirled from every direction. They converged on the Shadow Prince and crowned him true again as he rose.

Aros's hand stretched toward Ninli, and she jerked backward as the tip of the scepter grazed her chest and a strange light lit, but Kaveh's shadows were already diving. With only two moments of breath from the freed lock, they were moving as extensions of his will, as if he had never lost them.

Aros scrambled backward in outright terror and fell through a hole in the ground a mere moment before the shadows hit. The shadows hit the ground, then soared upward and screamed.

The Shadow Prince pulsed. The disbelief in his gaze as he stared at Rone did nothing to hide avarice and relief as he sucked shadow greedily into all his pores—like a desiccated sponge given new liquid life.

Fehl's gaze remained locked on his. "You have the emperor's gift."

Rone kept his gaze locked as well. He could not bear to look elsewhere. He knew what Taline's terror meant. He had always known what lay at the end of this path.

"Gift." Rone laughed without humor. "I can take magic. I can lock it away. Or use it—like a night hag steals breath."

"He didn't know."

Rone's smile slashed his face. "Never."

Fehl's head tilted, shadows swirling around, power filling him like the colossus he had always been. There was no worry about Aros returning. Not at the moment, not here. Rone had not needed Ninli's soft prodding to understand the power vacuum. There was a reason Aros had made sure the Shadow Prince was powerless before he had made his move. It was the same reason why Rone had felt no desire to return Fehl's powers.

"The emperor would have taken you," Fehl said. "Scooped you into his blessed ranks. Raised you above all." Shadows shot from the underbrush to coil at his cloak hem and around his familiar's remnants. "You could have become his favorite."

Rone's smile grew tighter. "It was a lovely joke—to watch the hordes compete."

Fehl observed him silently for long moments, then he looked at the broken shadows where his companion had fallen, carefully gathering the pieces in a living, shadowed cage that easily came to his command. "Irsula knew your power."

Rone wondered what Fehl was doing—and what part of a connection was being made in his animal mind. "Yes. She almost killed me for it." He had felt her desire to do it. She hadn't been without reason, with what the emperor's power had done to her. "I do not know why she spared me."

Fehl's fingers drifted through broken shadow—as if he could piece together his companion—or piece together his own troubled thoughts. "I begin to."

Fehl looked up, gaze fierce. "Why? Why did you unlock my power now?"

Rone did not want to think about Taline's reaction and what he would see when he finally looked at her. So he thought about Ninli's understanding face instead and the calm acceptance she always wore. "Ninli will sacrifice herself for that stupid ritual. Taline will follow. You are the only one who can stop Aros."

"Why now?" Why now and not before?

Rone looked down. "It was time."

"Valeran—"

He finally looked in the direction of the girls.

Ninli's expression was all things concerned but positive—encouraging, grateful, relieved. Her hand pressed strangely to her chest, and blood seeped around her fingers.

He forced himself to look at her sister. Taline's face was pale and sick. And her magic...

Self-loathing and horror crashed. He had locked her magic. He reached out and snapped free his mistake—the mistake he had made when he had tried to hit Darkness. Her eyes blew wider and he stumbled backward.

Rone shuddered. He had to get away. "I will leave at sunrise."

"You—"

Rone stumbled toward his things. "I will be gone as soon as I know you are—"

"You stupid man." Taline staggered forward.

He reached for her, then flinched away. He held his ground though, held still as she drew closer. He deserved her retribution. He welcomed it.

"You stupid, stupid man." She put her hand on his forearm.

Perhaps she would break it. Perhaps she would inflict a pain curse in his blood. He wouldn't even heal it later, if so.

Her hand stroked upward slowly, up his arm, over his shoulder, and curled around his neck—gently, as one would approach a wounded animal. She pulled his cheek to lay against hers. "I'm sorry."

His mind went blank and spotted. He couldn't remember how to breathe.

"I'm so sorry," she whispered.

A strangled sound—between a laugh and a sob—blew from his mouth across her neck, and he tried to catch a breath. "You—"

"I am careless with my words, Rone." She held his cheek to hers, her mouth moving along his ear. "I am quick to judgment. I am defensive. I have years of damage that I will be working to overcome forevermore. But I feel regret and I feel friendship deeply and I feel love, and once someone is mine, they are mine forevermore. And I will work to never hurt that person again. I didn't know," she finished on a whisper. "I didn't guess, and I should have."

"I never wanted this."

"I know." She stroked his neck, letting him gather himself against her, letting the spots resolve into visuals that made sense without forcing him to meet her eyes. "You think your powers make you abominable. You made that clear weeks ago, even if you didn't say why. My words and fear made you believe it more."

"You—I am... You should be scared. I can make you powerless. I did."

She stroked his neck again. "Yes. You meant to hit Darkness. But you can make me powerless in ways that have nothing to do with magic."

He stilled against her.

He didn't... He couldn't believe. He—

Taline tucked her head into his nape, resting on his shoulder.

He rested his head slowly and carefully on hers and gave a shudder. He put his arms carefully around her. It felt dangerous, illicit, and yet—

"That's it? That was your big secret?" she said against his neck, voice light.

"You wound me." He forced the drawl into his voice. But his shoulders relaxed, and he wrapped his arms more firmly.

And, for once, he let himself believe.

KAVEH

Shadows swirled around him, regaining their spots, welcoming him back to the fold, brushing against his skin. Nin fell to her knees in front of him.

Taline was stroking Valeran as if he were a wild animal while calling him stupid and repeating how sorry she was, but he couldn't concentrate on them.

He had almost lost Nin.

He had lost Ifret.

He stared at the place where Ifret had died. To look at the wisps where Ifret had been. He clutched the shadow cage to his stomach.

He had been so stupid.

His fingers curled into the cage. He had felt her as she had lunged, as tear had dripped from her, too. He had felt her magic as she had taken Kaveh's bargain upon herself, fulfilling the terms. Nin had sidestepped the question of how similar Irsula and Ifret felt. He had been so stupid.

Ifret had been part of Irsula.

Ifret...had been a piece of Irsula.

Ifret, who had always been with him—who the emperor had always looked at with consideration and caution. A slim shadow containing little power at first and too much rage, but one who had grown and become more powerful alongside him. And at five, the total eclipse that happened during the fifth month of his fifth year had increased the power they both had, and it had cemented them to each other.

Ifret, who was made from Irsula.

Did that mean Irsula actually cared for him? In the measure of humanity, no—or very little. But in the language of Darkness...

Irsula had given him a piece of herself—carved it from her flesh. She had sent a part of herself, and that part had grown into shadow. Perhaps it had been out of curiosity, initially, or a desire to see whether she could free herself by putting a piece of herself outside the cage, but Ifret had stayed with him. The shadow had grown alongside him. Ifret had become Kaveh's.

Ifret had become the dominating maternal figure in Kaveh's life—vicious and protective.

Nin knelt in front of him.

"Ifret..." He couldn't finish. Nin's hand wrapped around his. "You knew—you knew what she was, didn't you?" He stared at Nin's hand wrapped with his, around the cage. "That she was a part of my mother?"

"A part she broke off and sent with you," Nin said quietly. "Yes."

"How did you know?" How had Kaveh never guessed? Irsula had never even given a hint, not that she ever had much to say to him.

Nin looked at the wisps of dissipating shadow, the embers of dark fire. "I recognized the maternal spark of a mother who didn't know how to show maternal warmth, one who wasn't inherently connected to that type of humanity but was still...interested." She squeezed his hand. "And when I healed her, I could feel it. Ifret felt like you, but different. The way people with the same roots do."

"She warned you not to tell." He remembered the coded glances between them. He had just thought them something else.

"She did. We made an accord." She tilted her head forward so their brows rested against each other. "Are you unhappy with me?"

"No." He understood accords. He understood promises made. "That you keep your promises matters to me. Even if those promises are to others."

She wrapped her hand around his. "I will keep my promises to you."

"I know." He touched the top of her hand, wrapped around his. "I know you will," he said, voice gone strange.

Kaveh looked at where Ifret should have curled, and he thought of the reasons Irsula might have spared Valeran when he had entered her den. All of them were disquieting. Earthshaking, if he let himself dwell upon it.

But Irsula was only half-human and to attribute fully human characteristics would be a mistake. To attribute "sometimes" characteristics would be far more fruitful. Whimsy, perhaps. Curiosity. A desire to understand humanity, like Darkness did.

The knowledge settled quickly. Deep down, perhaps he had known all along. The corporeal shadow had been snappish and disdainful when he had been young. But she had taught him how to harness the shadows, she had eaten all who would do him harm, and eventually she had turned into a bloodthirsty companion who wouldn't be moved from his side.

"Come, let us gather the rest of her remains and move them to a container that can be transported separately from your shadows."

A container that did not rely on Kaveh's magic. For his power was fallible. Kaveh looked at Valeran—a man who could take his powers again if he was not careful.

Nin unstoppered a wide bottle and Kaveh carefully moved the embers of shadow inside.

Nin capped the bottle but didn't look away from it. "Why—?" She shook her head. "No, I know why you stepped in front of Taline. You said it as you did it. I just—"

He had almost lost Nin.

He touched the unshed tears at the edges of her blood-red eyes. The remnants of the bond pulled, as if tightening its grip—the underpinnings of the bond kept viciously intact by both of them despite the spring. They had accepted the bond into themselves. Nin had accepted Kaveh into herself. He looked upon her, at her eyes, her compassion, her magic, her ingenuity, her hands, her heart—everything that made up the most glorious of creations. Nin.

Something that had been gathering in him exploded. Kaveh gathered her face in his hands, fingers stroking her cheeks, and pulled her mouth against his. His mouth touched hers and it was the feel of regaining his power all over again—overwhelming, magnificent, fierce. Touching her was consumption and excess—better than eating the most decadent figstee after tasting years of nothing but bland bread.

Shadows swirled around them. Nin pressed into him as hard as he tugged, fingernails digging into the skin at the back of his neck, mouth moving with his. A stroke, then another, and the kiss gentled until they were merely breathing the same air.

He stroked her cheek and looked into her eyes, answering the question she hadn't finished asking. "You sacrifice yourself for the ones you love. Why should I not do the same?"

Nin shuddered and gripped him tighter. "Kaveh. I can't—I don't know if I can change."

"Why would you change?" he asked, mystified, stroking his thumb along her cheek. "You are perfect as you are."

A small sob escaped her. And a tear slipped over the lower bounds of her eye. "I sacrifice because I owe—"

He caught her face in both hands, rubbing the smooth skin beneath the rough pads of his fingers and tracing the tear. "But do I not owe far more than you?"

"But you—"

He tugged a lock of hair beneath the crook of one finger, bringing it to rest between finger and thumb, and rubbing it between the two while keeping her face cradled in his other hand. He couldn't bring himself to stop touching her. "It cannot be one way for you and a different way for others. If you feel that I do not need to sacrifice all to make amends, then it is the same for you."

"Kaveh—"

"No."

A strangled laugh caught her throat. "No? You do not accept?"

"I accept that you, too, have things to learn."

Her breath caught and tear-filled eyes met his.

"We will learn together," he said, as solemn oath.

She swallowed. "We will?" It was said a little brokenly.

"Yes." The feeling tugged at him again, pulling him forward as if she were true north. His lips pressed to hers and her mouth opened beneath his. Shadows swirled, starlight glittered behind his eyes, and everything was right.

He pulled back slowly, flesh not wanting to part from hers. "I can feel you again." He touched her lips, her cheeks, her hair. "And I would have accompanied you until the end of my days without magic, but Nin, I can feel you again."

She looked between his eyes and smiled in the way a person who was assured of losing something precious looked at something they desperately wanted to keep. He had seen it on countless faces of men and women at imperial negotiating tables enough to recognize it. He had derided people for the same expression—for the same hope—before.

"I will be better," he said.

Nin blinked, and her gaze softened. "You already are." She leaned forward and her lips grazed his. "I think it would be okay," she said, repeating his words from the night of the spring. "To fall in love with the same person over and again."

"Forever."

Nin drew back and the faint smile on her face was unbearably happy and horribly sad. Her hand pressed her chest. When she drew her hand away, it was sticky with blood. The mixed expression on her face—resignation, sickened relief, acceptance—was inconsistent with the amount of blood and her high healing abilities.

He grabbed her—pushing her back to sit while steadying her. "Aros hit you with the scepter?"

He touched the cut. The slice across her upper chest split the fabric and her flesh with a line of red. Vengeance and desire coiled in two tight ribbons within him—he would kill Aros, and he would dance upon his remains.

"He did." She wet her lips, tucking the bottle containing Ifret's remains into her bag. "But he fumbled the ripgate he was opening beneath me when he saw Rone was about to fix your magic."

Unease slipped through Kaveh. "Why did he slice you?"

Nin looked at Valeran and Taline, but it was as if she wasn't seeing them, looking beyond, resignation and acceptance descending. "He was shocked. He panicked. Scrambling. But he already had the spell—"

"No."

Kaveh tugged her closer and sent his shadows swarming over her. It felt like regaining limbs and senses—the feedback from all of them telling him everything about the spaces around them—and everything inside Nin.

She looked up at him, expression resigned as Kaveh found the thread, the unwanted bond already sunk deep inside her blood and magic.

Cold—all he could feel was cold. "How?" He had seen this before. He knew what this was.

Nin's gaze slid to the side. "Life-force bond. Unwillingly set. The same one that killed my family. If Aros dies, so do I. It looks like Aros learned something from Crelu ul Osni after all."

CHAPTER SIXTEEN

THE CURSE OF THE CARRES

TALINE

(The Land of Darkness)

"He put the Curse of the Carres on you?" Fehl's sudden swearing would have raised the dead, had he such power.

Taline's gaze swung away from Rone, all rising feelings of contentment turning to horror.

Fehl held Nin's face in his hands. "Tied to his life-force. Of course he did." Fehl's eyes closed and shadows pulsed everywhere.

Taline took a stumbling step forward. "Nin?"

Nin smiled at her, but her eyes were sad. "Everything is well, Tali."

Taline tracked the explosion of angry shadows and the way that a knot of them hovered over a slice in Nin's chest. Taline had thought everything was well, finally. After all, the Shadow Prince had his powers back, and Aros was terrified of that. The four of them could simply swan in and stop the Festival of Blood now.

"Tied to whose life-force?" Taline looked at Fehl, and for once, finally, there was no question in her mind about whether he would turn on them—turn on Nin. Perhaps it was time to start calling him Kaveh, like Nin had been advocating since she had taken an oath with the man.

"Aros?" Rone asked Fehl.

"It is the same spell. Unwilling participation. Blood magic. He tied her life-force to his. If he dies, so does she."

Taline pressed her hands to her stomach, everything going painfully cold inside her again. She couldn't keep having these upheavals. Her body couldn't handle it.

Rone stepped forward. "We'll undo it."

"Yes." Taline went to Nin. "The spring. You can drink of two days past. We are still in the Land of Darkness. We can go to the vill—"

Nin looked up at her, red eyes tired. "It is a bloodline curse. An old one, inactive before now, but buried deeply within. And at one time, I wanted it. I allowed it to set when my grief was too overwhelming." She looked away. "It is like the imperial oaths that I accepted as part of myself—that did not wash away. Using the Ninth Scepter pulled me to the bloodline threads as surely as using any of them did to Aros. We have been entangled together as an active bloodline, easily tied."

Rone's brows furrowed. "Using the scepters? But then Taline—"

"No. I've always made very sure not to give her my blood," Nin said severely. Taline knew Nin had feared it. Feared the way her family had been destroyed—and the household blood-tied to them with it. Sisters of heart, not blood, she had always said so adamantly about her relationship with Taline. She had always given magic so freely, but kept blood carefully withheld. "We are not blood-tied. I have made certain never to do so with anyone. All my blood ties are gone, except for the one Aros was able to reignite."

"There must be a way to sever it. Crelu ul Osni survived." Rone's eyes were narrowed. "He removed himself from the household tie. Erased himself from the magic. He has to know how to undo your tie as well."

"Oh, I know how to undo it," Nin said decisively and without humor. "That avenue is shut."

The sacrifice of Farrah. Osni had sacrificed that which he still loved. A different deal with Darkness.

"But Osni was still able to wield the ceremonial scepters."

"With Carre blood. Osni was careful never to use his own. He would have done so only on the day he could tie all the scepters to him. But the scepters have become hungrier after so long with Carre blood but not Carre magic. When Aros and I took them up—"

"You had never used a scepter before," Fehl interrupted, realization cutting his expression.

Nin looked at him, gaze distant and sad. "No."

Shadows pulsed and grew. "I did this. You used the scepter to help me. To help the empire."

Taline looked quickly at Rone, uncertain what they would do if Fehl lost control. Where normally Rone might have piled on more accusations to crush Kaveh ul Fehl, though, in this moment, he simply watched the Shadow Prince's rising fury and pain with something remote in his gaze.

Nin's hand closed around Kaveh's, pulling Taline's gaze back. "I regret none of it. If we do nothing, because we are scared, then we risk everything we believe in."

Taline stared at their hands, and something strange worked its way through her system.

"Why do you believe in…?" Me, was the end of Fehl's—Kaveh's—question. A question he didn't seem able to finish, because Nin had never stopped believing in the Shadow Prince.

It wasn't her way. Once she found a spark in someone, she pushed until it emerged. Even Rone, even Rone had been ensnared by her belief, long before he was ever ready to change.

The strange feeling working through Taline's system was…acceptance. Kaveh ul Fehl was part of their set now.

"Because I know you will be extraordinary, Kaveh. You will lead the people and they will love you."

"Nin—"

She wrapped her hands around his. "We will learn together, for as long as we have."

"You keep your promises," he demanded. "Promise me you will not die."

Her steady gaze slipped, tears forming. She smiled through them. "We move forward," Nin said simply. "Or we let go."

"No," Taline said harshly. Taline was not done fighting. She never would be.

"Let go, little sparrow?" Rone said, and Taline felt a brush of his magic against hers—tentative, but welcome. "I don't think you've ever heeded such words."

Nin smiled at him, but her fingers skimmed the cut across her chest. "It has been waiting. The bloodline curse missed me once because of whim and timing. It missed Aros because at the time he was not hooked into the family magics. Even if there was something that could be done, the festival—"

Taline cut a hand through the air angrily. "Damn the festival."

Nin looked at Taline. "You don't mean that."

She did. She did mean it. And yet, the people...their people...

Nin's eyes softened, seeing the reflected turmoil—a mirror of her own. "Tali—"

"Nin. Stopping the festival isn't like snapping your—"

"I know." Nin swallowed. "And I should have broken the binds my family held upon the soil of Tehrasi years ago—in the magic of the capital city, and the people who called it home. I used those powers instead. My blood gave me power in Tehras."

"To do good. Those powers allowed you to talk to the city and to manipulate it in small ways—to save its citizens, to rejuvenate sections that needed improvements, to connect to the spells and manipulate oaths."

"But it is the failing of power—to act swiftly for the good, but to allow the bad in as well. The festival could not have been activated if I had destroyed my bloodline ability to disconnect and reconnect oaths. Those are directly tied together in the old spells." Her fingers curled. "My own hubris. I should have broken the bonds."

Taline remained silent for long moments. It was hard to know what to say. For there was a price for everything one did or said, and sometimes that price was hard to see. "You didn't know."

"I didn't see. And I wanted—I wanted justice, but the line between justice and revenge is so thin." Nin closed her eyes and Taline wondered what shadowed memories assailed her. "And there's a point where we can't just steal or break whatever will make our problems go away."

"Nin."

Nin opened her eyes and looked at her. "The blood festival is a Carre legacy that..." She shook her head. "I will not allow to occur."

"Aros knows your feelings," Rone said grimly. "He activated the festival in order to use it against you. That, and he is a Carre by blood. He will gain great power from the festival in the lines of magic that run through Tehras."

"As will I." Nin looked at them from red, shining eyes.

"Sacrifices open on a full moon's top rise," Rone said. "Then bleed through to the set before the dark moon."

"The full moon is in six days."

"I will be with you on the temple steps to stop it." Taline's chest moved. But stopping the festival meant sacrificing Nin in some way. Either to Aros or to death. "Nin—"

"There are other ways to secure Aros that do not include death, nor require him to be conscious." Nin's gaze slid to Kaveh. "Whatever else happens, I will not allow the festival to take place. If he dies—"

"No."

"We need help," Taline said, mind working.

"I—"

"Nin. If you want to survive the end, we need help to stop the festival and to stop Aros from killing himself and taking you with him."

"I will do it myself." Shadows spread from Kaveh, pulsing. "I will stop the festival. I will cage him in shadow. And I will save you."

And finally something seemed to break through Nin's expression as she looked at Kaveh ul Fehl.

NINLI

She had known. Somewhere. Deep within her. That it had only been temporary escape. That the curse and plague of the Carres would come back to grab her. It was fitting.

Sacrifice. Death. These were fitting ends to her tale. She had gotten a life double what fate had had in store. She had long believed that each day she survived was one more than she deserved.

One more than Heba. Than Reyi. Than Farrah.

Than Lorsali.

It was a fitting end to die to the curse. A fitting end, to save Tehrasi and put the Carres to final rest, even if she did not want to see the end anymore.

Only now, here that she had found a future—with Taline, Rone, Kaveh—did she want to survive. But it was hard to see past destiny and to see hope instead.

Kaveh's shadows opened to her, to her thoughts—but this time, only to those she wanted to share. And it was in the face of a man who had felt so little for so long, that when he had opened himself up to it and embraced it fully—fully, like all that he did, and quickly, like a babe learning, with lightning regard—that she could see the consequences of her own actions and motives in another.

She looked at Kaveh and the shadows surging around him. She looked at him and saw the crown upon his head. Not a crown of sunlight or darkness, but a crown of starlight—darkness illuminated with light.

And she could do this, before the end. She could make sure that Kaveh was on that path to greatness. He would have to walk it, but she could clear that path.

"No," she repeated. "We will seek others to lend us aid. You will be the leader the people need. The one they are desperate for."

Power swirled around him like the cloak it had always been. "A strong leader decimates all things in his path."

"And a stronger leader sees how that path can be used." She touched him. "Find your allies. Seek those who will support you. Save the empire."

He grabbed her hand. "I will save you."

"You already have."

"No. You will not sacrifice. You will not give in."

"I want to stay!" They all startled at her cry. "I want to stay," she repeated in whisper.

"Nin, please."

"Please. Let the people—our people—be part of the revolution. Let them make a single choice, a choice of their own volition, and they will be yours forever."

"I can set up a thousand shadows. I can wipe any enemy from the map. I don't need—"

"Hubris," she murmured, though it was fond.

But the word stopped him. It made him pause. And she felt him settle and listen. "What then?"

"Find our allies. Save us all."

Myriad emotions crossed his face. He looked down at her hand clasped in his. "You wish me to go to Baksis," Kaveh said distantly.

"And Simin. Omari. The others who observe and wait."

"They can't influence the festival."

"No. That has to be done another way, but they can help take down Aros—they have information, knowledge, and skill—and they can influence the world after he leaves it." They could help make Kaveh's reign strong. Unified.

He nodded slowly. "And as for the festival?"

"We will seek Qara and Larit first." She looked at Taline, who nodded firmly. Rone said nothing, but then, Nin knew where he sat in this. It was a different cushion from where he had sat before, but it was just as delineated. He would follow what Taline wanted to do and what Nin advocated—but he did not believe in seeking out others any more than Kaveh did.

She gave a smile of encouragement and was relieved when it felt strong. "As well as the others in our network. If we ask for a little aid from a lot of people, we will minimize their risk. We will give them the choice to aid or to hide." Warming to the topic, she focused on the others. She was best when it was this way. "The festival will begin on the full moon's top rise, and we will stop it."

She looked at Kaveh and thought of the great leader he could be. Not just a general who people slavishly followed for glory, but one who people followed for a better future. He would not be able to kill Aros, if by doing so, it would kill her. She was going to have to do something about that.

Peace settled within her. Ever since Aros had touched her, her end had become...inevitable. The curse she had avoided, the crushing guilt of survival and continuance that she had been given was finally coming to a close. There was bitter relief in it.

"It will be well." She was assuring herself of that as much as them. "We will seek allies and be victorious."

"They will all help." Taline looked into the distance. "Like Birsa, they will give up much to help you."

Nin did not want them to give up anything. But she swallowed down the immediate argument. It wouldn't do for her to argue one way when she was arguing for Kaveh in the other. She would accept others' aid and she would keep them safe.

"If I can get into the scepter room without alerting Aros, we can make a play." Aros would know as soon as she opened the ripgate, so they would need a—

"Diversion?" Rone spun a knife in his palm.

"A large diversion. Multifaceted. And one that...perhaps plays to expectation."

Rone's eyes met hers as his knife spun. She saw the understanding there—the realization and dawning anticipation. She clung to the anticipation. She would make this work.

"Where to first?" he asked.

"Tehras." Always.

Tehras. Tehrasi. Country. Blood. Sacrifice. The sacrifice for her country versus the desire to live beyond this moon cycle.

"Six days."

She hoped she didn't have to make that choice.

CHAPTER SEVENTEEN

DAYS OF BLOOD

KAVEH

(An underground compound in Tehras, Tehrasi)

Three days later, after a string of a thousand haunted steps to a hundred different doors, they were hidden in a secret compound below the streets of Tehras. Hidden by Kaveh's shadows and Nin's knowledge of the city.

But Aros knew they were in the city. Baksis had confirmed it. Aros had long kept track of Kaveh's shadows, and he would be able to feel Nin's oath. Only lingering threats—of Kaveh and Valeran, and answers unknown—kept him from tracking them down with the scepter.

Aros would await an answer to the move he had made by cursing Nin.

They were all playing a game now. A game of days and moves, but one with a solid endpoint. Nin would never allow the festival to begin. She would interrupt it on the eve of sacrifice and Aros would assume that move.

This game of moves and allies was fraught with an uncertainty that Kaveh hated.

Nin and Taline were speaking with their Tehrasian contacts above while Kaveh and Valeran stayed below ground to wait.

It reminded Kaveh of hunting the Hand so many moons ago, but he found he disliked waiting even more strongly when someone he cared for was threatened.

Kaveh had a hundred shadows around their position, watching and keeping an active eye on what was happening in the growing sunlight above. He could see the group of women embrace. Kaveh flexed his shadows, feeling the small delay between what the shadows saw and the information he received.

Kaveh could feel the small shadows slipping into place more and more, interlocking into a tight web—it was just a web that was taking twice as long to complete as before. An unfortunately timed delay, given the circumstances they were under. "I'm not at full capacity yet, Valeran. You pulled away from the unlocking too soon."

"Well pardon me, Your Imperial Highness, for not whipping you into perfect fighting shape. You'll have to do some work now, like the rest of us."

Kaveh nodded, letting Valeran's ire slide from his skin. Valeran was skittish about his powers still—uneasy and snappish when speaking of them with Kaveh, overly patient and understanding whenever Taline questioned him about them—but the dueling emotions over his own powers were Valeran's to deal with. Kaveh was thankful he had them.

He was thankful he could touch shadow again, that he could wrap them around Nin—who even now stroked one absently as she and Taline discussed their plans with the two other women aboveground—and that he could keep her safe.

He wondered whether Omari could cleanse him of these last delays in regaining his full power. He wondered whether the spring would have fixed this leftover effort. He wondered whether this was a repentance—a chance to relearn again.

He flexed his fingers. Perhaps he would let himself learn again. Valeran was not wrong—Kaveh had not had to work at his power for a long time. When Nin had provoked some effort within him in that alley so long ago, it had been a shock.

The shadows pulled and flexed, fighting for control. He embraced the fight. It had been a strangely peaceful relief to be without the constant struggle, but he embraced the burden—it was his burden.

He needed to get that burden into fighting shape. He looked at Valeran. "Spar with me."

A single brow rose. "No."

"You are frightened?"

Valeran's mouth slashed upward. "Are you?"

Valeran could take his power again. It was there in his mocking grin. It made it all the more imperative that Kaveh conquer it. "Spar with me."

"No."

"You've never used your powers in a fight. Not fully. You are scared of them."

Valeran's smile tightened. "The parallels to the emperor would have been too obvious. I don't have the hubris that you do."

"No? I think you do, just in a different way." Kaveh examined him. "You hold it as your final roll of dice in a weighted cup that you hate. In your mind, it is a last deceit that can get you out of trouble should something go too poorly. Like Nin. And yet unlike Nin, you have never trained your ability. You despise and are frightened of part of yourself, yet you hold it as the last thing that can save you." Kaveh tilted his head. "Yet you weren't able to use it against Darkness. Because you had not trained it. How do you know that it will save you when the true end comes? How will you know the depths of the power you disdain, but count as last rite?"

"You court your own destruction." Valeran's fists were white-knuckled tight.

"I have yet to see you wield an ability that I cannot contain." Kaveh rolled his neck, releasing the tension there. "The emperor could not have beaten me, had I not been willing to be subjected to his punishment."

Valeran's teeth flashed. "More hubris?"

"Yes." Hubris was a part of him—he had won countless battles with it riding his skin. But hubris had also made defeat far more painful when it had come. Hubris was what had gotten him into this situation—into losing his powers, into nearly losing Nin.

He would find a way to make sure to know his hubris, to own it, and to make sure it never ruled him again.

He looked at Valeran. He would also make certain that Valeran's powers could not make him powerless again. "Fight me, Valeran. And claim your power."

Valeran uncoiled himself from his spot.

To Kaveh's eyes, a knife appeared in Valeran's hand from seemingly nowhere, but Kaveh's shadows told him where all the steel on the other man rested. Instruments made of metal and blade were pressed to nearly every surface of the other man, beneath clothes that appeared to hide nothing.

The knife flipped around Valeran's hand. "It is true that I still would like to slip this knife in your spine."

Anticipation wound through him. He could see it reflected in the other man.

He had sparred with Baksis and other siblings of similar age to Baksis long ago. When Kaveh had been five, he had fought many of them to test their abilities upon Awakening. Outside of tests, contact had not been encouraged. As he had grown older, the emperor had deemed such tests a waste of Kaveh's skills as well. By the time he was eight, he was on the battlefield and sparring was unnecessary when real battles commenced every day.

He hadn't sparred with anyone again until meeting Nin in the alley, when his curiosity at abilities he was not familiar with had made him interested in continuing to allow her to live and fight further.

He was not certain the alley was what normal people called sparring, but then, he had never been normal. Kaveh didn't think Valeran had ever been normal either.

Kaveh smiled sharply. "Good. Try to slip in your knife."

They circled.

Kaveh let his shadows creep out. Valeran would be a scorch mark on the ground if he failed to make a move before he was surrounded.

Valeran's hand flicked and sunlight hit in a wide arc as he moved. Kaveh's shadows dissipated. He merely called more, reforming those taken beneath the boughs of the cavern shrubbery and crevices. The shadows were merely an extension of himself. They were not alive like Ifret had been. Sentience withered the longer he did not touch the shadow, and these shadows were new. These were extensions of his own will, and he could feel Valeran move through them.

Two knives struck hardened shadow over Kaveh's chest and fell to the ground.

Valeran was already broaching another sunlight spell.

Kaveh struck it from the air. "And next, in two or three hits, you will combine the two—sunlight upon blade, pushed to my chest."

Kaveh flicked the spells from the air and watched Valeran's mouth tighten.

"You will never beat me that way, Valeran."

"If I take your magic again, I may not give it back." There was some bite of truth to his voice. Fury underlined his words.

"Then don't give it back, for I will have failed to protect."

Valeran dove and flipped open two boxes—one to crush bones and the other to confuse. Kaveh crumpled them to dust.

"You already know which of us will win at this game, should you not show your true power, Valeran. We have already had this match."

"I feel slightly more upset about things now."

"Do you?" Kaveh pulled the air out from around Valeran. "I could crush you where you stand."

Valeran rolled out from the hold.

"You do not let loose." Kaveh let a shadow swirl around Valeran's throat. "Were this not a spar, held by a leash, I would have destroyed you already."

"Were this not a quest held by a leash, I would have slit your throat in the night when you were powerless."

"Strike. There is no leash to this quest anymore."

"There is always a leash, Fehl. A thing you haven't accepted yet."

Kaveh allowed Valeran to move without shadow. "I've always chosen the hand that holds mine."

"No." Valeran circled. "You were given that hand first and you accepted it. Not the same as putting that leash in another's hand."

"How long did you fight Taline, before you allowed yourself to be leashed?"

"I've been fighting nearly the entire time I've known her."

"Because of her beauty?"

Valeran thrust his mid-blade hard. "Caught your eye?"

"No. I find her of middling countenance."

Valeran blinked and Kaveh used the distraction to send him hurtling through the air.

Valeran flew back, but he used his momentum to push himself into a back somersault so that he landed ready, with knife still in hand. He issued a short laugh, real humor reaching his eyes. "As stupid as that is to believe, I believe such stupidity of you."

It was yet another oddity—that Rone ul Valeran relaxed at Kaveh calling Taline plain. "Did you think I would find otherwise?"

"I have always thought you lacking human discernment. Soulless. Saying that you find the most beautiful woman in the world middling is more on point than expected."

"Nin told me that I don't look outside my own goals enough. That I don't recognize the struggles around me."

Valeran's face did something complicated. "Nin is the smartest idiot I know."

Kaveh frowned and pulled a shadow to hand. "She is not an idiot."

"No, she's the smartest idiot." Valeran switched his knife hand. The shadows told Kaveh that another small blade had dropped into his other palm. "Trying to train you to be human."

"Irsula claimed me too human."

Valeran's face did something even more complicated. "I don't care."

"No." Oddly, Kaveh thought of Ishum and the things Kaveh had been forced to pay attention to just by having to do things slowly by hand instead of quickly with a wave of his wrist.

"I'm glad that you didn't return my powers right after I lost them," Kaveh murmured, looking at his fingers.

"I can take them again," Valeran said laconically, blade striking.

"We shall see," Kaveh said. Shadows swirled just a little faster around his frame in defense. "But if you had returned them, I wouldn't have…"

"Had a change of heart?"

Kaveh stared at his shadows as they licked up the walls. He shook his head. "I will get my revenge. That hasn't changed. But I did not…I knew not what it was to rely on others." Not even the emperor. He had relied on the emperor to lead all that Kaveh wanted nothing to do with, but he had not needed to rely on him for anything else.

He had only relied on Ifret. Then Nin.

"And you do now?"

Kaveh cocked his head. "I see the shape of it. Like a distant shore that I don't know if I will reach. I see it, but—" With shadows, he caught the charged blade a hair's breadth from his right eye. "Come, Valeran. This is pitiful."

"You are having a revelation. I was helping make a point."

"Make a better point. Fight me." Kaveh pulsed his shadows around the chamber—letting the ones that had crawled around Valeran's fingers shake loose everything within and to force him to the floor. "Fight me like you mean it."

The blades clattered to the stones, along with Valeran's knees.

"Like I mean it?" Valeran was looking at the stones.

"You are tired of holding back. You hate it. You hate it as much as you rely upon it—this seal of your power. This last facet that makes you Valeran and Fehl—for both sides of your lineage would have done anything to get you under their command, if they had known your capabilities. I know your power. There is no secret. Fight me like it's the end of your secret."

"A final fight?" Valeran asked, voice and expression remote. "One where I use all my power?" Though remote, there was a thin level of excitement that he could not hide.

"Yes."

Valeran sprang to his feet—a fluid motion that was both entirely within his persona and a visual show of what lurked beneath. "If I damage you, do not cry."

"You fear your power too much."

"And you don't have full control of yours."

No, but Kaveh knew his own power, whereas Valeran had only ever toed at his. "The emperor could nullify cities using relics." Kaveh circled. "In the early conquest, he imbued relics for the generals to use. It was how they captured the first cities, cutting their power."

"You are suggesting that I have Taline power boxes with my magic."

"Among other things."

"No."

Kaveh smiled. "You just aren't desperate enough."

"I do not feel that desperation is an emotion I lack at the moment."

"Unfold your magic."

"This is not a sleight of hand."

"Do you not want to terrify Aros?"

"I don't want to enjoy using it at all."

Kaveh cocked his head. "Don't enjoy it then. Accept its need. Practice stripping levels, so that you know the feel. So you can control it when you do use it."

Valeran grimaced.

"Strip the edges of this shadow." Kaveh pulled a newly formed shadow from the corner.

Valeran's grimace did not ease. "The edges?"

"It is how you only lock one portion of a person." Kaveh moved. "That was how the emperor stripped levels. He skimmed a magi's power and sliced—like slicing farther and farther down a river reed—hacking it down until it was no more."

"He used it to terrify people."

"Yes. It worked." Kaveh had seen the emperor use his power countless times. Never had he seen him use it in distaste. The emperor had found pleasure in his power. Valeran found only pain.

They practiced, then practiced some more. Kaveh never let Valeran strip his own powers, but he kept the shadows moving and rotating in target.

"I'm going to know your shadows better than you will." Valeran grimaced again.

"Then you will be able to put them back together again."

Valeran looked up at him. "If you don't win, Fehl—"

"I know." Nin would do whatever it took to stop the festival.

"Do you?"

"I will win." He curled his fingers. "I will hold Aros in eternal torment until he undoes the curse, then I will grant him a swift end."

Shadows pulsed and swirled in evil regard.

"You could kill Aros now," Valeran said, in a far too leisurely manner.

Kaveh frowned, making his shadows pulse and swarm. "Then Nin would die."

"But you could do it." Valeran twirled his knives between his fingers, ready on the balls of his feet. "If he stands before you with all that he is—if he taunts you about your father—"

Kaveh's fingers gripped. "I will hold him."

"Will you? Will you? He who crushes without thought?"

Kaveh watched his fingers curl, shadows slipping around his knuckles. He looked at Valeran. "I must."

Something settled in Valeran's eyes. "We'll see then, won't we." He crouched. "Again?"

NINLI

Scrolls and papyrus littered the small office space above the hidden cavern.

"The procession will begin here." Qara ul Polingsa tapped a marked route.

The logistics of the defenses—where Aros had shored up palace points, where there were still weaknesses—were detailed and mapped. His major backers in the elite were listed, along with who might be swayed to support another Carre.

But there was something tense riding beneath the plans. Qara and Larit had been sidestepping and glossing over it for the past ten minutes, concentrating the conversation on strategies and tactics.

"What is it?" Nin finally asked, unable to take the suspense any longer. Aros's smugness in the imperial communication orbs they had intercepted had been getting worse, and Nin knew that meant only bad things.

Qara and Larit exchanged a glance. "Aros has Birsa."

Taline went rigid next to her.

"Birsa?" Nin shook her head in denial. "But she's in the non-magic—"

Larit touched a scroll that had not yet been opened, drawing it slowly across the workspace. "Birsa is in a holding cell at the palace. As far as we have been able to piece together, Crelu ul Osni told Aros everything he knew about his time chasing the scepter."

Everything he had ever known, if the blood curse counted. But Osni hated Aros. He held Aros and Nera partly responsible for Bilen's death. Osni would never voluntarily aid the other man, so she could guess at how the information had been gained.

"He told them about Birsa aiding us," Taline said grimly, looking to the side. "And where to find her."

"Our intelligence says that Crelu ul Osni sliced out his own tongue upon the floor of the broken palace."

Nin touched her mouth. "That wouldn't stop the scepter. Aros would not need Osni's words. He needed only to follow Osni's scepter locations. Osni activated his scepter in Birsa's home. Aros had already stolen the other scepters at that point when you were with Birsa, Tali. The prime scepter can track the others. Aros already knew where Birsa was."

Taline's eyes closed. "I used the Scepter of Darkness, splicing through to her. I did this."

"No." Nin grabbed her. "You did not."

Taline opened her eyes and looked at her. "And where is the line then, Nin—the one that separates whose actions influence?"

Nin felt the hit. But Nin turned to the Polingsas. "Who else?" For that was not the only news that fed the tension in the air.

"The girls from the palace. The last ones we freed."

Nin nodded grimly. Etelian had already blamed her for the women's disappearance. It had been the reason she had been summoned to the palace so long ago. Aros had probably pieced together that the women still lived as soon as he saw her ripgate from the palace—if not before. He had probably found those women the week after. Nin shut her eyes. She had not been able to check on anyone while bound to Kaveh's side.

"What is his plan?" Taline asked. But Nin already knew Aros's plan.

"They will be the first sacrifices of the festival," Larit said. "The first of the festivities."

"A dual trap," Taline said, horrified.

Nin looked to where the banners were being erected in the distance and to where the festival lights were being strung. "Yes." It was all a trap. An elaborate, beautiful, bloodthirsty trap. Red or green? Would the streets run with blood or be filled by laurels of green—the festival completed before it could begin?

"Nin?"

Nin looked at her. "More than one plan can ride the same mantawings."

"We..." Qara and Larit took each other's hands and Qara lifted her head. "We expect we will be part of the half crescent's sacrificial slate, should a second week of the festival come to pass."

Yes. Aros was smart where Etelian never would be, and he saw patterns because he was looking for them—because he knew what and who Nin was. Aros would have no trouble figuring out the Tehrasian connections she had made that had slipped by his brother.

Nin wanted to open a ripgate beneath Qara and Larit's feet—Taline's, too. A ripgate to shove them through to safety—to shove dark hair and light into a world where they could simply be.

"But not the first week?"

"The elites need us to conform during the cycle of heavier moons. The crescent set always goes down so much easier when the first set is not pushed against."

"Run," Taline said to them, tension lacing her body. "Nin can undo your oaths right now. You can run."

"So can you," Qara said.

Taline's lips pressed together.

Qara nodded. "This is my city. As one of the elite, I have a duty to the people."

"A duty to the people who rejuvenated the festival after being free for years without?" Fury laced Taline's voice.

"Yes," she said quietly. "It is the duty of those who can see farther to support those who cannot."

"The people who are going along with Aros—with the festival—are partly to blame. If the populace rose up against the festival—"

"Revolution takes time to build and bodies on which a movement is built upon. In the beginning, no one believes they or their families will be the ones targeted. Shock and pretense freezes even the hardiest of souls."

"But it was only ten years ago—"

"A short time. And also one quite infinite." Qara looked out at the city. "The human mind stretches or condenses time depending on individual wants and needs."

"There are individuals who don't believe that the festival is actually being cycled again," Larit said softly. "They believe it to be rumor and pretense—banners being raised in taunt. There are those who hope to buy time for themselves by saying, 'Throw the first sacrifices upon the pyre and spit.' There are those who say we have brought it upon ourselves—sacrificing the old ways so readily."

"You are voicing reasons for me not wanting to save them," Taline said bitterly.

"But there's a second group who fight, who plan, who look for allies in the night." Qara stood tall. "A second group who is ever ready to lend a hand. And there are those of the third category. Too scared. Too powerless. Those who lament. Who whisper in the shadows, 'What can we do?' and 'Help!' and 'Why have we been forsaken again?'"

Taline looked down, fists clenched. "It is unfair. It is unfair that the second has to fight for the first and the third."

"Yes. And yet, you were once in that third forsaken group."

"Yes," Taline said bitterly. "And I will never forget."

Qara's hands curled over hers. "But you became a believer, a fighter, an agent of change. You were given a chance to change your own fortune, where so few find purchase upon such sheer slope. You were shown the way. You can show others theirs. One rarely survives alone."

Taline looked to the distance. "And the first group, who actively work against us?"

"There are some who will see the first sign of hope and become ally as long as its glow remains. There are others, though, who no amount of compassion will reach. Those are the ones we plan around. Who we see but do not mistake for the rest of humanity. An attempt to spite them will just bring pain. We plan around them."

Taline nodded sharply in understanding. "I will do it."

"I know you will. And know that you will face this again. Those people will remain, though perhaps they can be tempered by society. The decision to save such mulish, heartless people is always hard. It never becomes easier." Qara squeezed her hand again. "We move in morning's first light."

"I don't want you to be hurt," Nin said, touching Qara's arm.

Qara looked at her fondly. "We all play our parts in humanity's cycle. You bring hope, though it has always been hard for you to see in your reddened view."

Nin knew that Qara knew, and yet still the acknowledgment shook her. Nin had seen the knowledge in Qara's gaze, but it had never been voiced. Aros had spoken it aloud for all of them. And things of darkness seemed less harmful in the light.

"Nothing I say will deter you," Nin said as levelly as she was capable. "You will continue on."

"We will," Qara said. Larit nodded.

There would be no dissuading them. That meant Nin would just have to save them, too.

"Dealing with Carres is not a new task." Qara smiled at her. "Ferra's wishes upon you, Ninli. Taline."

Taline turned to her as Qara and Larit headed off, hand in hand, heads bent together in concert.

"I'm afraid they will die," Taline said, ache in her voice.

"No." Nin looked at the sun's shadows on the buildings. At the strings of fairy lights and softly bobbing encased flame that heralded the start of every festival—the good and bad. "We will save them. We will save everyone."

"Nin."

"I know, Tali. I know."

As they walked into the underground tunnels, Nin stared at Taline's tense back and ached. She let her view be filled with the pair fighting at the end of the hall instead.

The two men moved as they fought—a dance that was uncoordinated in movement, but beautiful all the same. Kaveh was the epitome of the motionless fighter who pulled everything around him to the bidding of his hands. Every line of his muscular body was fraught with tension, every muscle engaged—as if he were fighting against his own powers and had always done so.

It was interesting to see, for he had always looked as if he harnessed and wielded his powers with ease. And she supposed that he did wield them with ease—it was just that such ease to him would be impossible to anyone else.

In contrast, Rone was constantly in motion—a whirling, smirking dervish of flow, dynamism, and sleight of hand. He was a master at movement that was itself a smokescreen to hide other powers.

Together, they made a powerful pair. Kaveh, the solid festival pole, guiding and extending flowing ribbons of shadows outward in all directions, and Rone, skillfully moving and dancing through and around their lethal laces. It was an alluring, powerful, jaw-dropping tableau.

Looking at them work in tandem only reinforced the feelings inside her.

She would give Aros what he wanted while taking what she needed. And Kaveh, Rone, and Taline would survive to build a new world.

CHAPTER EIGHTEEN

ALLIANCE IN SHADOW

TALINE

(Tehras, Tehrasi)

The Feast of Sustenance and Renewal—colloquially called the Festival of Blood—was celebrated for half a moon's cycle—from the height of a full moon to its complete decay.

That meant days of festivities and parades in the streets leading up to the full moon. Taline waded through the throngs of people assembled, listening to their murmurs, gauging the feel of the district, while depositing scrolls in key locations to alert their allies of their plans.

"The first sacrifices will walk through here," a woman said to a small girl. "We'll be able to see them clearly. Saru, where are your petals?"

"Here!"

"I hope someone from the outer family is chosen for the second set of sacrifices," another woman with them said, clinically observing the banners being raised. "I dislike that branch and the magic still comes to the entire fam—"

"You are sick," a nearby woman spat. "You are the reason this is happening. Sacrificing someone else's child to boost your own pow—"

A fight broke out and the investigorii flying above dove to squash it.

Taline felt hope at seeing the fight. She felt hope that there was still resistance to be had in Tehras. Fire mounted in their allies.

"My mother is a first sacrifice," a girl said to another, tears in her eyes. "And they celebrate."

Taline scored her palms with her nails, then deposited another scroll into an exchange pocket. They would fix this.

"You will get..." The other girl swallowed. "You will get to choose one ward and four scrolls after she has bled for Tehrasi."

"A king's gift for her sacrifice," a woman said curtly next to them, her eyes containing that same cool regard as the woman who had spoken of hoping an extended family member was taken. "Be glad for your fortune, girl."

"I...I'd rather keep my mother," the girl whispered.

The woman's expression turned sour. "If you say that again, they may take away your gift. Be thankful they are giving you such riches. You look quite poor."

"I don't want to be thankful."

"Be silent, then," the woman said harshly.

In that single conversation heard on the street, Taline understood the source of Nin's motivation. This woman encapsulated everything that Nin opposed. The girl and her mother were everything she wanted to save.

Nin would sacrifice herself for them all.

It was Taline's mission to make certain that her sacrifice didn't need to happen. She would continue to make sure Nin survived. She had accepted that mission a half moon cycle after recovering in Nin's small home four years before—after she had seen and known the heart of the other girl.

Time slid through the sandglass faster now.

First Sacrifices would be paraded through the streets on the day leading up to their sacrifice, drumming up support and excitement from the crowds. Nin had told her there was a specific way sacrifices were chosen to best ensure compliance. The selections were never as random, or by the gods, as those in charge made it seem. The majority chosen were from poorer families who needed the legacy, but there were a few of middle and elite origin, who were chosen strategically. It was a neat way for the elite to trim their levels, especially of antagonists, while promoting the idea that they, too, were impacted.

Those who railed against the sacrifice were silenced and paraded forth with blank eyes, their will having been stripped. Those who met their fate with "dignity" were given extra gifts for their families. Treated with ceremony and honor—with a largesse of food and magic, and a legacy gift to the families they left behind. Many chose the second option.

Their compliance fed a toxic environment, however. Dignity and duty in sacrifice was applauded, and any questioning against it was derided by those most impacted. Those impacted were not the ones who gained from the festival, though. It was all an illusion given to them by those in power.

Nin, in her hopeful way, thought that those grasping onto the renewed festival with such fervor were the last lunges and dying gasps of a noxious tradition and way—the people who put forth the festival with such ardor were the dying breed of Tehrasian. Those who were helping them work against it, who were spreading a message of freedom for all, were the future.

Taline hoped she was right.

It was the smallest of boons that they were dealing with a Long Day's Moon instead of a Blood Moon. The Long Day's Moon was among the weakest of sacrificial moon cycles.

Traditionally, the festival was held during the Blood Moon, since elements of the Blood Moon made the effects stronger, but it didn't specifically need to be held then. It could be called at any time. In Carre lore, the activation of the festival meant that the next full moon would demand the beginning of the bloodlet required to "drain the full moon."

The sacrifices continued until the end of the half cycle, when the moon was "drained" to a slice in the sky. At this point, the new moon would begin to form, and a new, brighter future would spread across the lands.

Nin had told Taline how much she hated the festival story. It had become a tale that made a twisted sort of sense—the kind that promoted fear. For if they didn't drain the moon...

The belief that the gifted magic made the city and lands run—that without it, they would sink into oblivion and become a waste upon the land—was still entrenched. So much progress, and yet some things were not so easily rooted out.

Banners of solid red lined the streets, lifting into place one after another. The red of blood. The red of the Carres' eyes. The legacy of the House of Scepters.

Imperial red and black banners trimmed in gold flew beneath. And it was this, most especially, that Nin could not let exist. For it was a subtle show of a possible future—the Carres reborn, the empire superseded.

Taline delivered the last scrolls and slipped around the corner just before a hand reached out to retrieve them.

"The Lost Princess. She can save us," a voice said.

"She is a Carre. Why would she want to save us?" another said.

"Because some look beyond what they can have and look to what all of us can."

Taline headed back to their underground quarters, deeds done.

A cadre of boys from the imperial forces had found them—Taline had wondered how until she saw the shadows swirling at their heels. Nin was working with them on setting up disruptions around the city. None of them could be older than fifteen—all new to their full powers. Taline knew the head boy, Akel, had been responsible for keeping the Shadow P—Kaveh—alive while he had been without his powers in the camp.

The boys were looking at Nin with expressions far too solemn for Taline's comfort.

Nin was being shady. Taline had realized quickly, four years ago, that meant Nin was trying to keep others from harm, and that by doing so she was putting herself in the line of fire, as a target.

Taline's gaze swept to the other side of the area, where Baksis ul Fehl stood in the interior of Kaveh's thick shadows—speaking privately—before he opened up his shadows and the wispy images of a larger group of generals and Fehls appeared within. She had seen Kaveh talking through shadow with other Fehl siblings and generals—Simin, Omari, and Omari's guard Namir, among a dozen more—but it was disconcerting to see them all so close at hand.

Taline wasn't certain about trusting allies on the Fehl side. Would they betray them? It was a point in the Shadow Prince's favor that he was physically strong enough to discourage betrayal, but Taline did not have a lot of faith in Fehls, in general.

Rone sidled up to her. "Deep thoughts are happening in that magnificent skull of yours."

She gave him a rueful glance. "The festival is in rising tension and we are surrounded by Fehls. I thought I had only one to worry about three full moons' past."

Rone lifted a supercilious brow. "More than enough for anyone to worry over."

Taline let her cheek rest on his shoulder. He stiffened only briefly before moving the smallest bit closer. She slipped her hand in his. They were both a little awkward with the unaccustomed gesture, but then, like a sigh, they gripped tight. "I won't lose any of you."

Rone said nothing for a moment, then he let his cheek rest on her crown. "I accept nothing less from the wall that defends all."

"If Aros dies or raises the scepter against himself..."

"I know."

The voices in the corner grew louder—a high-ranking general interrupting something one of the quieter Fehls had been saying. "You want someone on the throne who will bring progress and peace. And if you find that in Kaveh ul Fehl, then that pleases us, now that we know he is in full possession of his powers once more. We will need a leader on the throne who knows how to fight and exceeds in warfare."

Desine ul Fehl, Padifehl of Cartha, said, "We—"

"Have a thousand Fehl children roaming this layer, many of whom have different views on the matter of worth, class, and station? We know, padifehl. And they will make problems if there is the slightest avenue for it. Having a threat and deterrent on the throne is more valuable than a benevolent emperor."

The quiet Fehl tipped her head. "So we will have both."

The general shrugged. "As long as the Imperator General reigns, we will follow."

Strength. It would not do to underestimate that some could not see beyond the strongest pillar.

"The more allies, the stronger we will look to some," Taline murmured. "Might. Some simply look to might and strength and are not concerned about anything else." She envied that lack of concern, though she did not agree with them.

"We could ask the people of the north."

"The Valerans?" she said sharply, looking up at him.

He shrugged, as if the subject was of no consequence. "They fear the empire. With assurances—"

"You would ask them?"

"They have armies."

Taline felt her lips part, eyes blown wide. "Rone." She contemplated him for untold minutes, then she took his hand between both of hers and squeezed. "If at some time you want to confront them, I will accompany you. But we will ask them for nothing."

"I would like to see those of the north encounter your stone wall," he murmured, touching her cheek with his free hand. "A balm for a long victim of it myself." A faint hint of a smile curved near his eyes.

She opened her mouth to respond, but the sudden surge of shadows forced her to look to the side.

Kaveh's gaze was focused on one of the Fehls with a promise of infinite death. "Will you betray me?"

Kinu ul Fehl—the Padifehl of Ethi—said nothing for a long moment, shaking free of the terror of Kaveh's pulsing shadows with sheer determination. "Will you betray us?"

"No."

And Taline felt something in the underground room loosen in response. It was a simple, but powerful promise. For the Shadow Prince had never promised anything he did not deliver. His word was his bond, and his dark eyes—death and shadows and predation—held oath.

Something loosened in Baksis, most notably. "I will follow you," he said.

"We will follow you," Omari intoned.

"And I," Simin said.

The rest slowly nodded. Taline watched Nin's eyes close and body shudder, her posture easing.

"We never agreed with the way that the empire treated conquered territories," Kinu said, "but there was never anything to be done about it. Not with you and Aros as the emperor's hands. You terrify even the hardiest of warriors. But as you stand now…" Kinu lifted his fingers. "I would have followed you from fear before. I will now follow you for championship instead."

Ilia ul Fehl, Padifehl of Loran, lifted her chin. "We would not have followed you without the regaining of your powers. And we are reluctant to trust." She inclined her head, eyes sharp. "This is a new way forward. And we will support you as a leader. Do not fail us."

"I cannot betray Aros," Selist, new Padifehl of Zaga and Raba, said. "I took an oath upon the scepter for the padifehl throne. Aros would have killed all in the new territories had I not. I acknowledge my seat will be short upon this throne. I eye another. With that said, we can offer other things. A sprinkling of eggs to let a dragon follow a path."

Murmurs became plans.

Taline and Nin had extensively studied the blessed children of the emperor. Fehls always played at their own games—like Selist, who obviously wanted one of the territories held by a child of Nera—but some were more easily trusted. The padifehls who had gathered had bonds to others in the group. Some were known to be harsh in word, but none were known to be cruel in deed. Taline's gaze slid to Kaveh. And this would be the man who would lead them.

Her gaze slid to Nin, who had taken the place at his side. Taline took a deep breath and prayed to Sehk-Ra.

Shadows dispersed, and Nin and Kaveh came forward to meet Taline and Rone.

"Baksis, Simin, Omari, Kinu, Ilia, Hali, and Desine have agreed," Kaveh said in his no-nonsense tone. "Six others, including Selist, will stay neutral during the clash."

Rone examined him through narrowed eyes. "Northern Ersine was well represented."

"Baksis and Namir make multiple plays."

Rone tapped a finger on his arm, gaze remote. "You are certain of them."

"Yes."

"The empire needs to support you," Nin said, gaze distant as she looked at the pools of shadow connected to distant camps.

"That is what we are discussing." The Shadow Prince's tone softened, as if Nin had gone round the bend. "The test Baksis put forth was passed."

Nin smiled at him, still somewhat absent. "And that is important—to have the support of the padifehls not directly aligned to Aros or Nera. But...the empire is more than the padifehls and blessed children. You need to pass the people's test, as well." She met the Shadow Prince's gaze and there was a wealth of communication there.

His gaze narrowed. "The generals will stand with their Imperator General. Even those with oaths upon their tongues."

A number of men in imperial guard uniforms had been visible through shadow throughout the last day. As long as Kaveh ul Fehl retained his powers, they would follow him wherever he led. Taline shuddered at that type of singular devotion. She was glad he was on their side now.

"One will slip or deliberately tell Aros," Rone argued, still untrusting at his core.

"Likely." Kaveh nodded sharply. "But it won't matter. I have only told them to await my signal. Aros has to await it as well."

"And the Scythians?" Taline asked.

"Their staffs of power and closely guarded mining secrets aid us immeasurably already. They will take their own back and provide assistance for three seats more."

Rone looked to the distance. "I am glad that the Scythians play their part far from here."

"You have concerns?" Kaveh asked.

"Concerns about them taking back their own territory and forcing Nera's child from the throne? No. About their agents pushing against three more seats of Nera's spawn? No. It is what happens afterward which concerns me."

Rone had told her that the Scythians had made it no secret that they had no intention of being part of the empire. Nin had made it no secret that she hoped they would find a way to entice them into some form of coordinated council.

"That means you think we will win," Taline said.

"A truly dark hope," Rone said dryly. "Aros still controls the Scepter of Darkness and all it entails."

"Irsula beat the emperor with his hand upon it," the Shadow Prince said.

"You aren't Irsula," Rone said.

"No, but I have you now, don't I," Kaveh said. Taline blinked. She wasn't certain she had ever heard such a sarcastic tone in the other man's usually dead-serious voice.

"I hardly have a flair for her dramatics," Rone answered. "And I look quite terrible in gray."

Taline looked between them, sizing them up like she did all potential allies or opportunists. Would they work together? Maybe. There was something deep there if they could relent enough to grab it.

"Aros has had longer to study and wield the scepter," Taline murmured. She looked at Kaveh ul Fehl. "The emperor had no time to learn its secrets."

Kaveh surveyed her. "We beat the Carres at full strength. With all the scepters in their hand and a lifetime of wielding them."

"You had Osni," she said.

Kaveh's eyes glittered with hard hatred. "We still do."

Rone's gaze clashed with Kaveh's, and something cold passed between them—an understanding and an anticipation. Taline looked between them, slightly disturbed by whatever they were silently agreeing upon.

"Osni will be kept in the cells," Rone said slowly. "Aros won't trust him anywhere else."

"All high-level prisoners are held in one tower," Kaveh said.

Rone looked at Nin. "Strong enough to hold even a Carre inside of a Carre stronghold."

"Yes," Nin whispered. They were plotting without Taline. That means she would very much not like this plan.

"Aros is overconfident with the scepter in hand," Kaveh said, "but his intelligence cannot be understated. Unless he is past the point of corruption, he will surmise our plans. He will count on both success and a trap."

The two men's gazes connected again. Both nodded slowly.

Disturbed, Taline looked between them. "Is this a creepy Fehl thing?"

That, at least, seemed to shake Rone from his trance.

"A plotting thing, narsumina. Worry not."

She narrowed her eyes. He only called her that now when he was trying to play off something else. "Plotting about what?"

Rone smiled. "Aros's expectations. I always find it works best when you meet others' expectations with your own."

Taline was now certain that she was going to hate this plan. Looking at Nin's pale face and shaky nod, she knew she was going to hate this plan.

She looked between the two men and their glittering eyes as they seemed to exchange some sort of wordless design. Would they be able to work together? Maybe. If they could do so...

She thought for the first time that they might succeed.

NINLI

Nin completed her fiftieth medallion, fatigued but determined. Determined not to think of her own part that had yet to play—a part that she desperately wanted to commence and desperately wanted to run from. It had always been there—her past ready to clash with her present—but she had put it off. She had put it off for so long, that before their quest for the scepter, Rone had scoffed that she would never call an end play.

She turned to survey the others.

Kaveh was slipping shadows into glass orbs. The men and women around him still eyed him in fear, but the fear was slowly diminishing to determined awe as he directed them without resorting to inflicting terror.

Taline and Rone had their heads bent together. Taline was carefully selecting glass, that would in turn become marbles—painstakingly crafted marbles Taline would create by hand—to be magically filled.

Obtaining the glassblower and craftsmen scrolls all those years ago had been priceless.

They had been two of the first items Nin had stolen after Taline had stated in no uncertain terms that she planned to stay. They had given Taline the ability to create pieces of great power. They had allowed her to replace the parts within herself that had been broken by Etelian. They had given her a means back—a way to survive and thrive.

And Nin had contributed her magic easily and eagerly to complete all of Taline's designs.

Nin looked fondly at Rone helping Taline fill the insides with his magic and power. She watched as he carefully held her creation with the reverence that Taline deserved. That Rone deserved—for giving himself leave to feel such things was a gift all its own.

She watched them, and she ached with it—with the way that things might end up, if she made the wrong move.

Uncertainty. There was so much of it. And Nin hated it. She had always hated uncertainty—had always derided things outside of her control. So little had been in her control in the first of her nine years, that she had sought it in her following nine. Maybe not in the way that Taline would—by keeping everything strictly to plan—but in her own way.

There were problems in the empire. Problems that needed to be solved. But that she believed in many of the empire's aims made her want to save it, to make it better.

She wouldn't let the dreams of her countrymen die.

She wouldn't let the legacy of her family consume them.

She wouldn't let her own fears determine her destiny.

She was Ninli ul Summora. And she would succeed.

CHAPTER NINETEEN

THE LOST PRINCESS

NINLI

(Tehras, Tehrasi)

Crouched on the rooftop in the warm evening air, she waited for an opening, while anxiously watching the Parade of Blood through the scope.

The first sacrifices would commence as the full moon rose. There was a little over an hour left between the moon's rise and the sun's set. An hour of dusk-ridden sacrifices would coat the darkening streets, if Nin failed.

The excitement of the elites who would benefit from those first sacrificed could not be hidden by their languorous pace, and the reluctance of the first group to be sacrificed could not be heightened by merriment. The split existed in opposite measure as well, though smaller in number—uneasy elites and rapturous sacrifices.

A country and a class were not comprised of just one type of magi. There were elites like Qara who wanted no part in the festival—who had argued for its dissolution immediately upon the downfall of the Carres. And there were those in the lowest classes who strictly enforced the best options for those in charge.

Nin sighted Aros at the volute, waiting for the procession to arrive at the sacrificial stairs.

Decades ago, Aros had been the most vocal supporter on the imperial side to halt the festival. After the death of the Carres and the weeding out and shuffling of the elite, the two sides—Tehrasian and imperial—had come together to negotiate the future terms of the province. It was something Sher Fehl had done in every conquered land.

Sher Fehl had never been a supporter of blood rites—a stance that Nin had admired about the man—but he had maintained a policy of allowing traditions to continue in countries where the structure of command bowed to imperial aims. So if Aros had not vocally supported the festival's halt, the elites could have lobbied for its continuance for a few years (or a few dozen) more under Etelian's ruling hand.

Nin fingered the edge of the scope. She had always considered it a point in Aros's favor. Even with her knowledge that he was undoubtedly Jisarek's son, she had hoped he might be swayed to be a good and just leader.

Now, as she looked upon her city, she wondered whether Aros, the chameleon, had not just played the long game from the start. Why give Etelian the power of the yearly festival when Aros could use the stockpile of fervor, enchantment, and blood at a later time? Why give Etelian a power when Aros could use the goodwill of the populace to end the practice, while stoking those who wanted it to continue to push against the empire itself?

The actions had given him a fertile field to step upon, ten years later.

Nin shook the thoughts free and looked through the scope. She would have time for "what if" and "should have seen" thoughts later.

For now, it was time to concentrate on today. Their plan was threefold: disrupt the procession, spirit away those to be sacrificed, then confront Aros.

It was on how to achieve the last task that she and Kaveh had argued.

And Nin would be a fool to think it would go the way she thought, but then, too, so would Kaveh. Plans, like life, were too often taken from one's control. But here were multiple paths to victory.

She looked at the moon as it rose. This full moon would only reach a third of the way into the sky on this night. It was either an especially heavy moon or an especially light one, depending on which way the ruling class wanted to speak of it. There was always a discussion among councilors on what the populace would bear best—a positive notion that the festival was working, or a negative notion that they had to sacrifice more.

Her parents had not liked to hear the councilors' words on anything. Few mouthy councilors survived Giran's reign. But Farrah had been mindful about teaching Nin of the past, and of other Carres who had taken the pulse of their populace and ruled in tighter fashion.

It was her time now. Her time to fix a mistake bled into the roots of her family's dynasty.

From her vantage point, she could see Taline positioning herself in the crowd. Her sister's gaze was tense, and she looked everywhere but where Nin was. No one in their group had voiced excitement about this plan. It required...a lot of small sacrifices. It required each of them to release control in some way.

It was time to begin.

Nin let power slowly flow through her, rolling it slowly through her system, from head to toe. As soon as she used it, Aros would pinpoint her position. So everyone had to move quickly and decisively. There was a single chance for the moment of surprise.

This would be her stamp upon the celebration she loathed.

Aros knew it was coming, but he did not know if it was this moment, or the next, or one twenty ticks from now. This was their advantage, for the tension was on Aros, and the pretension of battle was something that took energy and vigilance.

She let the energy gather, closing her eyes and feeling it flow until it circulated in a continuous loop, hitting every magical point and system in her body. She let the magic of the city connect. It told her exactly where each person stepped in the procession along the main street. It linked her with their speed and size and wobbles in their gait.

Every bit of information streamed into data that she would never be able to explain, but that she could feel form a pattern that her mind understood anyway. She let the city connect, let her magic connect, let the oaths and sacrifices that had bound her to the city and its people intertwine.

Then she opened ripgates beneath the feet of every person targeted to be sacrificed.

There one moment, gone the next.

A furious uproar waved through the procession. And the festival magic that wove through the streets sparked.

Aros, at the tip of the spire's stairs, smiled and waved the Scepter of Darkness.

"Go," Nin whispered into the shared spell spread between Nin, Taline, Kaveh, Rone, Qara, and Larit.

Explosions rocked the street and shadows flew. People screamed and shot in all directions—hitting each other and forming clumps in the crowd.

Aros thumped the scepter onto stone and magic shot from stone to stone through the promenade. Magic ripped through air and rock. Sections of stone flipped, and the first sacrifices flipped back with them. Shaking and weaving, the sacrificial citizens fell to the ground, some vomiting into the dust-filled clouds as stones solidified into place.

Nin felt the scepter's magic target her.

"Is that all you have, cousin?" Aros's magnified voice taunted loudly through the air. "Did you really think you could spirit them away?"

"Throw the one in your left hand!" she yelled, magnifying her own voice to boom over the crowd.

The shaking, confused sacrifices threw one of two magic-filled vials that had been given to them by Qara and Larit's people in the seconds that they had stood beyond her ripgates—left hands pricked by magic and vials clasped in their hands in the moments before the scepter's world-changing magic pulled them back.

The thrown vials—connected to the person who bled upon them—broke and sent their power out, asking for permission to exchange their sacrifice. Nin put her palms upon the city's stones and yanked the magic in sharply—telling the city to send the magic to her, as the person of the bloodline who wielded the spilled blood.

Shadows swirled through the crowd. Opening ripgates beneath the feet of the sacrifices and sending them elsewhere had been the first part of the plan—but it had been a plan that brainstorming had shown could easily be circumvented by a man wielding a scepter capable of doing the same. And Aros had done exactly that—he had simply opened ripgates beneath them, putting them back to where he wanted.

Playing to expectation, on both sides. The thing they could change—was what the sacrifices brought back with them. That, and the sacrifice's willingness to fight.

Each one who had been given a second vial had chosen to fight. Each sacrifice who had not accepted had been superficially cut instead—small drops of blood serving as replacement—and vial breaking on Nin's command, if not thrown.

"The sacrifice has been accepted," Nin yelled and yanked the magic within her. "I take the place of all within these rites."

As soon as it was done, each willing sacrifice threw their second vial—some in hastier or shakier fashion than others—and shadows whirled up and pulled. The first sacrifices—the girls they had saved, Birsa, other familiar faces—whirled in the gathering shadows from the processional path and into the crowd. Vials full of face and form changing spells blinked through the crowd, blending one person into another as shadows pushed at chunks of the crowd and redistributed people so that one could not tell themselves from their neighbor.

Taline, Kaveh, Rone, and Nin's magic were all within, working together.

With the tracking spell to highlight each of their positions, she could see Taline flitting through the crowd, pulling victims away. She could see Rone and Kaveh, moving people where they needed to go.

Aros appeared in front of her. Nin smiled, feeling the last victim swept away by shadow. She stood slowly—shaking and drained. Disrupt the procession, spirit away those to be sacrificed...only the confrontation before her remained.

Aros's glittering amber-bleeding-to-red eyes narrowed, but his smile stayed in place. "Well done on such a noble offering, cousin. But there are others, are there not? Many, many others you hold dear."

There were. And this plan would never work as a single strike. But the first wave of sacrifices were safe, their blood tied within her. At the moment, this was a victory.

"The festival continues, even with you putting yourself forth as the first sacrifice. You will not be able to save the next flight." Aros leaned forward and whispered, "And, dear cousin, you missed one important thing."

⁂

TALINE

Tehras, Sacrifice Circle

"Siran."

Taline had prepared. She had prepared to see him here, knowing that he would be somewhere in the vicinity of the girls he and Aros were using as bait to trap Nin. To trap Taline.

She had not expected him to see straight through her disguise as if it existed not at all.

Etelian smiled. "You came. Aros said you would."

"You are mistaken—"

"I can feel your magic. Aros gave me a gift, you see." The Second Scepter appeared in his hand. "Unlocking powers within this that I never dreamed of. Powers that allowed me to find you. And now, I'll never lose you again." He reached out and grabbed her, and she felt the tip of a Carre scepter press into her side.

The world blurred, then she was inside the palace—inside chambers she had never wished to see again. She wrenched free and backed away slowly.

Blank faces stared at her from their places around the room. New girls, and old girls caught in his evil web. The ones in the procession had been saved, but these girls...

Etelian looked at the scepter in his hand. "Aros keyed it for me. For we still share Mother's blood. There are lovely things to be done with this scepter, Siran, did you know?"

"I know." In preparation for this assault, all information on the scepters had been revealed by Nin and Rone. Taline knew the capabilities of what he held better than Etelian did, for Aros would never tell Etelian all.

"Mmmm. I suppose you would, with the company you currently keep. The Summora sisters. The Hand. What weakness this is, Siran."

Taline kept an eye on the scepter as Etelian vacillated between lazy and agitated motions. He was certain of his victory, yet incensed at the journey he had needed to get there.

"Do you remember when your father first gave you to me? How you objected and how I meted out punishment for that objection? And your objections to the next girl who came after you? You learned so quickly and so well to ignore the plights of others. What happened to you?"

Taline stared at him. "You saw solution in the act that you desired to see. I could not help them, for by doing so brought more punishment upon them. But I never ignored their plights. And in a household bound by fear, you never noticed anything else."

She smiled, harsh and tight. As long as Etelian hadn't seen it, looks and touches and moments of sympathy had been found in multiple places. There had been some who had thrown away the companionship found in twilight and starlight and dawn. There had been some who had gone straight to Etelian with whatever gossip or lies they could muster.

And after Taline had learned to hate them, she had learned to pity them instead. For they were always desperate souls, never to be satisfied—for Etelian would never give them satisfaction, only a vicious beginning, middle, and end—and they couldn't see the scraps thrown their way elsewhere, the bare slivers of companionship of simple touches or shared looks exchanged between victims. Simple gestures and acknowledgment that they were still human.

They were human, and those gestures had been there, if one knew to look and hide.

"You thought us cowed," she said, her words intended for the women rather than the man in front of her. "And we were. But you never understood anything outside your own selfish regard. You never understood that there were those who maintained the smallest defiance. Who, in simply not giving up, continued to mentally survive despite your cruelty."

Etelian smiled tightly—lips curving, eyes cold. "I'll make sure to separate you from the others, then, won't I? Can't have you forming such bonds, of even the slimmest of margins." He raised a hand, his power coiling.

Taline took a deep breath and a bauble slipped unnoticed by him into her palm. Calm fluttered through her—like a butterfly flowing with a good breeze. "You think to make me powerless again."

She thought of Rone. She visualized his face as he had opened his magic in front of her.

"Powerless?" Etelian's full lips curled harshly. "Do you not celebrate your power over me? That I issue such exquisite challenge and desperation to find you again?"

"I wish no such existent power. I wish you cursed instead."

"You will lose, Siran." He smiled—a god's wings flaring in light. "I always win."

She thought of Rone, how he had looked at her with tenderness and respect and how his words flowed with the same affection. Taline clutched the smoothness of the bauble, felt its familiarity, its power. Like the Eternal Spring, she knew this magic and embraced it.

"No." She could feel the voiceless girls around her watching, watching to see whether someone truly could win over the monster they served.

"All I can do, narsumina, is make sure he can't use his loaded dice. The rest is up to you."

Taline threw the bauble to the stone and magic burst.

A first step.

Courage would be second.

KAVEH

Tehras, procession crowd

Kaveh followed Aros and Nin on shadowed wings, even as Valeran yelled in the background.

"Fehl! Etelian took—"

But Kaveh had no patience for appeals, and he shrugged off the curl of power he felt aimed at him as he sped off after Aros.

He could win this here, now. With the sacrifices swept free, Kaveh just needed to figure out how to remove the blood spell on Nin. Shadow and darkness—filled with power—Kaveh had never failed.

Kaveh appeared on the volute in a whirl of shadows, letting them flare outward as curled wings to bite at the barrier the scepter had erected around Aros and Nin.

Aros smiled. "I knew you would follow. At one time I might have shared a throne with you. Had events gone differently."

Nin was barely standing. She looked at Kaveh and slowly nodded.

"I will be the life that takes yours, Aros." Kaveh said, holding his position on top of the volute and carefully pulling shadows into position, feeling the spells and tasting the blood of both of them. He needed them next to each other in order to parse the parameters. "You will be the last sacrifice of the Carres."

Aros touched the scepter to the crown of Nin's head. "Then you will take hers as well. Tied to me, she will be the last sacrifice."

The scepter pulsed, and Kaveh jerked fifty shadows to form a cocoon around Nin. Aros sent a blast that shattered the dome and pushed a pulsating wave of death straight at Kaveh.

Kaveh let loose a tight, tidal wave of shadow that met it. An ear-cutting boom split the air, sending fragments of statuary and marble in two glittering arcs.

The people gathered below screamed—the same people Nin had been trying to save. Kaveh yanked the shadows curling around their hems and in the crevices of their clothing and a full wave shot up—pure nets of shadow shooting straight into the sky, burning beneath the sun at zenith, then splitting the air with early starlight. Nets of shadow were lit by the flames of the ceremonial torches.

"What is this?" Aros smiled, slow and wide. "You? The Terror of the Battlefront, trying to spare the onlookers? What new weakness is this?"

Kaveh pulled the shadows lower, weaving them together so they interspersed between sun and shade—the best technique to save those below from burning beneath the harshness of the scepter's beams. The shadow nets looked like a living mass. Like knots of snakes squirming and writhing above points of flame.

In the night, shadows could be blanketed as one. During the day, other measures needed to be taken. In sunset, as the sun fell, shadows struggled in his hold. He had been fighting in sunlight his entire life. He knew how to counter the sun's rays. He had been told his shadows were even more terrifying for humans this way—seeing them writhe like snakes.

He could see the onlookers he was trying to save shout in the face of them. But he didn't care about saving them from their terror or fear—only saving their lives.

Aros shot a void-filled beam at the onlookers. Kaveh's shadows swirled up and around and ate the scepter's magic as the onlookers screamed and scattered in panic.

Aros laughed madly. "The Terror of the Battlefront. He, who has caused entire populations to become extinct, is trying to save the people?"

He pushed one hand toward Kaveh and sent the scepter whirling.

Kaveh cursed and sent shadows diving, splitting his focus between foe and savior.

"Zehra wanted to save the crowd on the dark moon. And now, here you are, wanting to save the crowd on the rise of the full. I understood her desire, but whatever has gotten into you? What is this weakness?"

Kaveh could obliterate and be done with a fight in less time than it took an opponent's head to fall. He could win with effortless ease as long as he didn't care about casualties or what he ruined in the interim.

The emperor had never concerned himself with such things in Kaveh's path—he had always said that structures could be rebuilt, populaces could be reseeded. The real win was in capturing territory and establishing the narrative—what other, future territories would learn from such events.

Capitulation was vast and quick when people knew the consequences of combat.

But when an enemy could sense that you cared, that there was something you wanted to protect, targets were easy to identify.

Aros was not wrong. Caring was a weakness. Kaveh had learned, though—where Aros had not—that it was also a strength.

"You will never win against me, having such weaknesses. Kaveh," Aros tutted. "Kaveh, Kaveh, Kaveh. What have they done to you? Where is the beast? The terror? The might?"

Aros sent another blast into the crowd and Kaveh used the energy and concentration he would have used to slice the spells from Nin's blood to save the crowd instead.

But he was as likely to slice her lifeblood as to cut the spell from her. He was a destroyer. His shadows curled around Nin's throat, gently stroking the skin there as the cocoon unpeeled.

Save them; trust me. Nin's gaze repeated the same mantra.

Don't leave me. Don't make me leave you, he sent back.

Trust me.

He trusted her, with everything, but he didn't want to fight on separate fronts. For all of the plans he had created with his generals and siblings and Nin's ducklings, Kaveh didn't know if he could do this. This sacrifice of letting her go. The past weeks of fighting alongside the others hadn't been on equal footing—he hadn't had his powers. Even sparring in the caverns with Valeran, neither had fully let go.

Kaveh was too used to relying on himself. He was too used to solving things with might. Even now, with Valeran swearing at him somewhere behind, trying to catch up without shadow or ripgate, pushing against the crowd, Kaveh had come on his own.

"What is this? Where is my vicious brother?"

It was as Nin had said to him a half moon cycle before—resisting temptation required a different type of sacrifice.

"Weakness. You had so few weaknesses, Kaveh. You had only the emperor before. But look, look what you have brought me? A weakness far greater. You can't kill me." Aros smiled. "Her life is tied to mine, in a way that makes resurrection impossible, and you refuse to see her dead."

Kaveh swirled his shadows into a cage between them. "I can hold you in a cage. One gilded."

"I will die before I wither in a cage, and her with me. All of you so keen to follow a man who put you in them." He sneered. "No one ever challenged the emperor or asked if the emperor was wrong."

"He was wrong. In many things. But simply disagreeing with him doesn't make you right."

"He would never have saved the crowd, Kaveh. Weakness." Aros's eyes glittered. "And your weakness is your downfall."

"You killed your son. Was it worth it?" Kaveh sent his shadows diving. Aros screamed and whirled the mass into the scepter. "You cannot bring him back."

And that made Aros focus solely on him—sending bolt after bolt of slicing, purple energy at Kaveh that ate every shadow and made him call deep within the hellfire of the city's crevices.

"I will. I can do anything now."

"Then why haven't you resurrected him? The scepter lies."

"Lies? You who has always believed in the emperor's drivel about expansion and ideas? Some of us just want to rule that which is our due."

"You think you will find your answers on the throne?"

"The longer I have this and meld with it," Aros spit, "the more I can do."

"The madder you become." Kaveh could see the same threaded spell streaming in the blood just under their skin.

"Oh, brother, I've always been mad. It's in my blood. Just as inhumanity is in yours."

The scepter swept forth and pulled Kaveh's shadows into its outer ring. Kaveh felt unease slip down the others of its cohort.

Aros smiled. "Nervous, dear brother? You should b—no," he hissed and grabbed at his arm.

Kaveh's shadows broke and fell from the scepter, as if Aros's power was draining beneath them. They broke and fell from where they had curled against Nin's neck.

Ripgates formed and fell, and Aros and Nin slipped between one then another. Kaveh watched Nin, who appeared to be in increasingly rough shape.

He didn't know if he could do this. She was going to—

"No," Aros yelled.

But Nin's bloody hands were pressed against stone.

Power rushed through her—so much that she glowed. This was power of a different sort—rolling through her system, from head to toe. The Carres gained much from the sacrifices—tied into the city as they had always been. Disconnecting it would cause the opposite—it would take much from her, yet it would weaken Aros temporarily, too.

Kaveh watched Aros and waited—waited for the blood spell to break. This was their chance; this was...

Aros and Nin disappeared into the air, leaving mere motes of dust behind.

No.

Kaveh's eyes slipped close. Nin was on a path outside of him now.

He could have killed Aros a moment ago. He could have ended him right on these stones. He could have had his revenge.

But Nin...

"Shadow Prince? Are you with us?" Valeran's voice was mild, but there was tension beneath, as he finally gained the top stair.

But Nin would have died alongside Aros. Unacceptable.

"What happened?" Valeran demanded.

The civilians below would have died, too. Not as unacceptable, but a work in progress.

"That wasn't part of the plan, Fehl, you going in with shadows flying and darkness clenching—"

"I could have won." He looked at his hands. He felt the thoughts swirling and connecting as if from a long distance.

"Shadow Prince? Are you with us?" Valeran's mild voice didn't obscure the real question.

Kaveh took a long moment to be certain of the answer. "I am."

This was a new path, and he would walk it.

Kaveh felt his shadows breaking from dozens of glass cages to swoop around the imperial cities held by padifehls of Nera's blood or the provinces firmly in Aros's grip. Baksis, Simin, Omari, Namir, Kinu, Ilia, Hali, Desine, and the Scythians were wielding the enchanted marbles across the empire.

The war had begun. He would need to go. Time ticked.

But he spent one moment more staring at the shadows swirling around his hands. What could it mean that Aros had nearly controlled his shadows? He stared at his hands, brimming with shadow and life.

"Taline?" Valeran asked, his voice far less mild.

Kaveh did not need to ask the shadows; they had answered as soon as she had been taken. "In Etelian's chambers."

Valeran's face went cold, but he held himself still. They had planned for multiple contingencies. No one liked these contingencies, but they had to believe in one another's ability during this next stage. "Ninli?"

"Being thrown into a cell in the most secure palace tower. Nin sent the signal before she disappeared. The civil war among provinces has begun. The padifehls attack one another. Aros is enraged and panicked. Our time begins. He must go to each rebellion to lay them low."

And Kaveh needed to follow.

The festival procession had never been the point where they had planned to unseat Aros, no matter what Kaveh had wanted and hoped for. They had made plans far beyond.

He nodded through shadow to Baksis and Simin and to all the others who had begun their attacks. They would not be able to hold out against Aros at a single spot, but Nin had created ripgate medallions to transport them between. If they kept Aros enraged and on the move for thirty moments more...

"Aros didn't take Ninli with him?" Valeran asked, recalling and securing his thrown knives.

"He didn't plan for so many to be against him so quickly. Hubris," Kaveh said with satisfaction, as he gathered the shadows in his mind across the many different lands.

"Are you ready?"

"Yes." He looked at his hands and curled them into fists as he rose, shadows connecting in an immense grid. "We finish this. And we win."

"Will we?" The mildness and tension remained in Valeran's voice.

"I know what you seek in answer, Valeran."

Kaveh couldn't save just Nin. He had to save all of Nin's people. He had to save what she was fighting for. He had to save his father's empire. He had to bring everyone together, unite them in the cause, instead of eliciting their fear.

"We will pass the people's test first, then we will save this entire cursed empire."

"Cursed, it is, I do agree." There was a hint of ease under Valeran's sarcasm.

Kaveh looked at his hands. "It is easier to promote fear. Saving people is difficult... I am uncertain how to provoke empathy."

When he looked up, Valeran was studying him. "You want to provoke...empathy?"

"We will win this empire back, Valeran. And it will be an empire that we will all rule."

Valeran stared. His fingers tapped restlessly against a blade. "Then we have work to do, and quickly. Ready?"

Kaveh extended his hand and Valeran grabbed hold.

CHAPTER TWENTY

SACRIFICE IN DARKNESS

NINLI

(The Palace of Tehras, dungeons)

"Whatever you have set in motion will fail," Aros snarled, grabbing Nin by the upper arm. "I have a lovely cage, prepared just for you. The emperor was wrong to use them only because he was the one doing so. Perhaps a few hours with your past will make you see whose blood you truly wish to spill. Perhaps you will feel all of their deaths and know that it was your fault that it occurred."

Aros threw her into the cell. "When I return, you will be begging for mercy for your friends. And you will show me how to read the secret Carre texts."

She looked at him steadily. "I cannot read them."

Aros's eyes narrowed. "You lie."

Satisfaction swelled through her. Aros had not learned everything about her then. She smiled. "I need Kaveh to read them. You don't understand why that would be, but you can feel the truth of my words."

Aros bared his teeth, but he had no time to argue. Using the scepter, he cast an additional barrier over the cell, then opened a ripgate.

Nin sent silent prayers to Baksis, Simin, Omari, Namir, and the others. Be safe. Don't die.

Rone would be on his way to them by now, with their finest gambit in his hand. They just had to hold upon the fields and in the palaces. Ripgate medallions blinked in her mind as they were used across the empire. Five uses remaining on one, three left in another.

She slipped shakily to the stone floor for a few moments, gathering her energy. She was a physical mess. But Aros had made the correct choice in leaving her behind—she would have done everything left within her to disrupt every motion he made and would have tried to unsettle every spell he cast.

Nin touched the shadowglass in her sash and looked at the stones beneath her hand—stones laden with spells that had been made to keep even a Carre prisoner. Lorsali had locked her inside one of these cells once. Nin touched the mortar enchantments.

"Come, Zehra, see what secret is below. It will make you beautiful, like me. That's what you want, is it not?"

Zehra had longed for the beauty and nobility of Lorsali, and Lorsali had longed for Zehra's power.

An early handmaiden had been lost to that episode—executed by Salare for allowing Nin to be tricked. Handmaidens had not lasted long before Nin had gotten smart enough and grown strong enough to understand and play the game. She touched the stones with shaking fingers.

Nin had only been inside such a cell once, but one time had been enough. It was like being stripped of power by the emperor—all ability locked within.

She crawled to the wall and began her search.

"I know you," a scratchy, strangely lisping voice croaked. "Though you look quite the worse for wear at the moment, little Carre."

Nin tested the enchantments and spells on her cell walls without looking at the man calling from the cell across from hers. Nin let her fingers linger in one crevice, then move to the next.

Her family had devised this block specifically so that other prisoners could see exactly what was being done to their compatriots. There was another block of cells that allowed only sound. Each had been used for maximum effect, depending on what emotion the torturer wanted to invoke.

This block of cells was strongest of all, one of the palace towers cut into four cells. Rounded back edges of stone and front curved bars laced with enchantments. Holding spells were strung everywhere—in the stones, in the bars, in the mortar that held it all together—spells strong enough to hold even a Carre inside of a Carre stronghold.

"The littlest Carre," came a lisping voice. "Alive this whole time... How you must have laughed."

"You know nothing about what others find amusing then." She did not look at him, focusing on the stones and how they fit together beneath her fingers.

"He chose to put you in here with me. Pity."

"Rumor said you lost your tongue. A pity."

"The scepter grows everything back, however the wielder chooses. Made by a worldbreaker, one who powers creation itself."

She finally looked at him, eyes drawn to the hand he had lost a decade ago. An animal's hand curved into itself now, nails carved into a bestial palm, and a forked tongue hung from his mouth.

"Do you know why he put you in here with me, Zehra Amanan Carre?"

She looked up at him and held his gaze. She had never seen him look worse. Black lines ran across his skin—his veins filled with poison.

Chunks of hair were missing, and gouges were wrenched from his skin. His stitched-together tongue hung from his mouth. "Because we know the spells to get ourselves out of any of the other cells, Crelu ul Osni."

"The beetle princess, alive all this time and working as a healer. Your parents must be screeching from the demonic lair I cast their souls within. Their daughter, little more than a street magi scraping before the masses."

Nin ran her fingers along the walls, looking for the notches that she knew should be there. She found one and marked it, then ran her fingers along searching for the next. "They are undoubtedly screeching from beyond. But I freed their souls years ago, so they are not doing so from your demonic lair."

"It was you at the revenants." His labored breathing spoke to aggravation.

She turned. "It was me in all your worst moments, Osni." She held up her hand and slowly flexed her fingers outward into the sign of the thief.

"You've caused me a lot of trouble, girl." He pawed the locket around his throat. The one that had contained the vials of blood. The one that contained the memory of her family's death. Taline had said she had taken it from him but had lost it sometime in the palace battle. Osni had regained it somehow.

Nin had seen the locket's memories from afar because Osni played them sometimes when he didn't know anyone was watching.

She looked back to the wall to investigate. "I am glad."

"Aros found those weakened spots you seek. It will do you no good."

Nin didn't answer, continuing to work her fingers slowly across the stones. Her fingers found the last one and she pushed.

An empty click echoed in the room.

Osni laughed wetly, coughing up blood. "I told you—Aros disabled all the tricks within. Carre eyes were always able to see." It was said with no little bitterness.

Nin returned to the first point, pressing in, then went to point three, then five, continuing the odd pattern with a count in her head.

"You will go mad from trying, Zehra."

"That's not my name." Thirteen, seventeen, nineteen, twenty-three.

"That was the name to which you were born. How did you survive?" He sounded agitated. "I've pulled it around in my head since Aros's first taunt. I watched the memories. I saw you die."

Nin did not answer.

"A substitution? Farrah mentioned once your trickery against that high witch you called sister."

"Don't say her name."

"You afraid of hearing about your older sister? I watched her d—"

"Farrah. You don't get to say her name."

"She was my wife."

"You killed her."

Osni said nothing for a long moment. "I wish you had been there so I could have killed you after you watched her die." He sneered as she paused. Bile rose and she had to work to push it away. "You were always around. Little Zehra. Always tugging at her skirts. I tried to sway you to my side more than once. I might have been willing to let you continue to power the gates, if you had just complied."

"Your words were poison. Like everyone else climbing the vines in the palace. You killed her."

"Farrah would have died in the palace coup regardless of my actions."

Nin gripped the stone beneath her hand. "You killed her."

"Your family killed her." Spittle flew from his mouth. "Killed Bilen. Made me kill my own son with my own hands."

"And then you took Farrah's life in order to slip out from your oath. You gave up your heart." She sneered, releasing the sequence so that she could turn. "I always thought it ironic that magic would take that as a fair trade. Intentions.

I wonder, at your deal with Darkness. You cared more about your revenge than all else."

"Darkness demands sacrifice."

"Not everyone makes others the sacrifice." In direct opposition to Osni, who had sacrificed Farrah in order to gain what he needed, Kaveh, when he had called upon Darkness, had not been willing to make the sacrifice of her, or of Taline.

"Your family did this."

"My family served their own ends." She could not justify a quarter of the things her family had done. She had never been able to. "The world is better without them."

Without Lorsali's bright laugh, without Jolan's exuberance with a sword in hand, without Allit or Memni's bookish study—no, no.

She took a deep breath. "Without them in rule. I cannot defend them, nor their actions, but you killed the innocent. Your hands are stained with the same blood as that you decried."

"And you? I see the vengeance in your eyes."

"I would sleep better at night for knowing that I've rid Tehrasi of you."

"You think you will survive the empire under any rule?"

"All I cared for at one time was that I survived for a single sunrise after killing you."

"Then you should understand my own need for revenge best."

"If I took your life, I'd be closing the loop. You at an end, and me to follow, both circles of revenge complete."

"There will always be some thread left. You can't close this loop, girl."

"No," she said quietly, fury making the words wobble. "That's what happens when you go too far. You leave no one standing behind you, Crelu ul Osni. Mistress Farrah, forever loving you, would not have followed you here. No one stands with you but your own cold soul."

"The souls of the righteous stand with me."

"You killed all of them. Every one of the staff." She looked at the dying light of the sun. "Why?

You could have made the spell specific to Carre blood, not to the Carre blood oath."

"They let Bilen die. All of them. They were all complicit."

"Unforgivable." She met his eyes. "Giran made you kill Bilen, who should never have died. But you chose to kill Farrah, to kill my handmaidens, the staff, and all the people who had no choice but to serve."

"Darkness awaits us all, girl. It is always waiting, ever ready to make a deal."

Nin would see on which side her own deal fell. She engaged the last of the sequence and instead of a dull thunk of a failed spell, this time there was a chime—tiny and clear.

Osni sat up in his cell. "What did you do?"

Nin looked at the remaining spells. She took a deep breath and started on the next set with the first of the series. It would take time. Everything did. As if in balance for her magic being ever ready and easily wielded, everything else in her life had required time and effort.

She knew that Taline thought she was naturally kind—that deep within Nin resided a good person who had always been there. But in reality, she thought it somewhat the opposite. She had been born bad and it had taken every effort she had ever made to cover that monster with something else.

She had remade herself from her own ashes. She had pieced the embers together one by one, gluing them into a patchwork of bound dust.

She had fallen to the street, broken—physically and mentally—and she had taken one stone, one bloody chunk of dirt, one clump of sand, and she had stacked and covered and armored herself.

But inside, inside in that small place she never visited, she would always be Zehra Amanan Carre. No matter how much she pushed against the name.

"What did you do?" Osni demanded.

"What would you do to be free of your cell, Crelu ul Osni?"

He narrowed his eyes. "What game is this? You free me in order to what—kill me?"

"Perhaps. Though if I had simply wanted to be your assassin, I would have long ago succeeded at such a task."

"I am not so easily gotten rid of, girl, not with the deal I made. I still have things to accomplish before I die."

It explained much—as to why Osni had survived for so long, and as to why he was still alive—barely—in his cell. Even the scepter wouldn't be able to negate a deal with Darkness—it hadn't negated Aros's. "Wiping the world free of Carre blood or any who birthed them?"

His silence spoke volumes.

"Surely you didn't think you had hidden it," she murmured, "especially from Aros?"

Osni's lips twisted. "I knew that there were only a few paths to victory. Aros was slippery. He always knew. And Nera is ever the guarded asp. But they couldn't kill me. No one could until my quest was done. And so we played the game. I simply had to make the others think my objective and deal was in the quest for the imperial throne—and to convince Aros and any others that we were allies, united in one goal, dispatched when that goal was reached. Killing the Shadow Prince was key to any plan that involved killing the emperor. I was not the only one with that thought. Victory couldn't be gained over the emperor without the neutralization of the thirteenth blessed son."

"You would never have managed it on your own."

Osni smiled. "No. But I didn't have to."

"You hate Aros. Yet you worked with him."

"Aros will die." He looked out at her. "Tell me that he won't."

She said nothing for long moments. "He will."

Osni closed his eyes. "But Nera will slip away."

"Nera will be contained."

"Nera must die. I will not die until she does."

"I am the consequences of my actions. But I am not your hand of death."

"No, you are the King's Hand."

"I am my own hand," she said, locking eyes with him.

He regarded her for a long moment. "Perhaps. Perhaps you are." He looked at his sleeve, picked at it. "Farrah would have been proud," he said gruffly.

"Speak not of her," Nin said scratchily. "You have no right."

"No. But I will make it up to her in the life after the next one. I will face my punishment, then I will find her again."

Nin swallowed. "You can never be forgiven for her death."

"I'd kill any who said I was." And it was there in the remnants of his lost voice—the man who had loved his wife and son.

"How could you do it?" she whispered. "She loved you."

"Someday maybe you'll understand."

"I never will."

"Maybe you won't," he allowed. "You were always the softest of them. Saving your servants. Praying for the souls of the ones they forced you to kill. Farrah loved that about you. You were an easy board for her to grasp onto in a sandpit of vipers, especially after... She funneled her rage and sadness over Bilen's death—and in me having to carry out the execution—into preparing you."

"She did. And I loved her," Nin whispered.

"But she didn't...she didn't understand. That there was nothing to prepare for. Our life was over. She was trying to piece together some semblance of a life after, as if there was ever a life to be had after Bilen—" Osni gripped his head in his hands.

And his grief was something Nin understood, even though she would never forgive him—or his grief's response. Crelu ul Osni had loved his son. Bilen had been all that was good in the world, and she knew what it had done to both of his parents to lose him.

Osni had been the one forced to wield the axe.

"I'm sorry," she said. "Bilen was beloved, and for good reason."

It had been the beginning of the end, really. The Carres never realized what their actions wrought, but in that one decision, they had made their most fatal mistake. In protecting Jisarek, in condoning and allowing his horrible lifestyle, in shielding him from the emperor's wrath, they had made their most potent mistake. And that one mistake had led to many others. But then, if her family had realized their actions at any time, many things would be different.

Factions had formed in Tehrasi—secret factions that had helped facilitate the emperor's victory. And Osni had found an easy ally to rally behind.

"I killed my son," Osni said. "No one else could wield that axe. I felt his soul in my hands as he passed on. And I swore that I would see your family dead. Farrah poured herself into you, as if that was a possibility. I needed to be the vengeful hand for both of us."

Nin shut her eyes tightly. "She was trying to live beyond her grief."

"She needed to be her grief. There was...another possibility that Farrah could have taken. That could have allowed her to live. I offered it while the knife was in my hand. As you were coming down the hall to visit—your footsteps echoing on the stones."

Nin opened her eyes, dread encasing her. "No."

Osni looked at her, poison pumping through the black lines in his skin. "She loved you. She could have wielded the blade. She could have gotten out of her oath by killing you. She could have made the deal instead."

"She could have killed me instead of you killing her." Nin thought she could not feel any colder.

"A foolish thought in a split's second time. I knew she could never do it. For all our traitor talk after Bilen died, she would never condone killing the younger royals—the last four of you—and the spell I needed in the end wouldn't work without connecting all of you. You were all to die. A surprise, to be sure, that you survived. She made certain you were disconnected from the spells, didn't she?"

"You killed her. Killed everyone."

"You would have been used by the empire. They would have enslaved you. Given you to Etelian." He looked at the wall. "I saved you."

"You killed us. You killed Heba."

He said nothing for a moment. "Yes. They all had to die. Their deaths are mine."

"For your revenge."

"For Bilen. But Nera still lives." He looked at her. "You cannot let her continue to do so."

"I'm not an executioner."

"You will learn to be. Carre blood runs through you."

"I will not be your executioner."

He stared at her with a distant gaze. "You were always Farrah's favorite. Her beetle princess."

"You will not use Farrah against me."

"If I could kill Nera…" He closed his eyes. "If I could know Aros was dead, I would be my own executioner." He shook his head. "It makes so much more sense now."

"Your madness?" Nin asked tiredly.

He shook his head, opened his eyes. "I had written it away, the last words of the two

602

princesses. But with the knowledge that you survived..."

He opened the locket and Nin drew in a sharp breath as the memory expanded into the air. From a distance, she had seen enough of the memory to observe her family and the household collapse. She had heard the last sentence Giran Carre had uttered. But she had never been close enough to see the expressions on their faces. She had never wanted to.

But Osni's captured memory was micro fine—his most cherished memory of revenge, kept in place around his neck, close to his heart. Naming herself the Hand had not been an accident. It had been a taunt for Osni to hear, rather than the emperor, and it had done its duty.

But she had always been at a distance from seeing the memory in full. She had never been privy to everyone's last moments, the actual death scene unfolding before her.

Lorsali's expression displayed a contrast of emotions as she looked at Heba, who was wearing Zehra's face. "Beetles run," she said scathingly.

"Beetles don't escape. Only phoenixes fly free," her voice said.

Nin's hand went to her throat. Heba.

Nin watched Jisarek fall. She watched Giran speak his words. She watched each member of her family die. She watched herself fall. She watched Heba die.

Osni played it a second time. Then a third. Then a fourth.

Osni had never focused on Lorsali when watching before. He cared about Giran, Salare, and Jisarek. But now, Nin got to see Lorsali's face up close and hear the words that had only ever been lip movements in the background. Heba's last words.

"Beetles don't escape. Only phoenixes fly free."

"It is so obvious now. Lorsali knew it wasn't you. They all did."

And Nin could see it reflected in their faces on the fifth time watched, in the stiff way they purposely weren't looking Zehra's way. In the words that Giran uttered and that she had later claimed for her own.

"Even the witch said nothing."

And she could see it in Lorsali's face. The knowledge as she looked directly at Heba wearing her sister's face. The bitterness, the loathing, the envy, the possessiveness, then the blaze of resolve. Lorsali turned and looked at Osni, at the emperor, at all of the imperial forces with the royal disdain only she, Salare, and Savvan had been masters of.

Lorsali had known, at the end, and she had said nothing. She had chosen not to take Zehra down with her. Perhaps she thought Zehra would save them?

But no. She looked at the memory. Lorsali had known, the same as the rest of them when Giran had dropped five moments after Jisarek, and Salare had followed five moments more. Just enough time to see what was happening, as the spell gripped each one's blood.

The imperial forces were scrambling, the emperor was yelling, but there was nothing to be done for any in the scene.

Lorsali stared disdainfully at Osni as Savvan dropped and the spell caught her next.

Lorsali's head tipped the slowest fraction toward Heba wearing Zehra's face. How hard it must have been for Lorsali to stare at the servant knowing she had taken her hated sister's place. To know that Zehra would be saved and she would not.

How easy it would have been for Lorsali to expose the ruse.

She watched the memory again and again as Osni thrust it forward. Watched the complicated expressions cross her sister's face. Watched them harden into something familiar. Lorsali had held determination as her standard. Usually that determination meant terrible things. But here...

Lorsali turned again to the empire and determination hardened her features once more. And she said nothing.

Lorsali had not exposed her. The Carres had ever been about eating their own. Never letting anyone else touch them—only another Carre could consume a Carre. And maybe it didn't matter in the end, that Lorsali could never love her outside an obsession bordering on hate. Maybe It was enough that Lorsali hadn't said anything at the end. That Lorsali's silence had allowed Nin to survive. And that her survival had meant that she could do good for their country.

Lorsali had hated her. Nin had no doubt of that. But she had not given her up to the empire. Lorsali's belief in blood or revenge or house had overcome the hatred she felt in her last moments. And her silence had given Nin life.

Nin thought of the assassin who had tried to kill her when she had been six. Lorsali had slit the man from tip to stern.

"I hate you," Lorsali had sneered at her afterward. "No one gets to hate you more. But I will be the one who decides when you die."

Lorsali had been incapable of softer emotions. But there was something that had rigidly held her to family. She wasn't a nice person, wasn't a good person, and Nin had wanted nothing more than to see her married and far from the palace, but...

Nin always lit star lights for her, on their death anniversary, all the same. Glowing yellowed and whitened tips rising and weaving up into the starlight blanket above.

Nin swallowed and worked her pin into the bars again.

Nin owed Lorsali her life the same as she owed it to the entire lineup of family and servants who had remained silent. Osni had not meant to show her anything but the last words as a realization of a puzzle piece that had eluded him—and likely sought to mentally obliterate her emotionally. But what he had shown struck Nin more deeply than he could realize.

Lorsali had known that Nin was not standing next to her, and that Nin—Zehra—would escape execution. And Lorsali had not given her up.

Nin lamented that she could never have had a real relationship with her sister. She lamented Lorsali's obsession and hatred. She lamented that she could never have been anything other than the thorn in her sister's side—the nexus of her rage.

She could never forgive Lorsali for Sora and all the others Lorsali had killed before Nin had figured out how to guard her own. But she could accept that Lorsali had chosen in the end to save her. And maybe that was enough to put the spirit of her to rest.

The Carres were her past. She knew that. She had known that. But staring at the memory as it faded back into Osni's locket, she found an acceptance that had always eluded her. Of her past, her present, and her future.

Nin clicked open the latch on the rightmost bar.

Osni stared at her in shock.

The spells upon the door needed someone with authority working from the outside to undo them—as she had done to free the Scythians. She would never be able to undo the spells from the inside. She had needed to go around all the enchantments instead.

No one ever seemed to remember that she was a thief.

Magic was so ubiquitous, that people forgot the basics. Especially people who relied upon power like breathing. But living with Taline had made Nin both humbled by the amount of magic she herself had and had given her an understanding of what Taline accomplished without it.

Osni launched himself at the bars of his own cell, gripping tightly even through the pain of the spells burning his wrapped flesh. "Throw yourself from the tower, when you are free."

Nin slowly turned her head to look at him from where she was prying open the second bar. "Pardon me?"

"You speak of sacrifice. You want Aros gone. You want to save Tehrasi. I tied the spell both ways. If he dies, you die, but he knows not that if you die, he does as well."

Nin froze.

"It only took three bitten-free tongues before I could take no more. Or so he thought. I could withstand a thousand tongues being removed. I told him the parameters of the spell I used. I told him that I specifically tied the original spell to Jisarek. That he needed to be the first one who died in order for my pleasure to be sated. In order for Giran to see his beloved brother drop. But that wasn't true. I simply knew Jisarek would fall first. I told Aros that it was the blood—that you needed to touch the blood of the person who would take the others with them. I tried to get him to place the spell on me." Osni closed his eyes and the smell of burning flesh grew stronger as he gripped harder. "It wouldn't be enough, not to get Nera, too, but it would be something."

He opened his eyes. "I didn't tell him that the spell he tore from memory was one that had no single hooked end. Anyone with that spell upon them will die with the others attached."

Not just that Nin would die if Aros did—but that Aros would die with Nin?

Nin stared through the four tower windows located between the four cells and at the banners flying through the streets stretching in all directions from the palace's mound. She could end Aros, the Carres, and the festival in one fell swoop. One swoop from the tower and all would be saved. For Kaveh would never be able to kill Aros if doing so meant her death.

She stared at the choice before her—at her past, future, and present.

The chains of her past, always coiling. Herself, born anew, then seen as someone else in the beloved eyes of those in the second life she came to love.

The streams of light of the future, always beckoning. To live for something other than righting the wrongs of the past.

The darkness of the present, always tugging. In forgiveness for surviving, forgiveness for her existence, forgiveness for redemption.

"You want to save them. You want to save them all! Do you not, girl?"

Nin looked at her hands. "Do you accept the sacrifice, Zehra Amanan Carre?" she murmured. "Or do you choose to move forward and believe in your allies, Ninli ul Summora?"

"Give the life that you stole. End the Carres. Do you not have the nerve, little beetle, to right your family's wrongs?"

She looked at the streets and banners and the conveyances that swept through the streets and flew through the skies. She saw the old, haunted city of blood opening to the new wonders of the empire. She thought of Farrah, of Heba, of Reyi. Of Allit, of Memni, of Jolan, of Lorsali.

"The guilt has hampered me," she murmured. "All my life. I have lived for others. And I do not think that bad, by itself, but others..." Others cared for her, too, and it was incumbent on her to do right by that. Another form of living for others, perhaps, but there was a part of her—a growing part—that wanted her own happiness. That wanted to be free.

She had sampled it when she had thought of giving up the Scepter of Darkness to the empire or running away with Taline. She had felt the curl of it, desirous and wanting. To live free.

"I...I wish for more," she said, the words strange on her lips. "I rely on those I love in the same way they rely upon me. I will not waste this opportunity."

"And when the first one you love dies?"

She saw the signal. The flare of violet purple in the wind. She felt hope curl. The people...

She looked at Osni. "Decision is a constantly changing action as new information reveals itself. I will make that decision as I go, Crelu ul Osni. But I will give the life that I was given by Farrah, by Heba, by Reyi, and...by Lorsali...and I will continue to serve my community and that gift. With the life I was given, and the life that I choose."

Osni's eyes sparked, but he stayed silent for long moments. "Will you kill me, then, beetle princess? With the knowledge I have given you and the knowledge of how these cells work?"

Revenge, offered to her again, as it had been so many times. But never where Osni would know exactly who she was, exactly how he had failed, exactly what was to come.

She stepped forward and Osni braced himself. Nin unlocked his cell, spells in hand from the outside.

Shock, dismay, hate, grief, glittering determination—all cycled through Osni's eyes.

She stepped back. "What will you do, Crelu ul Osni? With the life you have left?"

He said nothing and she turned to limp to the scroll room. Speaking with him to find answers had never been the only gamble she had. And knowing that the spell went both ways—tied by blood—opened far more resources and countermeasures. She was going to find the answer. It was within her grasp and through the sight of the shadowglass in her pocket. Then Kaveh could end Aros's reign.

They were going to win. Nin felt certainty settle within.

"Gatemaker," Osni said.

Nin turned slowly around. Explosions rocked the city around them.

Osni stood outside his cell. His stare was hard. "Before Bilen died, I had some fondness for you, knowing Farrah loved you. After, I was incapable of feeling at all. But Farrah believed in you. For all that I hate your line and wish it to the depths of despair, I find myself with this single break."

He ripped the chain from around his throat and threw the locket to her. If he had thrown anything else, she would have batted it away without thought. But like a bird caught in a too-strong wind, Nin caught the locket and stared, uncomprehending at the memory cage of her family's fate.

"You go to find the scroll I destroyed, gatemaker. But the knowledge only remains now in my mind."

Nin felt horror descend as she tried to look away from the locket, but there was a blood spell there, enchanting her, and she was incapable of looking away. Her blood tugged. With her gaze locked, she could not see him, but she could feel the movements of turning air as he drew closer.

"I can feel the forces moving in the city and palace, gatemaker. I am still attached to the magic, too. I see the purple flare—the signal you follow."

"And what do you choose, Crelu Osni?" she whispered, leaving off the imperial format of his name, gaze still glued to the cage in her hand.

Osni let out a wretched, lisping chuckle. "You were always like Farrah—kind and soft—willing to see the good in those who are without. You loved Farrah, and she loved you. She believed in you—that you could rise above your birth as a Carre." Faster than she could comprehend, Osni swiped forward and spilled her blood with a hidden blade. She watched it drip upon the locket, sealing to it. A spell rose, hissing into the air with intent.

"One gift for another. The Carre reign of terror ends with you. Farewell, gatemaker. I will see you in another life."

Nin fell with her blood.

CHAPTER TWENTY-ONE
CAGES OF SHADOW

RONE

(Skudra, Scythia, Bahra, Cuipsin, Herat, Syra, Loran, and beyond)

Rone dodged another lethal blast, then sent a glass orb flying. Fehl's cloak, encased in shadows, flared out behind him as he darted over the turret tips of Ancyra; then, with a quick flick of his wrist and a dodge of scorching air, he was cut from the fabric of Skudra's capital and flew above the sparkling waters of Tomyr in Scythia.

Aros appeared five heartbeats behind. Rone flung another orb and dove for the palace roof. He could feel the scepter blast coming toward him and realized he wasn't going to make it. He signaled one of the Scythians stationed below, then he vanished again in ripped air.

Wielding bits of Fehl's shadows encased in Taline's orbs and carrying a medallion that allowed him to draw upon Ninli's donated power, Rone appeared and disappeared throughout the empire almost at will, breaking prisoners free, destroying thrones, and taunting a man who wielded an object that could unmake him.

But Aros had to hit him first.

The people had been rallied, the imperial forces had been readied, and Rone was doing his utmost to tip Aros over the edge. Aros was trying to patch each palace break, but he was losing the grip he held on the empire. Shadows couldn't be gripped.

Aros aimed a blast at Krokola's citizens. Rone threw an orb and a shadow dragon burst to life, ensnaring Aros's attention as it roared above the capital city of Cuipsin. Rone mimicked what he had seen Fehl do in Tehras and sent the dragon diving forth to save the citizenry.

"Kaveh!" Aros yelled and the scepter flashed the blast aimed at the citizens at the dragon instead. Rone used those scant moments to raze three additional monsters that Aros would feel the need to target.

Aros turned. Rone whirled and disappeared. Before Aros could capture him—or target imperial forces in order to make "Kaveh" relent—Aros had to find and hold his attention first. Stabilizing a foe was the largest hurdle when one wanted to gloat.

So Rone ran. Open ripgate. Fling shadows. Dodge. Open ripgate. Repeat. Stay fast, stay ahead, run the gambit, hit the mark, flee. It was Rone's favorite strategy and he was superb at it.

The shadows around him and the spells that had been woven to make him appear to be Kaveh ul Fehl from a distance—beneath a hooded cloak, because nothing could truly hide Rone's hair color—faltered, but he used the medallion to move again, knowing Aros would follow. For these few ticks of time, Aros was baited and on the hook.

Baksis and Simin and Namir were creating similar distractions, while somewhere the real

Kaveh ul Fehl was preparing their last move, somewhere Ninli was unhooking herself from the blood spell, somewhere Taline was fighting Etelian.

Sehk. He hoped Taline was winning.

Trust. Ephemeral as it had ever been—a shadow of a cage he had long fought against—he had to trust so many today. He threw baubles filled with shadow and darkness.

Trust. He had enough power contained in the last medallion to reach twelve more destinations. But after that, it would be the end play. He tapped through to let Fehl know the countdown had begun.

TALINE

Etelian ul Fehl's chambers, the Palace of Tehras

Etelian screamed.

Etelian's magic whirled around him, then locked into place. The palace guards froze and looked at him with uncertainty.

Taline grimly smiled. "How does it feel? To have your magic locked?" She withdrew what she needed next, heart racing.

"You slenterfasi! I'll kill you! Guards!"

The guards surged forward, and she threw her hands forward, littering the ground in front of their running feet with her spell-filled marbles. They exploded upon contact, taking down the ones who had surged forward by foot. The guards who used the winds to propel themselves forward, or bounded off the walls, required different tactics, and she had prepared something for each of them, too.

She spread her fingers, baubles appearing in each as she activated the enhancer in her sandal with a twist of her foot. Simulated winds rose and shot forward, carrying the marbles on unnatural winds and slamming into guts and chests.

The guards fell as they carried out maneuvers that were old and predictable. Etelian never learned or changed. As aggravating as that was, it was also to her benefit. He trained his fighters using the same tactics—because he believed that he could always have his power go straight through.

Poor Etelian, who was fumbling with the scepter now, his powers locked.

She let free her bellow of rage and triumph, then whirled and bolted from the room.

The nullification was a temporary measure. There had not been enough time to figure out how to increase its range and time. Rone was still far too careful with his powers, especially around her, and she adored him for that—but in order to fight an inferno, Rone was going to need to let his true power show before the end.

"Guards!" Etelian screamed, and she ran for the best spot to make her next move.

The beginning of the end had begun.

KAVEH

Tower of Justice, Tehras

Kaveh could feel his shadows in the hands of his siblings and allies. He could feel his shadows in the palace watching as Taline led Etelian on a chase.

With the others baiting Aros across the empire and Etelian temporarily silenced, Kaveh was free to come out of the shadows and make a more public move in the place that would hit Aros hardest.

Kaveh looked out at Tehras and stroked the shadow tears he had placed upon the farhani of each person connected to the Hand—each person he had originally intended to kill after dealing with the thief.

The shadow marks had faded, but with a little push, they pulsed into dark, visible lines—and small gray beacons reached into the sky. The loveliest of magical sights. Kaveh drew the feel of them within—diving down into the marks and pulling shadows down to encase each marked form.

Nin had activated her secret forces, but she had done so by refusing to ask them for sacrifice. Kaveh planned to give them the choice.

He turned as the door opened behind him and the investigore froze. Kaveh smiled as the investigore slowly shut the door.

"Imperator General," the investigore said cautiously. A man who had held true fondness for Nin, Malik ul Malit had not been replaced. He was a man who was true to Tehras and keeping the peace, and at this point, he would have seen all evidence for and against their plan. He would be fully aware of everything that was happening—with Aros, with Nin, with the Carres, with the elite, with Kaveh losing his powers.

Knowing all that—the man looked at him with cautious hope, and Kaveh felt that hope reflected inside. Kaveh thought of Ishum's words, and Teir's.

"Might is also something that can be nurtured and can evolve into other aspects. Community, building, creation."

"I want my village to be strong. Asking for help in making my village strong does not show weakness."

Kaveh pulled at the strings of the encasing shadows and a hundred terrified faces formed in front of them—attached by the shadows tears he had once placed upon them.

"People of Tehras. You once stood by the Hand. Do you stand with her now? Do you support the dissolution of the Feast of Sustenance and Renewal and the next step after it—progress for all?"

Terrified faces formed into resolve.

"I wouldn't trust a Carre with anything." A man spat, his gaze never leaving Kaveh's, while he waited patiently for his judgment. "But I'd trust the Hand with everything," he said gruffly.

Kaveh extended his fingers and let his shadows swirl. "I will not fail you. Neither of us will."

Looks were exchanged—people seeing each other in the ether of the investigore's office and in their own shadows and light. Then, slow, deliberate nods were sent his way.

The investigore tipped his head forward as well, lips tight.

Kaveh felt triumph swirl.

"Then here is what we will do," Kaveh said. He would make certain that the citizens had a part in their freedom. He would save this city for Nin, and he would save the empire for them all.

Valeran's signal tapped violently. It was time. Kaveh sent a pulse back to Valeran, Baksis, Simin, and Namir; then he sent the purple bag of herbs up in a spiral of shadow and watched it burst into purple smoke over the capital city. A signal for Nin's allies to secure Tehras, and others to secure the outside empire, even as it drew Aros back to the capital.

It was time to beat Aros at his own game.

TALINE

The Palace of Tehras, Tehrasi

Taline skimmed past a window, clutching to the stones three stories high, and saw the purple smoke rising in the east. The countdown had begun. Thank Sehk.

Pressed against external ledges and stones, hiding in corners, evading a pursuer who made her skin crawl and who held her mind frozen with terror was never the way in which she wished to find herself again.

Taline looked through the balistraria into the empty room and slipped back inside the palace.

Nin would be making her escape soon and heading to the scroll room. The holding tower was far from Etelian's rooms, and Taline had made Nin promise not to come looking for her if she ended up in the palace at the end of Etelian's scepter. But Nin would assuredly check the palace magic and see Taline, and Nin would come for her anyway.

Taline would scold her but be grateful.

Taline waited a beat, then two, unease slowly working its way upward when Nin did not appear. Perhaps Aros had done something to her or taken her with him despite Nin's certainty that he would not. Perhaps Aros had taken her somewhere else instead of locking her in a cell designed to hold her. If so, Nin would see it through. She always did. Taline worried over her, but Nin always prevailed.

But it meant definitively that Taline was on her own, and that made old anxieties rear themselves. Taline curled her fingers around one of the medallions tucked in her sash pockets. She could leave. She could flee.

"Siiiiiran. You are all alone. And you are so weak."

She was. She was thinking about fleeing right now. She took a deep breath and felt the crevices in the medallions, counting the lines of the glyphs she had carved. Fear was not weakness. And she was not weak.

Plans flitted through her mind, terror turning to resolve. What to do? What outcome worked best? Revenge, madness, terror, pain—a thousand paths. And no Nin to rely upon to talk through it with.

But then, Taline had needed to come up with her own plans on the spur of a moment countless times when Nin had deviated from the plan to save someone or do something reckless and wild.

"Siiiiiran. I see you. The scepter tells me where you are."

That meant he had control of his magic again. Terror froze her, but Taline reached out and grabbed it by the throat, hardening her thoughts. She had devised her own plans many times and she excelled at it.

She rubbed at the packet of herbs tucked into the clinking medallions, letting the mixed herbs seep into the cuts on her palms. She visualized the palace layout and darted to the corner before shifting into a secret corridor that connected one part of the structure to another. From memory, Nin had shared many of the passageways—ways that the Carre servants had maneuvered through a household that served people who could ripgate.

The City of a Hundred Gates contained a palace with a hundred more. The palace gates within the structure could only go between, keeping them safe from external influence.

Taline was granted a half minute of maneuvering before Etelian crept close to her position. He knew many of the passageways, too. She wondered how often Osni had doled secrets out over the years—keeping himself useful and alive. She looked at the next doorway, which could be activated into a gate by pressing a particular glyph on the frame. She plotted her course.

"You have a way of temporarily hiding yourself and someone taught you palace secrets. Naughty, naughty girl. But it's a futile gesture. You can't escape. Come out now, and I will only remove your feet, to keep you from straying again."

Etelian thought her useless outside of her face and form, so her continued defiance would have seen her dead in any vessel less to his tastes.

She touched her arms—the strangely blemish-free skin still felt foreign. She had been one of the lucky ones. Though she had not held that opinion until years after Nin had saved her. It had taken a long time for her to see a life without a collar stretched before her.

"Come out, come out. You know I will regrow them on you, after I'm certain of your broken state. I can't stand to see imperfections in you that don't contain my name."

Her lips peeled back from her teeth in a silent snarl.

He turned a corner. She headed straight at the passageway, hit the glyph, then whirled through the closest exit—a mirror—as Etelian appeared behind her. Her brain scrambled to remember where this one went.

His fingers brushed her cloak, nullifying one of the spells there. She fell through the mirror and hit the floor.

Etelian's rooms stared back at her. A miscalculation.

One of the women stared hard, then reached toward Taline, offensive magic brimming in her palm.

KAVEH

Throne Room, Palace of Tehras

Kaveh appeared in the palace amid shadow and silence. He felt the shadows curling around the empire and he reached out and drew all those outside of Tehrasi back to him. One merged with another and then formed a larger one with another group of three, joining and coiling together into a blanket of darkness that pulled across the empire, then flew through the streets of Tehras and dove to swirl around him.

Kaveh pulsed the shadows en masse—pushing them outward, pulling them in, then pushing out again.

A presence encased in shadow, but otherwise utterly empty, appeared behind the throne. Kaveh could do nothing but smile in anticipation as a slicing ripgate appeared around Kaveh's body, heralding the start. Kaveh pushed both hands outward and the ripgate exploded instead of finishing its work of slicing him in half.

Aros appeared in the rose-golden light of sunset, the scepter deflecting Kaveh's thrown shadow. With another flick of the scepter, a barrier immediately crisscrossed the walls, the floor, and the ceiling of the throne room. "And here you are, finally. Alone. And now unable to flee. Such cowardly acts, disappearing like that across the imperial fields. What will your forces say?"

"That they found wielding shadow a laborious task, I expect."

Aros's eyes narrowed and he waved off another blast of shadow. "Goodness, brother, such deception. Are you trying to kill me with shock?"

"It was on my mind." But Kaveh wasn't trying to kill Aros. Not yet. He needed to give Valeran time, hidden as he was inside of the barrier Aros had formed upon the walls of the room. He needed to buy Nin time, for she was still in the holding tower working her way out of her cell.

"It has been on mine, too." Aros's eyes glittered. "I see now, the many participants I've been running after for the past tick of sun's set. The trouble they have caused me will be ripped from the life-force of each."

Kaveh tightly held the shadows, standing perfectly still in their seething mist. He had to keep Aros speaking. "Should you survive, you will have much to do."

Aros's eyes were darting around Kaveh's frame, looking for the smallest movement that indicated Kaveh would attack. Aros knew his style well. "I will survive, brother. I have a lovely protection—a lovely new family member—who carries my blood."

"She's not your family."

Aros smiled dangerously. "I've lived with Etelian as family for his thirty-one years, Kaveh. I can assure you I'd far rather claim a more useful one."

"So you can sacrifice her as soon as it becomes convenient."

"That's what convenience means."

"I will not allow it."

"You will have no recourse. You cannot flee, and neither can I. One of us will die here. If you don't want it to be her, choose your death."

Kaveh's shadows swirled into a cage.

Aros broke it. "Was that my cage, Kaveh? The one you said would be gilded?"

Kaveh allowed the break, using the ruse to hide what Valeran was doing behind the throne.

Kaveh felt along the broken lines and pieces of torn shadow that were joining and melding with the swarm at the floor. He pieced together another cage, stronger.

Aros's eyes narrowed as he destroyed this one as well.

But Kaveh had time. Time was an asset now, and he could play this game longer than Aros could.

Nin had helped him make his cages stronger while fighting against him. Fighting with her, together, had only strengthened them.

Fighting with Nin in the alley as the Hand... It had been the first time in so long that he had needed to advance any of his spells. It had been a rush then, as it was now—as it was with Valeran—to have a physical opponent to fight against who could challenge him.

He had been fighting far too many mental games in the past weeks. Having a physical one brought relief and brisk exhilaration.

Aros hissed as the newest cage incarnation burned his skin. The scepter waved and cut the cage with a raised dome. A great show of weakness that Kaveh would normally celebrate, and perfect for the moment, but he would eventually need to make certain that Aros dropped the dome so Valeran could do what was needed.

"You use her spells," Kaveh said. "As a barrier around you? Weakness."

"I use what knowledge is mine now. As all who wish to become greater do."

Kaveh did not bother to test the dome. He didn't need to. Better to let time seep for Aros through the last cracks of sandglass.

"This is your last hour, Aros. What will you do with the time you have left?"

Aros paced inside the dome, keeping Kaveh in view and the scepter in front of him. "You are stalling. What is this new madness? That you do not strike me with all your force?"

"Soon," he said in soothing promise. "I will have your head soon."

"You will not be able—" Aros winced and pressed a hand to his chest, face disturbed. His head whipped up. "What have you done?"

Kaveh expanded shadows inside the room, waking every nook and cranny, taking advantage of Aros's inattention—covering Valeran's machinations and embedding his own.

"Her blood has been spilled." Aros looked disturbed, but it quickly morphed into pointed dagger. "You wait for the girl. But she has failed. Her blood runs upon the stones."

No. Aros was wrong. Nin was fine. She was escaping her cell. Kaveh sent shadows automatically to pierce the barrier Aros had initiated upon entering the room in order to check, but Aros waved the scepter and the barrier Aros had wrapped around the room pulsed. Kaveh's shadows sizzled and fell to mote, unable to connect outside.

"I questioned my fate, Kaveh, seeing your powers return, but the girl...the girl has always been the key. And so she is. As long as I hold the key, I am invulnerable. And she is bleeding out upon the tower floor. What will you give to save her?"

Kaveh narrowed his eyes. The blood spell was still in place on Aros. It looked odd—like it was shuddering and trying to stabilize—but a tie still existed. He couldn't strike Aros without risking Nin, and he couldn't check on her state without disabling Aros. She had been fine in the moment before Aros had encased the room in his own type of cage. The shadows had said she had been stepping free of her cell.

Kaveh's magic tightened, demanding to be free—demanding to kill and maim and destroy. To destroy all that was planned, and all that they had laid down. Vengeance filled him. He touched the ribbon tied to his sash.

A small, remembered hand steadied him as his larger fingers brushed the silk. No.

He looked at the man in front of him and glimpsed the past. The emperor blinded by his revenge on Jisarek, had paid dearly for his vengeance.

Nin was the best of them all. He believed in her and the future.

Stick to the plan, keep Aros talking. He watched the blood spell shudder again. "How did you get Osni to tell you how to set the blood curse?"

Aros looked at his fingers oddly as he pulled them from his chest, but he shook his head as if to free disturbed thoughts. "She is..." He shook his head again. "With a loving touch of the scepter, all give their secrets. Crelu ul Osni never made secret that he set that curse. It was obvious from the way he watched them die."

Yes. It was why the emperor had punished Osni with the loss of his hand. It had always struck Kaveh as odd that the emperor hadn't outright killed the man, but the emperor had needed to keep Osni alive for being the last—amid a pile of dead Carres and palace staff—to know how to use the scepters and power the gates.

"The emperor knew Osni had been freed of his oath, since he had survived the massacre, but not how. He tried to kill him. Twice, that I saw. Neither worked. It was one of the only times I've seen the emperor look unnerved."

It was news to Kaveh that Osni had survived death twice. Unease curled. Why would Nin be bleeding on the tower floor? "You had to worry for yourself then, Aros, even with the mass of oaths the emperor attached to Osni and made him sign with blood."

"Osni has always wanted me dead. But I was still alive after the massacre. The blood curse hadn't touched me, and Osni had been freed from the spell. How had he done it? He never revealed how, even under torture, until he was delivered to my feet along with the scepter that rules all." Pleasure suffused Aros's face. "Over the years, I pieced together enough, though. Enough to seek Darkness. It wasn't hard to recognize Osni's desires and the path he might have tread. Curiosity held my hand against him, and I kept Etelian's from him as well. For Osni alone was left with the secrets of the Carres. So I watched and waited. I planted spies and followed threads. I saw where he went, then sought those secrets myself. The scrolls and records. And now? Zehra will help me conquer my abilities, and I will reign triumphant."

Nin had seen Farrah's body upon the floor. The sacrifice of his heart, his last tie of love. A deal with Darkness on a level a regular magi could exercise, but one that had not left Darkness satisfied. Still, his wife's death had enabled Osni to skirt his oath and place a death spell on the Carres.

"Withering in his tower, watching me rule, watching the Carres grow strong again, Osni will pay with his life. He will live his life watching the Carres rule."

"You wanted to rule with your son."

"The emperor stole him from me! He sentenced him to death! Mother made him unrecognizable and forced me to cast him aside. That she didn't kill him is the only reason she still lives." Aros took a deep breath. "I would have found Zehra, too, if I'd thought of the possibility that a Carre had survived. The performance in death was effortless. Why would I—or anyone—have thought otherwise? But it was there when you look at the memory with opened eyes. The way their eyes go to the youngest. The way the eldest princess looks at her. The words from the king's mouth. It is all there as a puzzle that is easily deduced when all the pieces are laid bare."

Aros gripped the scepter tightly. "I should have deduced it before. That one had survived is the only thing that makes sense when looking very specifically at the happenings of the past decade. That Etelian wasn't able to piece it together is no surprise. I'm disappointed I did not." Aros looked at the scepter in his hand. "I could have been a lot farther on this path, if I had scooped her up at the beginning. The treasure trove of real Carre knowledge. The holder of their secrets. My son could have survived."

"She'll kill herself and take you with her before she lets you rule in Carre image."

"But you have convinced her not to sacrifice herself." Aros smiled. "It was the truest coup in all this that the two of you formed a bond. That you have weakness in each other. For it keeps you here, it hampers you from true power and decision, and it keeps her as well."

"While you have no bonds."

Aros gripped the scepter tight. "My son was a necessary sacrifice.

"Did you love his mother?"

Aros tipped his head. "Nera killed the woman who bore him. Even being a Barrini couldn't save her. People would always wonder, she said. Blood runs true, and gatekeeping was strong in his blood. He could track the scepters—he could feel them as part of his blood, allowing him to follow the Scepter of Darkness in the non-magic world. It showed that my blood was strong."

Kaveh's stomach turned. These were newer emotions to Kaveh, and it took a moment for him to realize discomfort and disquiet—but not surprise. "Nera didn't want your abilities seen."

"The only reason he survived is because I pretended not to know what adoption house had taken him in, and I continued my own educational journey."

"Did you mourn?"

"What difference does it make? It was a good lesson. I could rely on myself alone. I do not regret the lesson that showed me what I needed to see."

Kaveh hated this feeling. Had hated it since Nin came into his life, and still hated it now—to see the emperor as anything other. As anything lesser.

The emotions that had infected Kaveh demanded he see fault in some of the emperor's decisions. And yet the emotions were something that he was unwilling to let go now that he had them.

"The emperor should have accepted you as the child of his favorite wife and a man who was once an enemy and made peace with that."

Kaveh would make peace with the emperor's more complex sides someday. To rule over so many people and so much land—to take one's armies and bring so many new territories under control, then to rule them successfully—that took sacrifice and hard decision-making.

To love one's people and land meant that each decision was that much harder. It was far easier to rule without caring. He looked at the ribbon tied around the sash at his waist. Far easier, but not richer. He would not give up Nin for anything. He looked at the barrier, unease running through him again at the thought of her bleeding somewhere near Osni. Where was she? She should have been here by now with cut blood tie in hand.

"Nera would never have allowed that," Aros said. "She has always had her own designs."

And Nera had owned much of the emperor's heart. "What is Nera's plan?"

Aros smiled. "She loved Jisarek. Just a little. She saw the power in him. She played both sides. She has ever been cunning."

"She wanted you on the throne?"

"Well, dear not-brother, she didn't want it to be you. And it was obvious to all who followed the emperor's reign that by the time you took over the armies, there was no other option in the emperor's mind. Nera failed. She bred spoiled children in a mass of thousands of options, and when reason and sanity are invoked, they are easily passed over for something better—once the emperor's love extended to others."

"And yet her children sit upon prominent thrones."

"For how long?" Aros slowly shook his head. "You pay little attention, but the council was starting to push against the padifehls of Nera's birth. They said they were threatening the empire in the long term. And there were other options... Better options to be had."

Aros smiled maliciously. "It was your fault, brother. If Sher Fehl had simply done what he was supposed to have done and left the empire to me, he would still be alive. I would have been quite pleased to have the two of you conquer the world before I replaced him on the throne. But he was not going to leave the empire to me. Everyone knew where the empire was going." Aros slowly stepped sideways, scepter in hand. "So, really, it is your fault that he is dead."

Kaveh held his shadows. "I don't play your games, Aros."

"A true pity. He might still be alive if you had." Aros smiled. "We could have worked something out, the two of us. I'd have kept you as my right hand. Sher Fehl did. And Sher Fehl always knew best."

"He was never going to give you your birthright." And Kaveh felt the smallest measure of sympathy. Kaveh had never been without. But

Aros's birthright had been taken, hidden, and used against him.

"I could have—"

"You chose your path."

"It was chosen for me."

We are all made. But some choose a path as different as starlight to the sun.

Kaveh looked at the ribbon, gleaming in the light. "Nin chose otherwise."

"She will do what I tell her to do."

"Like the emperor did to you?"

"The emperor died being disappointed in you, Kaveh, not me." The words cut where the others had not.

Kaveh nodded, pulling shadow from the throne. "There is no way now to make amends with Father. That choice and outcome have been taken away. By you. Forgiveness, or understanding, will never come. I have to make peace with that, that I will never get that from the emperor."

"Oh, brother, I could spare you some peace," Aros said with a slash of a smile.

"From my father," Kaveh said. "But I will let that thought sustain me as I rip from you all that brands you alive."

Kaveh felt the feeling of nothing reach forth from the throne along with the grid that Valeran had formed. Kaveh swirled shadow to hide its path.

Aros smiled sharply. "You or Zehra will die."

"I think not." Kaveh saw the edge of the spell twining and he raised his hand and let shadows fly. The dome around Aros broke. Now.

"You have no choice in that matter, Kaveh." Aros spun and the grid snaked toward him. "And no one will aid you now. Least of all the traitor."

Aros brought the scepter down upon the ground. A line of broken marble snaked toward the throne and magic leaped along the fissure, shattering the nullification spell.

They had failed in their cage.

If Kaveh didn't kill Aros—and Nin along with him—Aros was going to kill Rone.

CHAPTER TWENTY-TWO

THE HOUSE OF SCEPTERS

TALINE

(Etelian ul Fehl's chambers, the Palace of Tehras)

Offensive magic flashed from the woman's hand. The blast hit Etelian as he tried to come through after Taline. Etelian swore, the mirror broke, and Etelian disappeared. Taline didn't wait—sending four explosive marbles to knock out the guards stationed within the room. The rest must have taken off to search for her at Aros's direction.

Taline took a shaky breath—a breath too soon, as a blast of utter power lit the falling night sky through the windows and shook the foundations of stones. Taline swallowed hard.

Her link to the scepter was gone—washed away by spring water and ancient enchantment—but she could feel its power here, now.

Aros ul Fehl and the Scepter of Darkness had arrived in the Palace of Tehras, the heart and house of scepters.

Taline looked to the woman who had helped her, then at all the others. "This is your chance," she told them. "Run."

"He will catch us!"

"We will be punished!" Terrified voices spoke out, but most of the women stayed silent in their fear.

Taline looked at her bracelet and the four ticks that were showing proximity. Taline, Nin, Rone, and Kaveh were now all in one place—the palace. Rone and Kaveh's marks would be together fighting and caging Aros. Nin would be freeing herself from the tower and from the spell, in order to give them all a chance. And Taline...

"Etelian Fehl is about to face his downfall," Taline said brusquely, refilling her sash with the orbs that had been stored deeper within her cloak. "Run now and save yourselves from the fight."

"You should run," the first woman said.

Taline looked at the royal chamber chair where Carres had sat for two hundred years, then Etelian ul Fehl had sat for ten more. She felt the stir of magic in the bedroom throne. Connected as it was to the Carres, the scepters would be able to seek it.

Rone, Nin, and Kaveh were fighting their battles, and it was Taline's turn. "I will fight. It is up to you, if you choose do the same."

She threw handfuls of ice orbs—Valeran-crafted ice spells—into the three clumps of women. Hands reflexively gripped and caught them but she had no time to give instruction.

Etelian appeared next to the chair, the fingers of one hand gripping his glowing scepter tightly, while the fingers of the other curled around the crown of his chamber throne. "Back in my rooms—oh, Siran, you do know what is best for you."

"I'm simply surprised Aros let you keep your chambers." She backed away from the women, putting them out of range of a blast, and slowly ran her fingers along her sash pockets. "A pathetic pity for a worthless padifehl."

Etelian's smile slashed downward—harsh and promising pain. "Worthless?" The scepter flashed. Guards spilled into the room and the first to reach the women made to grab one.

"Now."

Four women who held an orb pushed theirs forward. The guards froze. The rest of the women scrambled and thrust forward their own, seeing the results.

One tried to get Etelian. She boldly shoved her orb toward him, and the scepter glowed; then he struck her, pushing himself back.

"You will pay for this, Siran. You will all pay." But he was eyeing them differently now—as though they were a threat.

The women who were holding the clasped orbs were shaking, but their eyes were narrowed and focused. Etelian's hesitation was allowing them to see options. Others cowered or hid, but no one was actively interfering against one of their own.

Etelian strode forward.

"I wouldn't." Taline spread her palms, orbs between each finger, as she held them up. One was beating with fire trapped inside; another held emptiness swirling within. "What will you do, Etelian, if I take your powers again? What will you do without your guards to restrain your victims?"

Etelian surveyed her fingers, and the selfish madness that always lurked in the back of his eyes gleamed. "Dear Siran, fire? Are you going to show me how you escaped my burning chariot alive?"

"No." She rolled the fire orb back and forth between the two fingers that held it, making certain to keep all of them gripped. "But perhaps I'll allow you that discovery as you flee your burning chambers."

"Siran, you truly think to fight me?" He laughed, beautiful and terrifying. He raised the scepter.

She pulled her stretched hand in front of her face so that he could see the swirls of the orb held between first and middle finger. "Yes."

Etelian's eyes narrowed. "Another nullifying spell. My powers already returned. Aros has been doing experiments on me, and though I will eventually kill him for it, they are proving useful at regeneration. All I need to do is wait you out. You think those my only guards? Two more companies are on their way."

"And yet you stand here, alone." She didn't want to exchange words with Etelian, but she had an audience—an audience who needed to hear.

"I am never alone," Etelian said, something cold in his eyes.

"Aros won't be able to save you."

"Kaveh and Aros will kill each other today, then the Carre girl will be taken care of in turn. No one will survive. And good riddance." He hissed. "And you, my dear, won't survive this visit intact."

Taline spared a glance around the room to make certain she knew everyone's position. "It sometimes feels that way—that I lose a piece of myself every time you open your mouth."

"You should practice closing yours again. There's only one good use for your mouth."

The room shook. Taline felt the shaking in her hands. "But I am worthless. Isn't that what you always said?"

Another wave of guards poured into the room.

"Combine your magic!" Taline yelled and leaped forward. She threw three of the marbles, keeping the fire and emptiness in hand.

Etelian screamed in rage as she whirled around three guards. He ruthlessly took them out in the melee to get at her, but she used her momentum around the last, spinning out at Etelian's side, and she crushed the nullifying orb against his face.

Blood poured from the wound and he screamed in pain and fury.

There were so many guards now, though, pouring into the master chamber—only stopped by the doorway allowing them to fit through awkwardly in melee formation.

Etelian was tripped by the woman who had shot magic in his face, and Taline kicked the scepter from his hand. Etelian grabbed a knife and swiped it at the woman who had tripped him. The woman kicked him in the face, then whirled around and was lost in the chaos.

A few of the girls were fighting—throwing spells and using objects to knock out guards—but their magic use was scarce. The girls had been drained and scraped of their abilities—Taline recognized the scars. But they could generate some. They were new, so even scraped and hurt as they were, there was still some magic there—and some could become more.

"Combine your magic!" she yelled again.

The fighting knot of girls jerked in confusion, but two were suddenly grabbing others and pooling abilities, and soon a weak wind spell also held thrown shards of metal and earth.

A weak wave of water became a lightning storm.

A weak mending spell became an enhanced bind. Strands became ropes and turned into plaster and cement.

Together, they began to prevail.

The guards piled up on the floor—used to dealing with cowed women and forced respect—but the girls also started to flag.

"Go," she yelled at the girls. "Now! Escape!"

Most of them took off running—the younger ones fleeing, terrified.

"You will all die!" Etelian yelled after them. He whirled toward her. "You'll never save them, Siran! I'll kill them as they flee the grounds!"

"That's why coming alone would have been foolish." She touched the metal disks swirling with shadow at her sash. She tapped twice. She felt the ripgates opening below.

Etelian did, too, and he was scrambling for his scepter. A terrified-looking fourteen-year-old kicked it from his path, face draining of any remaining vibrancy as she did so. She would die, if Etelian regained his foothold.

"Go," Taline said to the girl. "Anyone who wants to leave, you will find help at the entrance doors and paths to take you far away."

That was enough for a few of the still frozen ones to run. The older ones, though...the older ones who had been dragged back in the past weeks, stayed. The fear on their faces had long past hardened to resolve.

"You will die beneath my knife." He scraped his way along the floor. "The bastard Valeran and Kaveh fight Aros. I can feel them now. And the Carre girl is almost dead."

That made Taline go cold.

Etelian still had direct connection to the palace and throne and through that, he could feel what was happening within. Where was Nin? Taline looked at her wristband. Three strong lines and one wavering one.

Nin was...not where she was supposed to be.

Taline dodged the blast aimed at her chest only at the last moment and threw a wind-powered blast.

It was fine. It would be fine. Nin was consistently not where she was supposed to be. And they had known things might get mixed up. They had planned on it—if not the exact way this scenario had turned out. But plans were made for flexibility. It was something she had learned quickly with Nin. Set something in stone, and you will break upon its unrelenting hardness. Stay flexible and you will bend in the wind and come snapping back.

She felt wind surge through her veins. "This is your end, Etelian."

He raged and flew at her. His eyes were lit with madness. His perfect features were crunched into a rictus of fury.

She ducked and slammed a disk-filled palm against his chest. She let a piece of Nin flow through her and told the magic to dive inside and squeeze his lungs.

He howled.

Taline hit him, then hit him again—letting healing magic do its opposite. Kidney damage. Stomach tear. Something in her wanted to keep hitting him until he could move no more.

She took a shaky step back. No. She took a deep breath and pulled the disk free. She raised her hand, hard metal pressed beneath. The eyes of the woman nearest to her went wide. This was it. This would be the final act. "Etelian ul Fehl, for all that you have done—"

A hand caught her wrist, forcing the metal to drop, and long, sharpened fingernails dug into her throat. Poison. Poisoned fingertips. Taline's body went rigid with agonized pain. Jerked around by the neck, she saw a shark-like smile stretched beneath sinister sea-green eyes.

"I think not," Nera ul Fehl said.

"Mother!" Etelian's voice was angry and relieved.

Nera twisted her wrist, shooting poisoned fire through Taline's body, while her nails dug into Taline's throat. And Taline knew only pain.

RONE

Throne Room, Palace of Tehras

Rone leaped away from certain death but continued to stare at the face of it all the same as the magic sizzled along the lines of his body, revealing him to the room.

Aros smirked. "The bastard." He moved slowly. "Hiding in Kaveh's shadows and with shield of your own—the only one to show the true potential of Sher Fehl's powers."

"It is why you wanted me dead."

Aros smiled sharply. "I knew as soon as your magic nullified the scepter. You were the only way Kaveh could regain his powers. But you waited so long to do it. I will express my surprise, as days and nights went by without. I started to hope. Logically, if you hadn't restored his powers right away, it could be that you had a weaker strain of power—like Etelian—or something adjacent—like Omari."

"And you are always logical."

"No, sometimes I am quite emotionally vicious." He threw a beam of orange.

Kaveh's shadows intercepted and ate the beam, then melted to the floor as the beam consumed them from within.

Rone was very glad Kaveh ul Fehl was on his side.

But even that was not enough. Not when he and his only ally in this room were bound not to kill the man who wielded the weapon against them.

They had just failed their first plan. Time to engage their second. It was in the third—killing Aros before Ninli was freed—that they would truly lose.

But Ninli should be in the grand library now, searching—reading. There were spells in the library that only a Carre could read—activated by eyes and blood. Ninli had long thought them lost to her. In all the time Rone had known her, her mind had been broken of the ability. And yet, Kaveh ul Fehl had given her something that allowed her to use him to do so.

She should be consuming the texts right now and finding the answer to disengaging her blood.

Rone looked at Fehl—Kaveh, because Rone couldn't call him Fehl at the moment while fighting another—in question. Kaveh slowly shook his head and Rone gritted his teeth. That meant Ninli wasn't engaging the glass yet. What was she doing?

"Come, bastard, use your powers against me again."

"Lovely." Rone groaned. "You asking me to do so isn't portentous at all."

Kaveh started casting spells immediately and Rone let him run the field while Rone walked the edges, trying to discern what Aros was up to. They couldn't kill him yet, so Kaveh's spells lacked death, but he was hitting him enough to give Rone options.

One spell hit the shield around Aros with enough force to knock Aros sideways.

Rone immediately shot a spell to nullify him. Aros dodged and hit back, making Rone dodge in turn, diving behind the imperial throne with its sun crest.

Standing with the Crown of Sunlight upon his head, Aros's eyes had taken on the blood-spattered hue that Ninli had tried to hide for half her life.

For a monster could only become more monstrous upon a throne.

But the thought he had long held made him pause, and the hue of Aros's eyes made him think. Ninli had always agreed that those in power had to be extra cautious—extra careful of their power. She had been born too far into a powerful family not to understand that there would likely always be powerful people who ruled. She had always wanted to see better in people. To not give in to Rone's pessimism about those who seated themselves in power.

For a monster could only become more monstrous upon a throne.

He had always believed that.

But Rone looked at Kaveh ul Fehl and he wondered. He wondered at the changes he witnessed. At the things he had seen him do. At the way the man was playing his part rather than obliterating his enemy—the enemy who was the reason for his father's death. At the way he had protected the people in the streets instead of seeing them as pieces to be broken, or weeds to be pulled.

At one point, not so long ago, Rone would have killed Kaveh ul Fehl himself, given the chance. He had watched his back for an opening to strike. And now he was watching his back to make certain it was protected. That no other could make a strike against him.

How had they gotten to this point?

It was a question for a late night and a flagon of something brain-wrecking.

He watched Fehl's shadows swirl around the scepter. He watched each of the Shadow Prince's shadows as they curled around the ring.

The Shadow Prince tensed. Aros laughed. But the flick of the Shadow Prince's fingers showed a different tension. And a blast from the back caught Aros unaware, pushing him off-balance.

Another chance.

Rone let his power free. And this spell...this one was going to hit. Rone readied the hook—he had not been fully in control of his power bef—

Aros swiped the scepter through the air, catching the edge of Rone's spell. Aros swirled the spell around the outer ring, then dragged it forward, pulling Rone's power to him.

"Sehk." Bonds tightened around Rone—his own power binding him and dragging him forward.

Rone felt true dread as no power answered his call—he had always relied on his power to save him. As a just in case, as Kaveh had said.

"I've been using the scepter on Etelian," Aros said. "He doesn't have a quarter of your powers, but it was enough for me to get a feel for what the scepter could do to bind you."

A line of shadow snapped the scepter's pull and Rone went stumbling back. Part of Rone's power snapped into the scepter; the other part recoiled back inside him.

Oh, that was not good. Not good at all.

Kaveh shot another blast.

Aros swiped the scepter again, vicious glee on his face, and instead of just Rone's powers circling around the ring, Kaveh's did as well. Then he shot both powers back.

Rone dodged but the feel of his own power sliced the air around him. He saw Fehl dodge shadows initially called by his own hand.

Aros grabbed hold of Rone again using his own power swirling at the end of that cursed scepter. Rone laughed mirthlessly. He had been fighting against his own power for so long, and here was a physical manifestation put forth to test him.

Taline, be well. "To the demon pits with you, Aros. I hope you enjoy a good show."

The scepter sent a blast at his heart.

KAVEH

Kaveh looked at Valeran, held firmly where he was. He saw Aros cast his lethal blow.

Kaveh dove in front and threw a full weight of shadow to counter the incoming blast. Part of the blast made it through anyway, and pain radiated up his arms. Kaveh clenched his muscles and pushed away the pain, then swung back. He couldn't kill Aros without killing Nin, but he could seriously maim him.

Aros swung his arm back again and there seemed something strangely more powerful about him all of a sudden—as if something outside of him had given him a boost. Kaveh's bundle of maiming shadows swirled around the outer ring of the scepter. They pulled away, but they were caught in its magnetic grasp. Aros whipped them to the side; the shadows shot off and the chair they hit exploded.

Aros stared hungrily as he moved forward in exulted steps. "I have longed for this."

"Yes, I know." Kaveh paced back warily—confident that Rone would do so as well, while staying behind him. He had known Aros coveted his powers—had coveted both Kaveh and Irsula's shadows. As far as Kaveh knew, Aros had never successfully captured any until today.

"And I bet this is not the only thing that can be taken and used." Aros gripped the scepter and lifted it in the dying light of sunset. "My forebears. So small-minded. They could have had the world."

"No." It was something that Kaveh had only recently started to realize. "They knew, even in their insanity, that possession of such would remove them from power, not keep them there."

It was something the emperor had instinctively understood—that letting the people have their own agency encouraged them to accept the empire more easily. Change their way of life little at first, then slowly nurture and ease the empire's aims into the minds of the populace. That was the strategy that allowed him to maintain hold of his initial conquered territories before he had expanded outward.

Of course, Nin had helped Kaveh realize that conquering and leaving populations to fend for themselves one right after another yielded their own set of problems. A strong empire was not a patchwork of separate states.

The emperor had never been satisfied by what he had, though. He was always searching for more. And it was a good trait to an extent. The empire was strong in many ways. But the emperor had not concentrated on what he had as he had done in the beginning, and instead he only looked toward the vast shores beyond. He had been looking too far ahead—what to conquer next, what to make and recreate.

He had put his own flesh upon each conquered throne. And though that hadn't necessarily been a terrible plan, in the case of Nera's children, especially, the minds inside had been tainted.

"That was why the Carres hid it—hid it in a place where it could not be found again. Away from temptation."

"Temptation is so misjudged, brother. Why not have what you can and use it for all things good."

"That is not how temptation works, Aros. You know that."

Aros looked at him through glittering red eyes, washed free of any trace of amber now. "Come, brother, cast upon me."

Kaveh did. And the scepter did exactly what it had done to Rone—it absorbed, it used, it fought.

Kaveh fought himself. It had always been a fight, controlling the shadows. It had been a strangely felt relief when he had been set free. And it had felt like a benediction to gain the struggle back again. To be worthy of it.

"Your mother's cage is ready for you, Kaveh. Ready for you to take her place."

Kaveh fought his shadows.

"You left her there, Kaveh, all those years. Really, you are no hero."

He caught a shadow before it could stab Rone. "For twenty-two years? No."

"You think yourself a hero now?"

Instead of running forward and powering his spells, Kaveh waited. Instead of attacking, he evaluated. Instead of charging in on his own, he opened his mind and his magic. "No. But who is to say what will happen at twenty-three."

Overconfidence and hubris, invulnerability—all of Kaveh's flaws...easily seen in Aros now. Kaveh opened his pathways. Aros threw his magic back and Kaveh swirled it into a tight ball and deflected it sideways. It blew the column to stone debris.

There was nothing Kaveh would be able to do that Aros couldn't learn and use against him—and that included against Rone, who stood behind him, and Taline, when she eventually arrived, and Nin, if she ever got here.

Fighting against himself. He knew this fight. He knew control. But he had been taught release. And he had been taught a new measure of strength.

Together.

He turned and grabbed Valeran—Rone—this brother who he had only begun to understand, and he let go.

TALINE

Etelian ul Fehl's chambers, the Palace of Tehras

Nera's poisoned fingernails dug farther into Taline's throat.

"You think to harm my child?" Nera dragged Taline forward until their faces were inches apart. "I know your face. I will carve it from you and carve this ridiculous obsession from my son."

"Obsession?" Taline choked. "You would know."

"Oh my, and you were always so quiet before, in the years you served my son," Nera mused, tightening her grasp and making the blood recede from Taline's head.

Taline's thoughts grew hazy and she had to force herself to calm her mind and body before she passed out. She knew Nera ul Fehl, but not well. It had been the one area where Etelian had been cautious. He had kept his girls apart from his mother whenever she visited.

But sometimes Nera would sneak in and inspect his household. And Taline had never been under any illusion that Nera didn't keep track. As a favorite, and one who knew when to hold her tongue, Taline hadn't been harmed by Nera. But she had seen Nera kill girls who hadn't learned to hold their tongues—she had killed them with a flick of her nails.

Those nails curled into her throat. "You have caused my son pain. I can't let that stand."

"Mother—"

"Etelian. Wake your worthless guards and heal yourself with that scepter."

Nera waited for him to move before whispering in Taline's ear. "You are dying, girl." Nera's mouth curled in satisfaction against her cheek. "And I think I will make it permanent—so you cannot be revived afterward just because Etelian wants to play. You are better off dead."

The vial that hung from Nera's neck pressed against Taline's chest. A poison vial, everyone said, because Nera was immune to poison, so she wore it around her neck. What was it the staff had always whispered? That she liked to hold drops between her teeth and slide them into the waiting mouths of men?

But Taline knew better than most about spreading rumor. About using it to one's advantage. With Nera's ruthless reputation, no one would ever risk touching that vial. Nera counted on it.

Taline muscled up the last of her reserves, thought of Rone, and mentally rolled his dice of death. Taline could mend torn flesh and put her body back together—Nin had made certain of it—but spreading poison was not something she had the power to heal.

Nera squeezed. "I will—"

She ripped the vial from Nera's neck and pushed hard against her chest. She could feel the skin around her neck rip away along with other, more vital things beneath Nera's nails.

She popped off the sealed top of the vial with her thumb. Blood sprayed from her throat as she fell. She had less than five heartbeats of life left. She tipped the contents of the vial into her mouth. A gamble on death. So very Rone.

Two heartbeats left. The vial fell and she hit the ground, marbles breaking beneath her and magic leaping into her back. She threw the magic up and into her neck, knitting together the life-giving and life-keeping pathways in her throat. Anti-venom from the vial spread swiftly along the knitted paths.

Taline took a gasping, full breath.

"You'll just die another way then." Nera snarled and surged toward her with her hand raised.

Taline grabbed the last container from her sash and gave a whispered prayer that the others would be safe.

A pulse of blinding light lit the room. Nera's hand sheared from its perch, and she was sent flying sideways, screaming.

Soft hands grabbed Taline and she was dragged into a physical covering of soft, vibrant cloth and worried eyes. Healing spells flowed over her.

Healing spells she recognized—administered by those Etelian had tortured in the past. Tears spilled over. She put her own hand to her throat to finish patching the damage there and to stop her lifeblood from spilling free. She needed to move, but she couldn't in her current condition. Twenty ticks. She needed twenty ticks.

"Finally," a rasping, garbled voice said. "We are at the end."

There were too many girls around her, guarding her, for her to clearly see, but Taline forced her head to turn to the doorway where Crelu ul Osni stood, covered in someone's blood, his fingers gripping two things tightly in his palm. Taline's breath caught.

He held one of the shadow orbs and Nin's communication and status wristband—something she would never willingly part with.

No. Taline touched her own wristband, unwilling to look at the lines. To think of what the wavering one had meant. "Where's Nin?"

Osni didn't look her way, his entire focus on Nera with a ravenous expression of joy upon his face, but he said, "Zehra Amanan Carre is dead."

"No!" Worried hands pressed Taline back down as she tried to rise.

Osni smiled and stalked toward Nera, a forked tongue poking free of his lips. "The end of the Carres and the end of the witch's line is at hand."

Taline's hand shook as she tried to see her wrist. She didn't know whether she would be able to bear seeing three lines there. Or whether Osni holding the wristband would count as the fourth.

Soft hands pressed metal into her palm. Taline shakily lifted the medallion that Nera had twisted free from her hand. Cold metal warmed in her fingers. Someone thought she could do something. They didn't know what it was, but the girls believed.

Nera moved back slowly along the floor, her cleaved hand pressing to her wrist from where Etelian was trying to reattach it with the scepter—but his magic was only coming out in stuttered fits. Nera's expression turned exhilarated and joyous. "The end of the Carres? Then we are finally free."

Osni's smile grew. "Oh…I'd say we are about to set everything right." He raised his clay hand and the scepter flew from Etelian's grasp. Etelian was pinned to the floor. Darkness drifted upward from clay fingers.

Nera placed her good hand to her chest. "I was a victim. Just like you."

"You thought the Carres would win." Osni slowly moved forward, as if every step cost him and yet every step was filled with exhilarating pain. "When Sher Fehl rescued you, you were surprised."

"I thought I would be stuck here forever!"

"You were a willing plume." Osni's slow steps forward were agonizing. "Jisarek should never have taken you. But you should never have played his game."

She gave a brittle laugh, letting part of the facade drop. "I'm a survivor."

"And a selfish one, above all else. You killed all of the others in Jisarek's chambers."

Nera's eyes went calculating. "Why do you say that?"

"The palace has many secret paths, and many eyes."

Nera considered for a moment, then sneered. "They were easily dispatched. I would have the only child. I would be the one with the power."

"And you were."

Nera smiled. "For thirty years, I have maneuvered paths and parts of the empire so that my children rule. My children sit on the best thrones. And whatever has happened today, I will make all rue a hair out of place on any of their heads. And you will help me."

Magic rose in the air, enticing and pulling. And Nera smiled, a vicious smug grin.

But Osni moved another step and Nera's grin dropped. Magic rose again. And again. Osni continued forward.

He held out the shadow orb. "The Shadow Prince was the only one you could never influence, not for lack of trying." He wiped Nera's threads with a swipe of the orb. "You entice men to your bidding and their doom."

Another step. Then his clay hand reached forward and, almost gently, wrapped around her throat. "I had to wait until Sher Fehl was dead to get this hand in place. For I couldn't get both you and your Carre spawn if I killed one of you without the other, unless I had the scepter. I thought Aros's death would take quite a bit longer, but I will trust the Shadow Prince to see him done. And with him out of the way, your time is at an end, you vile witch."

"Aros won't die! He will rule! You—"

Power burst from the throne room below, shaking the stones. Frightened voices screamed around Taline. A great roar echoed, and glass shattered. The entire palace pulsed.

Osni's eyes closed. He took a breath, and when he opened his eyes, they were unnaturally calm. "Finally, we have reached the end."

"Aros! The scepter—"

Snap. Nera fell from his hands.

"Is not an impediment anymore," Osni said.

Etelian screamed and dove at his mother's corpse. Osni swatted him away like a fly, then he bent over Nera's body and poured something on her face. His determination had taken on a strangely peaceful edge. "No coming back. No more of you for this world ever more. There will be no possible resurrection for Nera ul Fehl."

Osni grabbed a knife and stabbed it into his flesh hand, severing a twisted green and yellow thread there. "At an end, finally, old enemy, old friend, this last oath of blood I make. Consume the hearts of this tie that was made. Hearts promised to you, this tie is complete." The twisted threads fell free. Darkness rose, growing monstrous from Osni's palm. Darkness pulsed, screamed, then plunged through the stones of the floor.

Osni's breath hitched. He touched his chest, then a smile bloomed across his lips—one unfettered and light. An unnaturally forked tongue lolled from the side. He dropped to a sitting position, as if he had nothing left holding him up anymore. "It is done."

Taline and the rest of the room remained frozen.

Osni looked into the distance, eyes gone hazy. "Truly done. The last of the Carres." Osni looked at his hands and he laughed. He curled his fingers inward and closed his eyes. "Farrah, Bilen, I will see you again. Not in the next life, for it is undeserved, but in the life after—I will see you again."

Power burst through the palace again. Darkness surged upward through Osni's chest, then through the roof. Osni dropped dead, without heart, a smile upon his face. His clay hand burst upon the stones.

"I will kill every one of you!" Etelian screamed through the unnatural, petrifying terror that had gripped the room. He lunged for the scepter, but one of the girls leaped forward—her body automatically responding—and kicked it across the floor.

The scepter twirled upon the stones and landed next to Taline. Taline wanted to find Nin; she wanted to find Rone. But she had to get this done.

Taline looked upon Etelian as he turned and lunged toward them. She wondered at revenge and healing. She wondered at tying up loose ends instead of leaving them dangling to ensnare another.

She wondered whether she had any right to be an executioner. It was something Nin had always pushed against—that her family shouldn't have had such power. And yet there was always an authority that existed to mete out punishment.

Why not let it be her hand?

She thought of Nin, whose struggle was always that she wanted to be in the forefront—not as a victor, but as a shield, shielding all she loved and was committed to. She thought of how Nin had changed herself and her view of her family—thinking of herself as the sacrifice to Tehras instead of Tehras being the sacrifice to her.

There was trauma in that way of thinking. And yet there were spots where Taline saw hope—in how Nin saw that hope for the Shadow Prince. How she had encouraged the Shadow Prince to find allies and deal Aros's end in concert with those he would lead.

Taline looked upon Etelian as he raised his re-powered hand.

She did not have to be his executioner, nor did she need to be his victim. She could make certain no other ever was the latter.

If vengeful thoughts were mixed within, so be it. She smiled, rising. "We are all a work in progress, after all."

Etelian curled his fingers in the starting sequence, as Taline lifted the scepter. She pressed the medallion between the fingers of her other hand.

She thrust the scepter head forward, and a line drew itself across the floor in fire.

Etelian stopped. The self-preservation instinct—what had always saved him—saved him now as he eyed the fire as it receded to form a simple red line.

Taline looked at the girls. "Will you fight with me?"

"They have as little power as you." Etelian sneered. "Less, as you bewitched me. And you—" He paced the line. "You couldn't kill me before. In the imperial palace when you appeared." Etelian's pretty mouth curled savagely. "You had the most powerful relic in your hand, and you couldn't kill me. Weakness."

Taline stared at him. "Weakness?" she said remotely. "Killing you with the scepter would have resulted in something far worse for me." She would have been taken by it. She would have killed others with it—quickly, without compassion or care. "And that would have given you power and import you little deserve." She straightened. "But you need to be dealt with."

"By you? I am important to you, and I will always be."

Her heart beat so fast that she couldn't grab hold of it, but her mind was narrowing. She tilted her hand. "By hand, I think, with nails and fingers flaying your skin in a death that will take a smaller amount of time than you deserve. But it will be done."

"By hand?" He laughed. "You can do nothing—you never could. I'll strip you of everything again, then make you beg."

"I think not."

"Get rid of this line, and I'll make you regret every word you've uttered in your pitiful revenge."

"You misinterpret this revenge. And you mistake the ability for us to pass over it."

She touched the medallion to the scepter, and she touched the bodies of all the women who had been part of the medallion's call to aid the women escaping.

Two dozen lights answered the call. Taline reached with the scepter, letting the power of the Second Scepter touch each of those lights.

Etelian's brows drew down sharply, watching her, but before he could ask, beams of light were forming, and women were stepping free.

"What is this?" Etelian watched the women advance. "How do you know how to do that, Siran?"

"I listen. I watch. I wait, Etelian ul Fehl. We all have waited."

The women advanced.

"What is this?" he asked, stepping back, hands up and ready. "Are you going to take my power, Siran? Make me powerless?"

686

"No."

It was something Kaveh ul Fehl had said to her when they had been discussing strategy—that Etelian could neutralize ten, but not twenty. And if fifty came at him...

Some of the women slipped away—and she would not begrudge them that choice. The effect of Etelian's power—the ability to strip power while freezing an opponent in temporary, crippling pain—was still in play. Feeling that again was something she would tempt no one with. And yet, in dealing with him as he was, there would be catharsis for some.

It was their choice. And there was power in choosing—no matter what choice was made.

"You can't do this, Siran!"

That choice had driven more than thirty to remain or to heed the call. They steadily crept forward.

"You've never held determination in regard, Etelian. I will spare you no more thoughts after this. And my name? Is Taline."

He grabbed power from one, then another, but the surge did not stop. "Guards! I'll kill you all! Cowards! Guards!"

"Farewell, Etelian ul Fehl."

And Etelian ul Fehl fell to his victims' hands.

RONE

Throne Room, Palace of Tehras

Rone automatically grabbed Kaveh's wrists. Shadows twined around Rone's fingers.

Your power. Nullification in all things. Aros celebrates that which will destroy him. Reach past the scepter. Stop its shield.

Rone stared at the shadows in the suspended moment of reality. He stared at the touch he would never before have allowed—one that echoed the Shadow Prince's mind words and read Rone's very thoughts.

Rone.

Yes. Rone let the thought fill him. He looked at the shadows, then he grabbed them and pulled.

He pulled the Shadow Prince's powers into himself as Kaveh fell to the side.

All that practice with stripping the shadows of their powers, of learning their little secrets and quirks—Kaveh ul Fehl had allowed him that—and because of that trust...

It was a strange reality. The Shadow Prince giving his powers and Rone reaching out to take.

Rone pulled the shadows around his body and let them flare.

They had been certain that constructing a cage was the answer. That by trapping Aros inside, they could separate him from the scepter after. Simply slicing him with a ripgate or cutting off his arm was out of the question because the scepter wouldn't let anything through. Irsula had cut off the emperor's head with a power that no one else wielded and they needed Aros alive.

All the thoughts on how Rone and Kaveh could use their powers in sequence to overcome Aros, and in the end, it was the simplest and most complicated solution of all. Two becoming a stronger one, gaining the trust and partnership of another, working together not to change power, but to enhance it. Giving trust to another and accepting them in.

Things neither of them did.

Things both of them had embraced.

Rone clasped the Shadow Prince's shadows as they swirled around him. He let the Shadow Prince assume the spot at his back...knowing Fehl would protect it. Thoughts that he had been so certain of in the past—never trusting the Shadow Prince, never letting his shadows touch him, never letting him be at his back—discharged, and he let his power coat him.

He took Kaveh's power and held it in his hand, then flipped the current of it with his power—turning the life, the curl, the substance—into its opposite. Sunlight and darkness glittered in his palm like starlight in the sky.

He held starlight for a moment. Then he thrust it at Aros's hand.

Aros waved the scepter through the bolt with a sneer, but when starlight connected with caught shadow, it met its reflection. The scepter pulsed, Aros screamed, and the hand holding the scepter disintegrated around the staff.

Light pulsed everywhere, the palace shook, and the barrier around the room cracked and fell. The scepter dropped to the floor with a clang. Rone sent Kaveh's powers whirling back into him.

Aros reached for the scepter with his intact hand, but Kaveh's shadows skimmed it across the floor to rest in front of the door. Aros stared at it for long moments, breath heavy, right arm curled against his chest.

"You have broken me of the scepter, but you still cannot kill me." Aros smiled tightly. "What is it to be then, Kaveh? A cage?" Aros suddenly grasped at his chest. "She…" Aros's face went a funny shade as he touched his chest. "She's trying to kill us both."

Ninli. "What?" Rone asked aggressively.

"It is nothing we care about," Kaveh ul Fehl said.

Rone jerked his gaze to the Shadow Prince, certain that he was going to see the end of the world. But it was like looking in a morning sky where the stars faded to dawning light.

The battle tension in the Shadow Prince's frame melted. A smile curved his mouth. Shadows swarmed, swirling to encompass. Rone could barely see for the amount that were whirling in the air, blocking the light as if starlight shone down upon them.

Aros looked at Kaveh, and his expression was strange. "You don't care? But...I know I did not read you wrong. You changed. You cared. It took twenty-two years for me to find someone you cared about other than the emperor and your familiar."

"Truly, brother. Tut, tut." Kaveh's smile was vicious, but also victorious, and Rone held his hope to the latter. "How could you have gotten it so wrong? Tut, tut, brother, perhaps you should spend more time on a battlefield rather than with your wits and wagers in the salons."

Then the shadows pulsed and Rone could feel the bond—he could see the silk ribbon glow. Kaveh passed the feel of the bond through shadow—and gently tugged the person his shadows had encompassed into the room.

Nin stepped from the shadows, a bloody locket in her palm—blood dripping from a deep cut in her hand.

"You are no longer connected to the blood tie." Aros sounded befuddled, shocked as he looked from his chest to hers.

"No. Another took it forcibly from me." She held up the locket. "Another who knew more about Darkness than you and I. Never make a deal with Darkness." She looked to the ceiling and Rone stiffened as Darkness dove through the ceiling and consumed Aros's heart in one massive, uninterrupted stretch of eldritch teeth as it dove through Aros's body and through the floor, before turning and flying upward again with a horrible scream.

The scepter pulsed a last time for its wielder, then went still.

"Farewell, Aros." Kaveh released his shadows and closed Aros's eyes.

"Taline?" Rone asked tightly, staring upward at where Darkness had flown.

Kaveh's gaze was on Ninli, but he tilted his head Rone's way. "Alive." He extended his shadows to Rone, who automatically accepted them. Through them, he could see the remnants of Osni, his chest a duplicate to Aros's fate. He could see Taline standing strong and Etelian and Nera on the floor.

Rone let himself physically grip the column nearest to him in abject relief. "A drink."

"Nin?"

Rone tensed again, looking at Kaveh first—whose brows had descended into a sharp vee—before following his concerned gaze. Rone looked to see Ninli's small hand lift the Scepter of Darkness.

Blood dripped from the hand that gripped the scepter's staff. The scepter lit. Lifting the scepter again had not been in any plan.

"Ninli!"

"Nin."

She looked from the scepter to them and hazy, mesmerized eyes pulsed bright red.

NINLI

The scepter was on the floor, then it was in her hand. Blood dripped along the staff, along with her muddled thoughts.

Osni's blade had taken her blood and he had swapped it with his inside the oath that he held. He was now dead. She could feel it in the last dregs of the spell. He had taken her blood, and now her blood was coating the most powerful relic the Carres had ever ordered someone to create.

Created by a worldbreaker, who had been tortured to the bitter end. Created for one of her blood to wield it to glory.

Use me. You will become the most powerful being with me in your hand.

Madness. Madness had been imbued within the instrument of destruction, chaos, and creation held within her hand.

You will wield the scepter to rule all.

Perhaps it was why the villagers held the worldbreaker in perpetual stasis—forever a boy, never Awakened—so that he could not be used to create something like this.

Nin looked at Kaveh. Kaveh would help people like Teir. He would rule the empire and ensure that no one of such abilities could be used for ill.

A ripgate opened and Taline appeared in the room, the Second Scepter in her hand. "Nin."

Kill her.

Nin looked at Taline, who had never thought twice about the darkness to which Nin had been born.

Kill her.

No. Nin pushed back. She would not succumb.

The world will quail in terror.

The power of this scepter had imbued the Carre line. Nin thought of Lorsali's cruel words, her ghost always following her. She thought of Lorsali's held tongue and the last image of her inside Osni's locket.

Nin called the other scepters to the room with a flick of her wrist. They clattered to the floor. She eyed the Ninth Scepter, now an old friend. She eyed the Fourth Scepter, with its pristine beauty—the perfection of its previous owner with none of the chaos of the girl who might have one day held it in her hand.

"Lorsali was right," she whispered. "I will never wield her scepter."

The great scepter in her hand pulsed. You will wield **me.**

The madness, the voice—she knew it well. She had always wondered whether she was infected. If one day she would wake, power hungry and mad. If the curse of her family was lying in wait, waiting for an opportunity to strike. If all the positive things she did would ever make up for a tenth of the damage her family had done. Wetness streaked down her face.

And in the next instant, fingers were wrapping around Nin's, then wrapping them around the staff with hers, gripping it together.

Nin looked up and saw Taline in front of her, Etelian's scepter dropped to the floor with the others.

Taline's fingers wrapped and squeezed, and in that shared control, some of the feelings of panic and power receded and a feeling closer to calm slid over Nin.

There were things worth more than power—there always had been. Power, birth, family... Taline was her sister and Nin loved her. And she had always tried to shield her—from the moment she had pulled her broken body from the burning chariot. She had tried to shield Taline and take all the sacrifice within herself.

Taline stared at her, face set, and Nin nodded. "Together."

Nin reached out to the gates. There was enough power to sustain them. Enough power to start anew. Nin lifted the scepter. Madness swirled and she pinned it under the bond she could feel between Taline's skin and hers. "I release you."

The shard of the magi who had made the scepter—he of creation Tand rebirth who had been tortured by her ancestors—and that still resided in the scepter screamed. Nin screamed. Taline screamed. And they both held tight.

"I release you."

A wisp of sound and memory rose. The feel of a broken spirit being laid to rest.

Thank you, whispered along the skin of their joined hands. And the scepter burst into glittering shards of starlight.

"Nin." Taline's voice was exhausted and Rone caught her and they both tumbled awkwardly to the floor.

Kaveh touched her wrist, but Nin was not done. Just a little more. One more thing to start anew. To make the last sacrifice—an act of redemption.

She grabbed the connection that had always been a part of her and pinched it closed.

"Nin! Don't sacrifice yourself!"

Nin grabbed the threads and lifted them. "No. Not this time." And she disconnected Tehrasi from her blood. Slow pulses—like final heartbeats before death—pulsed outward. The wards and magic of Tehrasi slipped from her grip.

She could feel...nothing. The lifeblood of the city was as any other.

She felt the connection break, then shatter. Kaveh caught her as she fell.

"Nin."

She let her other enchantments sear away, leaving behind simple fellowship oaths to the others in the room.

"It is done." She closed her eyes, feeling calm descend. "It is done."

She would never wield another Carre scepter. She looked at Taline and they gripped bloodied hands close. They would build new tools. Better ones. Ones not created in madness, power, and despair.

"I will be an asset to Tehrasi for all my days, but I will live a full life as well."

Kaveh pulled her head against his chest. "Never again."

"Hubris," she whispered with a smile, watching Taline and Rone, who were leaning their foreheads together, whispering words that she didn't need to hear to understand.

"Never again," Kaveh promised, gripping handfuls of her hair and forcing her to see the promise in his eyes. "Not even arrogance will make that promise false."

She smiled against his lips. "Together."

CHAPTER TWENTY-THREE
A CROWN OF STARLIGHT

NINLI

(Throne Room, Palace of Tehras)

The palace staff moved in quick motions, removing bodies and rubble. There was visible relief on many faces that they were still alive—that they hadn't gone the way of the Carre household before them. Osni had spared this household, who had nothing to do with Bilen's death. And with the scepter in hand, Aros hadn't thought it necessary yet to tie all to his death in order to keep the staff in line.

In madness, at some point, he might have tried to tie the entire empire to him. But Osni had beaten him—he had sealed their choices back to Darkness, completing the ring.

Choice had consequence.

That Osni had chosen to take Nin's blood tie and make it his, had been unexpected. That he had somehow believed her words and chosen to treat the person she was now as someone separate from the Carres was even moreso. That Aros had believed Osni's words about the blood tie to be the full truth was what had doomed him in the end. Osni had taken the tie upon himself and used it to bring about the full end.

Aros's body had been removed and placed with those of his mother, brother, and Osni, and the throne room became the gathering place for all those who had fought, and all those who needed to be healed. The broken scepters sat in a pile upon the floor, surrounded by swirling shadow to keep them untouched by outside hands.

It was done. And yet like all things completed, there were effects that would spread. A life to live, a time to spend, memories to fight or gather.

She looked at one of the men "helping" to rebuild the throne room, edging ever closer to the pile of scepters, even with the threat of the swirling shadows to dissuade him. More than one person cleaning wore a face that did not belong. Sending spies and sniffers to suss out the developments in a kingdom changing leadership was a common tactic.

She walked quietly over to the one getting ever closer to the scepters. She crouched next to the pile, letting the shadows swim over her skin. He stiffened but continued to gather rock chunks for the city masons who were affixing each back into place on columns and walls.

Nin had broken her ties to the city, but some lingered longer than the others. Knowing a citizen's identity was a tie that would be purged more gradually. She could see the faint lines of his oaths, and she knew who was hidden beneath the spells.

She was sure that Kaveh and Rone had noticed, but other than the increased feel of shadows in the hem of her cloak, there was no interference as she addressed the man.

"You should join the new council that will form, Pentalayerist ul Toru." She looked at him. "Better to have a say in the open, don't you think? To be involved as advisory council to the new emperor and to all the territories that he commands?"

The pentalayerist leader looked sharply back. His birth name was a guess, and it appeared the guess had struck true. The Torus had been one of the gatekeeping lines consumed by the Carres...and his features fit what she remembered of their faces.

He turned to face her. "You suggest an alliance with magi who seek to expunge you, Zehra Amanan Carre? Who will continually seek to rid the world of relics like the scepters?"

She touched the broken pieces of the Scepter of Darkness that Toru had been not so stealthily working his way toward, then looked at the pile of broken scepters. The gates were already flickering. They would be allowed to fail, then they would build them anew. They would build them stronger.

"We will build better relics," she said. "Ones that everyone can use. Ones born of hope, not pain."

Toru stared at the pile of broken scepters for long moments, then looked at her. "I still cannot believe my own vision when I stare upon oath and thread," he murmured. "You broke the Carre hold on the city. You gave up your own advantage."

She waited until his gaze connected again with hers. "We will build something better. Something that will not hold people in fear."

He stared at her for long moments, then finally murmured, "I believe you, gatemaker."

"Then join us."

He rose, then stepped toward the door. His fingers flicked and other "staff" members rose and followed. "Perhaps."

She watched him leave, her fingers touching the locket that had been wrapped in a spare piece of linen and tucked into her sash.

"Nin?"

Nin smiled at Taline as she crouched next to her. "All is well."

"What do you have in your—is that Osni's locket?" Taline's expression was touched with quiet horror. "Nin—"

"There's nothing left inside," she said quietly. "The memory is gone. Gone with the spell. My blood…"

Taline touched her hand. "I'm sorry."

"No." Nin slowly shook her head. "It was time. It was time to be at rest."

She had seen the memory enough in that endless loop. It was hers now, if she wanted to review it.

"What happened?" Taline asked.

"Osni made a choice. He took the blood spell upon him. He could have killed me instead. The spell worked both ways—if I had been killed, Aros also would have died. Though I think Osni wasn't certain the scepter wouldn't keep him half-alive."

"Aros didn't know."

"No. He would never have allowed it."

"It would have made things easier if he hadn't set the blood spell on you at all."

Nin tipped her head and looked at the locket. "Choices have consequences, and Aros found his." She looked at where Kaveh and Rone stood, discussing something in low tones. "And we found ours."

"Would you say we have successfully 'scrutinized' the choice of Fehl for the throne?" Taline asked dryly.

Nin smiled warmly, remembering the conversation from so long ago. "And you said negotiating positions weren't my strong point."

"They aren't." Taline's gaze was pointed, but she was smiling, too.

Nin clasped her hand. "We'll heal these lands. And the people will thrive. We will look out, open and free, and we will see an engaged world stare back."

Taline's gaze drifted to where a number of the women had gathered, speaking closely. The expressions on their faces were ones mirrored in Taline. Survival, determination, hope.

Her hand gripped back, warm and firm. "Yes. We will."

KAVEH

Kaveh stared at the crown in his hands—carefully taken from Aros's head.

"The Crown of Sunlight," Rone said. "A powerful symbol."

"Yes." He touched the facets and depictions of the sun. Kaveh looked to the dark sky in contemplation—sunset having fallen, the full moon rising and starting its upward path to reach its midnight peak. "The emperor would have loved to see his legacy live on."

Rone grimaced, but the expression was...less intense. "You can still save your father's legacy."

Kaveh regarded the crown. "No. The time for saving is past. The emperor's legacy was one of conquest and progression. Mine has always been a legacy of terror. The time for something else has come. I've been told building houses builds character."

Rone grimaced. "Pass."

Kaveh let a smile through.

"If—" Rone looked to the side where the others had gathered and were healing the wounded. "If I had released your powers weeks ago—"

"It would have been a tactic that I would have taken every advantage of. I know the reason you didn't release me. You owe no conciliation or consideration for the past."

Rone grimaced. "Maybe—"

"No. I would have shown you no mercy a month ago. I'm glad that you didn't return my powers right after I lost them." He repeated his words from the underground compound.

"It may have been fine. It takes but a second for lightning to strike."

"And yet, I am not someone who takes change lightly. No. It was a gift." He looked at Nin. "I regret none of it."

Kaveh's gaze slid back to Rone. "And you? It is a powerful talent you wield."

"Your father used it well."

Kaveh looked down at the crown, then back up at Rone. "You will use it better."

Rone's breath shuddered, but his shoulders relaxed. His gaze went to Taline—always to Taline—watching the two women hunch over the broken scepters, quietly discussing what to do with them.

"We could make new ones," Taline said.

"Do you think people would associate them with the old ones though?" Nin frowned, cocking her head.

Rone put his hand to his chest and called out, "Not if you make them out of love, compassion, and togetherness."

The two girls exchanged a look.

"That was sarcasm," Rone said. His face took on a beleaguered expression that was increasingly familiar. "Sarcasm."

"It is perfect," Nin said, far too seriously, back.

"I hate you, Ninli."

Kaveh saw her smile as she looked down. His chest tightened.

"But truly," Nin said. "If we recrafted them with—"

Taline hefted a piece. "We'll put it on the list along with—"

"I can't stand this. Well?" Rone motioned at the crown in Kaveh's hands. "Are you going to put it on?"

Kaveh tilted his head, looking from the girls to the crown with Valeran's words swirling in his mind. He lifted one of Nin's medallions—crafted by Taline and powered by Nin and their allies—and held out his hand to Rone. "Lend me your power, Valeran. Both powers of your lines."

Rone lifted both brows. "I think not."

A brief smile slipped over Kaveh's mouth. "Lend me your powers, Rone."

The other man let the consideration sit for another moment, then held forth a ball in his hand—mixing ice with emptiness. He did so with tense muscles, but his eyes held certainty and sharp understanding. Mind reading shadows flowed between them still.

Kaveh lifted Rone's nullifying magic—the step before creation—and mixed it with his own, then curled the medallion inside, mixing it all together—Nin's spells and Taline's handicraft, along with Baksis, Simin, Omari's, and the other threads that had been given to make the medallions work for any person they had allied with. He let his shadows break the elements down and piece them back together into liquid and smoke.

He set the mixture upon the crown and the elements fused with iced strength. Shadows glittered in pockets of light all throughout the surface. Kaveh could feel his shadows mixed with the power of so many others.

Rone looked at it, tilting his head. "I'm not sure we can call that a Crown of Sunlight anymore."

"No." Kaveh looked at Nin. Warmth consumed him. "It is starlight. The Crown of Starlight."

CHAPTER TWENTY-FOUR

A GIFT OF HOPE

KAVEH

(The Land of Darkness)

Finding Irsula and navigating the Land of Darkness was nothing with the power of shadows and gate.

"The new emperor," Irsula said. There was no surprise in her face or voice. The shadows would have told her everything—about when he had regained his powers and what had happened after. "How lovely for you. And for the man who made you."

"Yes." Kaveh wouldn't deny it. "He would be pleased."

Irsula smiled viciously. "Why do you come?"

"To thank you." He carefully retrieved the jar.

She stilled as she saw what was inside. A tendril of shadowed wing reached out and brushed the glass, which held pieces of broken shadow inside. "I felt it. When Darkness..."

Silence descended and Irsula stroked the glass once more before withdrawing.

"You have always been with me," Kaveh murmured. "And you saved me. I thank you for that."

Shadows pulsed. She stared at him for a long time. "I care nothing for you, spawn."

"I know," he said gently. "But you gave me a piece of you that did. You put emotions into the shadow that became Ifret."

Irsula smiled tightly. "What good would those feelings have done me, within that prison? A bargaining tool with which to make me a weapon? No, I neutered my own use as a weapon. I ripped those feelings out. And I felt nothing for you as the boy who stood before me on each Feast of Shadow, and I feel nothing for you as the man who stands before me now."

"I know." And he did. He held the jar against his chest.

Irsula stood for a moment more, then she reached forward, and her shadows unstoppered the glass. She touched Ifret's shards inside. They stirred beneath her fingers. The tear had been crystallized inside and he could see Irsula's fingers brush it. "There are two choices I can offer. I can absorb your companion and have her feelings returned to me—maybe I will feel affection for you even—or you can keep her, taking her with you wherever you go."

Emotion curled in the choice before him. "I will keep her. I will take her with me." Always with him. Like Nin, who would always be in his heart, even if separated by distance. "But I offer you her tear."

Shadows pulsed, and the swirl of dark shadow became a targeted thunderstorm whirling up into the trees. The sky cracked with sound, then the shadows dove down.

Shards snapped together inside the jar and sound became nightmare. Ifret rose and dove, wrapping around Kaveh's shoulders, hissing and showing her displeasure. She bit him. Kaveh smiled, unrestrained, and touched her head.

"This changes nothing," Irsula said. But she carefully lifted the tear and tucked it into her wings. "I will not accept the empire within my borders."

Kaveh stroked Ifret's head and she bit him again. He smiled. "No. That will not be a problem. Though—" He looked north. "The people of this land, in the village... They look to you as a steadying influence, even now. They respect your power."

"You want me to care about the people within this land?"

"They are of this land, and they live within it as elements, not as conquerors. You will long outlive them, and yet, perhaps they will surprise you with how long lived they can be as allies."

She watched him for extended moments longer. "Send one of them to negotiate. I shall see what such alliance holds."

Kaveh nodded. "Thank you."

She tilted her shadowed jaw. "Go and bring darkness, spawn."

Kaveh tilted his in response. "I've chosen starlight instead."

Irsula pulsed her shadows. "Then curiosity will follow your path."

Kaveh smiled, then walked back to Nin, who was waiting outside Irsula's den.

She looked to him in question, smoothing her hands down her imperial regalia. She hadn't given him an answer yet as to whether she wanted the title of empress. Kaveh was patient to wait. He knew he would convince her.

Ifret peeked around his throat and hissed at her. Nin's smile was fond and relieved. "It is terrible to see you as well."

Ifret bit Kaveh again. He anticipated that this would be his future.

He was not displeased.

They walked through forest and shadow back to an area where they wouldn't disturb the surroundings or Irsula's wards by ripgating out. "Are you ready?" he asked.

"I'm nervous. What if they look at me and think—"

"That you are beautiful?"

"That I am..." She shook her head. She didn't have to say—he knew her fear of showing her abilities to the masses and being rejected as evil.

He took her face between his palms. "Light shining in the darkness...that's starlight. It illuminates the dark, and shows its beauty. It shows that a canvas of darkness bespeckled by light can be a glorious sight. And you are my light."

Her shoulders loosened. Kaveh wrapped his hand around hers. "We could also just conquer them instead. Say the word."

"And ruin all the plans? Taline would be vexed." She opened the ripgate to their horses that would take them to their destination.

Nin was smiling again. He felt everything in him settle. He gently squeezed her hand. "It might be worth it. Imagine Rone's face."

It was all worth it, just for her laugh.

NINLI

Arriving by horseback—a path traveled without magic or artifice—they entered Tomyr to the roars from an enormous crowd. They slowly made their way to the palace and to the entourage who stood in front of the newly built stone archway—built by Scythian artisans and built with Scythian hands.

"The gatemaker. Can you see her eyes?" came the whispers from the crowd.

Nin raised her chin. Confident, not conflicted. Open, no longer hidden. She removed the veil from the headdress that Taline had bought from her in the shop of Tehras so long ago.

The gazes of the crowd blew wide.

She let her red eyes warm as she smiled at the children.

The Scythian king joined them as they approached the arch and dismounted. Baksis and Simin, here as the council's representatives, joined as well.

"Your council is a pointed bunch," the king said dryly.

"The expansion is only for those territories who choose to join," Kaveh said.

"So they tell me. We will be added to the council, they said, with a say in the entire empire."

"Representation and provisional status—something that can be negated on either side, at the end." Countries united, agreements to work together, tentative allies.

"And we will retain the gate, no matter the fate of the agreement?" The Scythian king eyed Ifret who was sleeping in Kaveh's cloak, wrapped around the happy tear she had captured from Nin on the way.

Kaveh nodded. "And the controls to use it."

"As thanks for our help?"

"As new allies for a better world."

The king studied him. "The rumors spread—they say the sun and moon rise on this new council, and the Emperor of Starlight will hold the world together."

"We will hold this world together. Do you accept?" Kaveh's shadows held up the scepter that had been crafted by parties on both sides.

"I do." The king held up his hand.

And Nin took a deep breath and put her hand upon the archway.

It wasn't her first gate. She had rebuilt ten in Tehrasi—along with the first of the new scepters there, the new Prime Scepter of Tehrasi, wielded by the new padifehl.

But it was still so new—using her powers so freely. In front of their imperial party, the Scythian royals, and the whole of Tomyr, Nin opened the gate.

The power of her ancestors flooded her. It would be a gift used for all. She opened the gate to Tehras—the Scythians' choice for their first gate—and their Tehrasian welcoming party stood on the other side.

Nin looked at Taline, standing on the other side of the gate, holding the new Prime Scepter of Tehras, standing in front of the Throne of Tehras—a place where Etelian had once sat with her at his feet.

The throne looked fresh and vibrant. It would gather new, better memories and magic to overlay those of the past.

Taline nodded regally, eyes sparkling, and looked sidelong at Rone, who was also wearing ruling robes. He sighed far too theatrically. Akel nudged him surreptitiously and made an encouraging motion to Nin from his guard position at their side.

Nin grinned and anchored the gate, feeling Tomyr and Tehras join together—the first of many connections to come. "Let us begin."

EPILOGUE

"Tell us, tell us, the tale of the Crown of Starlight... Of the crystal tears that were shed and the promises that remained unbroken..."

For sixty years of peace and prosperity, Kaveh ul Fehl sat the imperial throne with Ninli at his side. The bloodiest of beginnings turned into a reign of growth and economic fortune. Magic flowed, knowledge was shared, and peace was cherished.

Worthy Fehls sat the throne for many generations more, and even as every dynasty has an end, the end of the Fehl dynasty transitioned in peace, becoming part of something even greater than what it was before—a worthy and harmonic end to a turbulent start.

Nin and Kaveh's children and Taline and Rone's children became great magi, powerful in their own ways, and even today, there are descendants roaming the layers, with the gifts of their ancestors in their hearts and hands.

One has only to look inside to see starlight shining back.

About the Author

Anne Zoelle is the pseudonym of a USA Today Bestselling author who loves writing about college-aged protagonists who get embroiled in complicated adventures. Split between the midwest and west coast, she writes books for all ages that feature sentient libraries, rock guardians, and people finding family.

You can find her at www.annezoelle.com.

Or contact her directly at:
anne.zoelle@gmail.com

Glossary

Terms, Places, Characters, and P anteon

TERMS

Ameni Tribe: a tribe of renowned horsemasters to which Taline was born.

beldrake: a type of dragon.

blessed child of the emperor: an imperial child, who is blessed by the emperor in a ceremony that bestows upon them the ability to control imperial oaths. Imperial children given this designation may also be selected to serve as padifehl of an imperial territory someday. The blessing ceremony takes place when the emperor deems it time—usually when a powerful child has come into their powers, generally upon an Awakening from age 10-17. Children, like Kaveh ul Fehl, who come into their powers at an early age and show rare amounts of power or extraordinary gifts are blessed at a very young age and are raised accordingly. There are hundreds, perhaps thousands, of imperial children residing in the imperial palace and living in far-flung streets and lands, but the honor of being "blessed" means something far more elite and powerful. The emperor has been decreasing the number of blessing ceremonies and increasing the requirements as more and more of his children are born with great power. The order of blessing does not correspond to the age of the child or their power, it is simply the order in which a child was blessed.

Chrimoa: an elite crafter of decorative glass and ceramic pieces.

coriolen: a being related to banshees that can produce a high-pitched shrieking sound.

crouel: a person with little or no magic.

croupa: a sickness not unlike croup.

farhani: a necklace worn in imperial territories that signifies a magi's power level and has the magi's imperial fealty oaths embedded within.

The investigorii can use the oaths to detain individuals in their territories for questioning.

fehlta, **fehltan:** a unit of currency used across the empire. Prior to its use, "measures" were used: five measures, three half measures, two quarter measures. Fehlta are similar to the Magahda coins used in ancient India. In the Fehl Empire, there are 5 magi coinmasters keyed to the treasury whose responsibility is to create the coins using personal, magical stamps. When a coinmaster dies or retires, another is keyed to take his place. The five stamped signatures have to be correct for the coin to be legitimate. Counterfeiting coins is extremely difficult and punishable by death.

gate medallion: an object which has been imprinted with coordinates to transport a person to a specific place and contains a one-time activation. They are incredibly rare and expensive because they can only be created by a gatemaker or gate relic.

gatekeeper: a magi who cares for and repairs already created gates, and who is able to switch internally embedded coordinates to open through other created gates (connecting already created gates together). A rare ability.

gatemaker: a magi who creates ripgates and who is capable of tethering ripgates to physical objects and locations—making an arch or object with an open interior into a semi-permanent gate between two places. An extremely rare and coveted ability. **See also: ripgate**

imperial names: names given tocitizens of the empire. The census requires all magi in the empire to receive designations based on the following name scheme: First Name **al** Power Level **el** Occupation **il** Birth City **ol** Oath Temple **ul** Family Name. These get shortened in informal use to First name **ul** Family Name.

Example formal: Ninli al Six el Healer il Tehras ol Gomen ul Summora

Example informal: Ninli ul Summora

For people living outside of the empire, individual society naming schemes prevail.

imperial professional titles: the professional designation that precedes one's imperial name. Professional titles eschew many of the imperial naming scheme elements brought by the census. Title + Family Name is most often used. If there is more than one person of the same profession with the same family name in the room, the power level is given in the middle. The first name would be added as well if the power level is also the same.

Examples:

Healer Summora

Healer Six Summora and Healer Four Summora

Healer Ninli Six Summora

investigore: head of the law enforcement, similar to a director. Investigore Malik ul Malit when formally addressed.

investigorii: a law enforcement unit or an individual officer (singular and plural).

imperator: title for the head of an army unit.

karogi tiles: tiles used in karogi (a game).

khursifa (khursifas): a spell-woven conveyance mat that can connect and use wind enchantments in a city and through its own woven magic. A type of flying carpet. Under the hands and skills of a specialist, they can be made to do wondrous things as a mode of transportation.

Kore: a fictional, powerful eastern dynasty.

layer, layers, layer split: The split of one world into five, each duplicate existing on top of the next. Three creation magi (worldchangers) working together split the Earth into five identical layers of land. Four layers have magic, while one layer (sometimes referred to as "the first") is without. This first layer contains all the humans and creatures born without magic and is protected from the magical worlds by ruthless groups of devout magi. **See also: pentalayerists**. The Fourth Layer was created specifically for beasts, creatures, and hybrid beings and is sometimes referred to as "the land of the beasts." Five layers of the same world, existing each on top of the next. Four steady layers and one of chaos—not fully settled during the event that produced them. One of no magic, two of plenty, one of beasts and power, one of chaos.

magi: a user of magic.

mancaleh: a classic board game, sometimes referred to as mancala.

majex (imperial majex): the wife of the emperor. The high imperial majex is the ruling wife.

mūdû: a type of magi who can tell the power, acquisition, and talents of others. It means "wise" in Akkadian.

narsumina: a pet name Rone calls Taline (used in much the way someone would call another "princess"). The reference is to the beautiful, vestal temple attendants of Narsum, the god of beauty, youth, age, and time.

padifehl: the leader of an imperial territory, usually a child of the emperor.

palmera: a palm spring drink that is highly intoxicating.

pentalayerists: a group who seek to protect and preserve the layers as they were designed. This includes protecting the non-magic world from magical influence. Their goal is to eradicate magi and relics that can open gates between layers. As a precautionary measure, and if given the opportunity, they will also destroy any relic or magi deemed too powerful, who may disrupt the status quo.

Polingsa Manuscripts: manuscripts and scrolls that contain powerful spells created and kept by the Polingsa family. Qara ul Polingsa encourages Nin to steal them so that they can be added to the library for the masses, while still giving Qara a reasoned voice among the elite.

revenant: one of the undead.

ripgate: a temporary gate created by a gatemaker or relic. It is different from a gate, which is a permanent or semi-permanent fixture.

sandrake: a type of sand dragon.

sandpronga: a large worm-like sand creature with immense teeth.

Sanskrine: modified Sanskrit

scholari: the head of knowledge or science in an imperial territory.

scepter chamber: a curved chamber at the heart of the Palace of Tehras that holds the twelve scepters of Tehras. Four per "wall" in the curved chamber.

shadowshaper: one who can use and craft shadows to enhance sensory perception and who can control shadows by pushing their own sensory output through them. A shadowshaper can connect their senses through a shadow to affect whatever the shadow is touching. In this way, shadows become extended limbs of the shadowshaper and are able to do whatever a regular limb can. A thousand shadows could become a thousand separate swords when wielded by a magi whose mind is able to control a thousand different limbs at once. Only two shadowshapers are known to exist. Neither is fully human. It is speculated that a regular human mind is incapable of wielding as many separate entities as shadowshapers have been observed to wield.

sirens, nerens, potamens: beings of the waters

slenterfasi: a slur

stormbrewer: a magi who controls storms.

string: a signature, the feel of a person's magic—how one magi sensitive to it can identify another.

sunmaker, sunchaser, suncatcher, suntaker: a magi who manipulates sunlight or light for specific civic tasks (enforcement, agriculture, leisure, etc.).

Swee: a fictional, powerful northern dynasty.

windcatcher, windmaker, windchaser, windtaker: a magi who manipulates the winds for specific civic tasks (chasing people using wind spells, crafting directional breezes for city travel, routing weather for agricultural means, etc.).

PLACES (story + modern equivalents)

Anarta: a region of ancient India.

Ancyra: the Latin form of Ankara, Turkey.

Antequere: Antequera Dolmens Site in the province of Málaga.

Assaka: a kingdom of ancient India.

Axšaina Sea: the Black Sea.

Babil: Babylon.

Bekli: Göbekli Tepe.

Bilbat: an ancient Sumerian city.

Caire: a district in Tehras noted for gambling.

Campistel: a fictional setting where the Spread of Verdis occurs.

Casp Sea: the Caspian Sea.

Dernholm: the fictional city where Rone and Oralia lived in exile.

Dozine: a fictional place set in ancient Syria.

Ersine: the Continent of Africa.

Fehlaka: the imperial capital. Modern day Failaka Island, Kuwait.

Gerod: a fictional place where the Festival of Marsk is held.

Idiqlat: the Tigris River in Sumerian/Akkadian.

Kailāsa: Mount Kailash in Sanskrit.

Kastoni: a fictional place set in Jordan.

Kiš: Kish, an ancient city in Sumer.

Krokola: Karachi, Pakistan.

Lisso: Lisbon, Portugal.

Magadha: a kingdom of ancient India.

Memfi: Memphis, Egypt.

Purattu: the Euphrates River in Akkadian.

Sarg: a fictional place set in northern Oman.

Tehras: the capital city of Tehrasi. Roughly Tehran, Iran.

Tehrasi: a province of the Fehl Empire that approximates modern day Iran.

Temple of the Scepter: a Second Layer temple that contains three chambers—the key chamber, the lock chamber, and the antechamber. The antechamber contains a gate to the scepter's actual location in the First Layer. The temple is located in the Caspian Hyrcanian Mixed Forests in northern Iran on the southern border of the Caspian Sea. But the scepter itself is in India. The temple gate did not just go through layers, but across them as well, in order to conceal the hiding place.

Telb Mountains: Alborz Mountain Range.

Ur: an ancient city in Sumer.

Uruk: an ancient city in Sumer.

CHARACTERS

Ninli ul Summora, Ninli, Nin: (age 19)healer and thief, gatemaker. Incredibly powerful magically and physically gifted in movement. Is unable to read (pure alexia) due to brain trauma at age 9.

Taline ul Summora, Tal, Tali: (age 20)healer and thief, spellcrafter. Highly intelligent with an excellent memory, but magically weak due to repeated stripping of her abilities when younger. Can recreate the bases and glyphs for spells she sees even a single time but is unable to power them.

Rone ul Valeran: (age 21)relic hunter, gambler, and trickster. The bastard son of two magically gifted lines, Valeran and Fehl. He is blessed/cursed with a distinctive hair color that cannot be magically or physically altered.

Kaveh ul Fehl: (age 22)thirteenth "blessed" child of the emperor, head of all imperial armies, and the emperor's favorite. A shadowshaper who is undefeated in battle, he answers only to the emperor and has ties to no other. He is known as the Shadow Prince,

Imperator General, Imperator General of the Empire, Terror of the Battlefront, Nightmare of the Empire, and He Who Has Never Failed.

Ifret: corporeal creature of shadow, companion to Kaveh.

Sher Fehl: (age 52) emperor, The Fehl, Great Fehl, Emperor of All He Touches.

Nera ul Fehl: (age 48) High Imperial Majex, favorite wife of the emperor. Born Nera Erias.

Aros ul Fehl: (age 32) first born of Nera, first blessed child of the emperor, no current territory.

Etelian ul Fehl: (age 31) Padifehl of Tehrasi, second born of Nera, second blessed child.

Carsue ul Fehl: (age 30) Padifehl of Moru, sixth blessed child

Shiera ul Fehl: (age 30) Padifehl of Cuipsin, eighth blessed child, beloved by her country.

Zorus ul Fehl: (age 30) Padifehl of Kemet, ninth blessed child

Urful ul Fehl: (age 30) Padifehl of Shoune, twelfth blessed child

Rayd ul Fehl: (age 28) Padifehl of Bahra, third born of Nera, eleventh blessed child

Baksis ul Fehl: (age 27) imperial prince, twentieth blessed child, no current territory.

Simin ul Fehl: (age 26) imperial prince, eighteenth blessed child, no current territory.

Voiya ul Fehl: (age 24) Padifehl of Fehla-da, fourth born of Nera, fourteenth blessed child.

Omari ul Fehl: (age 11) Padifehl To Be of Cuipsin, hundredth blessed child.

Namir ul Mero: (age 24) Personal Guard of Omari, distant cousin to the Queen of Kush.

Akel: a fifteen-year-old boy who becomes the head of Ninli's "ducklings." Akel is a budding spymaster.

Barrinis: a deceased family line of gatekeepers and gatemakers.

Ber ul Hon of the First Guard: the investigator into Shirsk and Siru ul Teg's death.

Birsa: a "seeker" whose enslavement bonds to treasure hunters was broken by Ninli. Birsa has been living in First Layer India for the past two years. She has been given the name "Luriandur—Devotional of Sea and Storm" in her new community.

Bilen Osni: Crelu ul Osni's son, Bilen was leading a revolution to upset the Carre Dynasty due to Jisarek's increasingly dangerous actions. Crelu ul Osni was forced to execute Bilen in order to prove his own loyalty.

Crelu ul Osni: Scholari of Tehrasi, worked for and betrayed the Carre Family; now rules Tehrasi from the shadows and hunts scepter lore.

Farrah Osni: Crelu ul Osni's deceased wife, and Ninli's tutor and primary maternal influence.

Kūruš: Cyrus the Great

Goran, First General Goran: one of Kaveh's generals on the battlefront

Gursuf Sule: a villain from Rone's past.

Heba: a master of courtly enchantment, makeup, and dress, and a loyal handmaiden to Ninli. Heba was the handmaiden who wore Zehra Amanan Carre's face when the Carres were killed.

Irsula of Denz: Night Terror of the Land of Darkness, Mistress of Shadows; mother of Kaveh ul Fehl. Born to Darkness and a human woman, she is half-human. Imprisoned, and with no oaths taken, she has no imperial census designation and no surname. Denz is the place of her birth.

Larit ul Polingsa: bondmate of Qara ul Polingsa, healer.

Malik ul Malit: Investigore of Tehrasi. Head of the investigorii—the law enforcement branch of Tehras.

Oralia Valeran: Rone ul Valeran's mother

Pikerens: the family that Oralia Valeran married into after abandoning Rone.

Qara ul Polingsa: an elite of Tehras, politician.

Reyi: a loyal handmaiden to Ninli who was killed in the Carre massacre.

Siran Bey: Taline's birth name.

Siru ul Teg: The First General in charge of the northern section of the front in Kaveh's absence. He was the lead point on Shirsk.

Sora: a loyal handmaiden to Ninli who was killed by Lorsali.

Carre Family (in order of age):

Giran Carre: former King of Tehrasi.

Jisarek Carre: brother of Giran, kidnapper of Nera ul Fehl.

Salare Carre: former Queen of Tehrasi.

Savvan Carre: former crown prince.

Lorsali Carre: former first princess.

Fein Carre: former prince.

Allit Carre: former prince.

Memni Carre: former prince.

Jolan Carre: former prince.

Zehra Amanan Carre: former princess.

PANTHEON

Sehk-Ra: two-faced god of death and chance (shadow wielders, undertakers and embalmers, death rite clerics, touch killers, gamblers, thieves) and god of the sun, rule, order (rulers, head of households, judgment/truth speakers).

When face names are used individually: Sehk for death and chance, Ra for rule and order.

To be Sehk-Ra-blessed is to be in total control = the god of dominion.

Ferra: goddess of birth and health (healers).

Akkan: god of winds, travel, and travelers (port mages, paladins/finders, some weather mages).

Gripna: goddess of domestic matters/hearth/estate/money (homemakers, merchants).

Narsum: god of beauty, youth, age, and time. Depiction varies—sometimes shown genderless, sometimes shown possessing all genders, sometimes shown as an infant, sometimes stooped with a cane. Narsum is the representation of all things experienced in a lifetime—change both physical and spiritual.

Narsumina is the title given to the vestal tenders of Narsum's shrines and temples—usually beautiful, young women.

Marsk: god of war and victory (warriors, rulers, politicians, etc.).

Oceana: goddess of all waters, the seas, rivers, rains and snow (fishermen, some weather mages, etc.).

Verdis: god of flora and fauna, forests (hunters, herbists, farmers).

Called upon by imperial citizens, prayer usage varies:

A healer might pray to Verdis to find herbs, but to Ferra to bless a procedure.

A sailor might say: May the winds of Akkan bless us and the waters of Oceana hold us.

Godly names are used as swear words often, especially Sehk-Ra, Sehk, and Ra with any combination of descriptive terms attached. Sehk-Ra-be-damned, Sehk-damned, etc.